FAREWELL

Originally published in Turkish as *Veda* by Everest Yayınları, Cağaloğlu, 2007
Copyright © 2007 by Ayşe Kulin
Translation copyright © 2012 by Kenneth J. Dakan
First edition, 2012

Library of Congress Cataloging-in-Publication Data

Kulin, Ayse.
[Veda. English]
Farewell : a mansion in occupied Istanbul / Ayse Kulin ; translated by Kenneth J. Dakan.
-- 1st ed.
    p. cm.
ISBN 978-1-56478-758-3 (pbk. : alk. paper) -- ISBN 978-1-56478-724-8 (cloth : alk.
paper)
I. Dakan, Kenneth. II. Title.
PL248.K7755V4413 2012
894'.3534--dc23
                                    2012004228

This book has been supported by the Ministry of Culture and Tourism of Turkey in the
framework of the TEDA project

In cooperation with Barbaros Altug and Everest Yayinlari

Partially funded by the National Lottery through Arts Council England, and a grant
from the Illinois Arts Council, a state agency

www.dalkeyarchive.com

Cover: design and composition by Sarah French

Printed on permanent/durable acid-free paper and bound in the United States of America

FAREWELL

A Mansion in Occupied Istanbul

Ayşe Kulin

Translated by Kenneth J. Dakan

Dalkey Archive Press
Champaign | Dublin | London

— 1 —

A Mansion in Occupied Istanbul

Snowfall loses its grandeur out of season. Instead of transforming Istanbul into a shimmering city of mother-of-pearl, the snow—which had arrived at the end of a long and arduous winter, just as the flowers were expected to bloom—resembled confectioners' sugar haphazardly scattered across the muddy streets and peeling wooden houses. In the Beyazit district, the driver of a two-horse carriage—his face red, his fingers numb with cold—drew back on his reins at the top of the second street leading down to the sea. The carriage slid several yards before stopping. Wary of shod hooves on patches of ice, the passenger, Ahmet Reşat, had decided to spare the horses and finish his trip home on foot. He descended from the carriage, paid the driver, and picked his way with cautious footsteps down the street, across the scattered snow. Soon it would be time for the morning call to prayer. Reşat Bey was worn out—his meeting had been prematurely concluded, the participants far too exhausted to think, let alone speak. He paused for a moment in the middle of the street, silently praying that his wife was still asleep, before slipping into the stately home on the right. He was in no condition, at this early hour, to answer questions.

His fingers had barely grazed the garden gate when it opened beneath them. "Good morning, sir," said Hüsnü Efendi.

"What are you doing in the garden at this hour," said Reşat. "Didn't I tell you all not to wait up for me?"

"I was getting up to pray in any case. And I saw you from the window. You're worn out, sir."

"Of course I am. How many days have we all gone without sleep? God help us."

"Amen."

The look Ahmet Reşat gave his manservant was intended to re-assure. Not only were Hüsnü Efendi's eyes filled with anxiety, he was obstructing his master's passage.

"There's no bad news, Hüsnü Efendi—business, that's all that kept me. Business. Go on now, pray. Off with you."

Hüsnü raced ahead to open the front door. Stepping across the threshold, Ahmet Reşat caught a sharp whiff of disinfectant. He grimaced, sank down on the footstool beside the door, removed his shoes and placed his fez on the appointed shelf, handed his coat to Hüsnü, and entered the *selamlık* in stocking feet. Hoping to nap for a few hours, he threw himself onto the divan before the window, face down, resting his forehead in the cupped palms of his hands. He had a splitting headache. Casting from his mind the discussions and events of the previous twenty-four hours, he tried to relax as Mahir had counseled him—clearing his mind, taking deep breaths. He drew one, released it slowly . . . and another . . . and another. Yes, his friend's advice had been sound. He stretched and yawned, rolling onto his back, placing the cushion he'd tossed to the floor beneath his head. But he'd barely dozed off when he was startled by the tobacco-coarsened voice of his aunt.

"What kind of person stays out until this hour, with an invalid in the house?"

Collecting himself as he sat up, Reşat muttered, "It's not for my own pleasure."

"Well then, what exactly is it that's been keeping you away until dawn?"

"You know the state of affairs."

"Affairs of state are best handled by day, my son. Nights are for prayer, for sleep. Your grandfathers' duties were no less exalted than yours, but come night they slept in their own beds."

"And how lucky they were that our country wasn't under occupation, Aunt."

"That's all I hear—the occupation! What's done is done. There's no fighting the past or death. But your nephew, he's still alive. Less concern for the health of the nation and more for my grandson, if you will. He coughed all night again. Soon he'll be spitting up blood. He needs to get to the hospital directly. Today."

"But he'd recovered—aren't you exaggerating?"

"Don't believe me, Reşat? Night after night he coughs, and you're not around to hear it. I've been trying to catch you for days. Kemal's cough syrup is nearly gone, and we're running low on coal. We can't even heat the house properly."

"I'll see if there's any syrup left in the Pera pharmacies. As for the coal, Aunt, even the Palace is running short. We'll have to burn wood."

"But there isn't any wood to be had, either. And we've got to keep Kemal's floor warm."

"Have the gardener chop down the trees at the end of the garden." Ahmet Reşat got up from the divan and patted his aunt on the back. "I'll go have a look at Kemal," he said.

"Looking at him won't help. Take him to the hospital."

"You know that's not possible."

"Why?"

"Because he'd be arrested on the spot. His photograph's been posted for months; he'd be recognized immediately."

"Are you calling my grandson a traitor? Which of you went off to freeze in that white hell? Which of you took up arms for the nation? *He's* a traitor—the rest of you are heroes. Is that it?"

"I'm no hero. But the police aren't looking for me, either."

"The government that issued his arrest warrant has fallen, hasn't it? Does the present government have the power of decree? What are you so afraid of?"

"Aunt, governments rise and fall, but the Sultan remains."

"All I know is that Kemal needs medical attention. Now."

"Look, you brought him into this house without my knowledge or consent, and I turned a blind eye for your sake. So he wouldn't be suffering out on the streets. But don't expect me to jeopardize my family. If it's consumption, there's nothing the hospital can do for him beyond the customary tending. Thanks to you, Kemal is well cared for here at home: Mehpare is at his bedside night and day. We'll do our best to get him medicine. I beg you, let's end this discussion once and for all."

"Reşat, you rat!"

As his aunt stormed from the room towards the staircase, Ahmet Reşat sank back onto the divan, his newly throbbing head cupped helplessly in his hands.

Ahmet Reşat was indeed besieged by a host of troubles. His fugitive nephew couldn't be taken in for treatment, and the only doctor they could call was Mahir, a close family friend. Were it to become known that Ahmet Reşat was sheltering Kemal, he would face immediate exile, with no regard for his explanations, his years of service, or his position. He was caught between his oblivious and aging aunt and the protests of his wife, who was terrified that their children would be infected with consumption. The two women agreed that Kemal should be sent to the hospital, if for very different reasons. Kemal's condition wasn't improving at home. The disastrous misadventure of Sarıkamış had left him a broken man. Guilty of politically-motivated crimes, the scalawag had sided first with the partisans of the Committee of Union and Progress (CUP); when they were swept to power after the revolution of 1908, he'd turned his back on them, alienating not only CUP supporters but their opponents as well. Kemal was a true liberal, and the rift with CUP had been wide. But the damage had been done, and he would be forever associated with their cause. In fact, information of an unsettling nature had recently reached Ahmet Reşat: some of his colleagues had taken to referring to Kemal as "Reşat's mutinous nephew."

While the nephew may, in fact, have deserved all the contempt he received, the uncle did not. Kemal had been mired in trouble since his first day at the *lycée*, associating with agitators from the

Young Turks to the Masons. He'd also become friendly with opposition writers, going so far as to have articles published under his own name in a magazine known to be disagreeable to the Palace.

Kemal had been thrilled when CUP took over the reins of governance, but it hadn't been long before he'd made enemies of them as well. So much so, that he had volunteered to battle the Russians in faraway Sarıkamış just to get away from them—as well as to serve the homeland, of course.

But Kemal and thousands of his fellow soldiers had had no idea of what awaited them in the North. Istanbul's soldiers departed from Haydarpaşa Station to the accompaniment of fluttering handkerchiefs, a marching band, prayers, votive offerings, and the sacrificial slaughter of livestock. The pomp and high spirits proved to be short-lived. First came the long train ride to the furthest reaches of Anatolia, where mobilization to the front continued in the ice, by oxcart. When the soldiers finally reached camp, the hell that greeted them wasn't one of flame, but rather of glacial whiteness—a scalding cold that burned their arms and legs and faces, that raised blisters and opened wounds on their unprotected skin.

Few of them managed to survive the catastrophe of Sarıkamış. Kemal's relatives had braced themselves for news of his death, and were relieved to learn that he'd merely been captured. Nine months later they found him in front of the garden gate, barely alive, physically shattered. While they'd succeeded in slowly nursing his broken body back to health through many months of treatment at the hospital, followed by a year of devoted care at home, all the patience in the world had failed to heal his spirit.

Ahmet Reşat had disapproved of his nephew's imprudence, but, in light of the boy's sufferings in Sarıkamış, he did his best to forgive and forget. Allah had spared his life and reunited him with his family; perhaps the Palace would be equally forgiving—surely he regretted his foolhardiness. Kemal was well-educated, well-versed in languages; he'd seen the world; he was a skilled writer: surely he could be of use as a translator? Through the force of his good name and connections at the Palace, Ahmet Reşat had managed to secure a position and save his nephew. But sadly, this solution hadn't lasted.

Kemal's sufferings seemed to have taught him nothing: this time, he got himself mixed up with the Nationalists. Even as the uncle was applying for clemency to the Grand Vizier himself, the incorrigible nephew was penning articles critical of the government for publication in the *Vakit* and *Akşam* broadsheets—again, under his own name. Finally, the palace issued an arrest warrant.

Reşat Bey had absolved himself of any responsibility for his nephew, and promptly evicted him.

He'd been enraged to discover that Saraylıhanım had smuggled her grandson, whose health had deteriorated once more, back into the house, and secretly installed him in the attic with the servants. More than anything, Reşat was furious with his wife for having colluded with her. He could well imagine how his aunt had cajoled, bribed and threatened the rest of the household into silence, but surely Behice wasn't so easily bullied. As he listened to her defending herself through a flood of tears, he couldn't decide if she'd been motivated by pity, as she claimed, or if it was the extremely valuable diamond brooch, presented to his aunt some years ago by one of the Sultan's adoptive mothers—a Circassian, if memory served—that had finally won her over. Reşat knew only too well that his aunt was as adept at bribery as his wife was fond of baubles. Still, his conscience wouldn't permit him to throw his convalescent nephew back into the streets, and so he was allowed to remain in the servants' quarters until he had regained his health.

Ahmet Reşat was drifting away from his family. It had been weeks since he'd seen his daughters or spoken to his wife. He would arrive home while everyone was asleep and set off for work in the early morning darkness, before anyone else was awake. So removed was he from the grievances and tribulations of his household that he felt as though he lived in another city.

Reşat sighed. These domestic worries were nothing compared to the trials his country was facing. The city had been under occupation for nearly two years. High Commissioner Admiral Somerset Arthur Gough-Calthrope, who had signed the Armistice of Mudros on behalf of Britain, had promised Rauf Bey, his Ottoman counterpart, that no foreign forces would be deployed in Istanbul. He had failed to keep his word. The Allies had set in motion their secret plan to dismember the Ottoman Empire.

The invaders' fleet of fifty-five warships had dropped anchor in the Bosphorus just nine days after the leaders of the Committee of Union and Progress—that unfortunate trio of pashas mocked as "The Father, the Son and The Holy Ghost"—Enver, Talat and Cemal—had fled into exile. Troops were dispatched into the streets of Istanbul without delay.

Clutching Greek flags, throngs of Hellenic Ottomans turned out to give the invaders' ships a boisterous welcome. Even worse, in the dark month of February, the wretched residents of Istanbul were forced to endure the cries of joy and the raucous applause of the minority populace as the French commander pranced the entire length of Grand Rue de Pera, a strutting conqueror on a white steed.

The Ottoman Empire had begun to pay a heavy toll for decades of errors. The Christian minorities of Istanbul were cooperating with the occupiers. Muslims were denounced at every opportunity; occasional shows of resistance were quashed and the ringleaders subjected to horrific torture at the city's police stations. The Muslim residents of Istanbul were cowed, drained, distraught. To make matters worse, demoralizing accounts of the rowdy behavior of the Senegalese soldiers were becoming exaggerated into rumors of general ill treatment of Muslims at the hands of the minorities, who were even said to be tearing at women's veils.

While most of the rumors might have been false, they contained certain unbearable truths. Homes were undeniably being seized for billeting troops, and the conceited and arrogant English didn't hesitate to humiliate and rough up not just members of the general public, but government officials—members of parliament and ministers of state. Because pashas Ali Rıza, Salih Hulusi and Tevfik—the successive holders of the office of Grand Vizier during the occupation—had surreptitiously resisted the conditions outlined in the Amnesty, pressure from the English had led to their removal from office. Ordinary citizens had begun to face harassment at the hands of their neighbors. Fifteen days earlier, Dilruba

Hanım, a distant relative, had set off to visit the home of Reşat Bey. Sitting in a tram car she was poked in the shoulder by a *madam* and ejected from her seat with the words, "You've been sitting for long enough, Hanım; now it's our turn." In tears, the poor woman had flung herself from the tram at the next stop and walked all the way to Beyazıt.

Despite the provocations, the oppression, some were still determined to resist the occupiers. The states of Europe had received official notification of the establishment of a less compliant, rival government in Ankara. And while it was true that the Istanbul Government had issued a death sentence for one Mustafa Kemal, signed by the Sultan himself, no one dared to travel to Ankara to arrest the leader of the Turkish national movement and self-styled chairman of the new parliament. In fact, certain members of the Cabinet were known to be secretly wishing for his success.

Resistance was all well and good, Ahmet Reşat thought to himself, but without arms and soldiers, it was an exercise in futility. Certain adventurers imagined they could liberate not only Istanbul, but all of our lands—and backed only by half-starved, ill-clothed troops completely exhausted by eight years of combat on a thousand and one fronts. They were doomed from the start.

After a futile search through his jacket pockets for his cigarette case, Ahmet Reşat let loose an oath and blushed, even though he was alone in the room. Events beyond his control were turning him into an irritable man. Yes, he'd changed. He'd never been one for swearing, but now found that curses leapt to his lips with startling regularity. He was smoking more frequently. If his limbs felt heavy when he finally arrived home—and that was almost always the case these days—he'd taken to indulging in a single glass of *rakı* just before bed, the sharp scent of anise on his breath supplying his wife with yet another pretext for complaint. He himself was unhappy with his new vices, but these were trying times, demeaning, demanding days. The Treasury was unable to pay the salaries of its civil servants: the Ottomans were up to their necks in debt. Ahmet Reşat found himself having to answer to creditors every blessed day. All signs pointed a doubling of the yawning budget deficit of the previous year. Compensation for the alleged losses suffered in the World War would push that figure higher still.

Rising again, Ahmet Reşat began to stretch, pacing the length of the small room. If he went up to bed, he'd awaken his wife. His daughters were also certain to be asleep. The wooden treads of the staircase squeaked horribly, alerting light sleepers to any descent to the kitchen, the *hamam*, or the tiled entry hall. This was yet another item in his wife's litany of complaints. "Saraylıhanım is sitting with her ears pricked up yet again, trying to tell whether or not we're going down to the hamam," she'd grouse. But how to afford replacing the worm-shot wood or having the creaky hinges oiled?

He considered tiptoeing to the middle floor, but the prospect of an encounter with his nagging aunt led him to conclude that napping in the *selamlık* for a while longer would be the safer course of action. He needed to rest in order to brace himself for the pitiful sight of Kemal, whom he'd reared from infancy. He couldn't bear to watch as his nephew slowly slipped away. These days, each time he saw that ashen face, he nearly broke down and forgave the young man his innumerable faults.

Ahmet Reşat sat down on the divan and surveyed the front garden. Snowflakes still clung to the glossy leaves of the magnolia huddled just beyond the window like a mournful bride. The apple tree a little further past had been deluded by the March sun into sending forth early blossoms—lifeless now, in the wake of the cold snap. A bitter smile. Stupid apple tree, Reşat thought. Just like us. Rejoicing at the first glimmer of light.

Hadn't they all been similarly rapturous at the prospect of the liberties awaiting them after the deposition of the Red Sultan, Abdülhamid II? They'd been beating their breasts in regret a short time later. Better the devil you know, indeed.

The vacuum left by the exile of the CUP leaders was now being filled by the Freedom and Unity Party, with their propensity to exploit religious sentiments. Well, the people would soon tire of them, too. Reşat could see that the Freedom and Unity Party— upon which the Sultan relied, but which had declared him pro-English—was becoming less attractive by the day in the eyes of the people.

Many of the political prisoners exiled during the rule of the Committee of Union and Progress had returned following a recently enacted amnesty, and opposition forces bent on vengeance were flourishing. As if that didn't complicate matters enough, the Istanbul-based Greek and Armenian Patriarchates were simultaneously doing all they could to ensure that the invaders gained control—not only of Istanbul, but of all Turkey. That would only happen in an atmosphere of general chaos, which was why all the means at their disposal were being employed to incite the Greek, Armenian, and Muslim communities. The Greeks in particular had grown unruly and willful. So much so that when Deputy

Mayor Cemil Pasha had attempted to inspect a kebab shop in Karaköy, the Greek owner had chased him off with a stick.

As Ahmet Reşat recalled that unpleasant incident, a sharp twinge of pain lanced from the back of his neck to his forehead. He slowly rotated his neck to the left and right, seeking relief. Events were becoming increasingly difficult to stomach, even for those with deep reservoirs of fortitude. The Turks had been the very model of patience since the beginning of the occupation, turning a blind eye to the excesses of their fellow countrymen and neighbors, striving to maintain relations as before. Ahmet Reşat had retained both Aret Efendi, his Armenian gardener, and Katina, the young Greek seamstress who came by every fifteen days to do the mending and the ironing. Jewish civil servants under his supervision at the Finance Ministry continued to discharge their duties as though nothing had changed. The same was true of Christian ministers in the Cabinet and Christian deputies in the Parliament. Some Greeks and Armenians were promoting rebellion, but most of them were above suspicion; happily, the loyalties of the Jewish community remained with the Ottomans. While the Greek press struck an openly anti-Turkish tone, the Jewish press and community continued to show respect for the rights of Turks. And this despite the best efforts of the Greek High Council to incorporate the Jewish community into the recently-established Greek-Armenian Federation.

In all of this, Ahmet Reşat was both participant and spectator. His hands were tied. He was powerless to stop it, any of it. That hopeless, headlong rush toward an uncertain future. The sudden, violent fluttering of his left eyelid.

– 2 –

Behice, Mehpare and Saralihanim

As Mehpare crept silently down the stairs carrying a basin heaped with cheesecloth, she happened upon Behice Hanım, who was on her way to the toilet. Behice was wearing a *paçalık*, the muslin gown customarily worn by Istanbul brides on the first morning of married life. It was a faded pink, the collar lined with badly frayed rose-colored ribbon, the buttons straining against breasts grown heavy since the births of her two children. Up until just a few months ago, the paçalık had been carefully laid away along with her bridal gown. Then Behice had taken it out of the chest to be aired, washed and ironed.

It wasn't that as the wife of a civil servant she lacked the means to have new gowns made. No, she'd begun wearing her paçalık because it reminded her of a time when her husband had worshiped her, kissed and caressed her nearly every hour of the day. As the worn fabric slipped over her head she felt as though her youthful figure was restored, as though she'd been transported back to happier times, when unpinned hair had cascaded past her waist and her husband's eyes had been for her alone. She longed for the days when Reşat Bey returned from work early, and dragged his feet with regret as he left in the morning; when entire weekends were spent in his wife's arms, and his devotion to her aroused the envy of the other women of the household, especially Saraylıhanım. Everything had changed with such dizzying speed over the past five or six years, both at home and in the homeland. Her husband no longer listened, rapt, as she played the *ud* in the evening and sang, no longer found time for their daughters. Now when he came home his face was perpetually drawn; the responses he furnished his aunt, the only one who ever dared to question him, were terse; the meals hastily assembled for his enjoyment went untouched; instead, he forced down a bowl of soup and went straight to bed, where he tossed and moaned until dawn.

As far as Behice could remember, her husband's depression had begun when Kemal went off to join the Sarıkamış campaign. Reşat Bey had always been an imperturbable man, the sort who wasn't discouraged in the least by military mobilizations, the hardships of war. He'd been completely unruffled when, in September of 1914, Enver Pasha's Government had declared war on England, France, and Russia. The sons of the Ottomans had always been at war; they were accustomed to the privations and bloodshed that went with it. What did another one matter? That had been her husband's attitude, both to this most recent war and to the stream of bad news from the front. But when Kemal had joined what was clearly a lost cause, and subsequently been captured, Reşat Bey was shattered. And it was then that a grim-faced husband and a continuously weeping aunt had begun to make Behice's home life unbearable.

Finally there came the long-awaited news of a victory: the decisive defeat at Gallipoli of the combined armies of the British Empire and France. A festive mood swept the land, celebratory desserts and *börek* were sent to the neighbors. Houses filled with morning visitors extending their best wishes and congratulations, as though it were a *bayram* holiday. But the rejoicing was short-lived. Behice's buoyant spirits were deflated as Reşat Bey told her that, in order to exact revenge for their defeat in Gallipoli, Britain and France had secretly reached an agreement to give the Twelve Islands to Italy: "How could they do that without so much as consulting us?"

Behice turned and spat: "Bosnia and Herzegovina are gone, the Balkans are gone, and you're sighing over the loss of a few Aegean islands."

Just as people grow accustomed to life's pleasures, they become inured to its miseries. Fate had decreed that war was to be a part of their daily lives, and they had adapted and adjusted, even under occupation. And through it all, they prayed only that Allah permit them to keep what little they had left; that their troubles be reparable, their maladies curable.

Behice was primarily concerned with the safety and well-being of her immediate family. As providence would have it, she'd been born into a prosperous one. In fact, the mansion in which they lived had been provided by her father the same year she'd given birth to Leman, her eldest daughter.

Behice's mother had died in childbirth, and her father, İbrahim Bey, had always doted on his only child. He could have given the hand of beautiful blonde Behice to any *ağa*, any landowner or tribal chief, in Beypazarı, but instead he chose to marry her off to an Istanbul *beyefendi*, the son of a genteel Circassian family that had served the Palace for generations. His son-in-law had followed in the footsteps of his ancestors: education at palace schools, service to the state. He'd never been stricken by that insatiable thirst for bribes that afflicted so many Ottoman bureaucrats; his moderate lifestyle attested to that, to his integrity. The question of character was crucial in İbrahim Bey's selection of a son-in-law. Like himself, Ahmet Reşat was big-hearted and a true Muslim. A man who couldn't be bought off was a man who would resist other temptations. He would treasure Behice, and he would never take on a second wife. İbrahim Bey's appreciation for his son-in-law's virtues led him to provide material aid far in excess of his daughter's needs. Careful not to injure his son-in-law's pride, he'd had to resort to clandestine means to send his grandchildren secret gifts and fill his daughter's pantry with supplies from Beypazarı.

Behice sighed deeply. Sometimes she couldn't help wondering if, instead of having been sent to Istanbul to become the wife of a man continuously distressed by bewildering affairs of state, she wouldn't have been better off as the queen of Beypazarı. The man she'd loved in their first years of married life was gone—in his place was a new Reşat, one who'd grown heartsick over his nephew's misfortunes, who'd become increasingly irritable since the occupation, who seemed to grow more distant by the day.

Saraylıhanım's hiding Kemal in the attic had only made matters worse. Reşat Bey had never forgiven Behice for turning a blind eye to Kemal's secret arrival. But what could she have done? Throw a sick relative into the street? Now, as Kemal's condition worsened, she bitterly regretted her earlier complicity. But it was too late. Not only had she caused a rift with her husband, she'd allowed a disease she feared more than anything in the world to enter her home. How was she to protect her children? She issued instructions for all surfaces to be wiped with rubbing alcohol, constantly monitored the cleanliness of Mehpare's hands, and struggled to ensure that Kemal used a separate set of dishes and cutlery. Saraylıhanım, who was notorious for her fastidious ways, had opposed this last measure on the grounds that her grandson would be heartbroken if they treated him like a leper. And now she, Behice, the mistress of the house, had no choice but to station herself in her own kitchen to ensure that her children weren't served on contaminated dishes.

Behice was tired—a few months had passed since her husband had begun staying out until dawn. Even worse, his rare evenings at home were spent in lively political debate with Kemal. What a peculiar thing it was, this solidarity among men. When it came to discussing matters of state, he preferred the company of his infuriating nephew to that of his devoted wife. And this after she'd worked so hard to ingratiate herself by brushing up on her French, by poring over every periodical and newspaper that came her way. When she'd finally felt ready to venture an informed opinion on the opening of a second front, having concluded that it would be ill-advised to do so before the wounds of the Balkan wars had fully healed, she'd been rebuked by Saraylıhanım with the words: "What business do you have poking your nose into men's affairs?"

And so Reşat Bey had found a companion not in his wife, but in Kemal.

With all the enthusiasm of youth, Kemal had invariably rejected every last one of his uncle's opinions and positions. When the accursed Enver Pasha had declared war on Russia, Kemal had taken up arms and rushed off to the front, ignoring his uncle's objections and Saraylıhanım's histrionics. A typical Mad Circassian. The price Kemal paid for his failure to listen to his elders was two amputated toes, ruined lungs, infected kidneys, and a shattered mind. Saraylıhanım was deeply aggrieved by Behice's view of Kemal as a deranged soul. But surely the description was apt for a man who thrashed convulsively and howled until dawn, who shivered helplessly even in well-heated rooms, and who was always huddled over the brazier, staring at the glowing embers.

Even so, Saraylıhanım would allow no one to speak ill of her grandson. Like many former members of the court, she herself was of somewhat unsound mind. Behice couldn't decide whether to attribute Saraylıhanım's dottiness to her court background or her Circassian ancestry. For example, she was so fastidious that her hands were always raw with incessant washing. No one was permitted to enter her room or touch any of her possessions. She'd raised Reşat Bey, and he revered her. After losing a son to war and a daughter in childbirth, she and her grandson had moved in with him, promptly making life difficult for the rest of the household. In deference to Reşat Bey, they showed his aunt respect, but Behice could never bring herself to call this elderly woman—who was considered her mother-in-law—*mother* or *aunt*. In moments of tenderness, she occasionally managed *valide*, but "Saraylıhanım" was how she typically addressed this difficult woman, whose caprices she endured only for the sake of her husband. Happily, the women had recently found common cause: the transfer of Kemal to a hospital.

Mehpare was waylaid on the stairs by Behice, her eyes bleary from a sleepless night, her voice tinged with resentment at not knowing whether or not her husband had come home.

"Kemal coughed until morning again," she fretted. "That syrup you gave him was useless. Has he still got a fever?"

"He was on fire all night long," Mehpare answered. "I kept dipping strips of muslin into cold water, putting them on his forehead and his arms, and the fever dropped a bit. He's sound asleep now."

"For goodness sake, go boil those cloths. Give all his utensils and clothes a good scrubbing as well. And be sure to wash your hands three times . . . We've got children in the house, heaven forbid anything should happen to them. I can't make Reşat Bey see that this just won't do. Patients belong in the hospital."

"Don't worry, ma'am," Mehpare said. "I'm scouring everything."

Once Behice Hanım had closed the toilet door behind her, Mehpare heaved a sigh of relief and raced downstairs. As she immersed the laundry in a tub of steaming water and flaked soap, she muttered, "*Patients belong in the hospital!* We've got a whole house full of people, haven't we? It's not like we can't tend to a patient ourselves."

She put the washbasin back on the fire and prepared a cup of milk and honey for Kemal. Then she carefully placed it on a silver tray. She was just preparing to carry it upstairs when Saraylıhanım flew in.

"The poor boy coughed through morning prayers. He coughed; I wept. Did you apply the cupping jars?"

"I did, madame. No good. He had a bad fever."

"Was he coughing up blood?"

"No."

"The truth, now."

"He wasn't, I swear. Just coughing dry."

"The district doctor isn't enough—he should be taken to the hospital. I told Reşat, but he wouldn't listen."

"They won't take care of him in the hospital. He'll get cold. The Master knows what he's doing."

"He knows nothing. He's angry with Kemal for being so independent; that's why he's doing this. We need to get him to professionals."

"They'll only do what we're doing. They'll give him the same medicine . . ."

"That's enough out of you, Mehpare! Why do you think I chose you out of all your sisters, your cousins? Because you were polite, obedient—you'd set a good example for my grandchildren. If all I'd wanted was a servant, I'd have found a Greek or Armenian girl, and she'd have been literate . . ."

"I can read and write too."

"Only because I let you attend Leman's lessons. Which I paid for."

"God bless you," Mehpare said. *Not out of the goodness of your heart. Just so I could read you those women's magazines aloud and, most importantly, any letters from Kemal.*

"Fortunately, my efforts didn't go unrewarded," Saraylıhanım allowed. "You learned to read before Leman did. You're a clever girl, Mehpare. But you've got a sharp tongue. You'll go off to a husband one day, and if you talk back to him you'll be sent packing directly."

"I don't want a husband, ma'am."

"Hush. Don't speak in front of your elders. Keep your thoughts to yourself. Just listen. Now tell me, did you perform your prayers this morning?"

"I haven't found time yet. I'll get Kemal to drink his milk, and then I'll pray."

"Very good."

Mehpare's slight form slithered away, so eager was she to escape Saraylıhanım. Had she believed that Allah would restore Kemal's health in exchange for morning prayers, she would never rise from her rug. But the case was hopeless. It wasn't just his lungs—his mind had been wounded. After returning from Sarıkamış, nearly a year had passed before he was able to sleep at night. And when he did manage to nod off, he'd wake screaming, shivering, winter and summer. Over time the nightmares abated, the trembling stopped, and he began leaving the house, going to the newspaper offices. He'd even found lodgings, when Reşat Bey suggested it would be more appropriate for a bachelor to live elsewhere. Just when it seemed that Kemal was fully restored to health, he'd been stricken by this accursed disease, forced to return to the family mansion. "What a pain!" Mehpare muttered to herself, then bit her cheek, ashamed. The doctors had said Kemal's illness was the result of lungs grown frail, that he needed a long period of convalescence. But it was impossible not to fear the worst. Uncomplaining, untiring, Mehpare had been nursing him ever since.

She rushed up the stairs to avoid encountering any of the other family members. The patient should drink his milk while it was still piping hot. As she entered the room, the stench left by a long night of fever, sweat, and anguish struck her in the face again. She set the tray down on a table and approached the sickbed. Kemal was sound asleep, his thin yellow neck like a reed on the pillow, his hair plastered over his forehead. His mournful eyes usually made him look at least a decade older than he was—but they were closed now. Asleep like this, sighing and mumbling, he made you think of a child. Mehpare didn't wake him. She set the milk on the windowsill and was just leaving the room when Reşat Bey entered. Mehpare lowered her head and stepped aside to let him pass.

"He was awake all night, is that right?" Reşat Bey asked, closing his eyes to the nightdress peeking out from beneath Mehpare's long shawl.

"He was running a fever, sir."

"Nightmares?"

"No, the nightmares have stopped, praise God. The syrup the doctor gave us has done him good. He'd been doing so well lately . . . But . . ."

"But what?"

"He met with a visitor last week, down in the *selamlık*. It's a cold room, so I lit a fire in the large brazier and took it in to them. But it wasn't enough to keep back the damp. He must have caught a chill."

"Who was this visitor? Why wasn't I informed?"

Mehpare bowed her head. "I don't know, sir."

"Mehpare, listen. No one is allowed in when I'm not here."

"But they went to the *selamlık*, not here . . ."

"You're not to admit visitors to the *selamlık* either. No one."

"The housekeeper said he was an army friend of Kemal Bey's . . . He gets bored here all alone, and his grandmother gave her consent."

"With the exception of Leman's French and history tutors, no one is permitted to enter this house, even if he claims to be the son of the Sultan himself. Is that understood?"

"Yes, sir."

"Now go to your room and get dressed. We're well into the morning."

Mehpare slowly backed out of the room, knees trembling, mortified at having been caught in her night dress. Then she ran all the way to her room.

The housekeeper, Gülfidan, was producing her usual clatter in the kitchen as she prepared breakfast. Whenever Mehpare made the slightest sound, even the clink of a spoon on a tea glass, she was roundly scolded. But Saraylıhanım would countenance no criticism of the housekeeper she'd brought to Istanbul from the Caucasus. Mehpare herself was Circassian, but she had been born in the city. For that reason, and even though she was a distant relative, she would never attain the standing of the housekeeper in Saraylıhanım's eyes. Saraylıhanım had filled the house with native-born Circassians. She wanted no Christian servants—she countenanced only Aret Efendi, who tended the garden three times a week in the summer and once or twice a month in the winter, and Katina, who was responsible for Behice's ironing and needlework. And Saraylıhanım wouldn't even greet Katina. Upon being sent into service before age twelve, Mehpare had been warned that "palace types" were a bit odd. She'd been told they split hairs, became fixated on the tiniest things, were cantankerous. And it was all true. Saraylıhanım's continual grousing also exasperated Behice Hanım, whom Mehpare had overheard on multiple occasions wailing: "If she were my mother-in-law, maybe it wouldn't be so unbearable. But she isn't even Reşat's mother."

Mehpare stepped into her room and spread her prayer rug on the floor. Then, a towel draped over her arm, she headed for the ground floor hamam to perform her ritual ablutions.

Ahmet Reşat sat at the foot of Kemal's bed and laid the back of his hand on his nephew's neck, his forehead. Kemal's fever had broken. His forehead and upper lip were beaded with sweat.

It had been thirty years since Ahmet Reşat had first caressed those pink cheeks with his fingertips, terrified he would wake the sleeping baby. Kemal's late mother had brought him into this world, then traveled on to the next well before the customary forty days of confinement following childbirth had ended. It was a fate repeatedly visited upon Ottoman Turk families: the women died of massive blood loss or infection; the men died on the battle-field: the infants were surrendered to the care of aunts and uncles. Kemal's father had been martyred in the Greco-Turkish War be-fore he'd had the chance to see his newborn son. Reşat, himself an orphan, had still been a young man when he took full responsibil-ity for his nephew. He'd considered Kemal his son, and arranged that the boy be looked after by his great aunt, Saraylıhanım, and educated by the most reputable tutors in Istanbul. He had done his best to raise Kemal but had utterly failed to exert any influence on him

At the touch of the hand now resting on his forehead, Kemal's eyes fluttered open.

"Uncle," he murmured.

"How are you feeling? They tell me you couldn't sleep last night."

"I was feverish. But I vaguely recall Mehpare trying to lower my temperature with cold compresses."

"Should I call a doctor?"

"I don't want you to. I'm fine now, uncle."

Reşat Bey reached for the glass of milk and honey resting on the window sill. "Try to take a sip or two; it'll soothe your chest."

"Later, Uncle. Don't worry, Mehpare will definitely make me drink it."

"That poor girl's been an attentive nurse. Your aunt brought her up so well."

"Eh. When I became too much for her, she found someone else to enslave, that's all," said Kemal, with a weak chuckle.

"You've been too much for me too. Kemal. Look at the condition you're in. Why didn't you listen to us?"

"My condition is nothing compared to what's happened to the motherland. I still have nightmares about that damned General d'Esperey, trotting to the French Embassy on horseback, triumphant, like a commander of the Roman Legion. And on a white horse, no less! The insolence of it! Alluding to Mehmet the Conqueror's entrance into Constantinople! As if to say, you took this city on a white horse, and on a white horse I'm taking it back . . ."

"Come on. Try to think of happier things. You'll give yourself nightmares."

"Better to have died in Sarıkamış than to witness that terrible day."

Ahmet Reşat squirmed in exasperation.

"Just be grateful you're still alive," he managed.

"They say Maraş has taken up arms against the French. Is it true?"

"Yes. We've received reports."

"That's wonderful, Uncle!"

"Kemal! Even after the armistice was signed, some of the pashas refused to surrender their arms, and the commander in Mecca fought on for another two months. And to what end? None! On the contrary, the more we oppose them the tighter they clamp down."

"This time might be different. Anatolia has begun organizing. If resistance builds in the hinterlands, Istanbul will spring into action too."

"And then? I fear what the English will do to us."

"So you've started to think like the Sultan too? Disappointing."

"What you need to understand is that the Sultan is no worse than most of his predecessors. Ill-starred, that's all. This invasion came to pass during his reign. He's doing all he can to protect a throne that has endured for six hundred years."

"And what about us? Is he protecting his subjects?"

"That throne represents us all. If it falls, we go down with it."

"Well let's say it does fall. What do you plan to do? What are your thoughts?"

"I'm a civil servant, a treasury official, authorized to act only by proxy. I'm not even a member of parliament. My thoughts don't matter."

"They matter to me."

"Kemal, you already know what I think. We've been at war for years: Russia, the Balkans, Tripoli . . . And on and on. As for the

Great War, it destroyed us. Nobody wants to wage another now. Our weapons, our ammunition—it's all gone. Seized. Under these conditions, I naturally support the Sultan, I believe that the occupation will have to be resolved through diplomatic channels."

"You support the Sultan even if you admit he is at fault, don't you?"

"For generations my family has served, and been served by, the Palace. Don't expect me to betray or defy my *Padishah*. And I have to advise you, my nephew, not to betray him either. It would be most unbecoming."

Kemal was silent. He was too frail to argue further, but hoped his uncle would remain here for a while, chatting, giving him news of the outside world. He'd been surrounded by women ever since his confinement to this room. He'd begun to find them unbearable.

Reşat Bey rose to his feet. "I woke you up. I'll go now and let you sleep."

Kemal stretched his hand towards his uncle. "Don't go yet. Stay with me. Let's talk a little longer."

Reşat Bey took a seat again at the foot of the bed. The two men held each other's gaze for a moment. In his nephew's exhausted eyes, Reşat nearly caught a glimpse of his late mother.

"Kemal, who visited you last week?" he asked in a soft voice.

"When?"

"You had a visitor last week. Who was it?"

"Uncle, you'd think Abdülhamit had entrusted his secret agents to you as he was being deposed. How on earth did you hear about that?"

"I have my ways."

"Do you really have spies in the house?"

"Don't upset me, Kemal. I want to know who it was."

"An old friend from the army."

"Your army friends froze to death."

"This one was captured; and now he's back."

"What's his name?"

"Cemil Fuat. A distant relative of Fevzi Pasha."

"Is he a member of the Committee for Union and Progress?"

"Are there any left? Almost all of them who went to Sarıkamış froze, and the few survivors repented. Those who remained behind were strung up, here, by the occupiers and Damat Ferit."

Reşat Bey ignored his nephew's bluntness. "What does he want?"

"He came to see me. Must he want something?"

"Every time you receive visitors something abominable happens."

"Look, uncle: am I in any state to involve myself in something dangerous? You know perfectly well that the only thing to emerge from this room will be my corpse."

"Heaven forbid! You're still young. With enough rest and nourishment—if you keep your nose out of danger—you'll be burying me one day, God willing. As things stand, there won't be anyone else left to do it. War has claimed all the men of this family."

"Don't fret about your corpse, dear Uncle. Your daughters are pretty enough that before long your house will be bursting with husbands. Who knows—maybe this time the boy you've always hoped for will come into the world, and push me off my throne."

"That's enough of your prattling. Just promise that you won't invite anyone else to the house."

"Well I certainly won't invite anyone who might put you in danger."

"I've heard that before. But I haven't forgotten the night our house was surrounded by the police."

Kemal had opened his mouth to speak but he was wracked by a fit of coughing. When it had passed, Reşat Bey held the glass of milk out to his nephew. After several gulps, Kemal was able to speak again. "Uncle, I've heard that the Sultan's son-in-law, İsmail Hakkı Bey, has sided with the Nationalists, that he's been trying to make their case at the Palace. Is it true?"

"How do you hear these things in this garret of yours? Or have you been sneaking outside?"

"My visitor told me."

"His account was less than accurate. Adventurers like you and İsmail Hakkı will be the end of us. The streets have filled with Greeks and Armenians in British uniforms gathering information for the English. They have eyes everywhere. All this nonsense about French sympathies and Nationalists assembling in Anatolia is just that: nonsense. It's over, Kemal. We're finished. Parts of Anatolia, too, are under occupation. We'll be lucky to save Istanbul and the Caliphate. The Sultan has consented to British administration, but only temporarily. It's better than being dismembered and destroyed. And that's why we're simply going to have to get along with the English."

"Can't the Sultan remain on friendly terms with the English even as he supports the resistance in Anatolia? Don't underestimate that movement, Uncle. They say that some have already left Istanbul to join them."

"What difference would it make if all Istanbul were to decamp to Anatolia? We have no boots for our feet, no control over our own armories."

"Our hopes rest with God."

"Exactly. The treasuries are absolutely bare, our civil servants unpaid. We were able to pay the wages of the clerks and cleaners this month, but only after ransacking our own buildings, selling off bags of sand, axes, shovels, leather, scrap-iron, anything else we could get our hands on."

Kemal's head fell back onto the pillow.

"You need rest. It's early, and I've worn you out," Reşat said. "I'll have a quick bite and get back to work. If you're still not feeling well, send word and I'll have Doctor Mahir stop by in the evening."

Kemal didn't respond. The cries of the street hawkers and milk-men had begun to penetrate the room. Istanbul was stirring; her populace waking to yet another day of occupation, shame, dejection. The carpet grew brighter and brighter under the bands of light seeping through the shutters.

Reşat Bey stood up and crept out of the room, careful not to disturb his nephew, who, no longer eager for conversation, was feigning sleep. As he descended to his room on the floor below he braced himself for the complaints of his wife. He was painfully aware that he'd been arriving home at dawn for nearly a month, no explanations offered; that Behice was wondering what could possibly keep a treasury official busy at all hours of the night.

But Ahmet Reşat was in no position to enlighten his wife on his clandestine activities. Moreover, his own feelings concerning his work were ambiguous. Mahir was the only person to know that the Grand Vizier had entrusted him with a special task; and only because the doctor himself had been charged with similar secret duties. A number of prominent bureaucrats, all of whom spoke excellent French, had been encouraged to cultivate friendships with high-ranking French officials. To that end, they were expected to attend dinners and to engage their new friends in games of bridge and chess. Ahmet Reşat had tried, and failed, to reassure himself that his duties were not, in fact, those of a spy. And it wasn't as if he was expected to rummage through safes and chests of drawers for secret documents and the keys to the Allied Forces' ciphers. It had merely been observed that relations between the British and French had grown increasingly strained, and there was curiosity as to the cause. When Reşat Bey had been informed by the first aide-de-camp that his presence was requested by Grand Vizier Ali Rıza Pasha, he'd armed himself with a stack of documents and arrived at the appointed hour prepared to discuss the empire's finances. But the Pasha made no mention of receipts and expenditures. The exchange of pleasantries over coffee completed, the Pasha came straight to the point. In two days, Reşat and Mahir were to attend a dinner at the mansion of Count Ostrorog, on the shores of the Bosphorus. Among those dining with them would be the French High Commissioner, and Reşat Bey was asked to keep his ears open throughout the evening.

Ahmet Reşat had a deep aversion to subterfuge of any description, even in service of the motherland. He was a straightforward man, well-bred, guileless. However great his reluctance to attend the function, he was somewhat comforted by the sight of Mahir, and absolutely overjoyed to encounter, in Ostrorog's salon, his old friend, Count Caprini.

"Caprini Efendi! How fortuitous! It's been so long. You're in good health, I hope?"

"My dear friend," said the Count, "the sight of you has improved my health no end. Now why don't you join me in a corner and we'll catch up."

Count Caprini reputedly held an administrative position at the Italian Commissariat, but had in fact been deployed to Istanbul to command the Italian Military Police and to prevent them from clashing with the Turks. He was known to be a friend to the Ottoman Muslims. As fate would have it, he had been serving at a gendarmerie in Crete during the massacre of the Muslims there and was subsequently rewarded for his humanitarianism by Sultan Abdülhamit II, who presented him with a medal and the title "Count Caprini Efendi."

The friendship between Ahmet Reşat and Count Caprini went back even further. Ahmet Reşat had held a government position in Thessalonica at the same time Count Caprini was employed there to help organize the Ottoman Gendarmerie. The two young men met and became fast friends. Together they enjoyed the diversions of the bustling port city, attended chess parties, and went riding. Many years later their paths had crossed on several occasions in occupied Istanbul. But, aggrieved by the treatment of his city, Ahmet Reşat had chosen to avoid his old companion. Now fate had united them once more, and they found time to exchange a few words before they were seated for dinner.

"If an emergency should ever arise, please come to me, Reşat Beyefendi," the Count said.

May Allah save me from having to depend on any of you, was what Ahmet Reşat thought to himself, but merely smiled and said, "How kind of you, Caprini Efendi."

After dinner, the men broke up into groups for bridge and chess. That first evening, no information of any kind was divulged. Still, the Grand Vizier thought it best for Reşat to cultivate any acquaintances made that day. A useful social connection might still emerge. Who knew?

Over the next few days, they spent a great deal of time with the French, one day attending a dance performance in Pera, followed by a trip to a bar. And it wasn't long before an apparently indifferent Ahmet Reşat heard lips loosened by drink convey some interesting information. His eyes fixed on the stage, his ears focused on the chattering Frenchmen, he had learned that even though the French were members of the Allied Forces they objected to being under British command, for which reason they were bedeviling General Wilson.

Ahmet Reşat's stomach churned as he began writing up his report the following day. What if the document fell into the wrong hands? He, Ahmet Reşat, was no spy! He was a finance officer. He tore the report to bits and went to the office of Ali Rıza Pasha, where he presented an oral account of what he'd overheard.

From that day on, he found himself frequently invited to play chess and bridge with the French, who were themselves cultivating closer ties with Ottoman bureaucrats, in order to spite the

English. He couldn't bring himself to sound out Count Caprini, though. After all, he was a friend.

When the cabinet of Ali Rıza Pasha ratified the National Pact presented by a delegation of nationalists based in Ankara, Ahmet Reşat was suddenly hopeful that everything would turn out for the best, and that he would be relieved of these unpleasant duties. In fact, the forces of destiny were simply preparing fresh surprises.

– 3 –

Sabotage

Doctor Mahir placed his palm on the patient's bare back and began tapping the surrounding area with the other hand. Kemal
struggled to remain upright in bed and flinched at the touch of
the doctor's cool, freshly-scrubbed hands. Not yet content with
his diagnosis, Doctor Mahir placed his ear where his hand had
been, and listened for a long while as his patient drew in and expelled the air. "Put something on immediately, don't catch a chill,"
he said, straightening.

Mehpare scurried into the room with the underclothes she'd
just warmed by the stove in the hallway. Kemal slipped into his
undershirt and allowed her to help him into his pajama top, but
when she began doing up its buttons he gently pushed her away
with, "I'll do it myself." Shifting his gaze, he looked directly into
the doctor's eyes and asked, in an exaggeratedly mournful tone,
"So doctor, are my lungs singing the song of consumption?"

"Consumption's no laughing matter. And it doesn't sing."

"It kills."

"That's right. But it isn't the white plague that will kill you,
Kemal—it's your hot blood."

"So I don't have consumption?"

"When I come by tomorrow I'll bring my stethoscope. I don't think it's consumption. You've caught a bad chill. Not that it's possible to know for certain, without conducting x-rays.

"I could come to the hospital myself in secret . . . Maybe at night."

"You'd only attract more attention. The hospitals are never empty! There's always a doctor on duty, orderlies, nurses. It's best you remain indoors for a few more weeks. It's still bitterly cold outside."

"I'm fed up, Mahir."

"Of course you are. But if your lungs catch a chill again you're certain to get consumption, no question of that!"

"Am I going to have to live with that fear for the rest of my life?"

"Exactly. You've so abused your body that you've lost all immunity. Your lungs and liver are seeking any pretext for disease. Don't give it to them."

"Am I going to be confined my bed forever?"

"Of course not. And you can use your brain without fear of affecting your other organs. But you've got to keep warm, stay calm, avoid too much rakı and abstain completely from tobacco. Marry a good woman, one who'll take care of you, and you'll live a long, happy, uneventful life."

"And where's the woman who'll accept this wreck of a man?"

"I know of any number of nubile girls eager to give their hands to a handsome veteran, disabled or not."

"Let's say we've given consumption the slip . . ."

"We're not assuming anything until you've had a chest radiograph."

"Well let's imagine for a moment that I'm in sound health. What woman would willingly sleep beside a man who can't sleep himself, who has nightmares whenever he does?"

"The nightmares will pass. Haven't they become less frequent?"

"Not at all."

"Are you taking the syrups I prescribed?"

Kemal nodded in Mehpare's direction. "She's constantly forcing various concoctions down my throat. But I haven't asked her what they are."

Mehpare leapt at the opportunity to speak. "We've ordered everything you prescribed. And the Master always manages to get them refilled within a day or two. As for me, I administer them with my own two hands, I swear it. Punctually and without fail."

"Good, my girl. Is he sleeping better?"

"Yes, praise God. He still has nightmares, but not as often. Oh, and he no longer insists I set up a brazier right next to his bed. See, we've even been able to move it to the hallway. This tiny room used to be like an oven."

"It'll pass, all of it. Now that the fever's broken the most important thing is that he eats well, gets plenty of rest and stays warm."

"Yes, Sir," said Mehpare. But what she hadn't said was that the medicines weren't always available, that they had difficulty obtaining meat, that they were dependent upon the parcels of cereal and grain that Behice's father sent from Beypazarı.

"Go on now, Mehpare. Go downstairs and prepare us two cups of strong coffee," Kemal said.

"What's happening out there, tell me quick!" he asked Mahir the moment the girl closed the door behind her.

Drawing his chair up to the bed, Mahir spoke in a whisper. "The Underground hasn't been idle, Kemal. They assembled last night, at Tikveşli Farm. There have been critical developments. We need information from inside the Palace."

"But isn't that just what the Sultan's consort has been providing?"

"She isn't privy to Cabinet meetings. Only to the harem. Is your uncle so very uncommunicative?"

"What do you want to know?"

"We'd save precious time if we had the inventories and locations of munitions and other war materials."

"Only to the Minister of War has that information."

"The Finance Ministry must know as well. They've been selling scrap weapons."

"I'll feel my uncle out as best I can. He thinks I've been too sick to get involved in any of this. He may tell me something."

"Ah Kemal, if only he'd join us. He'd be such an invaluable addition to the cause!"

"Mahir, my uncle is absolutely loyal to the Sultan. He'd never betray him."

"Your uncle has every reason to believe he's on the side of right. No one expects us to succeed."

"But what else can we do? However long the odds, we have to try, don't we?"

"Plenty of people believe that the Anatolian resistance is being led by former CUP partisans. And everyone's fed up with them. When you consider the fiasco that was Sarıkamış, who would follow them now? In reality, of course, the resistance leader, Mustafa

Kemal Pasha, is as despised by them as he is by the Sultan. Unfortunately, this is known only to a few."

"They haven't disappeared, Mahir. I've heard that some former CUP supporters even hold positions of responsibility at Karakol. Is that true?"

"It is. We have no choice but to employ experienced hands. Not that they should necessarily be judged by their past support for CUP. Don't forget, you were one of them once."

"For goodness sake, don't remind me."

"You see? Ideas change along with leaders. Of course there are a few of the old guard among the Turkish Nationalists. But now they're . . ."

"Nationalists."

"It rolls off the tongue, doesn't it? *Nationalist*."

"It rolls off the heart, as well. I vowed to sacrifice all for this cause. I'm prepared to do whatever you ask the very moment I'm healthy enough to do it."

"You'd better get well first. And let me know everything your uncle says."

"Are they still staying at the farm?"

"No, the farm is too far away. They've rented a place in the city. It was convenient to move to, and it will be easy to flee if the need arises. Not to mention its proximity to . . ." Mahir fell silent as Mehpare entered the room carrying a tray. He removed a few French periodicals from his bag and placed them on the desk, saying, "I brought these for your amusement, but I'd appreciate your translating the lead articles."

"Your French is better than mine."

"But my time is limited."

Kemal smiled bitterly. "And time is all I have."

Mehpare placed the cups of coffee on the desk, picked up the blanket that had slipped to the floor, spread it over Kemal's legs and silently left the room. As she descended the stairs she whispered to herself: "Praise be—it isn't consumption. Even it were, I'd nurse him back to health. Allah, I beg you, add my lifespan to his. Don't begrudge him a long life, Allah!"

Mehpare was astonished to find Kemal fully dressed, freshly shaved and sitting at the writing table in the selamlık. As recently as a week ago, he'd been unable to leave his room. She tapped lightly on the wooden surface of the table.

"You summoned me, sir? Would you like some coffee?"

"Mehpare, close the door please."

Mehpare closed the door and returned to her place beside the table. "Last time you sat here you caught a terrible cold. Why have you come downstairs? I'll go and get the brazier . . ."

"Sit down across from me," said Kemal, pointing to the leather chair across from his.

"But the brazier . . ."

"Forget the brazier. Listen to me . . ."

"But you'll get cold . . ."

"Mehpare! I'm not cold! Now hush and listen."

Mehpare sat down. "Yes, sir."

"You see this letter? It's addressed to you."

"To me! Oh God! Who sent it?"

"It's from your family."

"Has something happened back home? Is someone ill? It's not my aunt, is it?"

"Someone in your house is both ill and not ill."

"What do you mean? I don't understand."

"This letter informs the reader of an illness. But no one is ill."

Mehpare sat there, speechless, eyes wide.

"Don't worry. I wrote the letter, Mehpare."

"You wrote it?"

"That's right, I wrote it. It says that your aunt has fallen ill and wants to see you."

"But why would you write that?"

"Because that way you'll be able to show the letter to Saraylıhanım and receive permission to go home to Beşiktaş."

"Oh God!"

"What are you afraid of? You're familiar with Beşiktaş. You grew up there, didn't you?"

"I know Beşiktaş well, yes."

"Fine then. You're off to visit your aunt."

"But sir . . . Why?"

"Because I wish you to, Mehpare. This letter will allow you to visit a certain address in Beşiktaş. I'll give it to you. You're to deliver the letter, and in return they'll give you an envelope to bring to me. That is all."

"Saraylıhanım won't let me leave."

"There's no harm trying. When she reads the letter I wrote, she's liable to give her consent."

"But she'll ask when it came. What should I tell her?"

"Doesn't the postman come at about the same time every day? At about ten in the morning?"

"Yes."

"Well, it's about ten o'clock right now and I'm sending you to the shops for tobacco. You'll meet the postman at the door. He'll give you the letter. You'll tear open the envelope and throw it away. And when you read its contents, you'll run, in tears, straight to Saraylıhanım. Don't even think about going to Behice instead. She'd recognize my handwriting."

"What if she doesn't believe me? What if she wants to see the envelope?"

"Like I said, you'll tear it up and throw it away. Into the waste bin in the garden."

"I can't do it, sir. Please forgive me, but I can't"

"You'll do it, Mehpare. And you'll be tipped for your trouble."

"I don't want a tip, sir. I'm begging you, please don't send me away."

"If you don't go, I'll have to."

"But you can't sir! Not onto the streets. You've only just got over your fever."

"The danger isn't my fever but my getting caught. If I'm arrested I'll go directly to prison."

"But you'd die in prison. Do you want to die?"

"Of course not. I've got too much to do. But if you won't help me, go I must, and either catch a chill or get caught. Either of those would be the end of me."

"Please don't sir, I'm begging you."

"Then do as I say."

Mehpare started weeping. Hands pressed to her face, she rocked back and forth. Kemal stood up, then kneeled before her. He reached out and stroked a lock of hair that had spilled from beneath her cotton kerchief and onto her forehead. Then he caressed her cheek.

"Don't worry, Mehpare, everything will be alright. Once you obtain permission from Saraylıhanım, you'll go to your aunt's house and then to a house in Akaretler, where you'll exchange one envelope for another, easy as that," he cajoled.

"And if they find out?"

"Blame me. Tell them I forced you. That's the truth, isn't it?"

"If they find out they'll send me packing."

"They won't find out."

"But if they did . . . Reşat Beyefendi . . .Saraylıhanım . . . My God, I don't want to think about it. My uncles would shoot me."

"No one will harm you. I won't let them. If they dismiss you, I'll take you under my protection."

"How?"

Kemal couldn't help smiling. He was, after all, still dependent upon the patronage of his uncle, and even Mehpare would attach no credibility to his words.

"I'll marry you."

"Ah! That would be out of the question!"

"Why? Would you refuse me?"

"They'd never allow it."

"Some undertakings don't require permission, Mehpare. You've nursed me devotedly. If it weren't for you, I would never have recovered. And what's more, you're a pretty girl. You're intelligent, well-mannered. What else could a man want in a wife? Of course, if you say that I'm sick and old, that you won't have me, that's something else entirely!"

"What kind of talk is that, sir? Don't say such things!"

"Then think it over. You have until evening. If you accept, splendid. And if you don't, I'll fend for myself."

"Couldn't you give the letter to someone else?"

"No. I told you, I'll go myself." Kemal stood up, went to his chair and sat down again. "Now I'm ready for that coffee."

Mehpare emerged from the room like a sleepwalker. She leaned her head against the wall of the stairwell. She felt dizzy. It was only by leaning against the walls from time to time that she was able to make it as far as the kitchen.

Saraylıhanım burst into her grandson's room without knocking. Kemal was writing at the little table he'd placed directly in front of the window. "Everything alright?" he said. "Thank God I managed to dress myself a few moments ago. Is the situation so very urgent?"

The elderly woman ignored his annoyance. "That girl is prattling on about something or other."

"Which girl?"

"Mehpare. She claims to have received a letter . . . apparently her aunt is ill . . . My eyes aren't up to the task. Read this to me."

Well aware that his aunt was illiterate, Kemal smiled softly to himself as he carefully examined the letter thrust into his hand. "Grandmother, Mehpare's aunt has fallen ill and asks that Mehpare be permitted to visit her today."

"Is the illness serious? We'll send Hüsnü Efendi."

"She asks for the girl, not Hüsnü."

"But how can Mehpare be expected to travel there alone? Hüsnü Efendi can go with our condolences and return with news of the patient. I'll give him a bit of money for medicine if necessary."

"If, God forbid, something serious happens you'll have to answer for it. The letter says Dilruba Hanım suffered heart palpitations last night. Let the girl go to her."

"But if she goes who will care for you, my boy?"

"Am I a child? Look, I'm better now, I can walk around the house on my own. Please don't coddle me like that."

"The girl can go if you wish it. But are you certain this isn't some ploy she's hatched? Where's the envelope? Some sort of assignation, maybe?

"The things you say! God save us from such suspicion. The poor girl hasn't so much as poked her nose out of doors for months, and all because of me."

"She's had ample opportunity to go to the shops. We also sent her to the doctor's house when you were having your fit of nerves. She's been distracted these past few days. She's been strange. I'm an old hand, not so easily fooled. I know a pair of moon-eyes when I see one. That girl's in love, I'm certain of it."

"I can't attest to the girl's eyes, but with my own I saw her tearing up an envelope."

"You see!"

"That's right, I was on my way to the kitchen to get a glass of water . . ."

"Why didn't you send Mehpare? Why go all the way down to the kitchen?"

"I was tired of sitting in my room. I thought moving my legs a little would do me good."

"So you're telling me the letter is authentic?"

"I saw her myself. She removed a letter and tore up the envelope. After she read it, she began crying."

"You didn't ask her why she cried?"

"No, I didn't. She was in the garden. I saw her through the kitchen window. Just let the girl go to her aunt."

"Not on her own. Hüsnü will go with her."

"While they're in Beşiktaş, they can pick up some tobacco for me."

"Hasn't the doctor forbidden you tobacco?"

"Not completely. I'm allowed it in moderation. If I'm denied my tobacco as well as everything else, I'm well and truly finished."

"Ah, my boy. You finished yourself off with your own hands. If we fuss after you now, it's only to restore your health. I'll arrange your tobacco if you promise not to drink after meals."

"I promise," said Kemal through gritted teeth. "Oh, and could you tell Mehpare to stop by my room before she goes? I want to give her the address of my tobacconist."

Letter in hand, Saraylıhanım flounced out of the room and promptly ran across Behice on the second floor.

"Is there anything you'd like from the shops, my girl?" Saraylıhanım asked. "I'm sending Mehpare to Beşiktaş . . . You mentioned yesterday that you'd run out of white silk thread . . . Shall I order you some more?"

"Why's she going all the way to Beşiktaş? Aren't there plenty of shops here in Beyazit?"

"Her aunt has taken to her bed," said Saraylıhanım, nodding significantly at the sheet of paper in her hand.

"Let me have a look at that . . ."

"What for! I've seen it. I had Kemal read it to me, since my eyes can't take the strain. I'm sending the girl. She'll return soon enough. Give her a shopping list and she'll pick it up for you."

"Does Reşat Bey know about this? Better not make him mad."

"Reşat Bey has more important things to do than concern himself with the servants."

That little minx turns up under every stone, the elderly woman muttered to herself. She's taken on airs just because her father sends supplies every month. Well, we'll see whose word is law in this house.

Determined to see her orders carried out before Behice could intervene, Saraylıhanım descended to the kitchen on the floor below, where she found Mehpare absentmindedly attending to a bubbling pot.

"Hurry up, girl. If you're going, better get an early start. Tell Hüsnü Efendi to get ready. Get into your *çarşaf* and onto the streets. I expect you back home before mid-afternoon prayers. No dawdling. Ask after your aunt's health, find out what she needs and come straight home. Oh, and pick up some tobacco for Kemal. Don't forget."

Mehpare didn't have to be told twice. Flinging a ladle onto the countertop, she raced to her room to get dressed.

Hüsnü Efendi and Mehpare were able to reach Beşiktaş only after changing trams three times. The streets were full of soldiers wearing the uniforms of various nations. While the dejection of the Muslim Ottomans could be read on their faces, the Greeks and Armenians were all smiles. There were few women, Christian or Muslim. Among the scenes streaming past the window of the tram, the ones that most frequently caught Mehpare's eye were a few turbaned *hodjas*, street porters bent double under their towering loads, beggars sitting cross-legged on the sidewalk, carriage drivers whipping bony horses, Gypsy women with babies slung onto their backs. But it was the swarms of migrants that cut her to the heart: dirty-faced, bawling babies pressed to their mothers' breasts, women dressed head to toe in black, white-bearded men with creased faces leaning heavily on ragged children. Ethnic Turks and Muslims forced to abandoned all they had, fleeing for their lives, forcibly expelled from the lands they'd once called home. Proud and uncomplaining, they sheltered in makeshift shacks as they set about repairing their shattered lives. Mehpare's own family had been torn from their land and resettled in Istanbul. Face pressed against the glass, she looked out at the downcast, despondent citizens of a city besieged.

Hüsnü and Mehpare got off the tram in Beşiktaş and walked together as far as the neighborhood where Dilruba Hanım, Mehpare's aunt, had her home. The shops had opened their shutters, but there was very little to buy. As they were about to turn into one of the side streets in Beşiktaş Market, Mehpare was amazed to see apples displayed at a green grocer's on the high street. Just a week earlier, their poor gardener had returned empty-handed when Saraylıhanım sent him out for some fruit. Mehpare immediately bought a brown paper bag full of apples, then led the way along a narrow lane lined with wooden houses sporting oriel windows and latticed panes. They stopped in front of a two-storey house completely devoid of paint. Mehpare struck the door with the knocker and waited. The head of a grey-haired woman appeared in a second floor window. As Mehpare pulled back her çarşaf to expose her face, the woman smiled and waved.

"Hüsnü Efendi, they're home," Mehpare said. "You can go and look after your business now. Come and get me before the afternoon call to prayer."

Hüsnü Efendi was anxious to do just that, but propriety demanded he delay his departure. "The shopping errands . . ."

"I'll handle them. I know where the shops are."

"You can't walk the streets alone. I'll wait for you right here at the door and we'll go together."

"It's freezing! You can't possibly wait here in this weather. I'll do the shopping with my cousin. She's the best judge of what to purchase and where. Why don't you go to a coffee-house, or just do as you wish."

Mehpare removed a large iron key from the wicker basket lowered from an upper window and slid it into the lock.

"Fine then. I'll get some seeds for the back garden. It'll be March soon and time to sow," Hüsnü Efendi relented.

"Knock when you get back and I'll come down directly," said Mehpare.

Key in hand, Mehpare stepped into a dimly lit hall. Happy to be free of Hüsnü Efendi, she fairly skipped up the narrow flight of stairs to her aunt, who was waiting at the top, head covered with a traditional white Yemeni headscarf.

She kissed her aunt's hand and ritually pressed it to her forehead. Then the two women embraced and kissed each other's cheeks.

"Has something happened, dear?" asked Dilruba Hanım. "When I saw you pop up out of the blue like this I didn't know whether to be fearful or overjoyed. I hope nothing's wrong."

"I dreamt of you several nights in a row, aunt, and felt the need to see you," said Mehpare, handing her aunt the paper bag. "I know how much you like apples. I found them at the grocer's by the public fountain."

"May this abundance be a blessing to us all, my child," her aunt smiled. "Come in and sit by the stove, your cheeks are frozen. Would you like some tea?"

"I'd love some."

"I've just put it on to brew, ready in a moment."

Mehpare beamed at the sight of chestnuts lined up on top of the stove.

"You're roasting chestnuts for me! Did something tell you I was coming?"

"You were always terribly fond of them, weren't you? They're just about done," said her aunt, as she turned each one over with a pair of tongs. "Tell me, my girl, those dreams you had, did they unsettle you?"

"I've been feeling troubled lately, and it's crept into my dreams, aunt."

"Has that mad palace woman been upsetting you, Mehpare? Or have you been unable to get along with the lady of the house?"

"No one has troubled or upset me. It's Kemal Bey who has me worried sick. He's not getting any better."

"For goodness sake, thousands of young men froze to death in Sarıkamış. Your patient has such a strong constitution that he survived. Be grateful that he came back safe and sound."

"He may be safe, but he's not yet sound. He's weak, he frequently falls ill. He still has nightmares from time to time. He recovered only at the end of last summer."

"So what more do you want? Is it so easy to escape death?"

"He left home when he recovered. They must not have looked after him, because this time his lungs caught a chill. Saraylıhanım had him brought back to the house. He was so feverish last week. Behice Hanım was terrified he'd come down with consumption, and wanted him sent to hospital."

"Behice Hanım reckoned that with Kemal Bey out of the house you'd have more time to mind her children."

"The girls have grown up, aunt. They don't need minding."

"The eldest is only fourteen."

"Leman turns sixteen this year. Her younger sister is nine."

"Still plenty of time to marry them off. You'll be the first bride to emerge from that house—that's what you're really telling me. With Kemal Bey on his feet, God willing, we'll begin preparing for a wedding . . ."

"I don't understand."

"What is there to understand? You've been of marriageable age for some time. Saraylıhanım promised me she'd attend to your prospects. Not yet of course. She's got Kemal Bey to think of. But the moment he's fully recovered . . ."

"Shame on you, aunt! I don't even want a husband."

"What kind of talk is that? What will you do if you don't marry? Become an old maid?"

"Exactly."

"God forbid! Once you've married it will be Mualla's turn, and Meziyet's. I have my own girls' future to consider as well."

"Why aren't they here today?" asked Mehpare.

"Meziyet is at school. Mualla stayed with her aunt last night. They'll be home soon. Listen Mehpare, it's no use trying to change the subject. The order in which marriages take place can't be changed. And you're next."

"The tea must be ready now, aunt. I'll have a glass and go," Mehpare said as she escaped to the kitchen. "I have to pick up some things for the house."

"You've come to do your shopping, not for me," her aunt grumbled.

"How can you say that! Only this morning I wept tears of joy at the thought of coming home. But, seeing as I'd be in Beşiktaş, I was given a list of chores to do. I'll come and sit with you when I'm done."

Mehpare gulped down her tea, anxious to attend to Kemal's instructions, her mind elsewhere as her aunt continued to chatter. She carried the empty glass to the kitchen and had arrived at the top of the stairs when her aunt dashed after her.

"Are you leaving so soon?"

"I'll be right back."

"Let me put on my çarşaf and I'll join you."

Mehpare fidgeted uncomfortably. "Aunt, I wonder if I could ask you for something . . . I miss your *gözleme* terribly . . . Could you prepare some before I return? I hope it's not too much trouble."

"Don't they make you gözleme at the house? There's a head cook, isn't there?"

"He's been discharged. And anyway, no one makes it like you."

"Flattery, flattery! The ones with cheese?"

"Yes, with cheese."

As her aunt bustled off to the kitchen, Mehpare rushed down the stairs and into the street. The snow had stopped. She walked towards the marketplace. She knew of a tobacconist there, but couldn't recall the exact location. It had been so long since she'd wandered through Beşiktaş Market. Some shops were gone, new ones had opened. And unless she also found a sundries and notions shop to buy some thread, she'd have to stop by the shops in Beyazit Market on the way home. She was hurrying along the street when she slipped and bumped into a sesame-roll vendor's circular tray. The ring-shaped rolls spilled onto the snow. She bought a few from the muttering vendor after he scooped them up off the ground and wiped them on his trouser leg. A sack of rolls under her arm, she cautiously proceeded to the high street and turned towards Akaretler and the address she'd committed to memory. *You won't have to walk far, it's on the right, not quite half way up the hill,* Kemal had told her. *The house with the dark green iron door and the green shutters. You'll know it the moment you see it.*

She climbed up the street, scanning every door and shutter, unable to understand why Behice Hanım continued to insist that the family relocate to this neighborhood, and why Saraylıhanım was so adamantly opposed to the idea. Saraylıhanım claimed that the district wasn't Muslim, but Mehpare knew that employees of the court lived in this double row of identical yellow houses. Saraylıhanım was really something! There was nothing she wouldn't say to contradict her daughter-in-law. In this case it was just as well, Mehpare thought to herself. There were no signs of life in this wide avenue. The narrow streets of Beyazit were filled with donkeys dragging carts of onions and potatoes, street vendors selling sherbet, fabric, women's clothing . . . The only sights here in Akaretler, were a few passing phaetons and men in fezzes strolling along the sidewalk. A couple of automobiles belonging to the occupation forces drove by. This was clearly a neighborhood for the wealthy, for those with palace connections. That must be why Behice Hanım wanted to move here. The wife of an acting minister, she no doubt claimed the right to reside in a fashionable district and put on airs.

Mehpare spotted a pair of green shutters a few houses along, and increased her pace. The door was just as Kemal had described it. She'd been given a street number, but no number was visible on the door of this house, just a small signboard. Mehpare sounded out the words "Spor Kulübü." So, it was a sports club of some kind. She continued walking up the hill, but couldn't find any more houses with green doors and shutters. She returned, rang the bell to the lone green door, and waited.

A moment later the door opened. "What do you want?" asked a young man.

"Is Cemil Bey here? Cemil Fuat Bey?"

"There's no one here by that name."

"But this is the address they gave me . . . I'm to deliver a letter to Cemil Bey."

"Who sent you?"

"Kemal Bey. Kemal Halim Bey."

"The one who fought in Sarıkamış?"

"Yes."

"And he sent you to Cemil Bey?"

"Yes."

"Give it to me."

"But a moment ago you said Cemil Bey wasn't here."

"I'm sorry, I misunderstood," said the young man. "I thought you said *Cemal* Bey. In any case, Cemil Bey is occupied at the moment."

"I'm to deliver the letter personally."

The man sighed. "Come in then. Don't loiter in the doorway. Wait here. I'll be right back."

Mehpare stepped inside and sat down to wait on a wooden bench in a narrow tiled hallway. She was the only person there. A few heads poked out and stared down the stairway at the woman in the black çarşaf. When Mehpare found herself looking into a pair of eyes, she lowered her gaze to the floor and kept it there. A few moments later a worn-looking man of Kemal's age, light-complexioned and curly-headed, came down the stairs.

"I'm Cemil," he said. "You've brought word from Kemal?"

"He sent you a letter."

Mehpare pulled an envelope speckled with sesame seeds out of her shopping bag, brushed it off in embarrassment, and handed it over. Cemil ignored the remaining seeds as he tore open the envelope and scanned its contents.

"He's expecting an envelope from you," Mehpare told him.

"Yes, I know. How is Kemal Bey? Well, I hope?"

"Not entirely. He caught a chill . . . He came down with fever . . . He's quite ill."

"I wish him a speedy recovery. I'll prepare the envelope and bring it to you. Wait here, please."

"Will it take long?"

"I'm enclosing some periodicals . . . I'll only be a moment." The young man went upstairs. Mehpare waited patiently.

When he returned with a large manila envelope, he pointed his chin at her shopping bag and asked, "Will it fit?"

"If I take these out . . ." replied Mehpare. "Yes." She looked around helplessly for a place to put down the rolls. "Would you mind taking these? Otherwise there won't be enough room for the envelope."

Cemil gestured in the direction of the waste paper basket.

"But wouldn't it be sinful, especially in these hard times?" Mehpare asked.

Cemil smiled. "Give the rolls to me," he said. "I'll share them with my colleagues over tea." Mehpare handed him the rolls. "Tell Kemal Bey that we haven't visited only because we don't wish to disturb him. God willing, we'll come to see him when he's well."

"And when the weather improves," added Mehpare. They held each other's eyes for a moment without speaking. "I'll be going now . . ."

"Give him our greetings . . . My friends upstairs also send their best wishes."

Cemil accompanied Mehpare to the door. Hands full of rolls, he was struggling to turn the knob when an explosion hurled them both backwards into the hall and stones, earth and dust showered down onto them from the ceiling—from outside, screams, barking dogs, automobile horns, wailing sirens, growing louder and louder. Mehpare tried to stand up but was pinned beneath Cemil's body. Her right shoulder ached, and her eyes and ears were filled with dust. Through the thick smoke she was dimly aware of people rushing about and shouting. What had happened? An earthquake? Doomsday? She fought to remain conscious and managed to disentangle herself from Cemil. She tried, once again, to climb to her feet. A roaring in her ears, as though thousands of people were speaking at once. Sheets of paper drifted down from above, along with stones and dust. She gathered up her çarşaf, which was tangled around her feet, and tried to cover her bare head. At last, she was able to stand. She felt dizzy. Her shopping bag had disappeared. Cemil was curled up near the wall, moaning.

Mehpare knelt down next to him. "Are you alright? Is it your head?"

"I think my nose is broken," he groaned from behind his hands, which were clasped to his face.

Mehpare tucked her arm under Cemil's back and tried to help him get to his feet. He clung to her with one hand, to the wall with the other, and slowly stood up. His nose was bleeding. The hall, which had been deserted only moments earlier, had filled with dozens of people, all of them pushing their way down the building's staircases, fighting to reach the street door. An acrid stench hung in the air.

"There must be a fire upstairs," said Cemil. "We've got to get out. Can you walk?"

"I'm fine."

"Go outside, get away as fast as you can," Cemil said. There was a second explosion, less intense this time. Mehpare raised her eyes and saw flames on the second floor. Her nostrils burned. Mehpare had just begun looking around for her shopping bag when she was gripped by the wrist. She wheeled round, terrified:

"What on earth are you doing here?"

She strained her eyes to recognize the face of a man whose lashes and hair were white with dust. But the voice was familiar: "Mahir Bey!" she cried.

"Come with me, to the door, quickly . . . Is anything broken?"

"No."

"Cover your mouth and nose . . . We'll go through that door over there . . . Then you can explain what you're doing here."

They joined the throngs jostling for the door. Mehpare nearly lost her balance as she was shoved and elbowed. After what seemed an eternity, they at last inched ahead several meters, reaching the door, the open air. But when they stepped outside, things were even worse. Hundreds of policemen and firemen swarmed the street. Mahir was holding Mehpare's wrist so tightly that her hand had become numb.

"What are you doing here, Mehpare Hanım?"

"I . . . I was just passing through."

"I found you inside. What were you doing there?"

"Looking for my shopping bag . . ."

"What bag?"

"My bag. It's still inside. Please, can we go get it? I've got to have it. Please."

"Were you carrying so much money?"

"No. There were some periodicals."

"It's just as well you lost them. Keep walking . . . Over here . . .. Come on, quickly. Don't let go of my hand."

"You're hurting my wrist, Mahir Bey."

"You'll be fine. If the police stop us, say nothing. You're with me. My nurse. Understood?"

"But I'm not . . ."

"You're caring for Kemal Bey, aren't you? He's my patient; you're my nurse."

"What's going on, Mahir Bey? For the love of God, what's happening here?

"A bomb was tossed into our building."

"A bomb? Why? Who did it?"

"You came to a dangerous place. Kemal should never have sent you."

"No one sent me. I was passing through."

"Fine. It's best you stick to that version of events."

"I was passing through, looking for a tobacconist."

"And that's exactly what you'll tell anyone who asks, Mehpare Hanım!"

At the sight of a pair of approaching policeman, Mahir released Mehpare's wrist and they accelerated their pace.

"Hey . . . Hey you . . . Stop right there."

They stopped and a military policeman came up to them.

"Go stand with the others, right over there," he ordered them. Not far from the bombed building a few municipal police were forcing a crowd of people into an orderly line.

"Where are we going?" Mehpare asked.

"To the police station."

"Oh God!" For the first time that day, Mehpare lost her composure. As darkness descended she felt her legs giving way beneath her. Mahir slid his hands under her arms for support.

"You can take me in, but let this young lady go."

"That's out of the question. She was in the building."

"She was not; she was outside."

"And just how do you know that?" the policeman asked.

"I was inside. I saw her when I got outside."

"You can explain all of that at headquarters. Stop wasting my time and start walking."

Mahir propped his semi-conscious companion against the wall. She was weeping, she could barely stand.

"Look here, sir. I'm a doctor. I was summoned here because of a serious heart attack. As you can see, the only woman you've

detained is this poor young lady . . . She's nearly fainted. She's terrified . . . She told me she was walking past the building when the
explosion happened . . . I found her crawling on the ground."

"Do you know her?"

"Yes, I do. She lives in Beyazit. She's a relative of Undersecretary
of the Treasury Ahmet Reşat Bey, a member of his household. She
can't possibly have any connection to today's incident. Let her go
or you'll be responsible for her when she faints."

"What was she doing here all alone?"

Mehpare's face was ashen and her entire body trembled. "I came
here to visit relatives," she sobbed.

"Her handbag was stolen in all the confusion," Mahir interjected. "The poor thing was looking for it. A black patent leather
handbag. Have you seen it?

"That's enough out of you! People are dying and she's asking
after her bag! The lady can go, but you're coming with me," the
policemen said.

"How will you get home?" Mahir asked Mehpare as she immediately began moving away. "Would you allow me to give you
the fare?"

As the policeman pushed Mahir into a police van, Mehpare
called out, "My aunt lives nearby. She'll help me. Thank you, sir."

Terrified that the police would change their minds, Mehpare
found the strength to dash down the hill, turn left, and walk rapidly in the direction of her aunt's house.

"Open the door, my hands are full," cried Saraylıhanım at the
top of the stairs, breathless, and bearing a tray of warm *poğaça*

buns and a cup of linden tea. Kemal rose from his desk and opened the door.

"Grandmother, you shouldn't have. You've climbed all these stairs."

"Mehpare's not here. I have no choice."

"There's the housekeeper. And the girl who comes to clean. Isn't Leman at home?"

"We have things to talk about."

"Is something wrong? What have I done now?"

"You can't get up to much mischief here in the attic, can you? I've come to discuss your health. Praise be your fever is gone and you're coughing less. You'll be out on the streets again soon."

"I certainly hope so."

"And that's why I'm worried. You've never been content to wander on your own. You're certain to find yourself in bad company."

"There you go again!"

"It's true. I know you well. Didn't I bring you up myself? Ever since you were able to think for yourself you've found something to kick against. You simply won't sit still. Now tell me, what have you been doing at your desk all these hours?"

"I'm translating a French book."

"A book on how to topple kings and sultans?"

"A book of poetry."

"Just who do you think you're fooling!"

Kemal burst out laughing.

"Your tea's getting cold," Saraylıhanım said, handing Kemal the cup. "Drink it up. I added some honey."

Kemal took a few sips of the linden tea. "Grandmother, if you don't want me to regain my health and get into trouble, why are you fattening me up?"

"Because the moment you're better you'll be sent to your uncle in Beypazarı."

"So you're decided, are you?"

"I am. You can't stay here. Your uncle says there's a warrant for your arrest. When you were confined to your bed you weren't in any danger. It would never occur to the police to search the home of Reşat Bey. But the moment you're out on the streets the Sultan's detectives will follow you back to this house. I'm not often of a mind with Behice, but here her concerns are justified."

"I'll leave. But I'll decide where I'm going."

"To Beypazarı . . ."

"No. I'm staying in Istanbul."

"Where in Istanbul?"

"With friends."

"Impossible. You need nursing. You'll need it for years to come. You'll be well cared for on the farm in Beypazarı. You may even meet a girl from a good family. A virtuous girl."

"How convenient for you—you'll have me married as well."

"You're a young man, of course you'll marry. And once you're well, once you're gone, I'll marry off Mehpare as well, God willing."

"Are there any interested parties?" Kemal asked, looking directly into his aunt's eyes.

"Of course there are. She's a rose of a girl. But she promised she'd stay with us until you were fully recovered. And I promised her aunt I'd attend to her marriage prospects the moment you left the house."

"You, a matchmaker? Have you got a basket full of potential husbands?"

Saraylıhanım laughed dryly. "I'm not a matchmaker, nor do I have a basket of husbands. All I have is my reputation, and a nose for information."

"Saraylıhanım" Kemal referred to his grandmother as Saraylıhanım only in moments of resentment or gravity: "when do you want me gone? Tomorrow? Next week?"

"I've upset you."

"I just want to know how long you'll allow me stay."

"This is your home too. Stay forever, if you like. But it would be best if you left as soon as you're well. That may be weeks, or months—it depends entirely on how you feel. But when you do leave, you're going to Beypazarı. I hope that's clear."

"In that case, I'm never getting well."

"In which case you're barred from the streets."

"Fine then. I'll stay in my room and write. And Mehpare can take care of me."

"Mehpare will not be nursing you indefinitely. She's twenty now. It doesn't take long for an unmarried girl in her twenties to acquire a reputation as an old maid. I've assumed responsibility for the girl, and I have to consider her future." Saraylıhanım softened her tone as she changed the subject. "Have a bite of your poğaça. It's spinach, the way you like it. Behice's father sent some more eggs and vegetables from the village, and I've used the last of them for these. Eat up, it may be a while before you have anything so fresh again."

Kemal took the proffered bun from his grandmother's hand and bit into it, happy that for a few days now his appetite seemed to have returned.

"The call to afternoon prayers has come and gone. What's keeping them?" griped Saraylıhanım.

"They'll be home soon," Kemal reassured her.

"I'm going down to my room to perform my prayers," said Saraylıhanım. "You'll finish the poğaça, won't you?"

"Yes. They're wonderful—did Mehpare make them?"

"She's much too busy waiting on to you to roll dough. Gülfidan baked them." Saraylıhanım set the remaining poğaça on the writing desk, put the empty tea cup on the tray and left the room.

Alone, Kemal allowed the anxiety he'd hidden from his aunt to bubble over. Where can she be? She should have returned by now, he said to himself. Standing on tiptoe, he craned his neck for a glimpse of the street through the dormer window. The snow had begun drifting down again.

Until late that night—when, accompanied by Hüsnü Efendi, Mehpare finally came back to the house with a torn çarşaf and terrified eyes—Saraylıhanım sought to avoid the accusatory glances of Behice by keeping her own eyes firmly on her lace- work. With so many streets closed, the tramways delayed for hours, the avenue stretching from Beşiktaş to Tophane being watched by the municipal police, few residents of Istanbul made it home on time that day. And Reşat Bey was not among their number. The members of his household hadn't heard of the bombing in Akaretler, and thus had no plausible explanation for Mehpare's delay. Perhaps her aunt was critically ill and she'd decided to spend the night? Or maybe the girl had finally grown sick of her duties and run home for good? But Hüsnü Efendi was missing as well. Had there been a tramway accident? Behice and Saraylıhanım spent long hours in worried speculation.

Eager to escape her rival, Saraylıhanım retired to her room early, and it was there that she interrogated Mehpare when the girl finally returned; it was there that, on the pretext of a headache, she climbed into bed without even going down to dinner.

Behice sat directly in front of the window, waiting, determined that her husband would hear her version of the dreadful events of that day before Saraylıhanım could speak to him; determined to kill two birds—both of them relatives—with a single stone. She would cite Saraylıhanım's advanced age, her failing faculties— clearly to blame for the day's disasters—and call for an end to her dominion over the household; and she would point to the terrible consequences of allowing Kemal to remain with them. Her husband may have been able to overlook the fatal disease his nephew was probably carrying, but Reşat would never be able to forgive Kemal for using the young girl under his protection as a courier. Of that Behice was absolutely certain.

When Reşat Bey arrived home that day at his usual late hour, he found his wife sitting in front of the window in the second-floor sitting room.

"Why aren't you in bed," he asked. "What's wrong?"

"I've been waiting for you. We need to talk."

"This late? It must be urgent."

"Impossible to catch you in the morning. You leave so early. When else do I have the chance to see you?"

Ahmet Reşat sat down on the divan next to his wife and stroked her hair. "I know I've been neglecting you, all of you. But if you knew what I've been doing, you'd pity me." He fixed his wife's eyes with his own. "I have something to say to you, as well . . ."

"Reşat Bey, hear me out first, please. This is important."

"I'm listening. Who misbehaved today, Leman or Suat?"

"For God's sake, Reşat. Would I have sat up until this hour to complain about that? Be serious. A letter supposedly arrived for Mehpare this morning, and she insisted on visiting her aunt. She asked Saraylıhanım for her consent, and received it . . ."

"So?"

"Naturally, I objected to letting the girl go off without consulting you. But, as expected, Saraylıhanım ruled the day. Anyway, off the girl went, with Hüsnü Efendi. Afternoon came and went and they hadn't come back. Late afternoon prayers passed. It got dark, and we were worried sick. It turns out that Mehpare was passing through Akaretler when a building was bombed . . . I don't know whether she was inside the building or not . . . She was able to get home only long after the evening call to prayers, and in a sorry state. I saw her whispering with Kemal. I suspect she was delivering information. She denies it, of course. I thought you might like to know what happens in this house when you're not here."

As her husband's scowl deepened, Behice rose lightly to her feet, drew her shawl tight across her shoulders and, the skirts of her dressing grown trailing in her wake, stepped across to the door, confident that her work was done. She was just slipping into the hallway when Reşat Bey broke the silence. "Send Kemal to me immediately. I'll be waiting in the selamlık."

Behice slowly ascended the stairs and tapped on the door opposite Kemal's room.

"Mehpare, tell Kemal Bey that Reşat Bey is waiting in the selamlık. He wants to talk to you, and then to Kemal Bey," she said.

Mehpare sprang out of bed, got dressed and ran down to the selamlık, where she hastily lit a fire in the brazier while attempting to respond to the dozens of questions being hurled at her. Then she climbed back up to the attic. When she entered Kemal's room she found him fully dressed in trousers and a sweater.

"I heard," he said, "and I'm going straight down."

"Wait here a moment longer, sir. It's still chilly down there."

"It doesn't matter." Mehpare rushed after Kemal carrying several blankets. Not a peep came from Saraylıhanım's room. Other than the creaking patter of footsteps on wooden treads, the house had been plunged into a funereal silence.

Ahmet Reşat sat bolt upright on one of the divans lining the walls of the selamlık; on the divan opposite sat Kemal. The brass brazier wasn't up to the task of heating the room, for which reason Kemal had finally consented to Mehpare draping his shoulders and knees with blankets. Under the wan light cast by the ceiling fixture, Kemal's face appeared even paler than usual.

"Mehpare has been with us for many years, and this was her first attempt to visit her old home. And, for the first time, her family has communicated information not to me, not to my aunt, not to your aunt, but to a girl who is still, in many ways, a child. Her aunt taken ill! Do you expect me to believe that?" thundered Reşat Bey.

There was no response from Kemal.

"As if the harm you've done yourself wasn't enough, now you've started endangering your family. How could you send Mehpare to a safe-house? How could you? Do you know what you've done? Speak up, man!"

"I have nothing to say in my defense, uncle. I know there's no point."

"So you acknowledge your guilt."

"It's not that uncle . . . please . . ."

"Shut up! How could you, Kemal? She could have been killed. Maimed. What's happened to your conscience? She could have been arrested. Could have led the police right to you. That would have been the end of us all. What kind of a man are you, anyway? Just who do you take after?"

Ahmet Reşat got up and began pacing, his entire body shaking with frustration and rage. He had no idea what to do. Sitting opposite was an invalid swathed in blankets, a pathetic figure with waxen skin, bloodshot eyes, trembling hands. An invalid who continuously threatened the safety of his family . . . a madman . . . a fool! Reşat Bey tossed his burning cigarette onto the glowing embers of the brazier. Stopping directly in front of Kemal, he waved his index finger in front of his nephew's nose.

"You've taken leave of your senses, Kemal. I understand now what I should have realized from the start. How can I be angry with you, when you're clearly out of your mind? I intend to surrender you to the doctors. Psychiatrists. It isn't your lungs, but your mind. The doctors will do whatever is necessary to prevent you from harming yourself, from harming us. I can't protect you any longer."

"Uncle . . . please . . . listen . . ."

"I've listened to you. Every time. And every time I forgave you. *He's learned his lesson, he'll mend his ways,* I told myself."

"Uncle . . ."

"You sent an innocent to Karakol with absolutely no thought of the consequences. The girl is so intimidated, or so mesmerized, by your powers of persuasion that she is prepared to sacrifice everything for you. Just passing by! On her way to a tobacconist! Don't you dare try to find consolation in the fact that Mehpare wasn't injured, killed or arrested. You've made that innocent girl into a bald-faced liar."

"Uncle, punish me. Throw me out of the house. It's true, I've gotten involved in a dangerous business. Yes, I'm working with Karakol. Because I believe that we need to do more to defend the homeland. I won't sit idly by and watch things fall apart. If you want to banish me, so be it. But for the love of God, don't punish an innocent girl, a bystander, someone who happened to be passing in front of Karakol when a bomb went off. I'm begging you. Mehpare was looking for Kerem Efendi's tobacco shop. I gave her the directions myself. That's her only crime."

"And what emboldened her to go out onto the streets alone?"

"She wasn't alone. Hüsnü Efendi went with her."

"When they got to her aunt's house she released Hüsnü. She entered the street unaccompanied even by her aunt."

"For God's sake, uncle, what of it? Women have begun to take up employment in this city. An organization under the patronage of Naciye Sultan herself even encourages them to do so. That is to say, even your conservative friends at the Palace no longer advocate imprisoning women in their homes. The Municipality of Istanbul has begun employing the wives of men killed on the battlefield, letting them earn their own bread. Are we, members of a free-thinking family, educated for generations at palace schools, really at odds on this? Mehpare walked down the street alone. So what!"

A single look at his uncle's face was enough to tell Kemal that his efforts to steer the discussion onto safer ground had been in vain. It was time for a direct appeal. Voice trembling with emotion, Kemal began: "I'm begging you uncle, don't allow Mehpare to be sacrificed in the feud between grand-mother and my aunt. Believe me, she hasn't done a thing. I'm expecting news within the week. I'll leave the moment it arrives, and your troubles will be over."

The door was still shaking on its hinges as Ahmet Reşat stormed down the hallway. Kemal listened to the sound of his uncle's footsteps pounding up the staircase. A few moments later he heard the door to the upstairs bedroom slamming shut. He stood up, switched off the light and staggered to the door, guilty and afraid, barely able to keep to his feet, let alone climb three flights of stairs.

But clutching the banister and pausing frequently to gather strength, he finally made it to his room. He was astonished to see a ghostlike presence illuminated by his bedside lamp rise from a chair and walk toward him. "Mehpare! What are you doing here? You still haven't gone to bed?"

"Listen to me, please, I didn't tell the master anything. I did just as you said, I told neither Mahir Bey nor your uncle that you sent me. I said I was passing by when the explosion happened. And that's what I'll continue to say, no matter what. I wanted you to know that. That's why I'm here."

"Mehpare."

"If Mahir Bey presses you for the truth, say nothing. He suspects you sent me. I denied it. I said I was passing through." She spoke quickly, in a choked voice, breathing hard. Kemal took her by the hands and led her to the edge of the bed. They sat down next to each other.

"Mehpare, don't worry, I won't say anything to anyone."

"But Ahmet Reşat Beyefendi thinks . . ."

"That's all he can do, think. No one knows anything for certain. He can't accuse you. Don't worry, he won't discharge you without being absolutely sure. I know him. He's a just man."

"It's not myself I'm worried about, I'm afraid they'll send you away."

"Were you listening to us?" There was no response. "Don't worry, Mehpare. Neither you nor I are going anywhere. This won't be the first storm to blow over in this house."

"If something should happen to you . . . because of me . . . I went there at the wrong time . . . I should have gone earlier instead of chatting with my aunt. Forgive me . . ."

"I'm the one who should ask for forgiveness. If you only knew how I frightened I was when you didn't come back. I was in agony. Until you appeared at the top of the street with Hüsnü Efendi. I made a terrible mistake, Mehpare, I should never have sent you there. My uncle has every right to be furious with me."

"What what was it, sir, what was that place?"

"A charitable organization."

"Why would anyone bomb a charity?" Kemal didn't answer. "You trusted me enough to send me there, but now you won't tell me what kind of place it was."

Kemal blushed. "Various political activities are conducted there."

"So it wasn't by chance . . . and the Karakol . . . I was petrified . . ."

Kemal started at the word. "Karakol? What are you saying? What have you heard about Karakol?"

"When the bomb exploded, everyone ran outside, and there were military policemen everywhere. They were going to take Mahir Bey and me in, but he stopped them, let me slip away."

"Why didn't you tell me this earlier?"

"I told you I'd seen Mahir Bey!"

"But you didn't say anything about his being taken in to headquarters."

"I didn't want to infuriate Saraylıhanım any further, so I said nothing."

"God, I'm such a fool!"

"How were you to know about the bomb?"

"I should have known. What if you'd been killed! Or hurt!"

"The bomb exploded on the floor above. We were hit by a little debris, that's all."

"God was watching over you."

"He must have been. Well, I'd best be leaving now, sir. Is there anything you'd like me to do? Shall I bring you a cup of linden tea before bed?"

Kemal rested both of his hands on the girl's shoulders to prevent her from rising. "You're an angel, Mehpare," he said. "My angel. It was you who nursed me back to health. Without you, I'd have died."

Kemal was silenced by the slender fingers placed on his lips. "Don't talk about death." Kemal kissed the fingers placed on his lips. Mehpare was too overcome to rise from the bed. Kemal pressed his lips first against her neck, then against her shoulder.

"Sir . . . Please . . . No," the girl moaned. Kemal retreated immediately.

"You're right, Mehpare. I shouldn't have. I'm ill. I may even have consumption. I had no right to kiss you."

"You don't have consumption. You don't. And even if you did," Mehpare said, moving closer. Hair was beginning to spill from beneath her headscarf. Kemal pushed her back and looked into her face, the face that had been there to greet him whenever he opened his eyes—for so many months now his only glimpse of beauty. How many times had he confronted death, how many times had he rediscovered the will to live when morning came, looking into these eyes? Kemal breathed deeply. Was he happy? Was this happiness? How long had it been? She sat before him, long throat slightly twisted. The top few buttons of her blouse were open. Her hair had fallen loose.

When Ahmet Reşat entered his bedroom, he found his wife undressed beneath the covers, her hair lit by moonlight streaming in from the tall windows. She appeared to be sound asleep. He closed the curtains, slowly undressed, and had barely crept into bed when Behice turned to face him:

"I drifted off," she murmured sleepily.

"Don't rouse yourself. I have something to tell you, but it can wait until morning."

Behice rested her head on her elbow and looked at her husband. "There's nothing wrong, is there, Reşat? I hope you haven't thrown Kemal out of the house. I wouldn't wish it on a cat, not at this hour. At least wait until morning."

Ahmet Reşat interrupted his wife. "It isn't Kemal I want to talk about."

"What is it then? The ministry? You mentioned that salaries were going unpaid. Have they come to seize our property?"

"No, nothing bad has happened," laughed Ahmet Reşat, "but only time will tell us how auspicious my news is."

"Well tell me, I'm bursting to know!"

"Behice Hanımefendi, you're now the wife of a minister."

Behice screamed as she sat up. "They offered you the position! And you accepted?"

"Salih Pasha has been promoted to Grand Vizier and he formed a new cabinet today. He pointed out that I have been the acting minister of finance for some time now and suggested we make it official. I raised no objections."

Behice threw her arms around her husband's neck. "But why did you wait until now to give me the good news—why didn't you tell me the moment you came in?"

"I'd intended to, but you were so preoccupied with your own affairs that I thought it prudent to resolve them first."

"I remember now, you said you had something to tell me. But how could I know it would be so tremendous? You spoke so calmly. Is that any way to deliver this sort of news? Well all I can say is, may your new station bring joy and prosperity. To your country and your family. Does Saraylıhanım know?"

"How could she? I haven't even seen her today. I'll tell her tomorrow morning."

"What about Kemal?"

"Kemal and I had less pleasant matters to discuss."

"Am I the only one who knows?"

"In our family, yes."

Behice inwardly rejoiced now over Saraylıhanım's decision to allow Mehpare to leave the house today. If the old woman hadn't taken to her bed early, she would surely have been the first to learn of the promotion. But this time it was Behice who had been told. And that was as it should be.

"We'll tell everyone tomorrow morning," she sang. "And Reşat, shall we send a telegram to Beypazarı?" As she rested her head on her pillow Behice couldn't help but marvel at her father's foresight. Throngs of wealthy suitors had lined up to claim her hand, but her father had declared: My daughter has no need for goods and chattels. The marriage I arrange will secure her future. Sight unseen, he'd decided to give his daughter to a promising young civil servant, one related to their neighbors and the son of an Istanbul family. And how right he'd been! Thanks to her father, Behice would arise from bed the following morning as the wife of a minister. She was flushed with excitement, no longer the least bit sleepy. As she drew her body closer to her husband's, she shyly sought his mouth and, for the first time in ages, felt his lips respond to hers. It was as though he were eager to shrug off all the unhappy developments of that eventful day. Reşat pressed his lips against his wife's and, when he lowered himself onto her warm body, he was astonished to find how very much he had missed her.

− 4 −

March 1920

The following morning, Reşat Bey shared the news of his promotion with the other members of his household. Saraylıhanım received her nephew's announcement with an air of indifference, as though she'd expected no less. "Reşat, my boy, the position has been yours in all but name, it's only natural that they give you the title you deserve," she calmly pronounced. "God has willed that my family shall continue to be of service to the state. Come here, my dear, and let me kiss your forehead."

As Reşat Bey rose from his chair his daughters leapt up with cries of joy, kissing their father's hand and embracing him. After permitting his aunt to kiss his forehead, he ceremoniously kissed her right hand and briefly drew it up to his brow.

"Don't neglect your prayers, mother," he said. "We'll need them more than ever now."

"Well, I rose early this morning to perform my ablutions and to read passages from the Koran for you," Behice interjected resentfully.

"A mother's blessings are superior to all others," said Saraylıhanım, "for motherhood is itself blessed."

"But I'm a mother, too," Behice protested.

Saraylıhanım failed to hear her.

Upon hearing the news, Mehpare, Housekeeper Gülfidan, Hüsnü Efendi and the other servants lined up to express their congratulations. Having been shut up in his room all day, only Kemal remained ignorant of the promotion, until Mehpare told him.

As Ahmet Reşat was leaving the room his aunt went up to him and asked: "Shall I tell Kemal? He'll be so proud of you."

"I doubt it," responded Reşat Bey.

"How can you say that! Kemal loves you like a father."

"I need more than affection, aunt; what I want is obedience."

"I'll speak to him. I'll explain that as the nephew of a minister he'll have to be more prudent." "Don't waste your breath."

"Please, Kemal isn't a child. Don't you think he knows that everyone will be watching us? May

Allah protect my family from the evil eye. I'd best have some frankincense burned today."

"You're exaggerating, aunt. Nothing has changed. Today I'll be charged with performing the same duties in the same office as before. The only thing that's different is my title."

"Godspeed and return in good health, my lion," Saraylıhanım said, nudging Behice aside as she lightly patted her nephew on the back.

Stepping outside, Ahmet Reşat turned up the collar of his coat. The sun had dispatched all of the snow, transforming the street into a sea of mud. Warmer weather was clearly on the way. With hansom cabs so difficult to find these days, he had no choice but to walk to work again this morning. Taking care not to spatter the cuffs of his trousers, he strode across the cobblestones.

Behice looked on, astonished, as Mehpare, clearing the breakfast dishes, tipped over a glass and spilled some tea. The girl was like a sleepwalker, her face chalk-white, eyes bloodshot. The poor thing must still be reeling at having been rebuked, Behice decided. Perhaps we were a bit harsh? She'd only been following orders. The poor thing was a slave to Saraylıhanım's every whim. And it had been Kemal who sent her to the bombing, Saraylıhanım who had assented. What was the girl's crime? She'd always been respectful. She'd lovingly cared for Leman and Suat all these years. She'd at stood at Kemal's bedside, vigilant, uncomplaining. Suddenly, Behice deeply regretted having informed her husband of Mehpare's transgression.

"Mehpare," she softly said. There was no response. "Mehpare, are you deaf, my girl?"

"Ah . . ." The girl had been startled from her trance. "Yes, what is it, Behice Abla?"

"What is it, my lamb? What's come over you?" Mehpare flushed scarlet, head bowed, eyes lowered. "Did Reşat Bey treat you roughly last night?"

"I deserved it, efendim. I shouldn't have gone without his knowledge."

"What's done is done. Next time, come and tell me of your troubles, not Saraylıhanım. She's not as young as she was, and her misjudgments cause trouble for all of us."

"As you wish, efendim."

"Mehpare," Behice continued, "Leman has some ironing, and as Zehra won't be coming today I wondered if you wouldn't . . ."

"Of course I will, Behice Abla. Kemal Bey doesn't need me as much anymore. He can take care of himself now, thank God. And anyway, he doesn't want to be waited on."

"If he's fully recovered, why are you giving him medicine? Does he still have a cough?"

"He's coughing less, but there are the restorative syrups prescribed by the doctor. And, as you know, I've been told to administer drops to soothe his nerves and help him sleep . . ."

"You'd still better keep his cutlery and dishes separate," Behice cut in. "Better safe than sorry."

"All right," Mehpare said, turning toward the kitchen with a large, round tray of empty tea glasses and dishes; and promptly collided with Saraylıhanım, who seemed to have appeared out of nowhere. Mehpare stumbled and fell to her knees; the contents of the tray crashed to the floor. Suat had a fit of the giggles and clapped her hands.

"Shameful," Behice scolded her youngest daughter. "Help her pick everything up."

"No, stay back. You'll cut your hand, there are splinters of glass everywhere," Mehpare said.

"I can't help her anyway," Suat said, "I'm late for school as it is. You haven't even braided my hair yet."

"Very well, go to my room and get a comb," Behice said.

"What's wrong with you this morning?" Saraylıhanım demanded of Mehpare, who was down on all fours, plucking slivers of glass and shards of crockery from the carpet. "Earlier, you nearly fell down the stairs."

Mehpare fled the room with her tray of fragments.

"She must have been shaken by yesterday's disturbance," Behice said.

"There's no point in exaggerating all that," Saraylıhanım said. "It was an unfortunate coincidence."

"Reşat Bey doesn't think so."

"Reşat Bey is looking for any pretext to vent his anger," Saraylıhanım said. "This endless winter has told on his nerves. And everyone else's."

"Reşat Bey's nerves are not contingent on the weather," Behice retorted. "He's been upset by the state of the country, and unpleasantness at home only exacerbates his state of mind. Never mind—we've all held up as best we could. And now we're coming to the end."

"The end of what?" Saraylıhanım asked. "The deterioration of the country or the unpleasantness at home?"

Behice had no idea what to say.

"We women can't be expected to understand affairs of state. But if you're referring to our domestic duties, we'll be sending Kemal to Beypazarı soon. And then you'll be able to breathe easy."

"How can you say that, Saraylıhanım? How could Kemal's absence possibly please me? He's like a brother to me."

"Brothers are treated with kindness and compassion when they fall ill."

"Didn't I tend him when he came back from Sarıkamış? I'd have expected a little more understanding from you. With two little girls in the house, an infectious disease . . ."

Saraylıhanım interrupted.

"Those two little girls of yours have long since become young women."

"They'll always be my little girls," Behice sniffed, rushing from the room. It was just like Saraylıhanım, she fumed, denying her the opportunity to savor Reşat's news. But the odd thing was, she was no longer certain how pleased she was by his promotion. Yes, she felt extremely proud, but then why this strange sense of trepidation? She settled onto the divan in the sitting room and extracted a thin sheet of paper from a silver cigarette case, carefully placed a bit of tobacco onto it, wet the edges of the paper with the tip of her tongue, leaned over to light it on one of the coals still glowing in the brazier, and filled her lungs with aromatic smoke. She had just released a soothing stream of it when the agitated housekeeper burst into the room. Am I never to enjoy a little peace of mind, Behice thought to herself, and said, "What is it now?"

"Ziya Pasha's wife, Münire Hanımefendi, has just sent word that they'll be calling to extend their congratulations."

"When?"

"Today, this afternoon."

"Tell them they're welcome," said Behice, feeling both flattered and uneasy. The second puff of smoke gave her none of the pleasure of the first, because the moment the housekeeper quit the room Saraylıhanım suddenly materialized before her.

"These visits aren't going to end with Ziya Pasha's harem. There'll be more, plenty of them. Soon enough the house will be overflowing with well-wishers. We've got to be prepared with trays of börek and jugs of sherbet. Don't just sit there puffing on a cigarette; it's not easy being the wife of a minister, and it's time to get to work. I'll send for Zehra. She's to get started scrubbing the house from top to bottom."

"And how are we supposed to prepare these refreshments? The pantry is bone-bare."

"A woman of skill can work miracles with nothing. We'll find a way."

Not be outdone, Behice said, "Let me remind you not to ask after Ziya Pasha. He was badly shaken by all those years in exile. He's never really recovered; in fact, they say his condition has deteriorated to the point where they thought it best to send him to relatives in Bursa. He's being cared for there." Behice extinguished her cigarette in the ashtray and slowly rose to her feet. As she swept past Saraylıhanım on her way to the door, she said, sidelong: "Since as you've taken such good care of the household affairs, I suppose there's nothing left for me to do but deck myself out for company. And that's precisely what I intend to do."

Having carefully climbed the stairs to avoid spilling the foaming cup of coffee she was balancing on a tray, Mehpare tapped on Kemal's door. At the words "come in" she slipped into the room and set the tray on the nightstand next to the bed. Flushing, she whispered, "I was making coffee for Saraylıhanım, and thought you might like one."

"It's not coffee I'd like," said Kemal, pulling her down into the bed and across his chest. Arms locked around her waist, he silenced her protests with a long kiss. Mehpare finally broke free.

"Stop it, sir . . . what if someone comes in . . . I'll be ruined . . . disgraced . . . Don't . . . Please."

As Kemal held her tight with his left hand he undid the buttons of her blouse with his right, and buried his face in her bosom.

"How do you manage to smell so wonderful, Mehpare?"

"Stop it, sir, I'm begging you."

"If anyone comes we'll hear their footsteps."

"The girls don't wear heels. We wouldn't hear Leman or Suat."

"They're not allowed in my room." Kemal pressed his lips to Mehpare's chest. With a low moan, she pushed him away. He stood firm, running his tongue slowly from her breasts up to her chin and back. And then he kissed her again.

"Don't you want me, Mehpare?" She didn't reply. Kemal rephrased the question: "Don't you love me?"

"I've loved you for years. Hopelessly. I love you more than my own life."

"Then why do you push me away?" He undid another button, and began nuzzling the breast he'd liberated."

"Have pity on me," said Mehpare, who'd begun to tremble.

"I'll release you only if you promise to spend the night with me again."

Mehpare's inner voice wished that Kemal would never leave her, that he would stay like this forever, her nipple in his mouth. Her body was overwhelmed by sensations she'd never known.

"All right . . . I promise." I can't sleep unless it's here at your side—if I can't see you, can't touch you, I can't live, she thought to herself. When Kemal loosened his grip, she reluctantly rose, smoothed her skirts, tucked her breasts into her camisole, re-buttoned her blouse and picked up her yemeni headscarf, which had fallen to the floor.

"Your coffee's getting cold," she said in a low voice.

"Well then, bring me a hot one."

"Really?"

Kemal laughed. "I dare say you want to kiss and caress me as much as I do you."

"Actually, sir, I came with important news."

"And what news is that?"

"It would be more appropriate if Saraylıhanım told you. She might get angry if I do."

"Tell me anyway, and I'll pretend not to know."

"Beyefendi has been appointed minister."

"My uncle?"

"Yes."

"Ahhh!" Kemal exclaimed.

"Aren't you pleased?"

"I'm not, Mehpare. Minister of the Treasury?"

"Yes."

"God help him," Kemal said. Then he was lost in thought.

As Mehpare crept silently from the room she decided she was in love with a very peculiar man indeed.

Behice received Münire Hanımefendi and her daughter, Azra Hanım, in the rarely used salon overlooking the back garden. Even with the moss-green velvet curtains fully drawn and the slatted shutters flung wide, the room was poorly lit, thanks to its northern exposure and the garden's numerous trees. The gloom, however, lent the room an air of respectable sobriety. In contrast to the selamlık and the bow-windowed sitting room facing the street, it was decorated not with divans and cushions but with gilded, crushed-velvet sofas and matching armchairs. The glass case sitting between the two windows exhibited fine Ottoman porcelain, Beykoz glassware and lead crystal dessert bowls. On the walls hung three antique china plates and two oils signed by the painter Civanyan. The room was decorated in the western style—more typical of a prosperous Christian or Jewish family. Behice was gratified to observe Azra Hanım glancing at one of the paintings. Nodding in the direction of the canvas, the young woman spoke in tones at once bold and gay: "I'm a devotee of Civanyan's night-scapes, too. I see you have discerning tastes. Do you paint?"

Saraylıhanım had opposed the hanging of pictures, and Behice reminded herself to recount the visitor's enthusiastic appraisal at the first opportunity. "Unfortunately no, but my eldest, Leman, is terribly fond of art. She paints and embroiders wonderfully."

She silently thanked Reşat Bey for having acquired the paintings some years earlier, and blushed at the memory of her words at the time: "For goodness sake, you could have bought a few carpets instead of paying so much for a pair of paintings!"

Until Saraylıhanım entered the room to offer around a tray of refreshments, the women occupied themselves in discussion of the difficulties faced by the wives of men of high station. As the wife of a former minister herself, Münire Hanımefendi took it upon herself to warn Behice of the tribulations that awaited her in the days ahead, the long separations from her spouse, the burden of sole responsibility for the children's wellbeing.

"I have been accustomed to nothing else for some time now," Behice contented herself with saying. "I have followed my husband, children in tow, to Damascus, to Rhodes and to Thessalonica. At least we're no longer in rented lodgings; we have our own house. We live near our friends and relatives. I have no right to complain."

Once Saraylıhanım appeared, the conversation turned to other topics. The elderly woman said she'd learned from the neighbors that Muslim women frequently faced insulting behavior at the hands of the occupying forces, for which reason she'd taken to doing her shopping at the local greengrocer's instead of at the marketplace, a sad turn of events which explained the substandard flavor not only of the meals prepared daily by the cook, but of the very börek she was offering her guests, with her deepest apologies for the lack of either spinach or cheese fillings.

"Hanımefendi," Münire Hanım consoled her, "it's no longer possible to find anything at the marketplaces either. Food shortages have broken out across the city. With the roads blockaded, deliveries of provisions from Anatolia have stopped almost completely."

"I had good reason to urge my son Reşat Bey to lay in provisions, but he paid me no heed," sighed Saraylıhanım. "If those reports about the occupiers, their harassment, hadn't reached my ears, I wouldn't hesitate to go to the Spice Bazaar myself. It's quite far, but I'm certain everything is still available there."

Münire Hanım had just opened her mouth to inform Saraylıhanım that these days even the Spice Bazaar was short of supplies when her daughter leapt into the conversation. "They're not foreigners at all! They're Greeks and Armenians wearing the uniforms of the invaders—that's why I'm out in the streets every chance I get. I dare them to harass me! They'd be made to answer for their insolence!"

"Young lady," responded Saraylıhanım," what could you possibly do? Surely you don't expect to thrash them yourself?"

"I don't, not on my own. But I would raise such a ruckus that the entire neighborhood would rush to beat the offenders black and blue."

"My dear young lady, you shall do no such thing. You'd only be asking for trouble. You should simply avoid them."

"I don't agree at all," said Münire Hanım. "Turning a blind eye and cowering has got us nowhere. This is our city, even if it is under occupation."

"You're really agreeing with the girl?" Saraylıhanım asked Münire Hanım, looking directly into her eyes.

"Azra belongs to a women's organization dedicated to opposing the invasion. They hold conferences, make speeches, all to enlighten the Turkish woman."

"What organization is this?" asked Behice.

"The Association for the Protection of Women's Rights. Are you a member of any organizations, Behice Hanımefendi?"

Saraylıhanım stepped in before her daughter-in-law could answer. "She is not. Behice Hanım is rearing two daughters. She's also responsible for running the house. She has no time for organizations."

"Many of the women at our association are married with children. Domestic duties don't preclude membership," said Azra Hanım.

Behice shot an irritated glance at Saraylıhanım and turned to Azra Hanım: "My mother-in-law spoke the truth, but my children have grown up—they're at school now. As far as running the house, my mother-in-law, God bless her, is far more adept at that than I am. She won't so much as allow me to place my hands in cold water after hot. I would greatly appreciate it if you would permit me to accompany you to your association one day."

"Behice Hanım! Without so much as asking the minister! I'd certainly like to know what he'd say!" objected Saraylıhanım.

"He'd be pleased, I'm sure. My husband approves of industrious women," said Behice. "Hasn't he demonstrated as much by hiring a private tutor for Leman and by sending Suat to school at such an early age? You know what they say about 'keeping up with the times.'"

Mehpare was all ears as she served the tea. The visiting ladies continued to mind their manners, but they allowed their facial expressions to indicate, ever so subtly, that Saraylıhanım was not be taken seriously. But the Cunning Circassian was not going down without a fight: "Some of your organizations are also engaged in charitable activities. If Behice insists on becoming a member of a society, a charity would be more appropriate; like the Red Crescent, for example."

"My dear," smiled Münire Hanımefendi, "the contemporary female is nothing like us. She's educated, she speaks foreign languages, reads literature from Europe."

"We too received education and instruction," snapped Saraylıhanım, drawing herself up in her chair.

"Of course we did," agreed Münire Hanım. "We learned to pluck the lute. We committed the Koran to memory. But neither we nor our mothers were equipped for the demands of modern life. Until a short time ago, we spent our days shut up behind four walls. We're only now—slowly—learning the ways of the world."

"There's also something called experience," said Saraylıhanım," and it's every bit as precious as raw knowledge. And, unfortunately, it's something youth does not possess. Mehpare, dear girl, pour our guests some more tea, would you? Can I offer you another slice of börek, my dear . . . do help yourself to shortcake."

As Azra Hanım passed the platter back to her hostess, Mehpare carried off the empty tea glasses, her mind occupied by the discussion underway in the drawing room. When she returned, Azra and Behice were sitting side by side speaking in subdued tones. As she placed a glass of tea on the end table next to Azra Hanım, she overheard, "We're fighting for more than our rights, now—we're fighting for the homeland. Nesibe Hanım and Saime Hanım are going to speak on this next week. Would you like to come and listen?" Behice looked dumbstruck.

Having passed the guests sugar, Mehpare placed the bowl back on the table and stood with arms folded beside the door. She had barely retreated into thoughts of her beloved when the sound of his name shook her out of her reverie and made her prick up her ears.

"Kemal Bey, may God protect him, has penned some wonderful articles on this subject," Azra Hanım was saying, "but unfortunately he now writes nothing at all."

"My nephew suffered a long period of convalescence upon his return from Sarıkamış," explained Behice.

"I do hope he's fully recovered."

"He's not in Istanbul. He's gone to his uncle's, where he's resting."

Azra turned an incredulous look on Behice, who flushed pink and bowed her head.

"If you're corresponding with Kemal," Azra said, "do write and tell him that we're all eager for more of his work. And please convey our greetings and our best wishes for a full and speedy recovery."

And who are you, anyway? Mehpare thought. What are you doing here? She was prepared to cope with consumption, with kidney pains and nightmares; she could handle bombs, police interrogations if need be; but she was utterly unequipped to deal with the young lady sitting over there, so full of herself, a lock of hair hanging over her high forehead. Mehpare unfolded her arms and silently left the room. She began climbing the stairs. If she dared to ask him, would Kemal Bey answer her questions? Would he tell her what his relationship was with the know-it-all down in the drawing room? Sophisticated, impeccably dressed, well-read, opinionated, the daughter of a former minister. Next to her, Mehpare was a nobody. She'd learned to read by sitting in on Leman's lessons, but her handwriting was abominable, her knowledge of current affairs negligible. She was pathetic—what did she know of the world but this house and its immediate vicinity? How could she possibly interest Kemal? He'd appreciate her for as long as he was confined to his room. And then? After he'd grown strong, after he'd gone on his way, would he remember she'd even existed? The kisses, the lovemaking—she couldn't allow them. Never again.

Just as Saraylıhanım had predicted, the well-wishers weren't limited to Münire Hanım and her daughter: the house overflowed with callers. For ten long days, Mehpare and the others members of the household didn't have a single free moment. Saraylıhanım was care ful to conceal from Reşat Bey the sale of three braided gold bracelets that had once adorned her arm, the proceeds of which were devoured by particularly distinguished guests in the form of tartlets from the patisseries of Pera, box after box of chocolates and—again, unbeknownst to the master of the house—refreshments prepared with ingredients acquired on the black market. Neighbors, friends and relatives were served freshly-baked trays of börek and bite-sized fritters soaked in syrup. All available chairs were hauled in to the selamlık, the middle salon and the anteroom, which did service as a dining room.

Important guests and foreigners were received in the velvet drawing room, while male visitors congregated in the selamlık and close friends gathered in the front room with the bow window. Once the guests were gone, order was restored, dishes scrubbed and preparations made for the next day's gatherings. Day blurred into night, and everyone was utterly exhausted. Even in the midst of such bustling activity, Behice found time to have Katina over to the house to fit and sew new dresses, skirts and blouses, the allowance urgently requested from her father defraying the cost. The left over fabric was used to make matching dresses, complete with piping and frilly collars, for Leman and Suat, and the girls were sent to the best photographer in Beyazit to pose with their father.

Naturally, ceremonial prayers were conducted as well.

Being the wife of a minister was tiring, expensive, but it had its enjoyable moments too. At Saraylıhanım's insistence, Behice invited her father to visit. Saraylıhanım had calculated both that İbrahim Bey would arrive for an extended stay laden with provisions, and that when he returned home he would be more than happy to take Kemal with him to Beypazarı. However, her plans were spoiled when İbrahim Bey cited work and declined the invitation. Though filled with pride, he considered it opportunistic and in bad form to arrive on the doorstep so soon after his son-in-law had been appointed minister. Meanwhile, the onslaught of visitors had severely depleted their resources, and Saraylıhanım was growing increasingly distraught. If guests continued to pour in, how was she to protect the reputation of her household? With the sacks of flour and other staples nearly gone, what were they to serve? There may have been a war on, but the neighbors were not under any circumstances to know that within the minister's family dined morning and night on nothing but soup—which often enough consisted of little more than dry bread and broth.

Ever since the confrontation with his uncle, Kemal had largely kept to his room. He had descended to the entry hall a few times hoping to extend his congratulations, but, having failed to encounter his busy uncle there, settled for sending a card, and was actually quite pleased to have avoided a guilt-stricken meeting. He spent his days at his writing desk, working at his translations and reading. Mehpare would bring up his meals, administer his medicines and enquire, several times a day, if master needed anything else.

Saraylıhanım worried that Mehpare was literally being run off her feet. The poor girl was growing paler by the day, and dark circles had formed under her eyes.

She was right: Mehpare was exhausted. Late at night, after she finished mopping and sweeping in preparation for another day of guests, she would climb up to her room on the top floor, more dead than alive, leaving the door ajar so that it wouldn't squeak later. Finally, when everyone else in the house was sound asleep, she'd steal into Kemal's room and slip into his arms. Kemal made love to her fiercely, as though determined to make up for the long years of military service, captivity and convalescence. He was insatiable. All through the night he nibbled her lips, breasts and shoulders, basking in her scent, allowing himself to run riot. And Mehpare, too, was ravenous—she submitted her body to his, fought back screams, clapped her hand over her mouth, sank her teeth into the pillow, writhed and flailed under his slender frame. Later, in the hushed hours just before dawn, she would float back to her bed, spent but sleepless, her soul still overflowing with vitality. As the sun came up, she would creep down to the hamam to perform her ablutions and return to her room for morning prayers. Then she would prepare breakfast and go again to Kemal, this time with a tray. He was usually sound asleep, and she'd kneel at his bedside, lightly stroking his cheek, running her fingers through his hair as she waited for him to wake. For the rest of the day, she would seize any excuse to visit him . . . I'll bring sir his lunch . . . I'll be right back after I take sir a cup of coffee . . . I think I heard him call for me, sir may want something . . . It's time for sir to take his medicine . . .

"Dear girl, between Kemal and the guests you've been worn to the bone. Be sure to take care of yourself or you'll get ill as well," Saraylıhanım admonished, as Mehpare grew daily more hollow-eyed and wan.

− 5 −

Flight

One morning, Saraylıhanım and Behice were sitting opposite each other on the low backless couches lining the bow window. They'd risen early and dressed to receive, but were enjoying their cups of coffee and the sweet languor that came from knowing that few, if any, visitors were likely to call that day. Wailing sirens had made for another restless night, but neither of them knew, or cared to know, the exact target of the raids conducted by the occupying forces, who seemed to spend all their time and resources chasing after members of the resistance—"the rabble rousers," as Saraylıhanım insisted on calling them. Both women had grown accustomed to the sound of distant gunshots, and were not at all rattled. Reşat Bey had long since left for work. Leman was seated in front of the piano practicing for the lesson she was to receive later in the day. Suat sat near her mother's skirts, scribbling on sheets of paper she'd spread across the floor, her morning classes having been cancelled due to a performance of some kind being put on by the senior girls.

"Don't disturb your sister while she's having her lessons today. I'll inform your father if you do, and he'll be very angry with you," Behice said.

"I don't bother her. I just watch."

"She doesn't want you to watch, so don't."

"She's scared I'll learn to play better than her."

"But you didn't want lessons."

"I did so!"

"No, you didn't! You preferred the violin. And it was a wise choice, too. You and your sister will be able to give your father a concert one day," said Behice, "and, even better, you can take your violin anywhere you go. Your sister has no choice but to play at home."

Behice was slightly ashamed of her words. The reason Suat had been denied piano lessons was that Leman wouldn't let anyone else touch the instrument, becoming particularly enraged when the trespasser was her younger sister. The piano had been purchased when Leman turned ten. As they were in no position to afford a second piano, Suat had been encouraged to take up the violin. Even so, whenever her sister wasn't at home Suat would rush over to the piano and do her best to replicate a melody she'd overheard.

"You'll also learn to play the ud, of course," said Saraylıhanım. "Every girl in the house should know how to play the ud. I taught Mehpare myself. She plays beautifully."

"Teach me too, nana."

"We'll begin just as soon as school lets out for the summer, my dear. And you know what? Your grandfather says he might come in June. He loves listening to the ud."

"I wish he was here with us now," sighed Behice. "He hasn't seen the girls for months. The last time he visited, Leman was a child; next time he'll find a young lady. She's grown so tall this winter."

"Never mind, he'll be visiting soon enough, once we're out on the island."

"I expected him to come the moment he learned of Reşat's appointment. We'd have been off to the island shortly afterwards, and we could all have gone . . ."

Behice stopped mid-sentence as the housekeeper rushed into the room looking unusually alarmed.

"What is it now?" Behice groaned.

Saraylıhanım immediately broke in with, "Mercy me, Gülfidan, don't tell me visitors have arrived at this early hour."

"Aret Efendi is here. He wants to speak to you, ma'am."

"How strange! What's he doing here today?" said Behice. "And so early in the morning? Tell him to wait. We'll be down right after we finish our coffee."

"Something terrible is happening in the city today, ma'am. He asked me to tell you immediately."

Behice and Saraylıhanım simultaneously leapt for the door. Suat raced after them. Behice made way for Saraylıhanım to exit the room first, and, eager as she was to get to the ground floor, tried to be patient as her mother-in-law slowly took one step at a time. Suat did what her mother could not: wriggling past Saraylıhanım on the stairs, she was the first to reach the floor below, where Aret Efendi and Hüsnü Efendi waited in a state of high agitation.

"What's going on Aret Efendi?" Saraylıhanım asked.

"Forgive me for the disturbance, ladies, but the streets are dangerous today. I thought you should know. You'd best stay indoors. I left home at six this morning, and I've only just made it here. The city's crawling with military police and soldiers."

"Why? What happened?" asked Behice

"Have the streets been blockaded again?" asked Saraylıhanım. "I was just asking myself where Leman's piano instructor could be."

"Don't expect him. No one'll be able to go anywhere today."

"Does that mean I can't go to school?" whined Suat.

"I'm told they've begun detaining people," Aret Efendi said.

"What about me? What about school?"

"Hush girl," Behice scolded, "and we'll find out what's happened."

"Are they rounding up CUP partisans again?" asked Saraylıhanım.

"I don't know, efendim. But they were everywhere."

"Who was everywhere?"

"Foreign soldiers. The English. They've cordoned off all the main roads. I made my way here through the back streets. The high street is closed."

"I'll go out there and have a look," Hüsnü Efendi volunteered.

"Go, bring us news. You have us worried now," said Saraylıhanım. As Hüsnü and Aret walked together to the door Behice gathered her skirts and began climbing the stairs. Suat managed to dart ahead again.

"Careful," Behice said, "you'll trip me up. You're nothing like your elder sister. Since you insist on behaving like a boy, would that Allah had blessed me with a son instead."

"I wish I'd been born a boy," Suat agreed, "I wish I could go climb trees in the garden instead of embroidering."

"As if that weren't precisely what you do anyway!" Behice had no idea how to handle her younger daughter. While Leman was serious and serene, Suat was quite the opposite: as impish, fidgety and exuberant as a boy. The name Suat had been chosen when

Behice thought she was expecting a boy, and she sometimes blamed herself, as did Saraylıhanım, for having insisted on giving that name to a girl. The pillow cases and tables embroidered by Leman when she was Suat's age were so beautiful that Behice couldn't bear to use them. Suat hadn't yet mastered even basic backstitching, but she'd shone at school, where she effortlessly studied with girls two years older than herself. Her writing abilities nearly matched her sister's.

So much intelligence, Behice thought. What a waste.

Behice and her daughter settled onto the couch in the bow window. Only fifteen days earlier she'd been able to scan the street from the left side of the window; the view was now completely obscured by the leaves of the almond tree. Saraylıhanım appeared in the doorway, looking worried.

"Go and join your sister, Suat. She's doing embroidery in her room."

"I want to stay here with you, nana."

"Your mother and I have something to discuss. Come on, off you go."

"Can't I listen?"

"No, you can't." Saraylıhanım opened the door and called up the stairs: "Mehpare, come down and get Suat. Keep her entertained for a moment . . . Mehpare! Where are you?"

Hearing Mehpare's tread on the stairs, Suat dashed out of the room unprompted.

Saraylıhanım made certain the door was fully closed and took a seat next to Behice. "Behice, hear me out. If what Aret says is true . . . if they're rounding people up, they'll come here."

"But what for! There are no CUP people here. We're all devoted servants of the Sultan."

"That may be true, my dear, but, were we to take precautions nonetheless, what would be our best course of action?"

"What precautions could we possibly take, Saraylıhanım?"

"We could help Kemal over the garden wall and into the neighbor's house."

"You mean Ebe Hanım, the midwife?"

"Yes."

"Would she agree?"

"Were we to request her help why shouldn't she! After all, it was she who helped to bring our children into the world."

"But Saraylıhanım, wouldn't we be declaring to the neighbors that we've been harboring a criminal?"

"Then let's consider the alternative. Is it better to surrender Kemal to the police or to endure a few wagging tongues?"

Behice was feeling sick at heart. They'd already been disgraced once in the neighbors' eyes, when the police had arrived at the house after Kemal's falling out with CUP. Would they never be rid of him? Had she no right to lead a peaceful life with her husband and daughters? Just as she'd begun rejoicing at her status as a minister's wife, this had to happen.

"I couldn't answer that. I suggest we ask Reşat Bey."

"We can ask him, yes, but where is Reşat Bey right now? And, with the roads blocked, what time will he be coming home?"

"Late, as always," was Behice's reply.

"Your husband is not the corner grocer. Men of high rank come home when they can. You'll have to accept that."

"I wasn't complaining," said Behice, desperate to put an end to the conversation. The last thing she wanted was to receive a long-winded lecture on the virtues and attributes of her esteemed ancestors. Saraylıhanım stood up, hands on her hips.

"This is now the home of a minister," she declared, "and nobody's going to enter it unannounced and uninvited."

"The occupiers and their municipal police force couldn't care less whose house it is," said Behice, who clearly hadn't had time to appreciate the significance of her husband's appointment.

"Behice, dear girl, your husband isn't just any Reşat Efendi—he represents the Ottoman State. If the invaders dare to enter this house they will be made to answer for it."

When the housekeeper announced that Hüsnü Efendi had returned they all went down to the ground floor.

"I hear they've forced their way into Parliament," said Hüsnü Efendi, looking shattered. "They're detaining anyone who's associated with the resistance in any way, and conducting house to house searches."

Behice blanched. Was her husband in danger? Reşat Bey is a smart man, she told herself, and knows how to keep his head even in desperate times. But what about the fugitive in the attic? If they searched the house and stumbled upon Kemal, there was no telling what would happen to the rest of the family.

When Saraylıhanım began ascending the stairs Behice assumed she was going up to Kemal's room, and followed her. The two women breathlessly entered the sickroom on the top floor only to find Mehpare stirring a cup of linden tea and Kemal busily writing at his desk.

"Son, the situation is dire. You must leave immediately," said Saraylıhanım.

"But where will he go?" asked Mehpare. "He'll catch his death out in the streets."

"Mehpare, stay out of this," Saraylıhanım snapped. Kemal rose from his desk and pulled out a footstool; perching on it, he peered out of the window. "Where am I supposed to go?"

"I thought it best for you to hide at the midwife's house. No one would search the house of an old woman living with her daughters."

"But would she agree to hide me? Why should she jeopardize herself?" asked Kemal.

"I just thought of something," Behice said. "Azra Hanım lives nearby. You could get there through the back alley. She's full of ideas, just like you, Kemal, and if we were able to let her know of our situation . . ."

"That sounds like a good plan," said Kemal. "Azra's a brave woman and accustomed to fighting back. She's done so much for the Association for the Protection of Women's Rights. She'd be happy to help me."

"No! Stay here," pleaded Mehpare, terrified. "We'll hide you. You can hide in the pantry. They'll never find you there."

"Don't be ridiculous, Mehpare," Saraylıhanım said. "They'll be searching every corner of this house. We've been blacklisted."

"Won't they search Azra Hanım's house too? If she's been poking her nose into those sorts of things, she'll have been blacklisted as well, won't she," argued Mehpare.

"Mehpare, has anyone asked for your opinion? Know your place, girl. And what are you doing here anyway? Go down to the children," Behice said. The girl was normally so reserved and respectful, but fear and excitement seemed to have got the better of her. Mehpare blushed and bowed her head, but refused to budge.

"There was a secret crawlspace in Azra's garden," Kemal said, "years ago, when we were children, we'd go through a doorway and all the way back to the house, without anyone hearing a thing. If the military police show up there, I'll use it to come back here. It isn't as though they'll be able to raid every house simultaneously. They'll be searching one by one."

"How could you possibly remember all this about secret passageways?" asked Saraylıhanım.

"How could I not! Don't you remember, Azra used to live right next door. We'd play together ever day, along with Ali Riza, may he rest in peace."

"Well wherever you're going, be sure to wear a çarşaf, sir," Mehpare said.

"Great idea! All right then, quickly everyone," Behice said.

"Mehpare, you're the tallest. Run to your room and get your çarşaf." Mehpare didn't move. "I'm talking to you. What's come over you today?"

"I'm going with Kemal Bey."

"Oh? And why's that?"

"We'll be two women on their way to the marketplace, arm in arm. And if anyone questions us, I'll do the talking. Kemal Bey won't have to speak. "

"Such a clever girl, didn't I tell you?" said Saraylıhanım, voice full of pride. She'd resented the way Behice had rebuked the girl a moment earlier. "Circassians are like that, clever as can be! Well then, it's settled. Now go and get a çarşaf. Hurry up, girl!"

Mehpare was off in a flash.

"And if you'll kindly leave the room, I'll get dressed as well," Kemal said.

Saraylıhanım and Behice went down to the floor below and reassumed their places in the picture window. But this time, both women were trembling with anxiety. Behice badly needed a cigarette, but knew it was inappropriate to smoke in front of Saraylıhanım. A cheerless silence descended until Saraylıhanım spoke in her sweetest voice. "Roll us each a cigarette, Behice dear. On days like this, we can be forgiven for dispensing with propriety for a moment . . . Go on, don't be shy. Time simply won't pass otherwise."

The old fox has read my mind again, Behice thought to herself. She pulled a tobacco case from her dressing gown and began preparing a cigarette.

"Dear girl, I have a request to make of you."

Fully aware that such fond terms of address were resorted to only in the name of self interest, Behice looked Saraylıhanım in the eye and waited.

"Would you mind accompanying them as far as Ziya Pasha's house? I'll explain why. It's better they don't encounter Kemal on their doorstep all of a sudden. We're old friends but there are no men in their household and it would be inappropriate for him to appear without warning."

"But Mehpare is going with him!"

"Dear girl, who is Mehpare next to you? You're the wife of a minister. Your words have weight. They can hardly turn you away at the door!"

"But the children are at home today . . ."

"Have they never been here without you before, my girl?"

There was nothing left for Behice to say. "I'll go and get dressed." She rose resignedly and walked to the stairs.

"For goodness sake, do hurry," Saraylıhanım called after her.

Not long after, three women dressed in black from head to toe, one of them quite tall, hurried out of the house and down the street toward the sea. Keeping off the main road, they walked past a burnt-out lot and through the back streets until they were back in the same neighborhood, at the home of Ziya Pasha. The garden of the stately mansion was much larger than that of their own. They rang the bell at a heavy iron gate, painted green, and waited. "Please inform Münire Hanımefendi that the wife of Minister of Finance Reşat Bey is here to return her recent visit," a blushing Behice told the manservant who opened the door. She was well-bred enough to know that return visits are not made unannounced, nor so early in the morning, but she was in no position to explain further.

The servant showed the guests into the garden, re-bolted the gate and ushered them to the house. They slowly ascended the steps to the front door, and stepped inside. Kemal instinctively headed for the selamlık on the ground floor, but, when the raised eyebrows of the servant reminded him of his female attire, followed his aunt and Mehpare to the reception room on the floor above. The moment the servant left the room, he tore off the çarşaf, determined not to let Azra and Münire see his ridiculous costume.

The tense wait in the reception room seemed interminable; clearly, the ladies of Ziya Pasha's mansion had not been prepared to receive guests. They were no doubt having their hair arranged and getting dressed. Azra Hanım entered the room alone, looking pleased and surprised to find Kemal there. Handshakes were exchanged all round, and everyone sat down. Azra tried and failed to conceal her puzzlement at finding the girl who had only last week served her tea now sitting among her guests. The mistress of the house, Münire Hanımefendi, was spending a few days in Erenköy, at her elder sister's, she told them, before asking how they took their coffee and passing on the information to the housekeeper. Kemal hesitantly attempted to explain the purpose of their early morning visit.

"Well, it's like this . . . We don't know what's happened, exactly, but it seems they've begun detaining people again. The roads have all been blockaded. We're told that houses are being searched here in Beyazit. And as you know, I'm a . . . a . . ."

"I know," Azra reassured him, "it's been obvious to me."

"Does that secret passage still exist?" Kemal asked.

"Yes, but now it opens onto Aksöğüt Lane, not the burnt-out lot. That waste patch where we used to play has become a street."

"Azra Hanım, would you object to my waiting here until the municipal police arrive? The moment they knock on the door, I'll leave through the passage."

"How could I possibly object, Kemal," said Azra. She turned to Behice. "Behice Hanımefendi, your nephew and I may address each other formally, as Bey and Hanım, but don't let that fool you. Kemal and I have been close friends for many years. He and my late brother were inseparable. As boys, they were both headstrong, adventure-loving. And as young men, they were no different: neither of them hesitated to go off to the front to fight in what everyone knew was a lost cause. In his infinite wisdom, the Almighty gathered Ali Rıza to his side and spared Kemal. Such is fate. God has watched over Kemal and now it falls on us to protect him."

"God bless you." Kemal cut in. "Azra, if you have any qualms at all . . ."

"None. I'll instruct Hakkı Efendi to stand guard at the front gate. If anyone arrives, he'll ring the bell. We won't open the door until you're safely out of the house."

"But what if they come to the back gate? Or if they station someone there?"

"A thief entered the house through the back gate last summer and stole my father's order of merit from the display case. Mother was so upset that she had the back gate removed and a wall built."

"As the city grows, those sorts of crimes become more common," said Behice. "In the confusion of that bombing last week someone stole Mehpare's handbag."

"My condolences. A city inundated with immigrants is a city less safe. Thieves and scoundrels are certain to be among the newcomers," said Azra. "But, as they say, there's a silver lining to every cloud, and, happily for us, the back garden no longer has a gate."

The coffee arrived in fine porcelain cups wrapped with filigree sleeves. They sipped in appreciative silence.

"I never expected to be playing hide-and-seek at our age," Kemal remarked

"Did you expect to see Istanbul under occupation?"

"Salt in my wounds," groaned Kemal, his light tone belying the sincerity of his sentiment.

"There are times when the devil says to me, *Get your grandfather's pistol and shoot some of those invaders down*," Azra mused aloud. Behice gaped in astonishment. What kind of young woman was this?

"No fear, Azra Hanım, for that's precisely what others will soon be doing," said Kemal. "Matters can't stand as they are."

"How can you say such things, Kemal, when there are no soldiers left to fight the occupiers? Weren't they all forced to surrender their weapons the moment they entered Istanbul?" Behice asked.

"Not all of them did," Kemal said. "Some of the commanders kept their weapons. And the remains of the demobilized units are still on the streets. There are efforts underway to form an organization."

"But what good would they be without weapons and ammunition?" Behice protested.

"That's the easy part, aunt. Money buys arms."

"Kemal! Even with money no arms are available. The depots are all under guard. Do you think the English or the French are going to sell arms that will be used against them? You're talking like a child."

"Few men can resist money, aunt," said Kemal. "Everyone has his price. Besides, the foreign troops are thousands of miles from home. It isn't as though they're defending their homelands! We'll get rid of them one way or another."

Azra listened admiringly to Kemal's words, unaware that she herself was being studied—somewhat less admiringly—by Mehpare.

"If there's any way that I can help, Kemal, just tell me," she said. "I'm ready."

"How on earth could you help?" asked Behice.

"I could act as mediator. A translator. A courier. I could raise funds."

"All extremely dangerous for a woman."

"I understand your reluctance to get involved, Behice Hanımefendi. You have two young daughters. Your husband holds a high office. But I'm not married, I don't have children. Ever since my husband was martyred my only concern has been the liberation of this country."

"I understand," said Behice, "and commend you." Everyone sat in thoughtful silence for a few moments.

"Aunt, there's no need for you and Mehpare to stay here any longer. Go home and send word with Hüsnü Efendi if the house is searched. I'll come back by way of Aksöğüt Street when the danger is past."

"No!"

Azra, Behice and Kemal all stared at Mehpare, who had opened her mouth for the first time.

"Please don't, sir. Don't stay here alone. Behice Abla can go home. I'll wait here with you."

"Mehpare, what are you saying, girl," Behice said.

"Kemal Bey is going to wear a çarşaf again, isn't he, when he's out on the streets. What if he's asked for directions, or anything at all? What if somebody asks what a woman's doing alone in the street? How could he possibly respond? If I'm with him, he won't need to."

"I hadn't thought of that," said Azra. "She's considered every detail."

"She's extremely intelligent," Kemal said.

"But how am I to return all alone?" asked Behice.

"We'll send someone with you, don't worry. And it's only a few hundred yards at most!" said Azra, a note of scorn creeping into her voice.

"Well in that case, I ask that you give me an escort immediately and let me go home. The girls are waiting and Saraylıhanım will be beside herself with worry."

As Azra left the room Behice murmured in a low voice, "Azra Hanım—she's like a man. So bold . . ."

"She's always been like that. She'd leave behind her dolls and follow us around, even climbing trees."

"God forbid our Suat should turn out that way. She's already a distressingly self-assertive little monster. Not unlike Azra herself, come to speak of it."

"Why this antipathy towards Azra, aunt?" asked Kemal. "She's a strong woman, and as intelligent as she is determined. Any other widow in her position would have withdrawn from the world, or remarried. Azra has done neither. She reads, she writes, she translates. Do all women have stay home with their needlework?"

"It befits them to do so, yes."

"Forgive me, but you're familiar with the expression, 'if you lie down with the blind, you'll get up cross-eyed,' aren't you? It sounds like Saraylıhanım has rubbed off on you."

"Just you wait until you're married yourself, then we'll see if you prefer a wife with a pen in her hand, or a rolling pin. These are bachelor's pronouncements."

Behice stopped talking when Azra reentered the room. Anyone listening would think Behice spent all of her time rolling out *yufka*,

Mehpare thought to herself. In fact, She spent her days playing the ud and the piano, receiving guests or doing needlepoint. She was rarely seen in the kitchen.

"Hakkı Efendi will accompany you home, Behice Hanımefendi," Azra said. "He's waiting in the garden."

Behice embraced Kemal tightly before putting on her çarşaf. "I hope everything goes smoothly," she said. Then, to Mehpare, "I'm entrusting him to you. You're far more prudent than he is. But for God's sake, be careful."

"Don't latch the garden gate from the inside, Behice Hanım. We may have to enter in a hurry," Mehpare said.

"I can't just leave the gate open, anyone might come in. But I'll arrange the latch cord—you'll be able to reach it through the hole with your fingertips."

Behice and Azra left the room.

"Mehpare, how can I repay you," Kemal said.

"Stay safe and healthy. That's all I ask," Mehpare replied.

Azra returned after showing Behice to the door. "Would you like to go the kitchen, Mehpare?" she gently asked. "Housekeeper Nazik is rolling out some dough; you might want to join her."

"I don't know how to roll out dough, ma'am," said Mehpare, remaining seated.

"Very well then." A bit taken aback, and not a little put out, Azra turned to Kemal. "Well in that case, come to the library with me, Kemal. The books I ordered last month have arrived and I'd like to present you with one of them. I'm interested to know if you think it's worth translating."

Kemal rose and followed Azra out of the room.

Mehpare was alone. She folded her hands in her lap, sitting expressionless, ramrod straight.

"The women of your household are extraordinary," Azra remarked to Kemal as they ascended the stairs together. "Your aunt is so pampered she'd break if you so much as sneezed at her; Mehpare's the opposite, a girl of steel. But she seems quite smitten with you."

"Ridiculous. She cared for me while I was ill. She was most attentive. Now she treats me like an infant, forever trying to shield me from harm. She follows me like a shadow, making sure I don't forget to take my medicine or keep warm."

"Patients habitually fall in love with their doctors, and nurses with their patients."

"How could the girl fall for me? I'm a crippled man, Azra."

"But you haven't lost your faculties, have you? I hope you still have the clarity of mind to see that the poor girl is head over heels."

"Well, what can I do about it?"

"Don't get her hopes up. Create the opportunity for her to marry someone befitting her station. Don't let her squander her future on you."

"You're as presumptuous as you've ever been. I remember the way you used to try to order Ali Rıza about. We used to call you pipsqueak."

"I've touched a nerve."

"You're upset with Mehpare because she refused to go down to the kitchen. That's what this is about. Let me explain something; she doesn't have the status of a servant in our household. She's a distant relative of Saraylıhanım's. Nearly every family has members who, for whatever reason, have fallen on hard times. In our family's case, Mehpare is the grandchild of an unfortunate uncle. She works hard, but does so by choice. Otherwise, Saraylıhanım would have long since arranged her marriage to a respectable public clerk or some such."

"Haven't you ever considered why she would choose service over marriage to a clerk?"

"No, I haven't."

"You men are all alike. Blind to the inconvenient facts. Well, here's one for for: the girl wants you. You are that clerk of hers."

"Generous of you to say so. But even an impoverished relative would be unlikely to want a man who's missing several toes, who's in poor health, and, to make matters worse, who's a fugitive from the law."

"I know what you're doing—you're looking for flattery. But I won't rise to the bait. Tell me, Kemal, what do you know about the bombing? It's interesting, isn't it, that Mehpare just happened to be wandering in the area that day."

"Her aunt lives in Beşiktaş. She was visiting."

"Oh really!"

"Azra, what do want to know?"

"I want to know how deep you are in all of this. You came here for protection: you must trust me. Sharing information could be beneficial to us both."

"All right then. Are you familiar with an organization called Karakol?

"The old CUP partisans run it, don't they?"

"They used to, but since then it's become inseparable from the resistance in Anatolia. The English have gotten the names of some of the high-ranking members there. They have no hard evidence, but their suspicions have been aroused. So they carried out the bombing, as an act of intimidation. But with little consequence, for the organization has simply shifted headquarters."

"Well, what are your duties?"

"Due to my illness, I'm barely of use to them. I try to be helpful by penning articles or translating secret documents."

"I'm not ill. I could liaise for you . . ."

"I'd never use you. But I can give you the name and address of a contact. You could apply to speak to them."

Azra leapt from her chair, pulled a sheet of white paper and a pen from a pigeonhole in the writing desk, dipped her pen in the inkwell, and waited.

Kemal gave her a name and address, adding, "Use me as a reference and let them decide how you might be of use. Once you've memorized the name and address, tear the paper to bits—in fact, burn it . . ." He stopped mid-sentence, paused and exclaimed: "Listen Azra . . . The bell's ringing."

Both of them rushed for the stairs as Azra folded the piece of paper and slipped it into her dress. By the time they reached the entry hall, Mehpare had put on her çarşaf and was holding out Kemal's.

Azra leading the way, the party of three hurried down to the floor below, entered the garden though the door next to the pantry and, crouching, scurried along the base of the wall.

"The passage should be around here somewhere," said Kemal. All three searched for a gap in the wall. Azra found it, and they set about clearing away weeds and other vegetation, exposing the entrance to a crawlspace. Kemal peered inside and said, "You'd better get back to the house immediately, Azra."

"Don't worry about me. You're the ones in danger. If you encounter any difficulties, you can come back here."

"God bless you." Kemal entered the narrow opening sideways. "Come on, Mehpare. It's your turn. Once you're inside, I'll cover it back up," Azra said. Mehpare sidled into the passage and reached for Kemal's hand. He tugged her into the darkness. They walked for a time, doubled over, cobwebs brushing their faces. A couple of bats thrashed past their ears.

"There's not much further to go," Kemal said. "We'll be at the other end in a moment."

Back in the garden, Azra hastily concealed the entrance to the passage and ran for the house. She slipped through the back door and raced up the stairs, only to see, through the window, the manservant attempting to explain something to a Greek Ottoman standing next to a uniformed foreigner.

"What's all this about?" she shouted down. "What's going on? What do they want?"

"Hanımefendi, they're searching houses . . ."

"What next! Aren't they ashamed to be searching the home of a pasha?"

"Pasha masha," the Greek interpreter explained, "no make difference for us. Today we go into all houses."

"I'll get dressed and be down in a moment. I'll speak to them."

"No need for talking. I told you their wants."

"Your Turkish is appalling; how can you possibly communicate in English! Tell them I'll be down in a moment. I won't rely on your language skills."

Azra couldn't help smiling at this opportunity to bring the Greek down a few notches. She stepped back from the window, took several deep breaths and smoothed her hair. Then she leisurely descended the stairs she had scrambled up only a moment before. Her back straight, her head held high, she walked to the door and entered the garden.

Kemal and Mehpare waited a long time in the long, narrow crawlspace. Then they exited, one after the other, warily surveying their surroundings. According to Azra's directions, they were now on Aksöğüt Street. The windows opening onto the lane were all closed and shuttered. Without speaking, they marched down this quiet, deserted street, which seemed poised, preparing to ambush an invisible enemy. As they drew closer to the main street, a clamor broke out: the sound of gunshots, shouting, screams, the tinkle of breaking glass, sirens, whistles . . . They exchanged anxious glances.

"Stay here. I'll go as far as the street and see what's happening," Mehpare said.

"No. You wait while I have a look."

"If you're caught you'll be thrown in jail. They won't do anything to me. At worst, I'll be questioned and released. Let me go."

Kemal had no choice but to consent.

"If you sense danger of any kind, go back into the passageway. I'll be able to find you there," Mehpare said.

As she moved off towards the intersection of the lane and the main street, Kemal squatted at the foot of the wall. As he waited there, hunched up, his head sinking into his shoulders, his eyes on the ground, he was suddenly overcome with a sense of weary disgust. He was fed up with hiding like a thief, with this endless infirmity. He was too weak to join in the struggle. He was of no use to anyone. After all his efforts to help liberate his country, nothing could be more damning than having to remain in occupied Istanbul. He'd long since given up on the dream of independence, was even prepared to settle for the despotism of the sultan—anything, so long as the enemy soldiers got the hell out of his country. If they stayed, he was better off dead. Or so he told himself. So he wished to believe. Even as somewhere within him a tiny protest registered: a faltering sense of misgiving, of stealthy dissent, a distant voice seeming to say to him: Don't die, not yet. And as dark as his thoughts were, he saw, in his mind's eye, a woman. And asked himself, was it this woman who bound him to life. He saw her. The slender form of a young woman.

Each night, long after she'd slipped away, even after he'd fallen fast asleep, Mehpare's scent lingered. Mehpare. He remembered Mahir mentioning in conversation that consumption was known to increase a man's sexual appetite. That was one of the reasons that he was convinced he had consumption. How else to explain the desire that he felt for this girl? Yes, it must be consumption. At first he'd held back, afraid to contaminate her. He no longer cared. It was shameless, craven, he had to have Mehpare every chance he could. He'd be dead soon enough. How could he deny himself one of the only pleasures left! As he sat lost in thought, Kemal became conscious of the cold damp wall pressing against his back, and leaned forward. He rummaged through his pockets for his cigarette case, but failed to find it. Mehpare and Saraylıhanım had been pilfering his tobacco ever since the doctor had ordered him to decrease his smoking. As he sat up straight a solider appeared at the end of the street. He sprang to his feet and began walking quickly in the opposite direction; then he broke into a run. Behind him came the sounds of pounding boots, shouts of: "Stop!". He fell to the ground in front of the secret entranceway and crawled in; piling several large rocks into the opening, he advanced a short way into the darkness and pressed himself to the ground. He could hear men talking outside. Speaking in a Greek accent, someone said, "He can't have vanished into thin air. He must have gone into that red house. Or the next house over."

"He must have escaped through one of the back gardens," a different voice said.

"Cut off the street. Search every house."

Kemal stretched out on the ground. Were they to find the opening and look inside, at least he wouldn't be immediately visible. He'd have to remain prone for a time on the cold earth.

He'd shiver and fever would follow and if he already had consumption he'd die and if he didn't have consumption he'd get it. Better to die of consumption than fall into enemy hands. Actually both scenarios would mean certain death. If he was lucky enough to make it home he'd take his grandfather's pistol out of the second drawer of the buffet and die a man's death. A bullet to the head—after he'd made love to Mehpare one last time.

Stripping off his çarşaf he rolled it up into a ball and placed it between his chest and the damp earth. A rat scurried along just past his head. It was too early for ants—he was lucky, at least he wasn't being swarmed by insects. He closed his eyes to avoid the shadowy sight of rats and tried to focus his mind on other things, but now it was tormented by dark thoughts: lying face down anywhere but in bed could only mean trouble. Like being prone in the trenches, thrusting your head above ground to shoot at the enemy; and then, if you yourself weren't shot in the process, assuming a prone position yet again, and again. Enemy fire or not, at least you could lift your head. If he straightened up now, he'd crack his skull against the stone ceiling. He was overcome with a sense of suffocation—as a boy the passage had seemed capacious, but now he was squeezed in a coffin, his heart constricted. He was desperate to emerge from this prison, to go home: he lost track of time, there was no sound but the scurrying rats, nothing but the walls pressing in. His only escape was sleep. If he could only sleep, sleep. Eternal sleep. Oh, to be like a white butterfly, driven by wind above the seven skies, a snowflake flying, wind-whipped—to be a snowflake, to be white and infinite. To be eternity.

– 6 –

White Death

In Sarıkamış, sleep meant death. Kemal could remember the rows of soldiers stretched out side by side on their bellies—the way they'd prod each other, babbling to stay awake, to stay alive, because death under a white shroud of snow was the best you could hope for, if you fell asleep. To those who succumbed in their sleep, death was a white cat come to claim their souls; but to those who resisted, it came like a woman, a bride—a beckoning hand, a glimpse of dark eyes behind lace, a skirt lifted to show white thighs, a pair of naked breasts. And they ran, those young men, they ran by the scores, by the thousands, to embrace her. Staying awake was an act of defiance, of resistance, but it was only the first step. When the white bride approached them, few could resist.

And how strange that Kemal had managed to withstand the lure of the white bride, but had yielded so completely to Mehpare. Though he'd defied death, he'd been undone by lust. Or was lust the fiercer of the two? Defying death means clinging to life, jealously guarding from the claims of Azrail the life temporarily granted by Allah. It means taking another breath; it means another exhalation, another circuit of blood pumping through the veins, another moment, another second, another heartbeat, here, on the face of a miserable world of maddening cold.

It was peculiar, this defiance of death. He'd tried to explain one night, to Mehpare. It was one of those nights, those restless nightmarish hours of darkness. He'd finally nodded off, only to wake after several hours.

"I'm cold, cover me. Cover me up. I'm freezing."

She'd piled blankets and quilts on top of him. "Do your wounds hurt, are your toes stinging? Let me rub your feet. If you're in pain, I can get you some of the drops Mahir gave me."

"It isn't my wounds, Mehpare, it's my heart. You wouldn't understand. You can't know what it's like. It's beyond your imagination."

"Tell me about it then. Let me feel what you feel. Share your memories with me, let them be mine, not yours. I'll shiver instead."

"There are no words to describe what I felt, what I'm feeling, the sense of revulsion, the sense of rebellion that grips me. Ever since my fellow soldiers froze to death, ever since they were abandoned to the wolves and bands of Armenian irregulars, I've been wracked with pain. Had we frozen to death for our country, I wouldn't grieve. But do you know why we scaled those mountains? For the Germans. We Ottomans were pressured to open an Eastern Front in order to act as a decoy for the Russian troops. And without a second thought, that madman Enver sent 90,000 young men up into the mountains. Some of them were being deployed directly from the Arabian deserts and wore uniforms of thin cotton; as for us, we tramped through the snow for days in our leather boots. The winds transformed our greatcoats into icy shells; we couldn't move our arms. It was as though we'd been sealed into coffins of ice. Our fingers went from cold to stinging to numb. And we froze one by one, without firing a bullet. Enver killed us."

"Please don't cry. Don't. It was their fate. It was written on their foreheads by Allah. Forget those days, those nights. Forget them."

"At first, the snowflakes drifted down on us like white butterflies, settling onto our heads, darting into our coats. Then the winds rose. I'll never forget that night, the night our greatcoats froze solid. If I put it out of my mind it enters my dreams and if it leaves my dreams it's still there, stuck fast in my mind, rooted down. The cold piercing my flesh, my soul. If I still have a soul. If there's some shadow of a soul left in this sheath of skin, it's a soul that trembles and shakes and shudders. Ever since that night I always sit right beside the stove, as close as possible, with a cigarette in hand, summer and winter. And when that family hid me in their shed, in Palandöken, I kept the brazier lit even when spring came, Mehpare. Not just to keep warm, but because it seemed the red glow of the flames would keep the white death at bay. I kept the fire going all summer long. The memory of that whiteness will never leave me. I'll never be free of it, Mehpare."

"Try not to remember. Look, you're home now. Warm, in your room. Close your eyes, try to drowse if you can. I'll sit here, I'll keep the fire alive. You won't get cold. Now try to sleep."

"Listen to me, Mehpare. I can't bear it anymore, not alone . . ."

"I'm listening. You have my ear, my heart, my mind. I'm listening. Tell me."

"Snow lifted and driven by the wind, filling our mouths, our noses, our eyes. We hugged each other for warmth, we leaned into each other and onto each other, a single body of men, marching through the night. We were hungry, ill, infested with lice, doubled over with typhus. Yet we plowed along, falling to our knees, struggling to our feet, advancing through the snow. Our commander thought it best to return to headquarters, but the Pasha in Istanbul wouldn't listen to him. The order came from on high. We were to continue. There'd be no regrouping, no rest. We were to circle behind the Russians, ambush them. We walked in boots worn to shreds and wrapped in rags and we couldn't feel our feet. Some of us went mad from the cold. Some of us dashed into the forest, and when we had the strength we brought them back so they wouldn't be executed as traitors or devoured by wolves. Our tears froze to our cheeks. And as we scaled the mountainside some of us fell to our knees, too weak to continue, intending to draw breath, gather strength. And the moment they did so they fell asleep. We pulled them to their feet, slapped their frozen faces with our frozen hands, hoisted them up by their arms and dragged them through the snow. Sometimes we were too weak to do anything but struggle up and on, leaving them behind, and almost immediately they were blanketed in white, those men kneeling in the snow, sleeping. Death taunted us. You know how they say Azrail comes in many guises to claim your soul. Well, on that December night, on Mount Allahüekber, death appeared to us in the form of a bride all in white. A malevolent, unblushing bride. Greedy. Grasping. Hungry for us all. And only a handful escaped. There was Sergeant Musa of Dimyat, İsmail, Hadji Hasso and me. I don't know why she didn't take us too. Hasso never used his frozen feet again, they cut both his legs off just below the knee. Sergeant Musa lost his mind. I've had no news of İsmail. That night, I lost two toes, damaged my kidneys, caught a chill in my lungs—and developed a strange affinity for hot stoves. That's all. They said I was lucky. That I got off easy. I suppose they're right, I got off easy enough, except for having to relive that terrible night every night since. And now, as I shiver and my kidneys ache and my nights are filled with terrors and I manage without two toes, I continue to draw breath and patiently wait for the day of reckoning. And on that day, I'm going to seize General Enver by the collar with my own two hands and demand he account for the 90,000 soldiers who froze to death in the mountains of Sarıkamış. That day is coming. Soon. Very soon. And when my soul, too, is a white butterfly flown up to join my comrades in arms . . ."

"Don't. I'm begging you, don't talk like that. Don't talk about death. Try to sleep. Sleep for a while longer."

And he did sleep for a few hours; soothed by Mehpare's whispering, his head in her lap, her hands stroking his hair. He slept. And he had another nightmare. And trembled and cried out. Until, finally, morning broke, and the sun filtered in through a gap in the curtains, and a small patch of carpet glowed hot. It was morning. The sun was out and he would live another day. Another night had passed, and he was still alive.

When Kemal opened his eyes he was overjoyed to see a beam of light trickling through the rocks he'd heaped up in the entrance to the crawlspace. The ground below him wasn't soft and inviting, like snow. Something was poking into his stomach, just below his heart and his back ached; but there was light, and where there was light, there was hope. Reassured, he closed his eyes and surrendered himself to a deep sleep.

"Sir . . . sir . . . Kemal Bey! Wake up . . . Wake up . . . God, why doesn't he open his eyes? Hey! Kemal Bey, Kemal Bey!

He was being slapped repeatedly on both cheeks. He opened his eyes.

"Thank God! You scared me to death!"

"Mehpare!"

"It's me, it's me. I know you've been waiting. Try to sit up. You've caught a chill. You must be numb. Let me help you sit up."

Kemal tried to move his limbs. His entire body was stiff and sore. Even in the semi-darkness of the passageway, the light hurt his eyes.

"I must have passed out. I had terrible dreams. Nightmares . . . about Sarıkamış . . ."

"Sarıkamış is long gone. Those days are over. Come on, sit up a little."

Kemal got up on his knees and leaned back against the wall. "How long have I been here? What's going on outside?"

"It's havoc out there. The occupying soldiers are everywhere. It's a bloodbath. They've searched all the houses in the area. They even raided the Red Crescent. They're looking for Nationalists. And for CUP supporters, too. I made it as far as the midwife's house and waited there. So many people are hurt. They came and took the midwife away."

"Who took her away? The foreigners?"

"No. Our people took her away. To tend to the wounded, probably."

"What time is it?"

"Late afternoon prayers ended some time ago. You've been here for a while now. When things seemed to settle down I came to get you."

"Did they search our house?"

"Last I saw there were still soldiers at the top of our street. Let's go back to Ziya Pasha's house. They won't go there again. We can wait there, and when it's dark we'll go home."

"I'm sending you home now. Unless it's too dangerous, Hüsnü Efendi can come and get me."

"I'm not going anywhere without you. I'm supposed to look after you. We're going together and we'll stay together."

"God, Mehpare! Am I a child?"

"That's not what I meant, sir. Come on, let's go together. Come on, try to get up."

Kemal massaged his unfeeling legs a bit and rose to a crouching position. Bent nearly double, he followed Mehpare towards the garden where they had first entered the passage. The entrance had been concealed with rocks and weeds, so it took them some time to find it. Finally, they were outside in the garden. Kemal raised his arms over his head and stood there like that for a moment. He shook out his legs, one after the other. How wonderful to stretch your limbs, to raise your head high, to take up as much space as you wish! He imagined confinement in a tiny cell, and shuddered.

"Stay behind that tree over there, sir, and wait for me. I'll go and take a look at the house. If the coast is clear, I'll come back for you," Mehpare said.

Kemal had grown accustomed to taking orders from Mehpare. He said nothing. As he squatted at the base of a giant plane tree, she ran for the house.

Uncertain whether to run away or to stay where he was, Kemal tensed at the sight of a shadowy figure approaching in the darkness.

"Kemal Bey, are you here? I can't make you out in the dark," came the voice of the old servant, Hakkı Efendi. Kemal got up and walked over to him.

"Follow me, sir," said the servant.

"I hope those foreign soldiers haven't harassed you," Kemal said.

"Azra Hanım gave them a good dressing down. They searched the house and left."

"Well good for her."

"Don't concern yourself, sir, they won't be back."

Azra and Mehpare were waiting for Kemal at the gate to the house.

"I'm so sorry, Kemal," Azra said. "Mehpare told me what happened. It must have been dreadful shut up in that hole all afternoon. But better that than getting caught. You must be chilled to the marrow; I've had some soup prepared. Shall we go straight to the dining room?"

"Has your mother returned?" Kemal asked.

"No. I didn't expect her back until Friday in any case. I'd been planning to take the ferryboat to Kadıköy tomorrow to see her, but I understand they've been cancelled."

"As far as I know neither the tramways nor the ferryboats have been running on schedule for some days now."

"For a housebound invalid you're most knowledgeable, Kemal."

"I may be confined to the house, but the members of my family are free to go where they will."

They entered a dining room in which the table had been freshly laid. Dining rooms had come into fashion, replacing the traditional common dining areas upon which rooms opened. Families favoring an *à la française* lifestyle no longer supped off large round trays, and were slowly growing accustomed to sitting at a table. Azra sat Kemal at the head of the table, took a seat to his right and showed Mehpare to the chair on his left. Doing her best to conceal her tension, Mehpare sat down, racking her brain to remember what she'd read in Behice's women's magazines—advice on table manners. "Sit fully erect throughout the meal. Do not lean your elbows on the table. Do not smack your lips. In fact, do not speak while there is food in your mouth," she'd read in *The Gazette for Women*. She tensed her back, sitting ramrod straight, and slowly removed her elbows from the table.

Kemal and Azra spent most of the meal talking about a secret organization. When Azra wanted to keep something secret from Mehpare, she'd speak French. It was maddening. As the meal drew to an end, Mehpare could take no more.

"They'll be worried about us, shall we go as soon as we've finished dining?" she remarked to Kemal.

"If you'd like, I could send Hakkı Efendi first, to check the streets," Azra offered.

"Is there any need?"

"Caution is always advisable," Azra insisted. "Hakkı Efendi will be back before we've finished our coffee. Would you like to go with him, Mehpare? You're looking a little peaky."

"No. I'll go with Kemal Bey. He's been entrusted to my care."

"Mehpare nursed me for so long she now thinks she's my mother," Kemal laughed.

"She's far too young and beautiful to be anyone's mother," said Azra. Mehpare blushed. She would have given anything to escape this disdainful woman. She gulped down the hot coffee, scalding her throat, and impatiently waited for Kemal and Azra to finish their conversation.

Soon afterwards, Hakkı Efendi came in to tell them the streets were no longer dangerous, and they rose to their feet.

"You'd best be careful, anyway," Azra advised.

"How will we ever repay your kindness," Kemal said to Azra as they made their farewells.

"You may have to hide me one day," she replied. "Then we'll be even."

As Kemal and Mehpare walked towards the garden gate, Mehpare couldn't help thinking that the blue-eyed woman was a dangerous type who would only bring misfortune to Kemal.

− 7 −

The March 16th Disaster

At the bottom of the hill sloping down from the Reşat Bey mansion, the shadowy forms of two tall women were silhouetted against an indigo sea as they walked up the street, side by side and in silence. They would have conveyed an impression of nervous stealth had anyone been observing them. But the street was empty and the neighborhood, which throughout the day had been alive with gunshots and screams and curses, was wrapped in an eerie calm. The women stopped in front of a large house and looked to the left and to the right. Mehpare inserted her finger into a hole in the gate, deftly located the latch cord and pulled it. There was a click. Pushing open the iron gate, they entered the garden, immediately shutting the gate behind them. Kemal slid the iron bolt into place, leaned against the gate and heaved a sigh of relief. Then he sank to the ground, back still propped against the gate, too exhausted to stand.

"Don't sit on the ground, you'll get cold," Mehpare admonished him.

"We've probably both caught a chill today, all those hours waiting in that damp hole," Kemal said.

"Come on sir, don't give up now, not three steps from the house."

Kemal took Mehpare's extended hand and struggled to his feet. Leaning on each other for support, they walked towards the house. Kemal started at the sight of yellow light filtering through the curtains of the selamlık.

"Why's the light on in the selamlık at this hour? Shhh, Mehpare, let's wait here. There might be trouble inside. We'd better be careful."

Mehpare and Kemal managed to roll a large stone over to the bottom of the window. Kemal climbed on top of it, and standing on tiptoe, tried to get a look inside. He could hear a strange sound. A strangled bawling? A suppressed scream?

Good God! Ahmet Reşat stood inside the room pounding the wall, again and again, as he kicked and stamped his feet. He kept his left fist clamped to his mouth, but even through the closed window Kemal could hear his uncle's muffled howls. At first, he assumed someone else was in the room as well. Though crazily tilted to one side, his uncle's fez still rested on his head. Amazing! His uncle always removed his fez first thing; first his fez, then his ankle boots. Always, day after day, the same routine. But here he was, pounding and kicking like a madman. While completely alone in the room!

Kemal raced to the front door, Mehpare hard on his heels, and was just about to press the bell when the door was flung open by the grimfaced housekeeper. "Where have you been? We were worried sick. We thought something had happened to you," she grumbled. As Mehpare ran to the floor above, the housekeeper planted herself directly in front of Kemal, who was trying to remove his boots.

"Sir, something terrible has happened to master. He's been beating the walls for an hour now."

"Where are the ladies? My grandmother, my aunt?"

"They're upstairs. Everyone's too scared to go near him. *Leave me alone or I'll make you regret it,* he roared the moment he stepped through the door. They're upstairs with the girls, weeping. Leman Hanım is especially torn up. Master's been so ill-tempered that Behice Hanım fears for his heart. Shall we call the doctor?"

"Let me find out what it is first." Any and all past misunderstandings erased from his mind, Kemal rushed into the room without knocking.

"Uncle," he said, "what's the meaning of all this? What happened?"

"What happened? I'll tell you what happened. Something dreadful! The English raided Parliament today! Can you imagine, Kemal . . . the English, without the slightest explanation or warning from their ambassador, allowed that man of theirs, the one they call Intelligence Officer Bennett, to raid Parliament and take Rauf Bey and Kara Vasıf Bey into custody! They handcuffed high-ranking government officials, subjected them to all manner of insulting behavior, stuffed them into trucks, and took them off. And as if raiding Parliament wasn't bad enough, they dragged Cevat Pasha and Doctor Esat Pasha out of their homes, without even allowing them to get dressed, still in their pajamas, hands tied behind their backs like a couple of common thieves. And the way they treated Esat Pasha is abominable . . . I can barely get the words out of my mouth. They beat him!"

"What!"

"And in the early morning they raided the police stations and martyred any guards who resisted. A private soldier at the Şehzadebaşı

Police Station was still asleep when they killed him. Not a single man was left alive at the Caucasus Division Headquarters. We now know the reason for the gunfire at dawn yesterday. It's only because our soldiers withdrew to their barracks that the bloodshed wasn't worse. The English seized all their weapons. A battleship was anchored next to the Galata Bridge, another one directly in front of the Palace, its guns trained on the Palace itself. The English surrounded their embassy and all their interests with machine guns. And as if that weren't enough, they plastered signs all over the streets notifying the citizenry that the city was under English occupation and that any resistance would be severely punished."

His battered hands clasped to the sides of his head, Reşat Bey began pacing the length of the room. He, too, seemed to have forgotten about the recent altercation with his nephew. While Kemal had been biding his time in the passageway, the city had been plunged into chaos! Which meant the sound of gunfire had been real— no nightmare, no trick of the mind, no surfacing of suppressed memories. He inwardly cursed at having been stuck in a hole while outside the world went mad. But it was no time for self-pity, his uncle was still distraught.

"Uncle . . . Uncle, please sit down. Try to calm down. No fear, we'll find a way to get those weapons back."

"I wish it was as simple as retrieving our weapons . . . They pressed a bayonet into the chest of the Minister of War and demanded he enforce their orders. It was only when the Minister informed them that under those conditions he would be unable to issue orders of any kind that they finally lowered their rifles. The Minister arrived in the Sublime Porte having been jeered at all the way by Greeks and

Armenians. He kept his dignity, immediately prepared a strongly worded diplomatic communiqué, one worthy of an honorable people. But what's the use? Istanbul has become a captive city. Our city has sunk to this! His Majesty has been forced to consult the English even on the subject of the Friday noon prayers. With arms forbidden to all, who would guard the Sultan's procession to the mosque?"

"If a visit to the mosque requires permission from the English, it is better he not go."

"But he very much wishes to go. *It's my religious duty*, he says." Ahmet Reşat raised his cupped hands in appeal: "Allah, what have we done to deserve this?"

"I understand your distress, but there's nothing to be done."

Kemal opened the door and asked the housekeeper—whose ear had been pressed against its wood, and who very nearly tumbled into the room in consequence—to bring a glass of water. She had barely taken two steps when the door was flung open a second time. "Bring some rakı too, and two glasses."

Ahmet Reşat sank down onto one of the divans and ruefully rubbed his aching hands together.

"A moment ago, you said there's nothing to be done, Kemal. That's what I find most maddening of all. Rumors are flying: the Greeks and Armenians are going to cut down the Muslims, they're going to put icons back into Haghia Sophia, Christian priests have seized Muslim orphanages, and on and on. These stories are nothing but outright fabrications and ridiculous exaggerations but they're still sufficient cause for a popular rebellion. And yet the people of Istanbul haven't been agitated into violence. And why? Because the government has always been a soothing influence."

"Would that the fury of the people had been unleashed and riots had broken out. That would give the invaders something to think about."

"It would be wrong. Retribution would be terrible. We've endured so much, Kemal! We've resigned ourselves to degradation. We've turned a blind eye to so much. We've avoided bloodshed at all costs. But they seize the homes and mansions only of Muslims, the only ones they accuse of wrongdoing. Believe me when I say that the only thing preventing these heathens from being lynched by the mobs is the Ottoman municipal police force, the only force able to maintain law and order. You'd have expected some slight show of gratitude on the part of the invaders."

"Uncle! We're talking about the English here."

Ahmet Reşat slammed his fist onto the end table. A glass ashtray fell to the floor and shattered.

"Uncle, difficult times always lead to better days. They've gone so far that even you have rebelled. You, who always said we had no choice but to fall back upon the English."

Ahmet Reşat closed his eyes tightly in response, as though willing away the unbearable. But to no avail. Images of the raid on Parliament and a sense of utter helplessness were with him still.

"What was the Sultan's reaction?" Kemal asked.

"Those who gave him the news had difficulty getting so much as a word out of him."

"Well what did he say?"

"He screwed his eyes shut and sat there, immobile and impassive, and when he opened them again he stared into the distance. He always does that when he's distraught . . ."

"Uncle, you mean that at a time when they're rounding up and insulting statesmen whose sole crime is love of country, His Majesty does nothing but close his eyes?"

"What do you expect him to do, Kemal? Were he to defy them he himself might be debased and humiliated. How could the Sultan run the risk of such treatment?"

"If the Sultan is personally unprepared to take risks he should offer his full support to those willing to risk death for their country."

"Do you think he doesn't back them? Who do you think has appointed Grand Viziers who overlook the disobedience of pashas who refuse to turn over their weapons? Please, don't criticize him without knowing the full truth."

"Be sure of this, uncle, were the Sultan engaged in preparing a plan of salvation I would be the first to offer my life to him."

"It's only to be expected that your confinement to the house has prevented you from learning of certain developments. Why do you think the invaders pressured Ali Rıza Pasha into resigning? Because they were mad with fury over the Amasya Protocol our Minister of Marine co-signed with the Delegation of Representatives."

Kemal looked at his uncle in astonishment.

"And what was in this memorandum of understanding, signed between the Ottoman government and the Turkish revolutionaries? The outlining of joint efforts to preserve national independence and unity. The rejection of any concessions to non-Muslims that would threaten Turkish sovereignty," Ahmet Reşat continued.

"That's true, but the Sultan . . ."

Ahmet Reşat cut off his nephew. "Do you really believe that the Sultan was unaware that the Ottoman government ratified the borders designated by the National Pact? Are you such a fool, my boy?"

"Well then why doesn't the Ottoman government act jointly with the Delegation of Representatives right here in Istanbul? They should join forces, and end this once and for all."

"After this deplorable turn of events His Majesty has, in fact, issued an imperial decree to establish communications with Anatolia. They could have reached an agreement earlier, but Mustafa Kemal Pasha has insisted that the Ottoman Parliament assemble in Ankara instead of in Istanbul."

"That's reasonable enough. Ankara isn't under occupation."

"Kemal, stop talking like a child. Istanbul is the seat of the Caliphate and has been the capital of the empire for centuries. Shifting parliament somewhere else would mean giving up on Istanbul."

"Is that the only reason you can't reach agreement with the Delegation of Representatives?

"Isn't it enough?"

"No, it is not, uncle."

"Stop it! The Sultan is Commander of the Believers and must remain in the seat of the Caliphate. Heaven forbid that the custody of the faith should fall into other hands. And he also has the wealth of the Ottoman Dynasty to consider. Let's keep this to ourselves, but Sultan Vahdettin is concerned that the English might seize the treasury."

"But Uncle, I've received information that the Sultan has signed a secret treaty with the English. They say the Sultan has agreed to be under an English mandate and has even pledged that he will employ his spiritual and temporal powers in service of English interests. The Sultan may be able to cling to his treasure, but he's apparently willing to sacrifice our future."

"The Sultan is buying time, Kemal. The Nationalist Movement will be able to continue their struggle for as long as he remains on the throne."

"I hope what you're say is true."

"It is. I also want you to know that the Sultan is emphatically opposed to the dissolution of the Cabinet—" Reşat Bey was interrupted by a knock on the door. "Come in," he said. Framed in the doorway was Behice carrying a tray containing a small decanter and rakı glasses. "Why have you inconvenienced yourself, Hanım? Is no one else in the house able to carry trays?"

"I was worried about you, Reşat Bey. Are you well? You alarmed us all. Have you quieted down?"

"I'm fine, just fine."

"We were worried about Kemal Bey as well. What kept him out so late? What happened? Mehpare is upstairs; she told us everything, but Saraylıhanım is determined to see her grandson for herself. Does she have your permission to come?"

"Tell her to come," Reşat Bey said.

Behice set the tray on the end table and left the room. She'd hoped to find her husband quarreling with his nephew, not sitting across from him, engaged in amiable conversation. After all the events of the terrible day, Reşat Bey must have decided to avoid unpleasantness at home, she speculated. "Everything's perfectly serene downstairs," was how she delivered the good news to Saraylıhanım.

"Oh! Splendid! In that case, I won't disturb them. If they've reconciled, it's best to leave them on their own for now. I'm going to bed, my girl, it's been a trying day," Saraylıhanım said as she slipped from the room.

"And I'm going to visit my girls," responded Behice. "Leman was so upset at her father's condition. She'll need comforting."

Kemal half filled two glasses from the decanter brought by Behice. Filling them the rest of the way with water from the pitcher, he handed his uncle a glass of the potent milky-white spirit. Ahmet Reşat drained his glass at once and handed it to Kemal to be refilled.

"Dear Uncle," Kemal said as he refilled both glasses, "let's toast the unification of the governments in Istanbul and Ankara and the liberation of our country from the invaders."

"To the prosperity and health of the state!"

They were just preparing to clink glasses when the nighttime silence was shattered by a series of gunshots. Both men froze and listened attentively. Ahmet Reşat rushed over and raised the window. Faint screams and shouts became audible.

"What is it now?"

"They're still rounding people up."

Ahmet Reşat peered outside. Hüsnü Efendi had come out of the shed in the back garden and was running towards the house.

"Hüsnü Efendi, where are the shots coming from?"

"I don't know, sir."

"Put something on and we'll have a look." Ahmet Reşat pulled down the window and strode out of the room. Behice and Saraylıhanım were bustling down the stairs.

"Something terrible is happening again," Behice said. "Where are you going? It's out of the question! For God's sake, don't go

out! You might get hit in the head by a bullet. Reşat Bey, I'm begging you, stay here."

Ahmet Reşat disentangled himself from his wife's arms and began putting on his ankle boots. He stepped back into the selamlık
to retrieve his fez, which had rolled onto the floor, placed it on his
head, and walked to the front door.

"Saraylıhanım, tell him not to! God forbid something should
happen to him. He'll listen to you," Behice cried.

"It's best not to interfere in men's affairs," Saraylıhanım said.

"I'm entrusting the family to your care. Look after them," were
Ahmet Reşat's parting words to Kemal. Then he joined Hüsnü
Efendi, who was waiting at the garden gate. A moment later, the
two men were out of sight.

After gulping down the last of his rakı in the selamlık, Kemal
went up the second floor, where he attempted to distract his tear-
ful grandmother and aunt by recounting in detail all that had
happened to him that day. He persuaded them not to wait up for
Ahmet Reşat, saw them off to bed, and headed for his own room.
He wanted to wait for his uncle's return, but his eyes were closing
of their own accord and he could barely stand. When he pushed
open the door to his room, he was astonished to find Mehpare
standing in front of the window in a thin nightgown.

"Is anything wrong, Mehpare? I thought you'd gone to bed long
ago."

"I didn't go to bed. I waited for you," she said. "I thought you
might want something."

"That's very kind of you. I don't need anything. You're as tired
as I am. You can go to bed now."

Mehpare didn't budge. She fastened her eyes on Kemal's and stared. When Kemal looked again he noticed that she was naked under the nightgown. What had happened to the girl who was too shy to lift her eyes from the floor except when they were making love in bed?

"What is it?" he asked.

Mehpare didn't have the courage to mention Azra Hanım. She opened her mouth to speak but couldn't.

"You'll get a chill here like this . . ." Kemal said, gesturing to her nightgown. "Go to bed. We're both exhausted."

Once Mehpare realized she wasn't wanted she found she could speak.

"If Azra Hanım were here instead of me, would you tell her to go, sir?"

Kemal was completely taken aback. "What on earth are you talking about?"

"You heard me," she said. "Azra Hanım would never come to my room uninvited."

"Perhaps. But she'd never give her life for you either."

"Well why should she? What am I to her?"

Mehpare's lip trembled. "She's your childhood friend. She's important to you. You
can talk about everything with her . . . Everything . . ."

"Mehpare! You're not telling me you're jealous of Azra Hanım?"

Mehpare's eyes filled with tears.

Kemal didn't know whether to laugh or cry. Azra had been right: the girl was in love with him. He was filled with a strange sense of pride. Taking Mehpare by the arm, he tugged her away from the window and threw her up against the wall, roughly pushing against her as he undid his trousers with one hand and lifted her nightgown with the other. Mehpare didn't protest as he pulled her lips to his and forced his way his inside; in fact, she wrapped a leg around his waist to get even closer.

Kemal was soon done, and withdrew. But Mehpare kept her arms and leg locked around him and it was only with some effort that he was able to pull himself away. He stuck his hand between her legs. "Is this what you want? Here, here…" She writhed under his hand, strands of wet hair glued to her forehead, her right breast bursting from her nightgown. Kemal leant over and took her nipple in his mouth. A moment later, he was inside her again.

At the sound of footsteps on the stairs he hastily withdrew. "Quick, put on your shawl, fix your hair," he whispered.

"Kemal," came Behice's voice from the second floor landing.

Opening the door a crack, "What is it now, Aunt," he wearily asked. "Has Uncle returned?"

"He's back. He's waiting for you downstairs."

Kemal pulled his trousers up from his ankles and did up his buttons. He splashed a bit of water onto his hands from the *ewer* resting on the chest of drawers and smoothed back his hair.

"I'm going down, get yourself together and go to your room," he said to Mehpare, who was still splayed against the wall, on the verge of tears and looking deeply humiliated. Kemal gave her a tender kiss on the forehead. "There's no need for jealousy, Mehpare. No one can hold a candle to you."

Kemal hurriedly tiptoed down the stairs so as not to wake his nieces.

In the darkness of the entry hall, his uncle appeared suspended in mid-air, a haggard ghost bearing a lantern.

"Uncle!" Ahmet Reşat looked and sounded bone-weary.

"There are still running battles going on out there, Kemal. Despite all the precautions of the English our underground resistance has not been idle. They've attempted to blow up the French barracks in Eyüp," he said. "Tomorrow will be another trying day."

In the white light cast by the lantern, Kemal couldn't tell from his uncle's drawn face if he was pleased or concerned by this most recent turn of events.

– 8 –

April 1920

"Münire Hanımefendi is stranded in Kadıköy," Behice announced. "When I was finally able to call on Azra Hanım yesterday morning, to thank her for the friendly reception she gave us, I learned that the ferryboats aren't working. Permission is required for travel between the European and Asian shores."

"Well I never!" erupted Saraylıhanım.

"It's God's truth. With her mother unable to return, Azra has been all alone in that big house with only the butler and the gardener for company. I feel so sorry for the poor thing."

"They've always had several female servants in attendance."

"Those were the old days, mother. When we last visited, only Housekeeper Nazik had been retained, and recent events have so worried her family that she's joined them in the village for a time."

"Well in that case, why doesn't she honor us with a prolonged visit? She really mustn't stay all alone in that mansion."

"The same thing occurred to me, but I hesitated to extend an invitation. It might be awkward for her to have to see the piteous state of our dinner table."

"Don't be ridiculous, Behice. Is there a household in Istanbul that hasn't been affected by the occupation? Even the grandest mansions are short of food."

"Where would she sleep?"

"Suat can stay with Leman," said Suat, "and Azra can sleep in Suat's room for a few days, until her mother returns."

"I'm not leaving my room. On no account am I leaving my room. And I won't sleep with my sister either."

"And I don't want her in my room. I won't let her."

"Leman! I'll pretend you never said that. And as for you Suat, hush or I'll give you such a hiding! You're to listen to your elders, both of you."

"I can't stay with Suat. She's messy and she pulls my hair every chance she gets."

"You're both big girls now and you're still bickering with each other. Just shameless, the pair of you!"

"I'm not staying in my sister's room. Why can't the guest stay in the music room?"

"No! She'll play my piano!"

"Either you both keep quiet or I'll tell your father everything you've been up to the moment he gets home. I leave it to you to consider the consequences," Behice warned.

"You haven't been doing your duty as a mother," Saraylıhanım chimed in. "The girls have grown up impudent, and all the chastening in the world won't change that now. When I was a girl, we kept our eyes on the floor in the presence of our elders, never mind speaking or making a fuss in front of them."

Suat crossed her eyes and looked at the floor. "You mean like this, nana?" Leman and Behice couldn't help laughing.

"Go on then, laugh. But mark my words, if you continue this nonsense you'll end up an old maid. No one wants a girl who disrespects her elders."

"I'm not getting married anyway, nana," Suat said. "Oh? And why's that?" "I'm going to be a poet."

"What's got into you?"

"There are women poets nowadays. I'm going to be one of them."

"Stuff and nonsense! Both of you, go to your rooms. Out of my sight!" Saraylıhanım said.

"And send down Mehpare Abla," Behice called after the girls. "She can prepare the guestroom while I write a letter for Hüsnü Efendi to deliver. Azra Hanım should come over immediately. If we move the piano into the anteroom we'll be able to set up a bed in the music room. Now why didn't I think of that to begin with?"

Because you don't think, Saraylıhanım sighed to herself as she returned to the subject of Behice's parenting skills: "This is what comes of sending Suat to school instead of having her tutored at home. Mark my words, that girl *will* end up a poet. Or worse." Saraylıhanım had often complained that the girls were overindulged, and considered Suat's education at a local school to be indicative of a dangerous predilection for modern ideas on the part of her daughter-in-law. Surely it was Behice who had corrupted Kemal and Reşat. Otherwise, what good Circassian family would dare pass judgment on His Majesty or agree to send their daughter to school. Behice was poisoning Reşat and Kemal. And it was most certainly her fault that only a moment ago Mehpare had grown pale and clutched at the door when told to prepare the music room for Azra Hanım. That poor girl was literally being run off her feet!

Behice was in high spirits as she searched her room for a pen and paper. It would be good to have a guest in the house, if only for a few days. She was tired of having the same conversations with Saraylıhanım and of being rebuked day and night. Azra would be a breath of fresh air. And, who knows, her presence might even do Kemal some good.

Ahmet Reşat was still in his dressing gown when he entered the second floor sitting room that morning. At the sight of him, his daughters put down their needlework and erupted in cries of joy: "Father's staying home with us today!" The women of the house were all assembled on the divans, drinking coffee with Azra Hanım. Saraylıhanım was trying to teach Suat the art of canvas embroidery while Leman's skillful fingers were busily employed at a bit of lacework.

"Aren't you going to the ministry today?" Behice asked.

"No."

"Why not? Are you feeling well?"

Ahmet Reşat wanted nothing more than to answer that, no, he wasn't feeling well, he was having difficulty breathing, his chest felt constricted, his heart ached. "The Salih Pasha cabinet has resigned," he calmly said, "and I'm unemployed."

"How can you say such a thing, Reşat Bey! May the wind snatch those unfortunate words from your mouth!"

"Don't upset yourself, Hanım. We'll be continuing with our duties until a new cabinet is formed. I won't be underfoot here at home, disturbing you ladies," Reşat Bey said.

"Ah, Reşat Bey, you know perfectly well how much we adore you. When I saw you were still asleep this morning I assumed you were exhausted, and couldn't bring myself to wake you even as I worried you'd be angry with me later. I wish you'd told me last night that you would be at home today."

"You were asleep when I got home. And I couldn't bring myself to wake you either, my dear."

"Well, since you're here, I'll have coffee brought for you," Behice said.

"Do that, and I'll sit among the ladies today and eavesdrop on their gossip."

"We weren't gossiping," Behice said.

"These days we women are engaged in far more important matters than idle chitchat," said Azra, motioning to the periodical resting on her lap.

"And what matters are those?"

"We have to do all we can for the betterment of our country. Wouldn't you agree, sir?"

"Without hesitation, Azra Hanım."

"I was showing Behice some of the articles written here by our valuable women writers. I particularly recommend that she read the one about Nakiye Hanım."

"What's written about her?"

Azra turned to the page in question and handed the magazine to Reşat Bey, who began reading aloud as he skimmed the article: "Hmm, Nakiye Hanım, the embodiment of feminine virtue . . . hmm . . . If a distinguished, enlightened and singular woman such as herself has set her heart and mind on advancing the national cause it can only be expected that her efforts will match or even exceed those of our gallant men . . . hmm."

"Who is this Nakiye Hanım, my dear?" Saraylıhanım asked.

"She's headmistress of the Fevziye School in Üsküdar, efendim," Azra explained.

"Are women now assuming the responsibilities of men? She should content herself with the welfare of her students!" Saraylıhanım exploded.

"It's not only headmistresses who have joined the cause: Naime Sultan, the daughter of Sultan Abdülhamit, and Fehime Sultan, the daughter of Sultan Murat, have seen no harm in working for their country, efendim," Azra said, after which she turned to Reşat Bey and added: "And isn't it true, sir, that during the World War your beloved English allowed their women to work not only behind the scenes but on the front lines as well? And didn't they labor in the shops, the factories and the offices vacated by their husbands, to prevent the collapse of the economy?"

"They did indeed, and they did well, but since when have I been known as an admirer of the English, Azra Hanım?"

"The Sultan is pro-English, is he not?"

"The Sultan might be pro-English. The Freedom and Unity Party may be pro-English. I, however, am neither a follower of that particular party nor the English. My only allegiance is to the Sultan. And that is because His Majesty is a descendant of the House of Osman, the sovereign rulers of these lands for centuries."

"I said nothing to the contrary, sir. My only desire is that our women are kept informed of events and permitted to take their places among the ranks of men to combat the enemy."

"Agreed, Azra Hanım. And I would also like you to know that the Sultan is a proponent of the education and greater visibility of the women of this land."

Bored by the conversation, Leman requested permission to play the piano and immediately began quarreling with Suat, who darted after her.

"Sit back down and do your needlepoint. Don't come upstairs and bother me."

"You really could treat your little sister with a bit more kindness, Leman," Behice interceded, trying to put on a suitably stern tone. "Would it be so bad if she sat next to you and turned the pages while you played?"

"It would be terrible. Her hands are always filthy. She dirtied the keys with her greasy fingers yesterday after she ate a bun."

This time, Behice scolded her younger daughter. "Suat! Haven't I told you not to touch your sister's piano? If I hear of this one more time I'll lock your violin in the cupboard and you won't be able to play it either."

"If you don't want me touching the piano why don't you lock that in the cupboard too?"

Azra failed to suppress a smile. Behice turned to her husband imploringly and awaited an appropriate response to Suat's impertinence. But Ahmet Reşat, a man who had for many years managed the depleted coffers of the Ottoman Empire, was at a complete loss when it came to managing the sharp tongue of his little girl. Mehpare saved him by stepping into the room with a cup of coffee on a silver tray. "Mehpare, my girl," he said hurriedly, "would you be so good as to go and inform Kemal Bey that valuable opinions on the state of the nation are being expressed at this very moment, right here in the sitting room, and that we would be honored by his illuminating presence?"

"*I'll* go and get uncle," screamed Suat, elbowing aside Leman, who was walking decorously to the door.

Mehpare set the tray down in front of Reşat Bey and left the room.

Pleased as she was that relations had improved between her nephew and uncle, Saraylıhanım had bristled at Ahmet Reşat for having mocked Kemal in the presence of Azra Hanım. She herself didn't hesitate to employ her sharp tongue on her next of kin, but to guests and strangers she invariably sang the praises of her family.

"Opinions should be respected, including those held by the young, Reşat Bey, my son," she began. "But there's one thing I know and do not hesitate to articulate: politics is for men, and I strongly disapprove of women who meddle in such matters."

Adopting the attitude of a patient tutor as she carefully enunciated each word, Azra began to explain why women should be involved in all avenues of life, including politics. Behice listened in amazement; Saraylıhanım stubbornly stared out the window. Reşat Bey, for his part, shared Azra's views: for far too long, Ottoman women had been as voiceless and characterless as if they'd retreated to an early grave. Fortunately, in recent years schools for girls had been opening one after another. In fact, girls were now able to receive university degrees even from Dar'ül-Fünûnu.

"Would you consider sending your daughters to this school?" asked Azra.

"I'd be happy to do so, although I naturally consult Behice first on the subject of the girls' future," he replied, looking to his wife for her endorsement. Behice, who was a firm proponent of marrying girls off at an early age, smiled somewhat abashedly at the carpet.

The sonata being played upstairs was audible in the room

"Leman is remarkably talented!" said Azra, and nodded approvingly at the ceiling. "She performed a miniature concert for me last night."

"She has a good ear," Behice said. "Suat's taken up the violin, but despite her initial enthusiasm for music, I'd venture she'll never be as accomplished as Leman. She insists on playing the piano."

"She's only just begun," said Saraylıhanım. "Give the girl some time, would you! She'll come into her own in a few months."

Behice raised her eyebrows at this spirited defense of Suat, a girl SaryalıHanım was forever reprimanding and of whom she had never seemed particularly fond. Well, there was no telling what the old lady would do or say next.

When Kemal joined the group in the sitting room, talk returned to the state of the nation. Many of the newly resigned members of the government had gone to Anatolia to join the National Independence Army and the general consensus was that the next Ottoman government would be headed by Damat Ferit Pasha, whose admiration for the English was exceeded only by his hostility for the National Independence Army.

"Damat Ferit is going to be Grand Vizier again? How unfortunate!" said Behice, only now grasping the implications of her husband's words. "Kemal's sympathy for the Nationalists has unfortunately led you to view them more favorably of late. That can only mean that your ministerial duties really are coming to an end."

"They are indeed coming to an end, though I've promised His Majesty that I'll continue to execute my duties until such time as a new minister is appointed. Cabinets may fall, but the wheels of the state grind on."

At this confirmation of her husband's certain loss of his ministerial position Behice went visibly limp, and seemed close to tears.

Azra deftly changed the subject. "I was planning to attend a visiting day event tomorrow at which Şükufe Nihal Hanım will give a reading of her poetry. With your consent, I'd like to invite Behice Hanım to accompany me."

"That's out of the question!" cried Saraylıhanım. "Behice Hanım has no desire to get mixed up in your organizations and associations. Why, what was that just the other day, women by the hundreds taking to the streets, speeches in Sultanahmet Square . . . for shame!"

"Saraylıhanımefendi," Azra said, "we're simply being received at the home of Makbule Hanım for a friendly social gathering and to listen to a little poetry. And furthermore, her mansion is very close to yours."

Displeased by his aunt's humiliation of his wife in front of company, not to mention the offence she may have caused their guest, Reşat Bey spoke in a tone of firm certitude.

"If Behice Hanım likes, she can accompany you tomorrow, Azra Hanım," he said. "As you know, the streets aren't entirely safe these days, and I only ask that you let Hüsnü Efendi accompany you."

"Sir, can I go as well?"

All heads swiveled in surprise to the speaker, who was none other than Mehpare, who was gathering the empty coffee cups with eyes lowered. "I'll escort the ladies. I'll accompany Behice Hanım . . . Please sir . . . I want so much to go and hear poetry."

Saraylıhanım's open mouth snapped shut at a stern look from Reşat Bey.

"Very well then. Please don't keep them out late, Azra Hanım. The women of this household are customarily at home by mid-afternoon prayers. I would hope tomorrow is no different."

"It won't be, efendim," Azra assured him.

Suddenly quite dizzy, Behice found herself torn between joy and distress. Even as she wondered what she would do at a meeting where ladies were discussing politics, she was pleased that her husband had so authoritatively informed Saraylıhanım of her right to do so.

When they reached the garden gate of Makbule Hanım's house, Behice asked Azra how long the meeting would last.

"If the recital takes an hour, and conversation and refreshments another hour..." Azra began.

"Hüsnü Efendi," Behice said, "you can go home now; come and get us in two hours."

The three women marched to the front door, Azra and Behice in front, Mehpare two steps behind. Makbule Hanım's salon—a series of adjoining rooms containing chairs arranged in rows, as though for an Islamic memorial *mevlit* service—was crammed with about forty ladies conversing in loud whispers and exchanging sheets of paper. Azra must have spotted many familiar faces, for she greeted, kissed, and asked after the health of everyone she encountered. Behice, Azra and Mehpare found three seats in a row and sat down. Servants circulated with trays of lemonade and sherbet.

Behice observed that most of the women had removed their *maşlah* and that locks of hair curled out of their headscarves and onto their foreheads and temples. She'd already seen this modern hairstyle in magazines and vowed right then and there that it was a look she'd attempt to reproduce in front of the mirror the moment she got home.

The young woman with auburn curls who'd greeted them at the door and who she'd assumed was the lady of the house advanced toward a clearing in the forest of chairs and declared in a loud voice, "Welcome to you all. We have some new guests today. Among those present are the new finance minister Reşat Beyefendi's wife, Behice Hanımefendi, and their relative, Mehpare Hanım. Let's offer them a warm welcome before we begin."

A wave of whispering rippled through the room. Behice flushed pink up to her ears, uncertain of where to cast her eyes or what to do. Azra must have told Makbule Hanım who they were. Tactless! Behice contented herself with a brief nod of acknowledgement as she glanced at Mehpare out of the corner of her eye. Mehpare was staring at the wall opposite, her mind elsewhere, her face expressionless, her back bolt upright. She seemed nonplussed by the exaggerated and unwanted attention.

Some of the women got up and came over to introduce themselves to Behice and Mehpare. Avoiding the eyes of the women who were literally at her feet, showering her with compliments, Behice did her bashful best to offer some kind of response. She was aware that the wife of a finance minister, even one who had recently resigned, had a role to fulfill. But she had no idea what that role entailed. With the exception of her immediate family, relatives and close friends, she knew nothing of the world and had cultivated no views, opinions or sentiments that she could truly

call her own. The consequences of having surrendered administration of the household to Saraylıhanım were suddenly painfully
clear. The little she had managed to learn from newspaper articles
and magazines seemed to evaporate from her mind. She was per-
spiring heavily. Although she did her best to conceal her panic,
she felt frightened and besieged.

"Our previous assembly was graced by Fehime Sultan, who
even deigned to play a piano sonata she'd composed in honor of
the new constitution. Your presence here today is such a great
privilege and source of strength for us all," gushed the lady of the
house. "It is our fervent wish that you honor us with your company at all future gatherings. Is there anything you would like to
say to the ladies?"

Behice thought she would die.

"Thank you so much, efendim. I'm afraid I'm not prepared to
speak. Forgive me," she croaked.

"Please get me something to drink," she implored Mehpare the
moment Makbule Hanım left her side. "My throat's gone dry. They
were passing round lemonade . . . I'd even settle for water."

Mehpare stood up and craned her neck to find a waiter.

"Behice Hanım, may I draw your attention to that lady over
there—the one walking toward us: it's the poet, Şükufe Nihal
Hanımefendi. She's going to start reciting in a moment or two.
Shall I introduce you?" asked Azra.

"Later, Azra Hanım. I'm feeling quite dizzy."

Azra didn't insist, for at that very moment one of the ladies
strode into the center of the room and, with the silver spoon she
gripped in her right hand, began striking the small tray she held
in the other.

"Shhh. Ladies, quiet please. May I request a warm round of applause for today's speaker, a guest we all hold in the highest esteem: Şahende Hanımefendi. Welcome efendim."

As a short, plump woman made her way to the middle of the room, Mehpare handed a glass of lemonade to Behice and sat down again. Behice took two large gulps and immediately felt sick. She handed the glass back to Mehpare.

"Take it. Get it away from me. It smells awful," she slowly mumbled.

"It smells wonderfully of mint."

"It's upset my stomach. Drink it if you like, Mehpare."

Şahende Hanım began speaking. Behice did her best to listen, but there was a buzzing in her ears, as though hundreds of agitated flies were swarming inside her head. Words like *motherland*, *country*, *freedom*, and *independence* pierced the buzzing, but the shapes of the sentences, their meanings, escaped her. She struck an attentive pose and kept her eyes fixed on the speaker, who occasionally glanced directly at her, the wife of a minister, for approval and endorsement. The fiery tone of the woman summoned up unpleasant images for Behice: marching hordes, fists clenched, hands clutching stones and sticks; ugly shouts in a language that, though foreign, sounded like curses; beatings and degradation, fear for her life! She broke into a cold sweat and gave up all pretense of concentration, waiting only for Şahende Hanım to conclude her endless speech. It was all she could do to keep down the two swallows of lemonade. Mehpare noticed the beads of sweat on Behice's forehead and put it down to the airlessness of the room.

At last, thunderous applause broke out, at which Behice weakly clapped her hands. The assembled women rose as one to congratulate the speaker. Behice wanted to join the line of well-wishers but her head was spinning so badly she feared to stand. Azra leaned over Mehpare and asked Behice, "How did you find Şahende Hanım's speech?"

Behice forced out a one-word reply: "Remarkable."

"She would be so very pleased to hear you say that. If you'd like, we can go over to her before Şükufe Hanım begins the discussion. Let's go."

"Take my arm, please," Behice whispered into Mehpare's ear. "I don't feel at all well." A bit taken aback, Mehpare stood up, took Behice's arm and began propelling her toward Şahende Hanım. The salon was crowded and stuffy. Everyone was speaking at once, their voices ringing in Behice's ears. After a few steps, she was horrified to discover that she couldn't feel her hands or feet. Her knees were giving way. Mehpare encircled her waist to prevent her from sinking to the floor.

"Behice Abla . . . Behice Abla, what's wrong? Oh, Behice Abla . . . . My God, you're collapsing . . . She's collapsing . . ."

"She's fainted. Good gracious, she's fainted!"

"What's going on here?"

"Get back . . . Out of the way . . . Let her through . . ."

"Who's fainted? Ah, it's Behice. Quick! Get help!" Şahende Hanım took command: after firmly ordering the other ladies to get back she was soon kneeling at Behice's side. Mehpare cradled Behice's head on her knees and with trembling fingers began unbuttoning her blouse.

"Get me some lemon cologne, is there any in the house? Please bring me some immediately if there is," ordered Şahende Hanım. "And kindly open a window. Let in some fresh air."

Turning to Mehpare, she asked, "You came here with Behice Hanım, didn't you? You're relatives I believe?

"That's right, efendim."

"Is she prone to fainting spells?"

"No. I've never seen her faint before today."

"Is she pregnant?"

"No . . . Well, I don't know that she is."

"Why do you think she fainted? Has she caught a chill? Is she ill? Is she having digestive problems?"

"No, she's not ill," Mehpare assured her.

"She may have been overexcited by your speech," Azra speculated.

"Don't be absurd!" snapped Şahende Hanım as she poured some of the cologne hurriedly brought by Mehpare Hanım into her cupped palm, splashing a bit onto Behice's temples and waving a cologne-doused palm under the patient's nose. Using Behice's silk headscarf, she wiped away the cold sweat on the patient's temples and upper lip. Then she lightly slapped each of her cheeks. Behice was coming round, and a moment later she surveyed her surroundings through astonished eyes. At the sight of Şahende Hanım's anxious face hovering above her own, she closed her eyes, certain she must be dreaming.

"Don't worry my dear, you're fine. You've had a turn, that's all."

When Behice realized where she was and what had happened, she could have died of mortification. Here she was in a strange house, surrounded by strange ladies, and she'd dropped like a stone. Such a disgrace! She nearly burst into tears. Mehpare helped her to a chair.

"Let's take her to one of the bedrooms; I'll examine her there," Şahende Hanım said. As the poet strode off, Behice asked Azra,

"Is she a doctor?" She immediately realized how silly her question was: how could a woman be a doctor? But Şahende Hanım seemed so sure of herself . . . she certainly carried herself as though she were a doctor.

"Şahende Hanım is a practiced midwife," Azra told her.

Behice was stricken with panic. The color, which had only recently been restored to her cheeks, drained away once again. "Behice Hanım, you don't have to submit to an examination if you'd rather not. I'll explain to Şahende Hanım," Azra said.

"Wouldn't it be bad manners?"

"No, not at all."

Behice slowly struggled to her feet. Her head was still spinning. Propped up on either side by Mehpare and Azra, she stumbled towards one of Makbule Hanım's bedrooms. Şahende Hanım was already inside the room, drying her freshly scrubbed hands with a scrap of linen towel. She smiled and came up to Behice. "Don't be frightened, my girl," she said, "I'll just listen to your pulse. Have you eaten anything today?"

"Yes."

Clasping Behice's slender wrist, the midwife carefully counted the thumps of the arteries beneath her finger.

"Stick out your tongue."

Feeling like a helpless little girl, Behice opened her mouth and did as she was told.

"Normal," pronounced Şahende Hanım, "which can only mean one thing: there's only one reason young women your age faint . . ."

"And what is that?"

"The obvious one." Behice reddened. "If I'm right, I'd like to be the one who delivers your baby."

"I strongly doubt that I'm with child, but I do thank you, nevertheless, for your kind attention," Behice said as she turned her own attention to Makbule Hanım. "I'm afraid I've been a great deal of trouble and have spoiled your gathering. It's time Mehpare and I went home. Azra Hanım can return later, when the discussion is over."

After profusely thanking the ladies gathered at the front door to enquire after her health, and rejecting her hostess's offer of a carriage on the grounds that some fresh air would do her good, Behice slowly walked home, leaning heavily on Mehpare's arm.

What had possessed her to go along with Azra? What did she care for liberty, justice and equality? She hadn't yet managed to seize the reins of her own household. Was it up to her to save the motherland? Free as she was to remain peacefully at home with her ud and knitting needles, why had she gotten mixed up with a band of overbearing women? And to make matters worse, she'd disgraced herself by fainting. She would have burst into tears right then and there if she'd been on her own. "For goodness sake, don't tell anyone what happened to me today. Especially Saraylıhanım," Behice begged Mehpare.

"I won't, Behice Abla," said Mehpare. "You collapsed. Don't you think you'd better see a doctor? Don't you wonder why you fainted?"

"It was the discomfort."

"No one faints from discomfort."

"The lemonade disagreed with me."

"The lemonade was fine. No one else got sick. Why would you?"

"I have a sensitive stomach."

"Look, I'll keep your secret on one condition."

"What is it?"

"That you're examined by a doctor. We can send word to Mahir Bey, tell him what happened and ask for his opinion. He can examine you in Kemal Bey's room."

Behice looked thoughtful. Actually, she did wonder if anything was wrong, but she didn't like the idea of taking Kemal into her confidence. Mehpare seemed to read her mind. "Kemal Bey wouldn't tell a soul, believe me," she said. "He knows better than anyone what a hypochondriac Saraylıhanım can be."

"All right then," Behice finally agreed, "Now can you tell me what Şahende Hanım said? My ears were buzzing so terribly I missed her entire speech."

"It was a wonderful talk. Anyone listening to her would grab a gun and race off to fight the enemy. She called on us all, men and women, to join the Anatolian resistance movement."

"So we're expected to run off to Anatolia, children and all?"

"We don't have to go anywhere. We can raise funds. We can send blankets, sweaters, shoes and food. We can roll bandages and buy medicines. That's what she said, anyway."

"Whatever you do, don't mention a word of this in front of Reşat Bey. If he found out that Azra had taken us to such a gathering he'd send her packing immediately."

"I think Reşat Bey loves his country too," Mehpare said. "So he wouldn't get angry with us, don't worry."

"What a peculiar girl you are," Behice said. "Is Kemal responsible for teaching you all this?"

"No one is teaching me anything, efendim," Mehpare said. "We're all born with love: love for our country, for our children, for our parents . . . for a man. When the time comes, the love inside sprouts and grows. At least that's what I think."

"And since when have you been thinking all this?"

"Since all those nights I spent at Kemal Bey's sickbed, alone with my thoughts."

"Blessed Mehpare! Stop thinking so much and take care to sleep at night. You're growing paler by the day. At this rate, you'll fall ill. You might even faint like I did," Behice said.

"Don't worry about me," Mehpare smiled. "Nothing will happen to me. We Circassians are used to suffering. Just look at Kemal Bey, returning safe and sound from Sarıkamış, when thousands froze to death. That's when I truly believed that God is looking after us Circassians."

"I vividly remember Kemal's condition the day he returned, and you would probably have to be a Circassian to describe it as 'safe and sound,'" said Behice.

As the new Grand Vizier, Damat Ferit Pasha, set about forming his new Cabinet, he retained the old finance minister. The position required technical expertise and experience, and Ahmet Reşat had not only served well for many years, he had never exhibited partisan leanings. After Ahmet Reşat learned that his dear friend, Ahmet Reşit, would be serving as minister of home affairs in the new government, Ahmet Reşat was rather less reluctant to accept a cabinet position under a Grand Vizier for whom he had little affection.

When Doctor Mahir arrived early one morning to congratulate his old friend on his reinstatement as minister, as well as in response to the letter of invitation sent by Behice Hanım, he first made his customary visit to Kemal's room. Shortly afterwards, Behice and Mehpare crept upstairs as well. Eyes on the floor in obvious embarrassment, Behice mentioned a recent fainting fit, nothing serious but perhaps it would be prudent to have a doctor's advice. She wondered if Kemal wouldn't mind waiting for a moment in Mehpare's room.

"Of course not, I'll just go downstairs," Kemal complied.

"No, no, don't go downstairs. Let's not attract the attention of Saraylıhanım. There's no need to worry her. Just go and wait in Mehpare's room."

When Kemal left the room Behice got to the point. As she'd mentioned in her letter, she had a special request to make of the doctor: it was to be kept strictly confidential, with no one else in the house to know.

With the examination completed, Doctor Mahir asked leave to go and wash his hands. Once he was gone, Behice sat up in Kemal's bed, rearranged her veil to cover her hair and turned her attention to Mehpare, who waited at the bedside. "Tell Kemal Bey that he can return to his room, would you," she said.

Doctor Mahir came back to the room and said, "You appear to be perfectly healthy, efendim. What the midwife told you was right: you are most likely with child. I'll need a urine sample to be absolutely certain and will inform you the instant I am."

"But how could that be? Good gracious!"

"Why not? This time, you may even be blessed with a son."

"It's for Reşat Bey that I want a son, Mahir Bey, not for myself."

"As far as I know Reşat Bey is perfectly content with his daughters."

"You also know that he sent Suat to school, as though she were a boy. If he has a son he might let the girls be girls."

"Is it so wrong for girls to receive an education?"

"Schooling and training are a different matter altogether when it comes to girls. Suat can barely embroider. She can't play the ud. She's never home long enough to learn anything. That school of hers has taken over her life."

"What about Leman?" laughed Doctor Mahir.

"Saraylıhanım was able to rescue her from Reşat Bey. You know, she sees herself in the girl, her eyes, her figure, her fastidiousness. She's forever teaching Leman Circassian cuisine. But Leman's quite lazy, she cares about nothing but her piano."

"It's a difficult age for girls," Mahir assured her. "The indolence will pass. She's betwixt and between at the moment. It's only natural that she's at something of a loss."

By the time Mehpare and Kemal returned to the room Mahir had long since re-packed his medical bag.

"So doctor, have you discovered the why and wherefore of my aunt's fainting spell?" Kemal asked.

"The why and wherefore is most likely seated at this moment behind his desk at the ministry of finance," Mahir chuckled.

"You're not serious!"

"A people constantly at war must constantly repopulate itself, I say!"

"Stop having fun at my expense," Behice protested. "I may well have fainted from all the excitement. I haven't been able to stand crowds of any kind ever since our flight from Thessalonica. They give me heart palpitations. So please, don't speak a word of this to anyone, not yet!"

"Don't worry, Behice Hanım, information of a confidential nature is kept between patient and doctor. I'll certainly let you know the results of the test, and the rest is up to you. You can tell whomever you like."

"And if I'm not pregnant?"

"Unless you faint again, everything is fine. If you do faint, it's best you come to the hospital, where we'll run some tests. But what I need you to do right now is to locate a bottle and supply me with a urine sample before I go back downstairs, please."

As Behice thanked Mahir and left the room Mehpare ran after her. "Behice, we had a bottle of cologne with a stopper. Shall I empty it and wash it out for you?" she asked

"And waste the cologne?"

"It's nearly gone anyway."

"Thank you, Mehpare, bring it to my room as soon as it's ready."

Behice withdrew to her bedroom. Locking the door she removed her blouse and examined her breasts in front of the mirror. Her nipples had darkened slightly. She had no appetite in the morning and her sense of smell had sharpened. She might be pregnant; but, then again, the gathering that day had been terribly trying, enough to make her faint. Never again would she set foot in such a place. Mehpare knocked on the door, freshly rinsed bottle in hand. Behice raced to the toilet.

With the women out of the room, Mahir gathered the latest batch of translations scattered on Kemal's desk, took some new journals out of his bag and handed them to his friend.

"Merely doing translations isn't enough for me, Mahir," Kemal said. "I feel perfectly healthy and strong. It's time I joined you and the others."

"I don't deny that you've made a recovery. But your body is still weak, Kemal. You mustn't take on too much."

"Confinement to a single room is taking its toll on my spirit. At this rate, I'm in danger of losing my mind."

"I know it's not easy, my friend. If there weren't a warrant out for your arrest I'd have had you sent to your uncle's farm long ago. But there are spies everywhere. It's become more difficult than ever to know who's a secret agent."

"I could change my appearance, Mahir. I could grow a beard, dye my hair, wear glasses. Saraylıhanım uses henna from time to time . . ."

"You know, that's not a bad idea. With your hair tinted red they'd take you for a Jew. You'd immediately be spared the wrath of the occupation forces: it's Muslims they're after, not minorities."

Mahir fell silent at a knock on the door. It was Mehpare, bringing Behice's urine sample.

"Behice Hanım asked me to give this to you," she said, extending the bottle to Mahir, who checked the stopper was secure before putting it into his bag.

"Kemal Bey, may I ask you something?" Mehpare said. "Go on." "What happened to Behice Hanım in Thessalonica? What did she mean, about her 'flight'? Did something bad happen?"

Kemal and Mahir exchanged glances. "It's a bad memory, yes," Kemal said.

"Can I ask what happened?"

"Why are you so curious about it, Mehpare?"

"I thought I might be of more help to her if I knew. If she's not pregnant, but still continues to have fainting spells, I might be able to do more for her than just offer smelling salts and cologne. I did realize at the gathering the other day that the size of the crowd disturbed her terribly."

"You were right. My aunt's been terrified of crowds, of loud noises, ever since that day. My uncle was posted to Thessalonica during the Balkan War and the Ottomans were given very little time to evacuate the city when we lost. He thought it best to send his wife and daughters, who were still very young at the time, on the first ship to Istanbul. Apparently, it had begun to be dangerous for Turks, subjected as they were to the insults and harassments of the Ottoman Greeks."

"Weren't you there with them, sir?"

"No, I was here, at boarding school."

"Did something happen on their voyage back?"

"Behice and her daughters were collected at the door by a phaeton belonging to the Russian Envoy, and taken to the port in his personal carriage. A Russian armed attendant sat next to the driver the entire way to protect them from any possible attacks. As the city was being evacuated, the local Greeks were throwing stones at the carriages boarded by Turks, cursing them, insulting them, roughing up and plundering the personal belongings of anyone they were able to get their hands on. After their rough ride to the port they were able to board the ship, but not before being subjected to vulgarity and catcalls. They were pushed and shoved. My aunt was pregnant at the time and lost her baby during the voyage to Istanbul. Ever since, she's been terrified of shouting and yelling, of demonstrations, of large crowds of any kind. She wasn't herself again for quite some time. It wasn't easy of course, a young woman and two children, without her husband by her side . . ."

"Why didn't Reşat Beyefendi return with his family?"

"He was in charge of organizing archives going back centuries. He returned a few months later."

"He came back to Istanbul with my father," said Doctor Mahir. "See, you're learning something else today, Mehpare. The friendship between our families goes all the way back to those days in Thessalonica. Not only were we neighbors, he and father were colleagues. They worked together at the provincial office of the director of finance and they shared the risky voyage back home to Istanbul. That's why they were so close, like family really."

"May God bless his soul," Kemal interjected. "Mahir Bey's father was Uncle Reşat's superior. You came to live with us not long after Aunt Behice had returned to Istanbul. My aunt was in a feeble condition after the miscarriage and unable to look after her children properly. My grandmother gave us the news that a young Circassian girl was coming to stay and to keep Leman and Suat amused. You weren't much more than a girl yourself, but you certainly knew how to keep those imps in line. What a clever, beautiful child you were, Mehpare."

Mehpare blushed. "I was hardly a child . . ."

"What do you mean? You were no more than twelve or thirteen."

Mehpare became agitated all of a sudden. "Ah, sir! I forget to tell you, now Saraylıhanım will become cross with me. Your grandmother will be wondering why you haven't come downstairs; she was going to offer refreshments to Mahir Bey in the selamlık."

"Go on down, Mehpare, we'll join you in a moment," Kemal told her.

With Mehpare out of the room, Kemal returned to their earlier conversation.

"Or perhaps I could dress up like a priest?" he mused.

"When it comes time to travel to the farm you can wear a çarşaf again. Everything will be fine once you get there."

"But then what I will do, when I'm out on the streets?"

"You'll have no cause to be on the streets in the daytime, Kemal. You'll be working indoors. Demobilization orders and identity cards are being prepared for the officers who have fled to Anatolia. You'll be helping with that."

"And running guns at night, right?"

"One of our divisions is responsible for arms smuggling. They're doing a great job. God forbid you should have to join them. Your duties lie elsewhere."

"Where?"

"There are some Algerian troops attached to the French army. They're staying at Rami Barracks. They visit Eyüp Sultan Mosque for Friday prayers. The sermons of the clerics there aim to persuade these soldiers of the treachery of taking up arms against their fellow Muslims. You'll translate the sermons for the Algerian soldiers."

Kemal's face registered his disappointment.

"Don't worry, you'll have other, more dangerous duties, too."

"Like what?"

"I'll tell you when the time comes."

"I want to go to Anatolia, Mahir."

"I know you do, brother. But if everyone goes off to Anatolia, who will handle logistics and shipping here? The arms are all being secured in Istanbul for transfer there. The demobilized soldiers are being regrouped and redeployed to the countryside from Istanbul. We've got to prepare their papers, raise funds, buy weapons from the French and Italians . . . These are vital tasks. As vital as taking up arms. When the time comes, you'll pass over to Anatolia, and you'll be healthier and stronger than you are now."

"You're right."

"The appointment of Reşat Bey to the Damat Ferit Cabinet is an excellent development, Kemal. You might have the opportunity to obtain some valuable information from your uncle."

"Do you really expect me to spy on my uncle?"

"Of course I don't, but it would be most helpful if you kept us informed of anything you learn about arrest warrants and detainments."

"I don't want my uncle to get into trouble on my account. Arrange my passage to the farm and I'll do anything they want. Mahir, once I leave this house I'll never be able to return. I have no right to endanger the others."

"I understand, but information obtained from your uncle would be so valuable to us . . . I wonder if you couldn't stay here a while longer?"

"I'm bored to death. And even if I stayed elsewhere, I could still . . . No Mahir, it's impossible!"

"I don't blame you, but I do think it's time to forget family loyalties. We're about to lose our homeland."

"My uncle will understand that. Believe me, he was badly shaken by the raid on Parliament and the massacre at Şehzadepaşa Police Headquarters."

"Well then, we'll let time take care of everything, Kemal," said Mahir, "but how much time do we have? That's the problem!"

Azra got a chair from the dining table, placed it next to the stool Leman sat on as she played the piano, and sat down next to her.

"There's a piece we can play together. Shall I show you how?" she asked.

"Is it two-handed?"

"Yes."

"Alright, but don't let Suat see."

"Why?"

"She'll want to learn it too."

"Would that be so bad? You could play it together."

"I don't want to, Azra Abla. She gets her hands all muddy in the garden and then she touches the keys without washing them. She annoys me."

"It seems you take after Saraylıhanım, you're a little bit fastidious."

"So what? I don't want anyone touching my things."

"Cleanliness and tidiness are certainly virtues, but only in moderation," Azra said. "You play beautifully, Leman. Would you like to be a pianist?"

"What do you mean?"

"I mean performing in great concert halls, playing professionally."

"Girls don't do that sort of thing after they're married, Azra Abla."

"They do if they want to, Leman. Are you thinking about marriage already?"

"Not now, but in a few years. Nana says a good match shouldn't be missed. They make the best matches when a girl is still young."

"Is that so?"

"Of course it is. Just look at you—can't find a husband."

"Is that what Saraylıhanım told you?" Azra laughed.

Leman shook her head and asked, "Why don't you get married, Azra Abla?"

"I already have, my girl. But my husband was martyred in the war."

"Couldn't you get married again?"

"I could, but I prefer to remain faithful to the memory of my husband."

"But Azra Abla, are you going to go through life without a husband, without children?"

"It wouldn't be easy for me to find a suitable man, Leman. Saraylıhanım has a point, the men my age are all married with children."

"Not all of them. Uncle Kemal is a bachelor."

"Oh! Now whose idea was that?"

"They were talking about it the other day."

"I see. So your nana wants to marry me off to your uncle."

"No, not my nana, my mother. She thinks you're suitable for each other."

"Unfortunately, we grew up as brother and sister. Marriage is out of the question."

"What a shame! I'm ever so fond of you, and I'd hate for a strange woman to come to the house."

"Rest easy, Leman, your uncle has no intention of getting married any time soon."

"But mother wants him married without delay. She says he won't develop a sense of responsibility otherwise."

"Is that so?"

"Yes. He'll settle down once he has a family, that's what mother says."

"And I've been chosen to bring him to heel, is that it?"

"Mother says only an experienced woman could cope with Uncle Kemal, but nana wants to find him a young maiden. That's what I heard her say."

"God willing, Kemal will find his own bride when the time comes. Now, shall we play that piece I told you about?"

They had just begun when Kemal joined them.

"Azra, could I ask you to join me for a moment, there's something we need to discuss."

"Leman and I are playing piano right now. Let's talk a little later."

"Please, Azra. It's important."

When Leman looked at Azra with a devilish sparkle in her eyes and said, "Go talk to my uncle, we can play later," Azra stood up with a sinking heart. She couldn't help wondering if she was being toyed with by Leman, at the behest of Behice. Had she fallen into a trap? She'd accepted the invitation to stay at the house without hesitation, never suspecting ulterior motives of any kind. She followed Kemal into the sitting room.

"And what is it that could be so terribly urgent?" she asked brusquely.

"What I'm about to tell you should remain confidential, Azra."

"Do you think I'll babble to the neighbors?"

"What's gotten into you Azra? What do you mean, babble?"

"I don't know! Go on, tell me your secret!"

"You're friends with Fehime Sultan, aren't you?" Kemal asked.

Azra was taken aback by the unexpected reference to the princess. "I am. What of it?"

"Would you be able to obtain information from her?"

"What kind of information?" asked Azra, her curiosity piqued.

"You're familiar with the association known as T.S. . . ."

Azra thought for a moment. "Which association? Ah, yes."

"Them. They've been financing religious schools and institutions as a way of opening a front against the Nationalists."

"So I've heard. The ladies in my organization have discussed it."

"Just think, Azra, this association has identified over twenty-five religious schools in Anatolia. With the funding from the Sultan, they're swimming in money. And how do you think the Sultan finances them?"

"How?"

"The money is provided by the occupation forces. The English disburse funds to the Sultan, who passes the money along to pro-English proponents of Shari'a, chief among them Sheikh Sait. If Fehime Sultan could only find a way to get the Sultan to admit as much . . ."

"But isn't it perfectly obvious, Kemal?"

"That may be so, but confirmation from the royal lips would be different. Otherwise, we might be forced to slander the Sultan."

And so what if we do, Azra thought to herself. Kemal looked troubled.

"Ah, now I understand! You're frightened of your uncle, aren't you?"

"I'm not afraid of anyone. I'd simply like to be absolutely certain that the Sultan knows what he does. If we're made to answer for our actions one day, I'd like to hold my head high with the certainty that I have slandered no one."

"Is it worth taking all this trouble for a Sultan who would accept money from the states occupying his lands?"

"It is. If my uncle were to hear the Sultan himself admit as much, he would join us."

"And then all would be saved?"

"If the person controlling the state coffers joined our cause it would certainly be a reason for celebrating, yes."

"But how can your uncle be so blind to what's so obvious to us, Kemal?"

"People are blind to the faults of those they love and to whom they've sworn fealty. Tell me, do you think Fehime Sultan can extract this admission during conversation with the Sultan?"

"I'll go home and have Hakkı Efendi deliver a letter to Fehime Sultan, telling her I'd to pay a call."

"Then please, go immediately. If we succeed, we'll have obtained a powerful recruiting tool for the resistance."

"Don't worry, I was planning on leaving anyway. My mother tells me that the Asian Shore is more secure, and wants me to stay with her at my aunt's in Erenköy. I'll have to visit Fehime Sultan before I go there. Nor do I wish to abuse your gracious hospitality."

"That would be impossible! You're always welcome here."

"Yes, I've gathered as much. There's some intelligence I'd like to share—shall I?"

"Out with it."

"Your aunt has been matchmaking; I thought you should know."

At first Kemal didn't fully grasp the implications of Azra's words. When he did, he guffawed loudly. "What makes you think that?"

"You know what they say about the accuracy of information from the mouths of babes."

"Did Suat tell you?"

"No, Leman did. She's overheard her mother talking about how suitable we are for each other."

"You know, she does have a point. Perhaps I'll give it some thought," Kemal said, still laughing.

"You wouldn't dare!"

"Am I so unworthy of you, Azra?"

"Don't say that even in jest. You're like a brother to me."

"And even if I weren't, you deserve far better than the likes of me. Someone healthy and wise, with an inheritance or a career."

"And does anyone you know meet that criteria?"

"Yes, as a matter of fact."

"And who is this perfect catch?"

"Doctor Mahir, for example."

"For goodness sake," Azra cried, "I thought I was visiting the home of friends, but it seems I've wandered into a nest of matchmakers. If I hear the name of that doctor again, Kemal, our friendship will suffer a serious rupture. In fact, I might not look you in the face ever again."

"Why so angry, Azra?"

"Promise me you'll never pronounce his name again."

"I promise! But I'd like you to promise you won't neglect to visit with Fehime Sultan."

"I promise."

"Azra . . . forgive me for breaking my promise so soon . . . But why are you so set against Mahir? Has he done something to disturb you?"

"Of course not!"

"Well then, could you explain the vehemence of your objecion?"

"It's a personal matter."

"I see. He approached you; you spurned him. End of subject. I won't mention him again."

"Kemal, don't be ridiculous!"

"Well I know the two of you were close friends as recently as a month ago. Whenever Mahir stopped by to see me it seemed he was always on his way from your house. You must have found his attentions excessive."

Azra bowed her head for a moment, then she suddenly looked Kemal directly in the eye: "No, it's the opposite. I understood that Mahir Bey didn't return my affections."

"The fool," said Kemal. "Forgive me for prying, Azra. I'll never mention him again."

"Kemal, I'd have no objection . . . I haven't made marriage to the doctor a question of my personal honor. I simply misunderstood the nature of our friendship."

"But his having failed to appreciate the charms of someone like you . . . It makes no sense."

"He appreciates me well enough, Kemal. But love is something else."

"Ah, Azra, don't I know it," Kemal sighed. "The heart knows no master. If only we could demand its obedience."

"The obedience of our desires, as well as our hearts. It seems to me that you men are far more captive to your desires than to your hearts."

"How did you reach that conclusion?"

Azra was preparing to respond, but fell silent when Leman entered the room with a silver tray of foamy coffee, Mehpare just behind her.

"Forgive me for interrupting," Mehpare said, nodding in the direction of Leman, "but the little lady insisted on bringing you your morning coffee."

"I did no such thing!" Leman protested. "It was Mehpare Abla who wanted to make coffee."

"And a good thing she did, too," Azra smiled. "I haven't had a good strong cup of coffee for ever so long. Mehpare, I wonder if you wouldn't mind reading my cup when I'm finished. Behice says you're a wonderful fortune teller."

"Reading coffee grounds is nothing more than a diversion," Mehpare said. "I simply make things up as I go along, just as Saraylıhanım taught me."

"Well let's see what my cup inspires you to say. Who knows, perhaps you'll divine a path leading directly to the Palace," said Azra, with a clandestine wink at Kemal.

The wink was not lost on Mehpare.

Leman cried, "Oh, Azra Abla, are you really going to the Palace? And will you take mother with you again?"

"I won't be taking your mother this time, Leman. Certain things of great interest to me seem to leave her quite faint," Azra laughed.

"To be fair to my aunt, she had other reasons to faint that day," Kemal said.

Mehpare took a cup of coffee from the tray in Leman's hand and placed it on the end table in front of Azra. But as she was handing the second cup to Kemal, her hand suddenly trembled, spilling most of its contents onto his lap.

"Ah! I'm ever so sorry, sir. Let me get you a napkin. And it was piping hot, too. I hope you haven't burned yourself!"

Tugging at the rapidly growing stain on the front of his trousers, Kemal leapt to his feet and raced out of the room. To Mehpare, who had followed, he whispered, "I *have* scorched myself, actually. And each passing day makes it clearer just how badly."

When Leman heard her father and uncle talking inside the room with the bow window on the middle floor, she tapped on the door. Saraylıhanım had admonished her since childhood not to enter a room until granted permission, so Leman waited outside for the words "come in". It was strange, she knew her father and uncle were behind the door, but there was no response from either of them. Her patience exhausted, she finally pushed the door open a crack and peeked inside. The two men were seated opposite each other on the divan and so engrossed in their conversation that they hadn't even heard her. She ran toward her father:

"Father, Suat and I have spent forever getting ready. She's going to accompany me on the violin. We're going to give you a concert after dinner," she cried.

"I won't be at home after dinner, my beautiful girl."

"But father, you said . . . You were mad at me for not helping Suat practice and that's why for days now I've been . . ."

"I'll be visiting the home of Ahmet Reşit Bey tonight. There are some documents we need to prepare. I'll listen to your performance another time."

"But father, we've been preparing for days . . ."

"Leman Hanım! You'll give your concert another day. Shut the door on your way out, please!"

Leman was on the threshold of womanhood, but the bowed head and pouting face with which she reluctantly left the room were those of a child.

"You've upset the girl, uncle," Kemal said.

"The women of this household, from seven to seventy, have all failed to grasp the seriousness of our country's situation," Ahmet Reşat grumbled. "Is this any time for concerts?"

"She's only a girl, uncle."

"You're right. I'm afraid I've been a little irritable lately."

"What's wrong?"

"We had such high hopes when we formed the Kuva-I İnzibatiye, and now we've decided to abolish it. Cemal Pasha will also be coming to Reşit Bey's house tonight to work on that process."

"Well, in any case, what need was there for a new military force when we already have the National Forces?"

"There was a need."

"I fail to see one."

"It's easy enough to blow hot air from the sidelines, Kemal! The occupiers issued our government a memorandum, a diplomatic warning if you will, instructing us to destroy the National Forces. Remember?"

"Of course I do! And you complied, just like that."

"Had we rejected the memorandum, the government could very well have been dissolved. We complied for that reason alone."

"Well, good for you, I say. And by doing so you agreed to suppress the so-called rebels who are in fact patriots trying to save their country."

"Haven't you ever wondered why we agreed to such a thing? The occupiers knew we had no military attachments of our own—they expected that our only recourse would be to cite our lack of weapons and invite them to stamp out the insurrection themselves."

"I wish you'd done just that. Then you wouldn't be cursed for the rest of your days with having once issued orders to destroy the National Army."

"Ah, Kemal. Don't you see, it was a trap! Had we rejected the memorandum they would have dissolved the government. Had we cited our inability to fight the resistance forces ourselves, that task would have been assigned to the Greek Army, ready and waiting in İzmir with 100,000 men. Affairs of state require a certain degree of finesse. Before a statesman takes a single step, he has to see his next ten. The only way to avoid the devilish trap they'd laid for us was to establish a new army and to pretend to suppress the insurrection, while in fact allowing the National Army more time to gain strength. And then, when the time came, we would deploy our new Caliphate Army in Anatolia against Greece."

Kemal scanned his uncle's face in astonishment. Was it possible that Ahmet Reşat wasn't blindly loyal to the Sultan? That, after all, he too was a patriot at heart? But if that were true, why, even though they lived under the same roof, hadn't he realized it before?

"Well then why are you abolishing the new army?" he asked.

"Unfortunately, our calculations proved to be wrong, Kemal. We were outmaneuvered. We'd expected like-minded ministers to head the government and the war ministry. But Damat Ferit swooped in like a hawk and persuaded the Sultan to give him both posts."

"Ferit is an opportunist extraordinaire."

"Married to the Sultan's sister as he is, he rarely leaves the Palace. Over time, he's become one of the few people the Sultan relies upon."

"And thus he's succeeded in having death warrants issued for the Nationalists."

"That's not all. The Caliphate Army didn't turn out at all as we'd imagined: they began using it to crush the Nationalists."

"But Uncle, surely you knew that Damat Ferit was a sworn enemy of the Nationalists? A man unable to discriminate between CUP and the Nationalists is a man too short-sighted to see the tip of his own nose."

"There's been another unfortunate development. The forces of the Caliphate Army were deployed to Anatolia via İzmit. When they arrived there, they were ambushed by a group of Circassians. It turns out the Circassians, too, have dreams of forming their own state. As you can see, absolutely everyone seems bent on betraying the Ottoman Empire, Kemal."

"Yes, I heard about the events there in İzmit."

"It seems you're intelligence is quite thorough."

"That it is."

"Then it's safe to assume that you already know about Damat Ferit's pending trip to Paris, where he'll be dealing the final death blow to the Ottoman Empire."

Kemal didn't respond.

"And while Ferit is away, we intend to destroy, with our own hands, this monster of an army we created—again, with our own hands. I am working on that very task with Ahmet Reşit Bey and Cemal Pasha."

"What about their weapons? It would be wonderful if they somehow found their way to the Nationalists."

"Let's focus on demobilizing the army before we concern ourselves with the disposal of its arsenal."

"You've got your work cut out for you, Uncle," Kemal said. "When I see you like this I'm deeply grateful I've been imprisoned in this house. I wouldn't like to be in your shoes."

"I've considered resigning many times. But I've been serving the state for as long as I can remember and I've been well-served in return: it's beneath me to flee like a rat from a sinking ship. I have no choice but to endure whatever comes my way."

"May God come to your aid," Kemal said.

"He hasn't so far, by God!" Reşat sputtered. "And as if one government split into two factions weren't bad enough, a second government has been established in Ankara. The Chinese have a proverb: A dog with two masters dies of starvation. May God watch over us to the bitter end."

He sighed, rose to his feet and said, "I'd best be on my way now. It won't do to keep Reşit Bey waiting, and the carriage I ordered must have arrived long ago."

Kemal was overcome by a surge of gratitude and compassion, but he resisted the impulse to throw his arms around his long-suffering uncle, knowing how much he deplored demonstrative shows of affection. Ahmet Reşat was nearly at the door when he turned round:

"There's something I meant to say, Kemal . . . Leman and her piano . . . I've upset her. Would you mind listening to the concert this evening in my place? Do you think you could endure Suat on the violin, as well?"

"Who could possibly replace you? It's for you they wish to stage their talents. Perhaps you'll listen to them tomorrow evening."

"Don't raise their hopes. You won't be seeing much of me in the coming days, I'm afraid," Ahmet Reşat said.

"When have we ever seen much of you?" murmured Behice, appearing in the doorway. "You requested a carriage, Reşat Bey, but Hüsnü Efendi has been unable to locate one. You didn't listen to me when I advised, way back when, that we get a coupe. And now you'll be walking all the way to Reşit Bey's house."

"Off I go then. Suitable retribution indeed for having failed to heed the advice of my wife," said Reşat Bey. "Thank God for the mild weather."

Alone in the sitting room, Kemal stretched out on the divan and placed his arms under his head. He was bone-tired, that exhaustion born of awaiting news that never arrives. He'd grown weary of life, of everything but his translations and making love with Mehpare. A breeze brought the smell of the sea through the half-open window. Kemal filled his lungs and gazed up at the deepening darkness of the evening sky. The white blossoms of the magnolia tree just outside his window had completed their brief lifespan and the tree was now covered with shiny green leaves. So, spring this year would be like its predecessors, diffident and noiseless as it passed through Istanbul, leaving hearts untouched and blood unstirred. High spirits and exuberance would have to await another spring, in this city.

Dear Brother Kemal,
I jot down this letter in some haste in the writing room of FS.

I visited FS the moment I received word that she expected me. She received me with her usual courtesy and we spoke at length on the usual subjects. I asked her about that matter of particular interest to both of us. In two days, on the occasion of a tea being held to celebrate the birthday of her cousin, she will be in the presence of the person of whom we spoke. She has assured me that she will find a way to raise the subject and will send me a report detailing His response. It is not yet clear when the ferryboats will be running. My mother is most upset and worried about me, as you know. FS has proposed that I travel as far as Üsküdar in her private *caique*, for which reason I must leave shortly without making my farewells. I enclose letters of thanks and farewell to Saraylıhanımefendi and Behice Hanımefendi. I will convey to you any information I receive, through Hakkı Efendi. I extend my heartfelt gratitude for your family's warm hospitality. Send my kisses to Leman and Suat.
Your Sister.
Azra Ziya

Kemal refolded the letter and put it back in his jacket pocket. He would have to wait at least a week for a second letter to arrive from Azra. If that letter confirmed his suspicions, he would attempt to persuade his uncle. He didn't want to sneak off like a common thief, to abandon the family that had cared for him so devotedly, or to burn any bridges with his uncle, who had forgiven him so many times in the past. He knew that if he left without making his farewells, he would never be able to return. But if he could get his uncle to side with him . . . If only he could . . . Or if his uncle could at least be made to see that he had been right all along, then he would be able to say goodbye properly. He'd embrace them all. Their prayers would go with him. He paced the length of his room, dismayed by thoughts of his grandmother, the girls, his aunt, his uncle. And Mehpare! Never to see Mehpare again, to hold her in his arms, to kiss her smooth skin. He heard footsteps coming up the stairs. A man's heavy tread, not Mehpare's. His uncle had left home early in the morning. Who could it be? Hüsnü Efendi certainly wasn't in the habit of wandering through the house! He grabbed a brass candleholder, moved behind the door and waited. There were two raps on the door.

"Who is it?"

"Mahir."

Relieved, Kemal opened the door.

"What is it, Mahir?" he asked. "Trouble?"

"Saraylıhanım instructed me to go directly upstairs, and that's what I did."

"You startled me, I wasn't expecting you. Only the women come up to this floor."

"I wanted to give your aunt the results of her test without delay. When I was met at the door by Saraylıhanım I told her I'd come to see you, and she sent me straight here."

"What was the test result?"

"Permit me to tell your aunt first." Kemal left the room and tapped on the door opposite.

When the door remained closed he called out to Mehpare on the floor below:

"She's making *ayran* for you and Mahir Bey. She'll bring it up in a moment," Saraylıhanım responded.

"Mahir, I received a letter from Azra," Kemal said. "Princess Fehime is going to see the Sultan today. She's going to send out feelers. I think she may even ask him directly. Sultan Vahdettin has never made a secret of his pro-English sentiments, so why shouldn't she simply ask him?"

"You do realize, don't you, that in these trying times, when everyone is hard up for money, Sheikh Sait is living a life of extravagance?"

"Are the English funding him?"

"I'm certain they are, among others. There are pro-English organizations other than Sait's. The Freedom and Unity Party is unhappy with Sait monopolizing all the funds. The English don't want to anger their supporters. They must be giving the Sultan a share of the money for redistribution to the others."

"Let's pray that's the case."

When Mehpare arrived with the ayran, Kemal asked her to bring his aunt upstairs. Mehpare ran down to Behice's room and soon returned with her.

"Come on, Mehpare, let's go to your room and let my aunt speak with the doctor in private," Kemal said.

Behice sat on the edge of the bed, folded hands trembling in her lap as Mahir broke the news.

"Congratulations, efendim, we've determined the cause of your fainting spells. You're preg-nant."

"Really?"

"Aren't you pleased? You'd been hoping for a son. God willing, you'll have one."

Behice stared blankly. "Leman's a young woman, nearly old enough for marriage. I'll be embarrassed to tell her."

"But you're still young yourself."

"We're at war. Our troubles are many. The child is untimely. It doesn't matter if it's a boy."

"Of course it doesn't. May Allah give you a healthy, dutiful child."

"Amen."

"If you're able to provide me with some dates, I can calculate when the child will be born."

"Don't trouble yourself anymore, doctor. I'll be seeing the midwife from now on."

"As you like," Mahir said.

"Now, by your leave, I'll be going . . ."

"Behice Hanımefendi . . ."

"Yes . . ."

"If they ask, what shall I tell them? What shall I say to Kemal, Saraylıhanım and the others?"

"Give me a few days. I'd like to give Reşat Bey the news first, then we'll tell the others."

"In that case, I know nothing. We haven't received the test results just yet."

"Thank you, doctor," Behice said as she left the room.

Mahir looked thoughtfully at the doorway. In a city under occupation, news of a husband's promotion to minister or of a baby is insufficient to gladden a woman. Even the Judas tree and hyacinth seemed to droop; a veil of melancholy had descended on young and old, everyone and everything. Mahir waited in the room a little while longer. He was in a hurry, and when Kemal didn't return he made his way to the stairs. The tinkling of a piano echoed up the stairs: Leman was playing in the anteroom. At the sound of footsteps she raised her head and smiled. Her light auburn hair spilled over her shoulders. Her head was uncovered. The light from the window fell full across her face, and Mahir noticed the reddish tint in her hair, the honey-colored flecks in her large green eyes. When had this girl grown up? When had she become so beautiful?

"How are you, Leman . . . Hanım?" he asked, pronouncing the word "Hanım" with some difficulty. It seemed such a strange term of address for a girl he'd once bounced on his knee in Thessalonica. But the young woman seated on the piano bench was no child, that much was clear.

"I'm fine, doctor. How are you? Have you come to examine Uncle Kemal?"

"Yes, but he has no need for me. Your uncle has regained his health, young lady."

"That's wonderful! And Mehpare Abla is going to stay here with us regardless."

"You're quite fond of Mehpare then, are you?"

"Yes. We understand each other."

"Keep playing Leman . . . Hanım. You play beautifully."

"Azra Abla taught me this piece last week. You know Azra Hanım, don't you?"

"Yes, I do."

"She plays well too."

"I haven't heard her play for a long time."

"That's a shame," said Leman, "she's far better than me."

"She's been practicing for many years. When you're her age, who knows how much more accomplished you'll be. You're still very young. A child, really."

"Better not let Nana hear you call me a child. She's trying to get me married off."

"That's absurd! Your father would never allow it. How old are you?"

"Fifteen, but I'll be sixteen in a few months."

"You've grown up, Leman. I hadn't realized how quickly," Mahir said. "I ask your leave for now, but I'll return one day just to hear you play."

"If you let me know in advance I'll play a duet for you, with Azra Abla."

Mahir descended to the entry hall, took his black sheepskin cap from the shelf, put on his shoes, retrieved his cape from the coat stand and threw it over his shoulders, and walked out the door. He resisted the impulse to look up at the window on the middle floor. Had he done so, he would have seen Leman watching his departure from behind the tulle curtains.

Mehpare picked up the jacket Kemal had forgotten to take with him as he hurried back to his room. She shook out the jacket, spread it on the bed and, with slender fingers, stroked and straightened its collar and sleeves. Ever since the arrival of Azra, Kemal had neither visited her room nor summoned her to his. She'd missed him. And every night Azra was in the house, after everyone else had gone to bed, she'd carefully listened for any untoward sounds in Kemal's room, even leaving her door ajar so she wouldn't miss the patter of footsteps going in or out. Kemal hadn't left his room and Azra hadn't visited it, of that much Mehpare was certain. But Kemal had virtually ignored her for the duration of Azra's stay. And now, this morning, when he'd waited with her while Doctor Mahir was examining his aunt, he'd confined himself to kisses. Mehpare had trembled inside as she asked him if he'd missed her.

"Of course I've missed you, but Mahir and my aunt are in my room. They might burst in at any moment."

"Burst into my room? For goodness sake!" she'd cried as she fought back tears. Was this the same Kemal? He must have tired of her. Once she'd given herself to him, he'd moved along, looking for new and lovelier conquests.

She snatched up the jacket she'd so lovingly straightened and hurled it against the wall. Unable to stop herself, she stamped on it, again and again. Then, as she felt the tears coming, she picked the jacket up off the floor, held it to her nose, buried her face in the plush fabric.

Mehpare had no idea how far this love of Kemal would take her, but she was prepared to follow him anywhere. If he remained in this house, she'd stay here until she died. If he were to marry someone—Azra, for instance—she would follow him to his new home as his servant, more than willing to be Azra's fellow wife as long as she could be a handmaiden, concubine, mistress, slave to Kemal.

She rose from the floor, spread the jacket on the bed, and was smoothing it again when she heard the rustle of paper in the right-hand pocket. She reached in and found a letter, folded in four. She paused for a moment. After opening and refolding the letter, she held her breath, opened it a second time, and scanned the handwriting. When the name Azra sprang out at her from the bottom of the page, she walked over to the bright light in front of the window. Her knees felt weak and her heart beat so fast that if anyone else were in the room surely they'd hear it throbbing. She began reading.

Then she folded the letter and sat on the bed. The relationship between Kemal and Azra wasn't romantic, as she'd feared—that much was clear, and good. But there was something between them that she could never share. Together, they were meddling in some murky business that could mean death for Kemal. That was bad, very bad.

She put the carefully folded letter back in Kemal's pocket.

Azra had gone home, thank God. But it was obvious that they'd continue to correspond, and that that appalling blonde, blue-eyed woman would continue to lead him into danger. What should she do? If she told Saraylıhanım, would it do any good? Should she go directly to Reşat Bey? But when had either of them been able to make Kemal listen! Perhaps she should knock on Azra's door and have a word with her. She'd explain that Kemal had been critically ill and only just recovered from his terrible fever, and request that Azra leave him in peace. There must be hundreds of fit young men prepared to endanger themselves in this way. Azra could choose any one of them for her games. If Kemal were arrested again or—

God forbid—relapsed, it would the end of him. Yes, that would be best: go directly to Azra and talk to her. Were Kemal to find out what she'd done, she couldn't rule out a beating, even though the men of this house were not in the habit of resorting to violence. Well let them beat her. If he found out, he'd never look at her again. So be it! It was enough that he survived. But hadn't Azra written that she was going somewhere? She withdrew the letter and scanned its contents once more. Azra had gone to the Asian shore yesterday. Would she be able to persuade Behice Hanım to allow her to visit Azra at home in Erenköy? Even if she failed with Behice Hanım, she might succeed with Leman: Azra was a skilled pianist, and Leman had grown to like her. They'd become friends. And if Leman set her mind on something, there was no stopping her. She'd nag and cajole until she got her way. Yes, she'd work on Leman until they were allowed to go to Erenköy.

After dinner, Behice retired to her room and put on her paçalık for the last time. It was a tight fit, but she knew she'd never wear the faded pink gown again. She brushed and re- brushed her hair with her ivory-handled hairbrush and lightly pinched and slapped her cheeks to bring out the color. Reşat Bey was late, as usual. Lighting the night lamp, she stretched out on the bed and lightly strummed her ud.

When Ahmet Reşat returned home that night he found his wife sound asleep on the bed. The ud had slipped from her hand and onto the floor.

"You'll catch cold, why aren't you using a blanket?" he asked. When his wife opened her eyes he added, "Your gown is so thin."

"I've worn my paçalık."

"You should wear something warmer in this weather."

"I wanted to give you the news wearing this."

Ahmet Reşat started. "I don't understand, Behice."

"I wore this gown the other times, and I hoped it would be auspicious . . ." Behice looked straight ahead, her lips trembling.

Her husband came over and sat by her side. "Behice, has something happened? What news? What is it?"

Taking a deep breath she spoke with her eyes on the floor. "Reşat Bey, I'm pregnant. Perhaps it'll be a boy this time." Her husband was silent for a long moment. When he failed to speak, Behice whispered: "You're not pleased?"

"May it be for the best," said Reşat. "It's a bit untimely, but Allah will help provide for its care."

"Of course He will! You're a minister, aren't you?"

"We're at war. Under occupation. These are difficult days and they're only going to get worse. All I can do is hope and pray for a healthy birth. And yes, God willing it will be a boy this time."

Behice realized she'd been foolish to expect the displays of delight that had greeted news of her earlier pregnancies.

As Ahmet Reşat stood up and undressed he asked: "Does my aunt know? Who have you told?"

Behice hadn't told her husband about her fainting spell or the doctor's visit, so she lied: "No one knows."

"In that case, we'll tell the other members of the household tomorrow. Mind your health and your diet, Hanım, you tend to have difficult pregnancies."

"I feel fine," Behice protested.

"Mahir shall come and examine you tomorrow."

"There's no need. I've called for the midwife."

"Behice Hanım, times are changing. Seeing as we have a family doctor there's no reason not to benefit from his services. The midwife can of course attend the birth, but do go and see Doctor Mahir."

"When I went to that gathering of women last week I made the acquaintance of Şahende Hanım. Of Recep Bey's family. She's a most enlightened woman."

Reşat Bey's expression soured and he said, "I've heard of her but I still think it best you apply to our neighborhood midwife."

Before Behice surrendered herself to Şahende Hanım, one of those women who meddle in men's affairs and caterwaul from behind lecterns, word would be sent—first thing in the morning—to Doctor Mahir, so that he might arrange a suitable time to examine her at home. His wife's previous pregnancy had ended in miscarriage. She was delicate. She required careful attention. He would also have to find a way to suggest to his aunt that she show special consideration for Behice and not upset her in any way. Reşat Bey knew that his aunt, although basically goodhearted, firmly believed that that the duties of mother-in-law necessitated the adoption of a critical stance towards the family's bride.

"I'm sending word to Mahir Bey," he said, stroking Behice's hair.

Behice felt alarmed. She didn't know whether to tell her husband that she'd already seen the doctor without his knowledge, or to keep it a secret. She felt quite flushed and attempted to mask her confusion and high color by murmuring, "Reşat Bey, I'm mortified at having to tell Leman about her new sibling."

"Why?"

"She's nearly of marrying age herself."

"In my house, no matter what Saraylıhanım says, no girl is going to be married before the age of twenty."

"But Reşat Bey, who would take a bride of over twenty? Everyone prefers a fresh-faced maiden. Did you wait for me to turn twenty?"

"If your father had refused your hand until then, I'd have waited. Let's keep the girls here with us for as long as possible. In fact, when they do marry, let's have them settle here with their husbands. What do you say to that?"

"I had no idea you were so fond of your daughters."

"For all these years of work, I've been missing them—when I retire I'd like them to be here with me. And I think it's important they're old enough to choose a husband wisely. Tell me, Behice Hanım, you were a mere girl when you were sent to me: Have you ever regretted it?"

"Never. I'd choose you again, at this age."

"Don't throw out that pink gown just because it's old, Behice," Ahmet Reşat said as he leaned forward and buried his nose in the hair spilling down her shoulders. "It will bring us luck if we have any more children. And it suits you perfectly."

Mehpare tapped on the door and stepped into the room without waiting for Kemal's invitation. Kemal was putting books in a suitcase he'd laid open on the bed. Mehpare quickly scanned the room before resting her eyes on the books.

"Sir?"

"What is it, Mehpare?"

"You summoned me?"

"No, I didn't."

"If you're packing your bags I'll help you."

"I can do it myself."

"Do you want me to go?"

"Yes, you can go."

Mehpare walked over to Kemal and snatched the book he was putting into the suitcase. "Why are you packing them up?"

"I'm removing them."

"But these are the books you always read."

"I've finished with them."

"Well in that case I'll put them on the top shelf of the bookcase tomorrow. You don't need to put them in a suitcase."

"Stop meddling, Mehpare!" Kemal snapped as he tried, and failed, to retrieve the book she was pressing to her chest.

"What's going on, sir? Are you going somewhere? You've had all your laundry done, and ironed. Why?"

"I thought it'd be nice to have clean clothes."

"You've never worried about that before."

"Look, it's late—leave me alone and get to bed, in your own room!"

Mehpare stood her ground. Kemal stared at her in stunned silence. She had placed the book on the bed and was slowly unbuttoning her blouse.

"Stop it. I'm not in the mood." When she ignored him Kemal grew angry. "I told you to go to your room, Mehpare."

Mehpare came directly up to Kemal. "You've been so distant. You don't even look me in the face. You don't care about me anymore. Maybe there's someone else."

"Ridiculous."

"Then why are you sending me away?"

"You can't force these things, Mehpare," Kemal said. "I'm out of sorts, confused. I'm expecting some news and it just won't come. I'm feeling a bit low and there's nothing I want right now."

"Well then tell me all about it. Tell me the news you're expecting."

"Some things are private."

"You can tell me anything." As they spoke Mehpare undid the final buttons, stripped away her blouse and camisole; Kemal found himself looking at her breasts, their tracery of blue veins. They seemed even fuller than he remembered. Mehpare's thick brown hair had fallen across her face. She was unfastening the clasp of her skirt. A moment later Kemal had pulled off his trousers, shoved the suitcase to the floor. He pressed against Mehpare until he was inside, all else forgotten.

"Tell me," she said, squirming free.

"What?" panted Kemal.

"What you're expecting."

Ignoring her, Kemal struggled to get back inside—and each time she wriggled away. "For God's sake, Mehpare, hold still!"

"Tell me and I will."

Kemal barely suppressed an oath as he tried to mount her. She slipped free again.

"I'll give you a good pummeling in a minute."

"Go ahead."

"Mehpare, please!"

"Tell me. Who or what are you expecting?"

"Look Mehpare, I've had enough of this. Didn't you come here of your own free will? Weren't you the one who wanted to make love?"

"I was. I haven't been able to sleep, I missed you so badly."

Kemal pinned her beneath him again. But she shook him off, sprang up from the bed and stood by the door.

"I'm going, unless you tell me."

"Like that, naked?"

"Naked. And I'll lock my door and you'll never touch me again."

Kemal looked at Mehpare helplessly. "Come here," he said. Mehpare glided over to the bed, and lowered herself onto him.

"Tell me."

And as Kemal rocked beneath her, he told her. "I'm expecting news… I'll be leaving to join the resistance."

"You're leaving *me*. You're going off and . . ."

Mehpare cupped his face in her hands, kissing his mouth, his nose, his chin.

Some time later, after gently slipping out from below Kemal, who had fallen asleep with his head on her breast, Mehpare picked up the scattered books and put them onto their usual places on the shelves, slid the suitcase back under the bed, wrapped herself in the blanket that had fallen to the floor, gathered up her clothes, and left the room. As though she believed that order was restored, that nothing, now, could change.

Mahir wasn't entirely comfortable as he sat across from Ahmet Reşat, who was still dressed in his Friday best, in the selamlık.

Reşat has just returned from the royal procession to the mosque for Friday services, where the Sultan was customarily drawn in a horse and carriage to the accompaniment of the Palace March, his officials following in order of rank. Lined up in the courtyard of the mosque where prayers were to take place were the Grand Vizier, ministers, members of the senate, civilian and military state officials, men who had married into the royal family, ambassadors, and various guests and dignitaries. Traditionally, it was an opportunity for the public to get a glimpse of the Sultan and Caliph, but the occasion had lost much of its pomp and spectacle when the occupying forces had banned the participation of the Ceremonial Guard.

Ahmet Reşat had been upset that morning to see that only a handful of people had turned out to applaud their Sultan. It could only mean that even the Muslim citizens of the empire, who had always been devoted to the Sultan, had begun to lose faith in his government. Reşat knew that he himself was a leading figure among this despised leadership, and was greatly saddened by the realization.

Mahir was disturbed for a different reason. He'd concealed the news of Behice's pregnancy, and as if that weren't bad enough, had kept secret Kemal's plan to leave his uncle's house and join the resistance. How could he have hidden so much from his old friend?

It had been impossible to persuade Reşat Bey to join them. He still believed that the Sultan would realize, sooner or later, his folly in trusting the English. It would happen any day now, he believed, as a faithful son believes to the end in a wayward father's reformation. Ahmet Reşat had no choice but to wait patiently, without resorting to betrayal, without turning his back, without doing his Majesty a disservice of any kind, until the Sultan saw the error of his ways.

Mahir hoped with all his heart that when that day came it wouldn't be too late for Ahmet Reşat. Taking another sip of his lemonade, he set the glass down on the mother-of-pearl inlaid end table.

"Delicious. My compliments to whoever made it," he said to Reşat Bey, who responded, "My eldest daughter made it." Mahir waited in vain for the conversation to turn to Leman, wondering as he did so how Ahmet Reşat would react if he knew that his closest friend couldn't help thinking rather frequently of his fifteen-year-old daughter.

"The lemons are from the back garden. It's almost as if we'd foreseen the food shortages and planted fruit trees well in advance. We've been dining on fruit from the garden all winter long, even sending some to the neighbors. It's impossible to find anything in Istanbul these days," said Ahmet Reşat.

"I certainly do know."

"Bless my father-in-law for having sent us supplies so frequently, but the roads are no longer safe; they're even impassable at times."

"So I've heard. Even officers find it difficult to travel these days. We're forever having to produce our papers at checkpoints. Who knows what we'll come up against before we reach our destinations."

"I wish you Godspeed on your journey but you'll be sorely missed here in Istanbul, Mahir Bey," said Ahmet Reşat. "We'll need you more than ever now that Behice Hanım is expecting another baby."

"I wish I could stay here with you, but the only way to prevent any more outbreaks is to work in the areas under quarantine. Your wife looked perfectly healthy to me. I don't anticipate any complications."

"You know, Mahir, we hadn't planned to have another child at a time like this. Even so, I've been curiously elated by the news. As though a baby were the harbinger of brighter, better days."

"God willing. But I'm afraid we'll have to wait some time for better days. The occupiers don't have the slightest tolerance for Muslim Ottomans. You wouldn't know, not being a soldier yourself, but they've found a new way to plague us: they expect Ottoman officers of whatever rank to salute any and all soldiers of the allied forces."

"I don't understand. You mean a high-ranking Ottoman officer is required to salute an allied soldier, even if he's a private?"

"That's exactly what I mean. Just imagine a situation in which an Ottoman Pasha is forced to salute a common soldier, whether English, French or Italian. Or even Greek."

"How long has this been going on?"

"For a month. They'll soon inform your government in writing and request your cooperation to enforce it. It's an intolerable situation for Turkish officers. Many of them have taken to wearing civilian clothing just to avoid it."

Ahmet Reşat was struck by a stabbing pain in his stomach. He felt like vomiting, and unconsciously clapped one hand over his mouth and the other over his midsection.

"What's wrong? You've gone ashen, Reşat Bey."

"A sudden wave of nausea. I don't know why."

"Would you allow me to examine your tongue?"

"I'm fine, Mahir Bey, just fine. I'm as fine as any of us can be. Don't worry, it's passed."

The two men sat for a moment without speaking, as though too weak or dispirited for words. Mahir broke the silence. "Believe me when I say how sorry I am to be going off like this, especially considering Behice Hanım's condition. I'll leave the name and number of a friend, just in case. Akil Muhtar is a good man, and a skilled doctor."

"Thank you."

"Leman Hanım has grown up fast, hasn't she? She seems to be a self-possessed young lady. I'm sure she'll be a great help to her mother."

"She would be, if Behice didn't insist on treating her daughters like children. She won't let them lift a finger. I think she's making a mistake, but the rearing of children is best left to women, and I don't wish to interfere. Mahir Bey, how long will you be away?"

"The cholera patients are gathered in Tuzla; those with typhus and venereal diseases are under quarantine at various other locations. And there's been an outbreak of the Asian flu among the most recent wave of immigrants. I'll be conducting a tour of inspection in Tuzla first, but it's not yet clear where I'll be going after that. I certainly won't be returning until the situation is under control."

"A city with this many immigrants and refugees was bound to suffer an epidemic," Ahmet Reşat said. "The numbers are staggering. During the Balkan War sixty-five thousand people arrived in Istanbul alone, not to mention some ninety thousand Russians and nearly one hundred thousand refugees from the Crimea."

"Well at least we were able to prevent an outbreak of the typhus brought by the Crimeans."

There was some sort of uproar outside the house, and Ahmet Reşat went to the window to see what it was. Hüsnü Efendi was standing in front of the garden gate in heated discussion with someone. The man, whose back was turned, was gesticulating wildly. When he turned towards the window Ahmet Reşat recognized him.

"Ah, it's Hakkı Efendi, Ziya Pasha's man. I wonder what he wants? Maybe Azra Hanım needs something?"

"Strange." Mahir joined Ahmet Reşat in front of the window.

Ahmet Reşat left the selamlık and upon opening the front door nearly bumped noses with Hakkı Efendi. The poor servant was trembling.

"Sir, the invaders have come. The invaders have come to our house. The invaders."

"Invaders? What are you saying, man?"

Thank God the ladies aren't home. They're on the Asian Shore. Come quickly, sir. Do something. For God's sake . . ."

"Hakkı Efendi! What are you going on about?"

"They're seizing our house. They'll listen to you, sir, don't let them do it. I'm begging you, please come with me, come quickly."

"Let me put something on and I'll be right back," Ahmet Reşat said. As he sprinted up the stairs he ran into Kemal.

"Mahir Bey's come and you haven't even told me. Uncle? What's wrong?"

Ahmet Reşat pushed Kemal aside and continued up the stairs. At the sight of Mahir, who was standing at the entrance to the selamlık with a distraught Hakkı Efendi, Kemal raced down the stairs.

"What's happened, Mahir?"

"They've seized Ziya Pasha's house."

"You're not serious! When?" Hakkı Efendi had begun a disjointed account of recent

events when Ahmet Reşat came back downstairs. The two men hurried off together. Mahir and Kemal were left dumbfounded and alone in the entry hall. At the sound of rustling Mahir turned round. It was Leman, frightened, standing in front of the garden door with a basket of blossoming branches.

"Ah, Leman . . . Hanım," Mahir said. "Was that you? We didn't hear you come in." A smile spread across the doctor's troubled face.

"I was in the garden, gathering some branches that have flowered early. I'm going to put them in a vase and sketch them. What's going on? Uncle Kemal, why do you look so upset? Where has father gone running off to? It's Friday, the offices are all closed, aren't they?"

"There's been some urgent business. Why don't you run along upstairs," Kemal said. "Uncle Mahir and I have something to discuss in the selamlık."

Annoyed at having been addressed as "uncle" in front of Leman, Mahir prepared to follow Kemal to the selamlık, but couldn't resist turning his head for another glimpse of Leman. Delicate and graceful—that melancholy face, those enormous eyes shot with green . . .

"When you're finished, come upstairs and I'll play the piano for you," Leman said.

"Do you enjoy playing the piano, then?" Mahir asked.

"Very much. Especially Chopin, but I haven't been able to find the sheet music I was looking for."

"Write down whatever sheet music you'd like. I'm going to Pera tomorrow, and I'll stop by the music shops for you."

"How kind of you, sir." She smiled.

"Enough talk about music," Kemal said, "we've got some important business to discuss."

Mahir found himself fairly shoved into the selamlık. The door was closed behind him.

Having returned to the European Shore to organize her house for surrender to the occupation forces, the Azra who was now staying at Reşat Bey's house was visibly thinner than the Azra of only a few weeks before. The dark circles under her eyes attested to the toll taken by recent developments, but she held her head high and concealed her sufferings as best she could.

"I admire you, Azra," Behice said, "you're taking this so well. I'd have been confined to my bed long ago."

"No you wouldn't. Calamity brings strength. When father was exiled, and again when I lost my elder brother, I expected my mother to fall ill and take to her bed: she did no such thing. She carried on for my sake. And now it's my turn to be strong for her sake. Besides, I don't want the enemy to see how upset I am."

"I have some news for you. I'm not a particularly strong woman, but I'm not so weak that a few vigorous speeches at a women's gathering can knock me out. I was embarrassed by my fainting spell at Makbule Hanım's house—but it turns out that I'm pregnant. Forgive me for having caused con- cern."

"Oh, Behice, it's wonderful news! Congratulations. I'm as pleased as can be."

"Would you like me to come along when you go to collect the furniture from your house?"

"Absolutely not! If you hadn't shared your news I'd have considered your offer. But now I think you should stay here, Behice. It would upset you terribly to see my house surrounded by enemy forces. And they're certain to have an insolent Greek translator with them. It wouldn't be right to distress you like that. Stay here at home."

"Take Mehpare with you, then. I'm sure she'll be able to make herself useful."

"It would be such a help."

"I'll tell her to get ready."

Behice found Mehpare in the small room next to the kitchen. She was ironing Kemal's underwear. "Would you mind accompanying Azra Hanım to her house, Mehpare?" Behice asked. "She needs to write up a list of the furnishings and get her personal belongings before the house is taken over. I'd hoped to go with her… but given my news, it wouldn't be wise."

"Let me put away the iron, Behice Abla," Mehpare replied, "and I'll be ready to help in any way I can."

Deciding there was no need to take Kemal's laundry up to his room, she stacked it neatly on the chiffonier, grabbed her cloak and raced off.

The most recent letter that Azra had sent to Kemal rested on Ahmet Reşat's knee. He'd put on his reading glasses and studied it carefully from start to finish. Other than one particular detail, everything conveyed at some length to Azra by Fehime Sultan was already known to him.

" . . . Sheikh Sait, in particular, enjoys close relations with the Association of Anglophiles, many of whose members are influential Armenians. A portion of the substantial payments he receives from them are spent on his own extravagant lifestyle while the rest is being used to fund the formation of a pro-English cabinet. The first duty of this cabinet would be the elimination of the Nationalist movement . . . Ferit Pasha is preparing a counterinsurgency against the Nationalists and has accelerated the frequency of his meetings with Kurdish tribal leaders, which are being arranged by Sheikh Sait, himself the head of a Kurdish tribe . . ."

After re-reading the letter, Ahmet Reşat returned to a particular sentence, which he read aloud, as though for confirmation: "Our Sultan is fully aware of these circumstances."

With a mild oath, he removed his glasses and looked at his nephew.

"You see, uncle!" Kemal said. "That's our Sultan for you! Had Mahir been able to summon up the courage he would have told you about this long ago, but he was disappointed in his efforts to find an appropriate opportunity."

"Intimately familiar as I am with your lunacy, I'm not surprised to find you in the thick of all this; but as for Mahir—he has a career! I'd never have expected him to get involved in an underground organization."

"Everyone in his right mind is on our side now, Uncle. And it's not just the patriots among us, even the French are supporting the uprising taking root in Anatolia."

"If the French support us it isn't for love of our black eyes. They're settling old scores with the English," Ahmet Reşat countered. "The Greeks are now demanding territories given to the Italians. English support for the Greeks has driven the French and the Italians, in particular, towards the Turks. I heard as much from Caprini Efendi himself."

"But it doesn't change anything, does it? The Sultan is on the wrong path; you see that, don't you?"

Ahmet Reşat was unable to respond. I see everything clear as day, were the words he couldn't bring himself to utter. The Sultan to whom he had pledged his allegiance had, upon falling into the sea, chosen to embrace a serpent in the form of the English, a nation whose ruthless designs on the Ottoman Empire were unmatched. But the Sultan's choice of serpent was unfathomable. It had for some months been so obvious to Reşat Bey that the English planned to establish a Kurdish state under the puppet government of Sheikh Sait on lands seized from the Ottoman Empire that he was truly astonished that the Sultan and the Freedom and Unity Party seemed unable to perceive what was happening under their very noses. No—in fact, he was no longer astonished: backed by money or propaganda or whatever else it took, Sait the Kurd had managed to enlist the services of a sizeable number of Ottoman intellectuals, and it was these intellectuals who were leading the Sultan astray. With each passing day, Ahmet Reşat found his faith slipping further as His Majesty invariably responded to disastrous news by closing his eyes and losing himself in mediation.

On numerous occasions he'd discussed this very matter with Home Minister Ahmet Reşit, and while neither man had been happy with the Sultan's blindly pro-English stance, they had at first found some justification for it in Sultan Vahdettin's emphasis on religion over country. It had become painfully apparent, however, in the days immediately following the occupation, that they had been wrong on that count: every one of their Christian subjects had toadied up to the state sponsors of their religions. The Bulgarians, Serbians and Orthodox Armenians had turned to Russia; the Catholic Armenians to France. And when it came to the Americans, they'd been thronging to Anatolia seeking converts from among the Ottoman Christians for years. Religion was like concrete, and it was the Ottomans who had failed to harness its adhesive powers to their own ends: had the Muslim tribes of Arabia hesitated to stab their co-religionists and Caliphate in the back?

Ahmet Reşat stood, ignoring the ash that tumbled from his cigarette onto the carpet as he wearily paced the length of the room.

What a shame, what a terrible shame! The officers of a mighty empire spanning half a millennium had been reduced to saluting lowly Greek privates. And the royal patronage of the Sultan had been extended to organizations clamoring for Shari'a. No, this was going too far! Things had reached breaking point; well, let them snap.

"Son," he wearily said to Kemal, "our people are divided in two: there are those who believe we must take up arms against the invaders, and those who believe it prudent to rely on diplomacy to soften the terms of the armistice. I'm fully aware that our finances can not endure another war, for which reason I have consistently counted myself among the latter group. But the events of recent months have convinced me it's in our interests to support those who want to fight."

"Now that you've seen the truth, please help us."

Ahmet Reşat went to his nephew's side and whispered his next words.

"The coffers are bare. If it's money for arms you want, there isn't any."

"We're not looking for monetary assistance. What we will need is the authorization and blessings of the government. That's when we'll apply to you for help."

"And when you do, I'll be of assistance any way I can."

"Thank you. I knew that one day . . ." Kemal kissed his uncle's hand and pressed it to his forehead "You've always been the father I never knew. Young as you were, you looked after me, you brought me, you forgave me my mistakes. If I'd been forced to leave this house without your blessing, and died somehow, I'd have had no one to close my eyes for me. But I'm at ease now. You've made me very happy."

"When are you going, my boy?" asked Ahmet Reşat.

"I'm awaiting word. I'll go the moment I receive it."

"I'll be thinking of you. Wondering how you are. And my aunt will weep for you every day. We'll be a worried house again, a house of suffering."

"I returned from Sarıkamış; surely I'll be able to return from Bakırköy."

"But weren't you going to Anatolia?"

"Later. When the time comes. Along with supplies . . ."

"God speed you on your way," said Ahmet Reşat, "and don't tell anyone else until the day you leave."

"I may be going in a few weeks."

"Well at least we'll have a few more weeks of calm. The women of the house are going to be in an uproar, and I don't have the strength to endure it just yet."

The two men fell silent when Leman entered with some sheet music.

"Look what the doctor sent me, Father."

"Oh, did he really? But Mahir Bey's left, hasn't he?"

"An orderly just brought it. If I'm able to learn all the pieces inside, I'll surprise him when he gets back."

"Well, you'd better get to it."

"Did he tell you when he was returning?" Leman said.

"When his work is done."

"When will it be done?"

"How am I supposed to know, Leman. The hospitals are overflowing with patients who've contracted everything from typhus to trachoma. He may not be back for some time."

"May God protect him."

"God looks after doctors," said Kemal, "just as He looks after children."

"I'm not so certain God looks after anyone anymore," Ahmet Reşat said. Kemal glanced at his uncle with raised eyebrows. His uncle had never been one for gloomy pronouncements. His disillusionment with the Sultan appeared to have spread.

Mehpare's back was cramped with constant bending and her fingertips had gone numb wrapping parcels. The contents of the salon, the office, and every bedroom in the enormous mansion had been tied into bundles. While she admired the many precious objects, Mehpare was thankful that her own house was less ostentatious. The foreigners had passed over the less grand mansions, with smaller gardens, that lined the street. Otherwise, finance minister or not, Ahmet Reşat and his family might have found themselves out on the pavement one winter's day. The English had seized the Taksim house of a family friend, Şakir Pasha. They'd been forced to move to their summer house on Büyükada Island, in the Sea of Marmara, in the dead of winter. Were the same thing to happen to Ahmet Reşat, they'd have no choice but to move to the island as well . . . And freeze to death. It had been difficult enough to heat the city mansion, and the cold northern winds sweeping across the pine-topped hills of the island would have killed Kemal, while causing Saraylıhanım and the girls to come down with pneumonia at best. Mehpare silently mouthed a prayer of thanksgiving she'd learned from Saraylıhanım; then she touched wood and tugged her right earlobe for good measure.

"We're both exhausted. Let's stop for some tea," Azra said as she struggled to secure the ends of a bed sheet she'd wrapped around a large Acem carpet.

"Let me help you," Mehpare offered, disposing of the task in a trice. Then they settled themselves side by a side on a sofa swathed in calico. "Could you bring each of us a tea, Housekeeper Nazik? The alcohol stove and teapot should still be in their old places," Azra said.

With the housekeeper out of the room, Azra and Mehpare were alone for the first time. Mehpare seized the opportunity to speak.

"Azra Hanım," she began, looking directly into the young woman's blue eyes, "I wonder if I could speak frankly with you for a moment."

"What about, Mehpare?"

"I have something to say about Kemal Bey."

"Please," Azra nodded, prepared to retort sharply when Mehpare asked about her relationship with Kemal.

"You may have guessed, Azra Hanım, what I want to ask of you."

"What?"

"You may not appreciate the extent of Kemal's illness, both physical and . . ."

"I'm well aware, Mehpare."

"You're not aware of everything, efendim. He was bedridden for two years. His lungs are weak. As are his kidneys."

"Why are you telling me this?"

"Because if he falls ill again he won't recover. He'll die. Doctor Mahir has told me as much. Other doctors have said the same."

"Then continue to tend him well. I've noticed how attentive you are."

"Azra Hanım, I'm begging you, don't drag him into this dangerous business."

"What are you saying? What dangerous business?"

"You know what I mean. You're a clever woman. I know you're working for the good of the country. I commend you for it. But if Kemal Bey were to leave our house, catch cold, wear himself out . . . He'd get ill and . . . and . . . I can't say it. He's already served his country. He was in the war. Please, leave him out of this. I'm begging you, Azra Hanım."

"You're worn out. You don't know what you're saying, Mehpare."

"Tell me, I'll do whatever it is you want him to do. I'm healthy; I'm strong."

"I don't want anyone to do anything. That's enough. Please stop talking nonsense." Azra sprang to her feet and began pacing the room.

"I'm upset enough as it is today, preparing to turn my home over to the enemy, and then this. The housekeeper will bring your tea. You've been of sufficient help to me, Mehpare, and you're free to go home when you've drunk it. Thank you."

Azra was walking through the doorway when Mehpare ran up and clutched her arm.

"Don't be angry with me. I'm only trying to protect him. And Azra Hanım, I'm ready to help any time you need me. I'll deliver messages. Drop off letters . . . Even weapons. Make use of me; I'm not afraid."

Azra was uncertain how to respond to the desperate young woman clinging to her arm, but she stopped and glanced around the room, taking in the salon that had once been brightly lit and airy, not at all like this place of empty shelves and shrouded armchairs, this reception room for ghosts. It was here that they'd celebrated her late brother's circumcision ceremony, and here that she'd been engaged to Necdet. In a few days, this room would echo with the stamping boots of English officers. The downstairs sitting rooms and anteroom would become classrooms for Christian children. And in that, Azra found solace . . . At least children would be racing through the house, much as she'd done at a happier time with her brother. It was a cruel life. And this woman clinging to her arm, begging. So many different kinds of suffering. It staggered you. A deep sense of compassion arose in her heart.

"Mehpare," she said, "I understand your concern, but there's nothing I can do. If Kemal Bey has made up his mind, he'll go and he'll assume whatever duties he chooses. I can't prevent that; neither can you. And if you think I'm a spy, I'm not. I lost my brother, and my husband, and the situation in which my father is spending his last days in Bursa is one he never deserved. There's nothing for me to cling to but my country, and I'd like to do my share to liberate it, that's all."

"I apologize. I never thought you were a spy."

"There's something else I'd like to say to you . . ."

"Please."

"Kemal Bey might leave home to join the war of liberation. And he might die in battle."

"God forbid!"

"God forbid. But thousands of men just like Kemal Bey are leaving their families and loved ones behind. And it's not just men, women are rushing off as well."

"But what can women do?"

"So many things, Mehpare. From preparing meals on the front lines, dressing wounds and rolling bandages, to taking up arms and standing guard, when necessary. There are many things women can do. Don't forget, soldiers need food, sleep and clothing."

"You're right."

"We have to think of our country, not our loved ones and sweethearts. Try to understand."

"Forgive me," Mehpare said, admitting defeat. "I hadn't seen it that way. But if Kemal does go, and if there is a place for women, couldn't I come?"

"Even if Kemal doesn't go anywhere you can join us. You know how to read and write, don't you?"

"Yes. And I know how to nurse."

"Good, I'll remember that."

"Are you going off to Anatolia?"

"My work here is done. I'll go when the time comes."

"I'd better get home before dark. If you need me, I'll come and help you," Mehpare said.

"Please stay and have tea with me. We'll chat a while longer and get to know each other better."

Head bowed, Mehpare re-entered the salon and reclaimed her place on the shrouded sofa. They were soon sipping tea from tulip-shaped glasses.

"Tea is normally served with cake but I'm afraid . . ."

"We've been making do without cake for ages," Mehpare confided. "It's ten days since we reached the bottom of the sack of flour, and supplies haven't come in from Beypazarı at all this month."

"We've still got a little flour. I'll tell them to give it to you."

"I wouldn't dream of imposing!"

"What do you mean, imposing! I'd planned to give everything in the pantry to the Housekeeper and Hakkı Efendi; you're certainly welcome to the flour. I'm not leaving anything for the enemy, I'd throw it out first."

When they'd finished their tea, Mehpare got up, threw her cloak over her shoulders and walked to the door.

"Thank you, Mehpare. With your help, we were able to pack everything up today," Azra said.

"Shall I come again tomorrow?"

"We're leaving the house tomorrow."

"Are you coming to stay with us?"

"I'm returning to the Asian Shore, to my mother."

"God grant you a safe journey," Mehpare said.

Azra embraced her, kissing her on each cheek. "Give my love to the family. And send my greetings and wishes for a safe journey to Kemal."

"Can I tell him we talked about my joining you?"

"Of course you can," said Azra.

"Send for me if ever you need me. I'll do whatever I can. Behice Hanım had so wanted to join you, but, with her condition . . ."

"Yes, I know."

"Goodbye Azra Hanım. Do take care."

"You too. We'll see each other again, Mehpare."

As Mehpare quickly walked home, a few paces ahead of Azra's manservant, her thoughts turned to their talk. If she went to Anatolia with Kemal she could protect him. She'd cook for him, make sure he stayed warm, give him his medicine. It was true, fighting for your country was a beautiful thing, but there was one point on which she differed with Azra: love came before country. First came Kemal, then country, then life, then pride, honor, morality, family, the world, paradise, whatever. But first and foremost came Kemal, always Kemal. If he went, she would follow; and if need be, to the gates of hell.

Taking Zehra with them, Saraylıhanım, Behice, her daughters, and Housekeeper Gülfidan moved to the house on the island at the beginning of June. This annual ritual took place around the time the first discarded watermelon rinds washed up on the shore: packages were tied up, suitcases slipped into dust covers, dinner plates stacked in tin boxes, and it was off to the island for the rest of the summer. At the first sign of the late September chill, back they would go to the house in Beyazit.

Life on the island was full of simple pleasures. Cushions were strewn onto carpets rolled out under pine trees, and from the sycamores hung swings for children, hammocks for adults. And all through the hot months, the many relatives of Behice Hanım and Saraylıhanım streamed in, stopping for the night or longer. İbrahim Bey was no fan of city life, and his visits to his daughter and grandchildren were timed so that he could indulge in the restorative, sweet-smelling air of the island. In addition to the overnight guests, neighbors were frequently invited to drop by for breakfast, late afternoon tea, a few hands of poker, a late evening chat over drinks, and their visits were returned, one after another. Fruit was picked from the mulberry, apricot, and peach trees, grapes from the vineyard, vegetables from the kitchen garden. The caretaker and his wife would snap into action after the slow winter months, racing here and there to maintain the household, but with the help of an extra cook hired to assist in keeping up with the many summer guests. At every hour of the day plumes of smoke curled up from the freestanding kitchen back behind the main house. Water was kept cool in glazed earthenware jugs; watermelons and honeydews were lowered in net bags into the garden well; but Ahmet Reşat had also had an icebox made for his summer house. Ice from the fishmonger was chipped, wrapped in salted canvas and placed onto the top and bottom shelves of the zinc-lined oaken cupboard, where rakı, as well as bottles filled to the brim with lemonade or sherbet, were neatly stacked. In this house, whose hosts were honored to be able to serve their guests icy cold juice and rakı, the flurry of refreshing offerings was without end.

The children had their dinner early in the back garden while the adults had theirs late, under the arbor out front, where, accompanied by saz and ud, they drank rakı and sang songs well into the night. Life on the island was devoted to entertainment and enjoyment, in stark contrast to the solemnity of the house in Beyazit. With its vineyard and vegetable garden, its pine grove and paved courtyard, the enormous green garden had always been five thousand square meters of paradise, as much for friends and relatives as for the children.

But that had all come to an end some years ago. War had taken its toll, and the family didn't dare allow Kemal to make the ferryboat ride to the island. Kemal would be spending another summer at the house in the city, along with Mehpare and Hüsnü Efendi. Except for weekends, Reşat Bey was too busy to join his family, a development that pleased Kemal as much as it distressed everyone else. Kemal looked forward to spending his last weeks in the house alone with his uncle, talking man to man and strengthening the bonds of their friendship. It also occurred to him that this might be just the opportunity he needed to win his uncle over to the cause.

− 9 −

July–August 1920

The summer of 1920 was unusually hot. Mehpare kept the shutters of the front windows closed and had arranged a shady spot under the linden tree for the men to sit in the back garden. Sadly, Reşat Bey rarely found the time to do so, even in the evening. The Grand Vizier and interior minister had gone abroad to negotiate the terms of the peace treaty, leaving Ahmet Reşat as acting interior minister. He'd stagger in to bed late at night and rush off in the morning without breakfast. The long man-to-man talks Kemal had imagined with his uncle were not to be, and he was sorely disappointed.

One oppressive July evening, Ahmet Reşat arrived home at an uncommonly early hour. Instead of going up to his room he washed his hands and face at the basin in the entry hall, asked Hüsnü Efendi to lay out rakı and all the usual accompaniments, without delay, and headed straight for the garden. It was immediately clear to Kemal that something had gone wrong.

He went out to the garden and up to the hammock where Reşat had stretched himself.

"Uncle, has something happened?"

"Why do you ask?"

"You never drink rakı without reason. Especially at this time of day."

"Today, my boy, the peace treaty dictated by the Allied Powers, the terms they've forced down our throats, was agreed to by the Council of State. Now do you understand what's happened? Do you understand why I want to drink myself under the table?"

"That I do, uncle."

"The Greeks marched into Tekirdağ yesterday. We've learned that an Armenian regiment entered Adana two days ago. Three days ago, the English occupied İzmir. Four days ago the Greeks invaded Bursa. The previous days saw Bandırma, Kirmastı, and Balıkesir fall one by one. Shall I continue?"

"No. Please don't."

"You'd think our land was a watermelon, out of which, each and every blessed day, some salivating infidel takes another bite. I feel like beating my head against the wall. And this, today, what happened today, has unnerved me like nothing else: today, it's become clear to one and all that we're expected to resign ourselves to whatever happens. In less than a week, the treaty will be signed. And so it ends . . . and so we're finished!" Ahmet Reşat rubbed his palms together. "Finished, just like that, the great Empire of the Ottomans, dead and gone. And God has willed that my generation will pay for its sins, whatever they've been, by signing the empire's death warrant. We're paying a terrible, terrible price. Hüsnü Efendi, bring me my rakı! What's keeping you?"

"Uncle, you've had a drink or two on the way home, haven't you?"

"And so what if I have? Has sobriety ever done me any good? If I stay sober will I prevent the invasion of yet another one of our cities tomorrow? Go on, run and get me some rakı, sit down and have a drink with me, would you?"

Helpless to console his uncle, Kemal circled the hammock. Hüsnü Efendi soon arrived in the garden bearing a large tray that he set on the table. Mehpare had lined little plates with tomatoes and sliced melon.

"The tomatoes are from our garden, sir," Hüsnü Efendi said.

"Then you'd best guard them with your life, Hüsnü Efendi, because soon enough they'll be all we have left," Ahmet Reşat responded.

"God save us!"

"God's not going to save us, efendi. God's forsaken us. God's been favoring his Christian subjects for quite some time now."

"Good Heavens, sir!"

"They've got money; they've got power; they've got science. What happened to us; tell me, efendi, what happened? No, never mind, let's say for the sake of argument that you don't know either," slurred Ahmet Reşat as he turned his attention to Kemal. "But what about you—a scholar, no expense spared for the best education; you, who claim to know more about everything than anyone: so tell me: why has God, in his infinite wisdom, deemed us worthy of this disgrace, this abomination? Why's He doing this to us and not to them?" He reached out his glass. "Fill it. And a glass of water. You drew it from the well, right? If you didn't, go get some. Might as well enjoy our well water while we can. Just so you know, its days are numbered too. And the garden, this garden, they'll take it away soon . . . Soon, very soon!"

Kemal and Hüsnü Efendi exchanged glances. This wasn't the Ahmet Reşat they knew and loved. Hüsnü Efendi had never seen his master in such a state, even on the ill-omened night of March 16th. He tugged Kemal by the arm, pulling him a step or two away. "Are we really finished young Master? Is it true what Beyefendi says?" he asked with trembling lips.

At a loss for words, Kemal reached for a proverb: "Patience, Hüsnü Efendi. We never know what may happen before sunrise. Only God knows what tomorrow may bring." Then he downed a glass of rakı, neat, like his uncle. His throat burning, a pleasant warmth spreading through his belly, Kemal sat down on the grass, next to the hammock. His uncle had long since finished his rakı but hadn't touched any of the food. His empty glass had been dropped to the ground; eyes closed, he lay suspended motionless in the hammock.

"Uncle . . . Is there no hope?"

"Kemal, Tevkif Pasha refused to sign the Treaty of Sevres in Paris. The Pasha detected the differences of opinion among the Allied Powers and hoped to exploit them to our advantage. He kept reviewing and rereading the treaty in an effort to buy time. But the invasion of Thrace has upset all our calculations."

"Uncle, I know all about that."

"There's plenty you don't know. The Council of Ministers reassembled today. We read each line of the dispatch they sent, poring over every word. It's even worse than we thought: the provisions they've imposed, both moral and material, are each harsher than the last. Not only are they exacting heavy reparations for our declaration of war and the subsequent loss of human life, they've added punitive payments for damage to property and goods. That much we could live with, but as far as some of the other conditions . . ."

Ahmet Reşat began coughing. As Kemal patiently waited for his uncle to finish, he retrieved and refilled his glass.

"For example, the Allies have decided to end forever our sovereignty over other peoples. From now on, we'll rule only Turkish subjects, and so, since we're the minority population in Thrace and İzmir . . . Just think, Kemal . . ."

Ahmet Reşat had taken another swallow of rakı and began coughing again. Kemal tried slapping the choking and spluttering man on the back.

"I think that last one went down the wrong way."

"In a show of magnanimity, they've deigned to allow Istanbul to remain our capital. But as for the Bosphorus . . . those sons of donkeys . . . The words stick in my craw . . ." Ahmet Reşat stopped speaking. His face had gone beet-red. He paused, not speaking, not coughing, not even breathing.

"Uncle! . . . Are you all right?" cried Kemal, as his uncle's scarlet complexion paled to pink, acquiring a greenish tinge. He dipped a napkin into the pitcher of water and dabbed at the beads of sweat on Ahmet Reşat's temples. "There's still a ray of hope, uncle. We're not finished."

"We're finished, my boy."

"No, we're not. The Ankara Government has announced to the world that it will never comply with the terms of the Sevres Treaty."

"We were in the middle of our discussions today when a telegraph arrived from Reşit Mümtaz Bey: Sign the treaty immediately, or the Allies will take Istanbul away from the Turks."

It was Kemal's turn to hold his breath.

Ahmet Reşat had spoken in such a low voice that Kemal wondered for a moment if he'd heard correctly.

"It's killed us, but we've signed the Treaty of Sevres."

Through an open window on the second floor came the sound of Mehpare softly singing as she accompanied herself on the ud:

> When I think of my fate, my sentence, I must tremble,
> Weep, though complaint will never cross my lips.

– 10 –

Confrontation

Her husband having failed to put in a single appearance at the island during June and July, Behice left her daughters with Saraylıhanım and, without waiting for September, returned to the house—a visit, she was shortly to learn, as untimely as it was early. In all their married life, Reşat Bey had never been this foul-tempered. Every evening, as soon as he got home, he'd sit under the arbor in the back garden and sip his rakı without a word to anyone, not even Kemal. She racked her brain for the cause: was her husband seeing someone else? He'd spent the winter in strange salons playing bridge. Had he been smitten by some strange and beautiful woman? No, that was impossible— Reşat Bey was far too well-bred to embark on an amorous adventure.

But men were men—and she was pregnant, her belly swollen, her breasts enormous, her cheeks puffy. Who knew? Saraylıhanım, though a troublesome woman, was the one person she could have unburdened herself to, and she was on the island. It's true that Mehpare was at home, but she shrank from such familiarity. Desperate, she decided to appeal to Kemal.

"There must be a reason Reşat Bey is so sad and subdued, Kemal, and I can't help wondering if it's an affair," she began, getting straight to the point. "I've always been like an elder sister to you, and would expect you to inform me."

"How could you think such a thing?" was Kemal's horrified response. "I hope and pray that my uncle never finds out you suspected him of something like that. He'd be terribly angry, and not a little offended."

"Well then what's the matter with him? I haven't seen a smile on his face since I returned from the island. If something's upsetting him, why doesn't he tell me? Aren't I his wife?"

"Listen to me carefully. What if my uncle were to say to you: 'I've been forced to sign the Treaty of Sevres. I've signed it knowing full well that it means the dismemberment of my country, the undoing of everything I hold dear, the termination of my own position, the blackening of my future. Still, we signed it at the Sultan's request—so that His Majesty wouldn't have to sign it himself, so that a door would be left open. That's why I don't want to speak to anyone. I want to be left alone with my shame and my sorrow.' Now, if he told you all that, what would you do?"

Behice stared at Kemal. "Why would he terminate his own position?" she asked. "And anyway, if he was acting at His Majesty's request, he wouldn't be responsible for any of it. The Sultan knows best. If he was simply obeying order, why should he be so upset?"

Kemal sighed through clenched teeth. "Forget everything I just told you, aunt," he said, as calmly as he could. "What you need to know is this: he isn't involved with a woman. Rest easy. His life is nothing but duty and heartbreak."

As Mehpare stepped into the garden with a basket of laundry on her arm she saw Kemal smoking a cigarette under the arbor. Hastily setting down the basket she bounded over to him.

"Put that out!" she cried, as sternly as she could. "Don't you remember what the doctor said? No more than three cigarettes a day, and only after meals."

"Let me finish it and I won't have one after dinner."

Mehpare reached out to snatch the cigarette. "Give it to me. It's finished anyway. Give it to me or I'll tell Saraylıhanım." Kemal threw the cigarette onto the ground and stubbed it out with his foot.

"I should have known you were up to no good when I didn't see you in the house. Every time you step into the garden you light up a cigarette."

Mehpare pulled a damp handkerchief out of the basket and began wiping Kemal's tobacco-stained fingertips, muttering all the while. "Your hands smell of tobacco."

"What's so vile about a cigarette?"

"It's bad for your lungs."

"What's done is done, Mehpare."

"A vice abstained from is a profit gained. And it was you, wasn't it, who was preparing to run off and save the nation? You need to be strong and healthy. You have to look after yourself."

"Without you by my side, there'll be no one to tend me and no one to jail me. I'll most certainly perish," Kemal joked.

"No you won't. I'll be looking after you."

"I meant after I left home."

"I'll be looking after you. I'm coming with you."

"There's no place for women where I'm going."

"Yes there is! Women are flocking to Anatolia, along with their fathers, husbands and brothers. And I'm going as well."

Kemal gaped in surprise. Mehpare never ceased to amaze. "Where did you pick all this up?"

"When I went out with Behice Hanım. And later, when I spoke with Azra Hanım. In fact, I went to another gathering with her."

"What kind of gathering?"

"A gathering of women."

"Does Saraylıhanım know about this? She'd never consent to something like that."

"When I told her I was going with Azra Hanım she agreed. She was staying with us, remember? That's when we went."

"Azra?"

"It wasn't her doing; it was I who insisted."

"And now you're off to Anatolia? Do you really think they'll let you go?"

"Sir, you're going. I wish I'd been able to prevent it, but you wouldn't listen to me, or to anyone else. I know you'll go, just as you went off to Sarıkamış without asking anyone's permission. Without you here, the walls of this house will close in on me. I won't be able to breath. So I decided I might as well leave and serve my country. Maybe now you'll have a higher opinion of me."

Kemal stood up and—without thinking of the spectacle he would present were anyone to spot them from the house—tightly enfolded Mehpare in his arms. The damp handkerchief fluttered to the ground. Mehpare pressed her face into Kemal's chest.

"I've always had a high opinion of you, Mehpare," he said. "Please, don't endanger yourself on my account."

"I want to go. I want to be of use. The girls have grown. There are servants for the housework. Let me go and become a nurse like the other women. They might even send me to wherever you've gone. So I'll be able to continue caring for you."

"I'll be leaving soon, but before I go to the front I'll be staying somewhere in Istanbul. I can't tell you where. I've been assigned some duties there. Then I'll be moving on. It's cold in the east and the unfortunate state of my lungs is no secret, so they'll be posting to an area with a milder climate."

"They shouldn't be posting you anywhere at all."

"How can you say that! They need everyone they can get. I'm a veteran, a trained soldier. My place is obviously on the battlefield. And you're set on going as well. State a preference for the western front. I'll find you, somehow."

Something was happening—Mehpare could feel it. Kemal was more than a bedmate: he was becoming a confidant, a collaborator. She'd been so envious of Azra, brokenhearted at the sight of Kemal lost in conversation, knee to knee, eye to eye with that blue-eyed woman. She'd despaired at the thought that there were some things she'd never be able to share with this man. But now, things were changing. She was changing. She'd gone from being the girl who runs errands, makes tea, to a woman like Azra. A savior. A patriot.

After taking a deep drag on her cigarette, Saraylıhanım flicked the ash onto her coffee saucer and fastened her eyes on Behice. "What's the meaning of this, Behice Hanım, my girl," she said. Behice knew what it meant to be interrogated by Saraylıhanım, and squirmed in her seat.

"I swear I know only as much as you. She's taking lessons. She's going to be a nurse."

"A nurse? Why does she need lessons? Hasn't she been doing just that all these years? Wasn't she the one who nursed Kemal the whole time he was ill?

"It was."

"She didn't seem to have these sorts of aspirations while she was actually nursing, did she? So why this sudden interest now?"

"Why are you so angry with me? Am I the one who put this idea in her head? Why don't you ask her, Saraylıhanım?"

"I have. She stares at me. Pigheaded. She won't answer my questions. I thought she might have told you something."

"She's set her mind on it. She's determined to become a licensed nurse. Azra may have led her astray."

"No doubt. But how could Reşat allow such nonsense! I told her she wasn't going anywhere, and she answered, impudent as can be, that he'd already consented. So it's come to this. We take her in, educate her, bring her up, do everything we can for her, and now she rebels."

"Well, maybe we'll get something out of it after all: her training may come in handy when I give birth. Not to mention that we're all getting older. Wouldn't it be convenient to have a nurse in the house?"

"The only person in this house who's getting old is me. I'm afraid I don't quite follow you."

"Don't imagine you're the only one affected by the passage of time. We're all growing old."

"That's beside the point. What really makes my blood boil is the way Mehpare follows Azra around, everywhere she goes, every blessed day of the week. If something were to happen to her one of these days, we'd be the ones held accountable."

"What could possibly happen? She walks the few steps to the Red Crescent and then comes straight back home. Suat cut her hand the other day. Mehpare bandaged it so beautifully you'd have thought it was Mahir's work. She did a better job than most doctors."

"The expression 'too clever by half' springs to mind. Mehpare was such a quick-witted little girl. It never pays to be too bright. A pity. May the Lord protect our girls."

"Saraylıhanım, why should He protect them from their own intellect?"

"Go on, laugh. A girl should know her place. She mustn't go round poking her nose into everything."

"I agree completely. But Mehpare simply wants to be a nurse. Surely there's no harm in that?"

"That's what you think! She was whispering with Kemal the other day. Mark my words, you'll see a lot more than nursing when all this is done and over."

"Do you mean you were listening to them?"

"I was, naturally."

"Where?"

"They were under the arbor. I walked over quite slowly and stood at the base of the linden tree. They didn't see me."

"How could you do that? It's beneath you."

"I couldn't care less what is or isn't beneath me. I learned what I needed to learn."

"And what's that?"

"As you know, our foolish Kemal is running off to save the country, yet again. Well, it seems that this time they're going to save it together. Mehpare will be treating patients on the front lines. And that's not the half of it. So much for imagining she'll be there to attend the birth of your child. Her intentions lie elsewhere."

"It's Azra's fault," said Behice. "It's all her doing. When she couldn't sway me, she must have moved on to the girl."

"Since when has it been the duty of women to save the country?" Saraylıhanım asked. "Men save the country. Women serve their men. A man who finds peace at home is able to save not only his country, but the world. Don't you agree?"

"But are you sure you heard them right?" Behice asked. "Does Mehpare really intend to go off to the battlefield?"

"That's what I heard. And I'm going to tell Reşat. Let's see what he means to do about it," she said, taking a final pull on her cigarette and extinguishing it. When Behice, who was sensitive to smoke, went over to the window and threw it open, Saraylıhanım scowled. Ahmet Reşat's bride had always been such a dainty slip of a thing. But they were all like that: either over-delicate, like Behice, or unbecomingly vigorous, like Mehpare. She had singularly failed to bring a proper woman into this house, and it vexed her. There was a time when she'd gone as far as to pair off—in her imagination—Kemal and Azra, but she'd quickly seen her folly. It was as though the Creator (heavens forefend) had set out to create a man and had, in a fit of absent-mindedness, molded Azra instead. May such a woman never set foot in this household again! Azra was out of the question, of course, but it was high time something was done about Kemal. If he'd had a wife, he'd never have embarked on this course of action. If the streets weren't filled with enemy soldiers she herself would venture out and, a mere three neighborhoods down, find a suitable bride for Kemal. But her hands were tied, thanks to these infidels. A new account reached her ears every day of their despicable conduct. No, it wouldn't do for a lady to venture out onto the streets, even one her age. Only madwomen like Azra had any business out and about these days.

"Depravity is contagious, my dear. Make certain Leman doesn't fall under the influence of Mehpare," Saraylıhanım said, "or she too may well be on her way to becoming a nurse before there's time to put a stop to it."

"Nothing could be more unlikely. Leman recoils from sickness. Fear kept her from so much as going up to her beloved Uncle's floor. Surely you've noticed the way she no longer sits on his lap. She won't even go near him."

"That's because she's grown up. She's far too old to be sitting on his lap. She'll be taking the veil soon."

"Mercy me, I'm not putting my daughter in a çarşaf just yet."

"Then what will you do? Have her wander about like those painted foreign hussies?"

"She's still a child."

"A child! Back in Beypazarı, girls her age are having children of their own. Didn't you see the way Mahir Bey was eying her last week?"

"Ridiculous. He could be her father."

"What's all this about his being her father? Do you think I'm not perfectly aware of Mahir's age? Back in the old days we were neighbors in Thessalonica. And it's always best for men to be ten or fifteen years older than their women. Women wear out so quickly, my girl. Why, I was no more than fifteen when I was wedded to my husband, God rest him, and he was almost forty."

"The times are changing, and traditions with them. I don't want my girls marrying old men. And as for Mahir Bey, he's a close friend of the family. If he looked at Leman, it was with the tenderness of a father, yes, a father admiring the sudden blossoming of his daughter."

That woman is pure malice, Behice sighed to herself as she arose from the divan and walked to the door. She turned round just as she reached it. "You'd be ill-advised to berate Mehpare, Saraylıhanım. She's attending nursing classes with Reşat Bey's blessing. A country at war is a country in need of nurses. If I weren't pregnant I'd be going to classes myself."

Without waiting for a response, Behice bustled up the stairs to her bedroom. Mahir had looked at Leman! Mahir Bey, a courteous gentleman, had made eyes at a mere slip of a girl! No, it was impossible. Saraylıhanım was absolutely intolerable at times. Behice stretched out on her bed and reached out her hand for a bottle of lavender cologne, which she splashed liberally upon her breasts and temples. She felt faint. When it passed, she placed her hand on her belly and waited attentively for signs of life. No, there was no movement at all. The infant in her womb was unusually docile. A clever, obedient son, just like his father. They'd name him Raif, after his grandfather.

Raif Reşat! Her son would be a wonderful person—he would grow to embody the meanings of his two names: Raif, "compassionate," and Reşat, "who follows the path of righteousness."

Azra was sitting next to Mehpare in one of the back rows of the classroom. They listened admiringly as Şahende Hanım wielded a long pointer to indicate on a map hanging from the blackboard the organizational structure of the Ottoman Red Crescent Association and described the various strategies for tending to the wounded and needy people of Anatolia. As the sons of the nation battled the enemy from the mountains and hilltops, their mothers, sisters and sweethearts must sustain and assist them. The women of this great land should lead the way, blazing the trail for their men. They should carry guns to the trenches, keep the cauldrons bubbling behind the front lines, assist in the dressing of wounds. Women's organizations, led by the Red Crescent and The Defense of Women's Rights, were organizing and opening branches in the countryside, where they would pass on their knowledge, skills and experience to their rural sisters.

At the conclusion of her lecture, Şahende Hanım asked her rapt audience if they were prepared to volunteer to go to Anatolia. There were thirty-three women in attendance. Among the seventeen who raised their hands were Azra and Mehpare.

"My honorable sisters, the bloodiest battles of all are currently taking place in our southern provinces. There is a dire need for nurses in the regions of Maraş and Antep."

"I'm prepared to go anywhere," Azra declared as she raised her hand a second time.

"If any of you speak French, please raise your hands." Azra's hand shot into the air a third time.

"Azra Hanımefendi, as you speak French, I'm writing you down for Antep, along with Necmiye Hanım and Neyir Hanım."

"What use will my French be there, efendim?"

"That entire region is under the control of France. Since all of the men who speak French are on the battlefield, there's a shortage of translators in the city. Your language skills will serve you well. Shall I jot down the name of your friend?"

"No, don't!" Mehpare cried.

"My friend's betrothed is being stationed on the Western Front. We would be grateful if you could arrange for Mehpare Hanım to be sent to İzmir."

"Ladies, we are at war. I beg you to rise above your eagerness to be reunited with your sweethearts and fiancés. Service must take priority over all else."

Azra rose to her feet. "Efendim, Mehpare Hanım wishes to be with her sweetheart only to serve him and to tend to his needs, if necessary. You see, Kemal Bey was seriously wounded in the Battle of Sarıkamış. He requires medical attention, even now."

Mehpare was deeply distressed as she braced herself for Şahende Hanım to ask what business a man in poor health had on the battlefield.

"All right then—I'm writing this young lady down for the Western Front," was all Şahende Hanım said. "And now I'm turning the floor over to Nakiye Hanım. For those of you who don't know her, Nakiye Hanım is the headmistress of the Fevziye Lycée. Please listen to her attentively, ladies."

As Azra and Mehpare were leaving the classroom, Şahende Hanım came up to them. "Azra Hanım," she said, "you will most likely be leaving quite soon. Before going off to Anatolia, where you'll be stationed with the others, you'll kindly agree to stay at a *tekke* on the Asian Shore. You'll be in safe hands there."

"Most certainly."

"You might have to wait at the lodge for some time. Our convoys are able to take the road only under certain conditions. We'll have to wait until a compliant sentry is on duty. You'll be boarding a wagon conveying supplies to Anatolia. Naturally, you'll be escorted by your husband."

"But, Hanımefendi, it's been many years since my husband passed . . ."

"A male escort will be acting as your husband. There are many men who are anxious to travel to Anatolia. They'd attract suspicion if they were to do so alone. You and the other women will all be traveling as a family. The *hodja* will provide you more particulars when you arrive at the lodge."

"When will I leave?"

"You'll be there by the weekend."

"What about me?" Mehpare asked. "Add your name and address to the list. When the necessary
preparations have been completed, I'll send word. You're a nurse, aren't you?"

"I am, but there's no work I won't do. I also know how to read and write."

"And you particularly want to go to İzmir?"

"To the Western Front."

"The Western Front is a wide one. First, I'll need to find out how we can be of assistance there."

"Shall I come back next week?"

"We'll send you word."

"You shouldn't take so much trouble, efendim. I'll come here and find out myself."

"You aren't intending to go off without your family's permission, are you? It would be inappropriate for you to join us without their blessing. When you come to the Red Crescent meeting next week, do be certain to bring a letter of permission from your parent or guardian."

Azra and Mehpare made their farewells and left. As they walked along Divanyolu towards Beyazit, they linked arms. They'd been fast friends ever since that day together, packing up Azra's furnishings. Reşat Bey had allowed Mehpare to enroll in the nursing classes Azra was attending. Twice a week they'd walk to class and back. Azra had been affected by Mehpare's unclouded intelligence, naïveté and sincerity; and in return, even if she still suffered an occasional fit of jealousy, Mehpare worshiped Azra, whom she embraced as a role model and elder sister.

Mehpare was deep in thought as they walked together on that particular day. "I'll ask Kemal Bey to write a letter for me," she said. "Şahende Hanım thinks I'm running away from home."

"Well aren't you?"

"Yes, but with Kemal Bey. I mean, he's running away as well, isn't he?"

"No, Mehpare. He's leaving home; you're running away from home. I think you should convince Kemal that it's best for you to leave together."

"We've already spoken about that. I'm going first, so I can be of benefit to my country. He was so pleased to hear me say that."

"Mehpare, you're not doing all this just to please him, are you?"

"I'm doing it to be with him and to please him. But Azra Hanım, believe me when I say I'm happy to be of service to my country. It's just that my love for Kemal outweighs anything else."

"You should go to your death only for your ideals, Mehpare."

"With Kemal gone, I'm as good as dead."

"Mehpare," Azra said, "I wish I could love a man the way you do."

"Didn't you love your husband?"

"I loved him a great deal, but not like that."

"There's still time for you."

"I doubt it. I'm thirty-two."

"That doesn't matter," Mehpare protested.

"How do you know?"

"I feel it."

Azra silently wished to herself that Mehpare's instincts were right. She was to remain at Reşat Bey's house for a few more days, then cross to the other shore. When they arrived at the top of the street leading to the house, Mehpare stopped walking.

"There's something else I feel, Azra Hanım," she said.

"What?"

"That you're going to fall in love. Like me."

"Really. When?"

"Soon."

As Kemal made his way up the stairs to his room he was surprised to see his grandmother on the landing. She was dressed in a light blue nightdress and a long, white, lacy head covering normally reserved for prayer. By the light of a flickering candle her elongated shadow danced across the wall.

"And for what reason, my Sultan," Kemal said, "have you honored this floor of the house with your presence? What brings you up here?"

"Into your room! We'll talk there."

"Okay, okay—I'm going. Why so rough, grandmother? What have I done?"

Kemal walked through the door and set his own candleholder on the desk. The electricity had been cut for some days and kerosene was in short supply. Candles were the only source of illumination, but even in the wan light cast by two small flames Kemal could read the anxiety on the elderly woman's face. Saraylıhanım closed the door, sat down on Kemal's bed and gestured to a place next to her: "Sit."

Kemal sat down as instructed.

"Now listen, Kemal."

"At your command, my Sultan."

"Don't interrupt. I'm in no condition for your jokes." Kemal listened with increasing concern. "What have you done to that girl?"

"Which girl?"

"How many girls are there in this house?"

"A lot of them, actually. Leman and Suat, and Mehpare, and Katina comes and goes . . . Azra's a frequent visitor . . ."

"Stop it. I want the whole truth and I want it now. What have you done to Mehpare?"

"I haven't done a thing."

"Don't lie to me."

"Why would I lie?"

"Mehpare's gone thick around the middle; her breasts have grown."

"My, what sharp eyes you've got, grandmother. I've noticed no such thing."

"Can you guess what's happening to her, Kemal?"

"She's getting fat."

"No, she is not, my boy. She's not getting any fatter at all."

"Well in that case, I'd say you're seeing things. You must be mistaken."

"I'm not easily fooled, boy."

"Then out with it, please."

"Mehpare's pregnant."

Kemal sat up, in genuine astonishment. He blushed, and with a quavering voice said: "You've decided she's pregnant just because she's put on a little weight?"

"No, that's not all. I've made some other observations."

"What?"

"Mornings, she's nauseated by the smell of cooking in the kitchen. And there are other signs, none of your business."

Angry and amazed at himself for not having considered the implications of his relations with Mehpare, Kemal bowed his head.

"Now, let's get to the crux of the matter. This girl grew up in our house under our supervision. If you are responsible for this, confess it immediately. It isn't in Mehpare's nature to enter into relations with someone she doesn't know. Though it's true she's been trailing around after Azra, walking with her to and from the Red Crescent, it's absolutely unthinkable that she would get up to any devilry outside the house. She wouldn't dare. That leaves you."

Kemal sat in silence, staring at the tips of his slippers. "Kemal, look me in the eye." Kemal reluctantly raised his eyes and looked at his grandmother. "Are you willing to place your hand on the Koran and tell me you aren't responsible for this?" Kemal didn't answer. "I'm going to my room to get my Koran. You'll swear. And then I'll believe you. If I'm convinced that you bear no responsibility, I'll do whatever it takes to make the girl talk. I'll find out what I need to know. And when I do, both Mehpare and that defiler of women are going to rue the day!"

"Leave the girl alone, grandmother," Kemal growled. "If she's pregnant, it's my doing. Don't do anything to hurt her. She's innocent. I coaxed her, coerced her . . . It's my fault."

"Aren't you ashamed of yourself? We were trusted with that girl's care."

Kemal was dumbfounded: Saraylıhanım knew full well that he had barely glimpsed a woman for many years; he'd had precious little opportunity to conjure up the image of a woman, let alone gratify himself with one.

"I'm sorry, grandmother. It's not what I wanted. I was overcome. It happened one night, while I was having a fit of nerves. I'm sorry."

"I'll speak to the girl tomorrow. If she's pregnant . . ."

"Weren't you absolutely certain of that just a moment ago?"

"I still am. But it's best she confirms it herself. If she does, you'll immediately inform your uncle that you want to marry her. And next week we'll hold the nuptials here at home. Your uncle must never know that she was pregnant."

"Why not?"

"You'll have disgraced yourself in his eyes. He'll never forgive you, or her."

Kemal sprang to his feet and angrily paced the room. "What difference does it make? My political views have lowered me enough in his eyes," he said.

"This isn't a question of your views. It's a question of purity, honor. If he finds out, you'll never be able to exonerate yourself."

"You're right."

"Pray that I'm mistaken. But if she's not pregnant, I'm sending her straight back to her aunt's. I'll find an explanation for her."

"But if she's not pregnant, why send her away?"

"To put an end to your relations, of course. With the daughters of pashas available in droves, is Finance Minister Reşat Bey's nephew to be snapped up by a maid?"

"But isn't Mehpare our relative? Are you telling me now that she's not?"

"Of course she is; she's my uncle's granddaughter on my mother's side."

"And aren't we direct descendants of the chieftains of Kamçeriko?"

"Naturally."

"Who could be more desirable than a girl of such noble lineage?"

"If I hadn't brought her up and educated her myself . . ."

"So she grew up under your supervision, was reared and tutored right here in the house."

"I'll permit you to marry Mehpare only if you're the father of her child. If she isn't pregnant, you'll end your relations, and I'll marry you off myself."

Kemal sighed in disgust.

"Enough of that," his grandmother said. "You've made your bed, now lie in it. Pray that I'm wrong and the girl isn't pregnant. But if she is—tell no one. Leave everything to me."

"I'm marrying her whether she's pregnant or not."

"There's no need unless she's pregnant. If not, I'll find her a suitable husband in due time."

"Don't trouble yourself. I'm marrying Mehpare."

"Look at you: as incorrigible as you are guilty! We'll decide what to do after the midwife's visit tomorrow."

Saraylıhanım slowly rose to her feet and strutted toward the door; before sweeping out into the hallway, she turned round, looked at Kemal, and said: "Idiot!"

He sat there listening as his grandmother creakily descended the wooden stairs. Then he bolted for the room opposite. Mehpare was sitting in bed brushing her hair. When she heard the door open, she held up a brass candlestick to see who it was.

"Oh, it's you. I wasn't expecting you. Can't you sleep?"

"There's something you need to tell me, Mehpare."

"But I told you everything the moment I got home. I'll tell you again if you like. We gathered at the school again today. You know Şayeste Hanım, the midwife and head of the organization . . ."

Kemal cut her off. "That's not what I'm talking about," he said. "There's something else you need to share with me."

"All right. I'll be leaving a few days after you, going to Anatolia. I'll be on the opposite shore, at the Özbek Dervish Lodge, for a couple of nights. When the convoy sets off, I'll head straight for İzmir. And then . . ."

"Mehpare!"

"What?"

"Tell me this: Are you pregnant?"

Mehpare leapt from the bed and stood across from Kemal. Her almond eyes downcast, a look of dread on her face, she spoke in a low voice: "I don't know, sir."

"What do you mean, you don't know. What's there not to know?"

"I'm not sure."

"Well, after we summon the midwife tomorrow, you will be."

Mehpare sank to her knees and clasped Kemal's legs. "I'm begging you sir, don't touch my baby. I'll leave immediately if that's what you want. I'll go to Anatolia before you do. You'll never see me again. Don't touch my baby and I'll kiss the soles of your feet."

"How can you talk like that?" Kemal said as he seized her under the arms and struggled to pull her to her feet. She'd gone completely limp and her face glistened with sweat.

"Mehpare, are you all right? You haven't fainted, have you? Don't you dare faint. Come on, lie down."

Kemal hauled Mehpare onto the bed and slid a pillow beneath her head.

"Mehpare, what are you so afraid of? Is it Saraylıhanım?"

"Sir, in God's name, don't touch my baby."

"Well, if you're pregnant, the baby's mine as much as yours. How could I let anything harm my own child?"

Mehpare started crying. "You mean you'll let me have it?"

"Of course I will! We'll get married as soon as possible, and you'll bring our baby into the world." Mehpare leaned her head against Kemal's chest and began sobbing. "What kind of man do you take for me, Mehpare? A monster? Why didn't you tell me?"

"I was afraid you wouldn't want it."

"Let's say I didn't. How did you expect to hide your condition?"

"I'm going off to Anatolia in any case . . . I hoped to make my farewells and leave everything else in God's hands."

"There's no longer any need for you to go anywhere. We'll get married this week before I leave this house."

"Married or not, I'm going to Anatolia. I'll wait for you there. All I ask is that you write me a letter of permission."

"Impossible, Mehpare. I didn't know you might be pregnant when we made our plans. Anatolia is no place for a woman with child. You can't go."

"I'm strong. I'll manage. Don't leave me behind, I'll be sick with worry."

"No. You'll stay here, you'll have our baby. This war will be just like all the others; it won't last forever. Then we'll be together. We'll raise our child."

"I'd die without you."

"You won't die, Mehpare. Neither of us will."

"Sir, please don't leave me behind."

"Anatolia is turning into a bloodbath. The occupation forces are everywhere, marauding, wreaking havoc. Disease is rife. People are starving. How can you possibly expect to have a child under such conditions?"

"What about you? How do you expect to survive such conditions?"

"I'm not pregnant."

Mehpare started laughing. Kemal pulled the blanket over the two of them, blew out the candle and held Mehpare tight as he murmured, "Good night. Let's get a good night's sleep, the three of us. We'll be busy tomorrow. I'll give my uncle the good news. We'll find a hodja, we'll begin preparations for the wedding. We've got our work cut out for us."

"I wonder what Saraylıhanım will say about this?" Mehpare asked.

"May God grant you both a lifetime of happiness, is what she'll say."

"What about your uncle? Will he consent to the marriage?"

"I'll do everything I can to get his consent." Kemal stared thoughtfully at the ceiling for a moment before saying, "I'll give him no choice but to consent, Mehpare."

"Please don't tell him about the baby, I'd die of shame."

"Don't worry, we're not telling anyone about the baby. But if Saraylıhanım realizes on her own, it's out of our hands."

"They'll all know the truth once it's born; all I ask is to hold my head high until then."

"These are terrible times: its father is off to war; its mother is worried sick. It'd be perfectly normal for the baby to come early, don't you think?"

Silent, they lay in each other's arms for a while. Then Mehpare quietly asked, "How did you know, sir?"

"Nothing about you could ever escape my notice," said Kemal.

Mehpare snuggled closer to her lover. It wasn't long before she'd fallen into her first untrou- bled sleep in months.

When Ahmet Reşat walked into the selamlık, Kemal closed the windows and drew the heavy velvet curtains.

"Are you chilly, son? It's nice outside, why are you sealing us in like this?"

"The matter we'll be discussing is private. I don't want anyone eavesdropping."

"Who could possibly hear us?"

"Female eyes and ears haunt every nook and cranny of this house."

"Alright, out with it. What's so urgent and private that you have to hide it from our women?"

"The long-awaited news has arrived at last. I'll be leaving the house on Friday."

"Oh?" was all Ahmet Reşat said; though he was shaken by the news, the face he presented to his nephew remained composed.

"I'll be traveling to the farm. There are numerous documents that need my attention: new identity papers have to be prepared for those traveling to Anatolia. Once we've procured sufficient arms, they'll be shipped to the front—and, as you know, me with them."

"Kemal, I advised you against going to Sarıkamış, but you paid me no heed and barely escaped with your life. Once again, I'm going to advise you against leaving. But since I can't stop you, I wish you a safe journey. Please keep us informed of your movements."

"When I leave for Anatolia I'll send word to Beypazarı. They'll be in touch with you. That way you won't attract any unwanted attention, uncle."

"You've thought this through."

"Any news I send will be conveyed via Beypazarı. You have family there, and it's only natural that you'd correspond regularly, isn't it?"

"It is."

"If I need money for any weapons we're able to locate in Anatolia, I'll ask you for help. 'Sugar' is the code for 'arms'. There's been a shortage of sugar in the city, and so it's sent from Beypazarı. If any of my letters are to fall into the wrong hands one day, they mustn't arouse suspicion."

"I doubt they'd read letters addressed to me. But it's best to take precautions."

Uncle and nephew both seemed to recognize that they might not see each other for a very long time. They were sad, but content to sit in silence for a few moments, breathing the same air. Ahmet Reşat thought back to the first time he'd held Kemal. He'd become an uncle very young. As he stood there that day, cradling Kemal in his arms, absolutely terrified of hurting him, he'd known, along with everyone else, that the infant's father would probably not be coming back. Ahmet Reşat would be the closest thing to a father Kemal ever knew. And as he gazed at the fully grown Kemal he wanted to blurt out, "Don't go; stay here. And if you can't work I'll look after you but I couldn't bear your death." He said nothing for several minutes, but when he did speak it was with a quavering voice.

"Son, they won't be able to look after you like we have. Mind your health. Remember to take your medicine. I must have had a premonition of some kind: I've already asked the health minister if he'd help locate some of the medicines we've been unable to find. He's sending me a box tomorrow. Take it with you. You'll never find any out in the countryside."

"Bless you, uncle."

They fell silent again. This time, Kemal was wondering where to begin. Plucking up courage, he finally said, "I have a favor to ask of you before I go."

"What? Do you need money?"

"No. I need your blessing and your consent."

"You already have them."

"Uncle, there's something else, something personal. I feel extremely abashed as I tell you this, but it's time I confessed. I've fallen in love with Mehpare. With your permission, I'd like to marry her before I leave home."

Ahmet Reşat stared with his mouth open. "Marry Mehpare?"

"Yes, uncle. With your permission."

"Mehpare's like a daughter to us. She's a blood relative, my boy. Would it be proper?"

"She's a distant relative. And it's most fortuitous that she's a member of our household. I leave confident that she'll be provided for while I'm gone."

"Your grandmother would never allow it."

"I'm the one getting married, uncle."

"She raised you, Kemal. She's within her rights."

"Saraylıhanım has pinned her hopes on an advantageous marriage for me. I'm ill; I'm wanted by the government; I'm about to embark on an adventure whose ending I can't predict. No one would want me but Mehpare, be assured of that."

"My boy, if what you say is true, isn't it rather hard on Mehpare?"

"She's as eager to get married as I am. We fell in love with each other when she was nursing me."

"I hope you realize that if you marry her over Saraylıhanım's objections the girl's life will be hell here. I myself wouldn't want to assent to this marriage without first obtaining her consent. She is our elder."

"Don't be anxious on that score. If you allow us to get married immediately, Mehpare will not remain here at home when I go to the farm. She's going to Anatolia with Azra, to serve her country."

"What!"

"You heard me, uncle. The daughters of every respectable family in the city are prepared to make the ultimate sacrifice. Plenty of them have traveled to the countryside to organize the village women and work behind the front lines."

"Good Lord, a girl from my house out wandering the roads . . ."

"She's going away to save her country, not to wander. You should feel honored, uncle."

"Abandoning home isn't the only honorable way to serve the nation."

"Mehpare has another reason for leaving. When I'm sent to battle I'm going to have her join me. She'll continue to look after me and my health."

"So that's it! That's what was behind Mehpare's sudden desire to attend nursing classes."

"Don't speak ill of her, uncle. She truly wished for her nursing skills to be of benefit to us all."

"Son, you seem to have arranged everything without consulting me," said Ahmet Reşat. "Once you're married she's your responsibility. I won't interfere. But if she weren't your wife, I'd never let her set off on such an escapade."

"You'll give us your blessing, won't you?"

"I'm damned if I do and damned if I don't," Ahmet Reşat grumbled. "Were she to have run off after you without having been married first, how could I possibly look her family in the eye?"

"It wouldn't be your fault. She's a grown woman. You'd simply explain that she was acting on her own."

"I hold myself responsible for any action taken by anyone under my guardianship. How else do you think you've managed to upset me so greatly over the years?"

"Uncle, with your consent, I'll arrange for Ömer Hodja to officiate at the nuptials. Again, with your consent, I'll send Hüsnü Efendi to Aunt Dilruba's to invite them to the ceremony. They can bring along their children and we can finish everything by Thursday."

"Arrange the hodja first, then we'll send Hüsnü to Dilruba's. Be certain to handle this before you leave home, Kemal," Ahmet Reşat said resignedly.

"As you wish, Uncle," said Kemal, bending to kiss his hand.

"Congratulations. May it bring you happiness."

"If it would upset you for Mehpare to go to Anatolia, I promise to persuade her to stay at home."

"I can't approve of our girls rushing off to Anatolia. I don't even want to think what could happen to a lone girl in a country at war, with soldiers everywhere. If Mehpare is determined to be of service, she can do it here, under my protection. She could work at a hospital in Istanbul. Why should she have to go out into the countryside?"

"I'll talk to her. I won't allow her to go anywhere."

"It would be best."

"I have one more favor to ask," Kemal said.

Reşat Bey muttered a prayer as he peered at Kemal over his spectacles.

"Would you break the news to Saraylıhanım?" asked Kemal, with a sheepish grin.

"Enough! I'm not telling her!" protested Ahmet Reşat. "You made me break the news of your leaving; I've done quite enough. Either pluck up the courage to tell Saraylıhanım yourself, or start making other plans!"

As Saraylıhanım left the kitchen, she called out, "Bring my coffee to the arbor, Mehpare."

"I'll send it with Zehra, efendim," Mehpare said as she looked up from the *dolma* she was busily preparing.

"Bring it yourself."

"My hands smell like onion—your coffee cup would . . ."

"Bring it yourself, I said." Saraylıhanım had been exceedingly bad-tempered for the past two days. Putting aside her work, Mehpare lathered her hands with soap. Saraylıhanım was waiting under the arbor in a large wicker chair. Mehpare cautiously set the coffee on the end table and slowly raised her brown eyes to meet Saraylıhanım's stern stare.

"I know the reason for this wedding, Mehpare." Mehpare lowered her eyes. "When I arranged for you to come to this house I thought you were an honorable girl, a clever girl."

"I am, efendim."

"An honorable girl would never do what you've done!" Mehpare waited with her eyes on the ground. "Regarding your cleverness, I have no doubt. May it serve you as well in the future."

"But I loved him, efendim. I loved him very much."

"Enough. I'd meant for Kemal to marry well. But you were too clever for me."

"Efendim . . ."

"Don't interrupt me. Now listen, Mehpare. No one knows about your condition, and no one will. I won't have my nephew disgraced in his uncle's eyes. I'll speak to the midwife, handle everything myself. Şayeste and her ilk are not to set foot in this house. I hope you realize that. Distress at the absence of a distant husband will induce a premature birth. Do I make myself clear?"

With burning cheeks and tear-filled eyes Mehpare replied, simply, "I understand, efendim."

"Tell me, how many months has it been?"

"I'm not sure."

"What's that supposed to mean? Are you telling me you don't know when this wicked act occurred?"

Mehpare didn't dare to say: If you mean the first time, of course, I know exactly when it happened. But I have no idea when I became pregnant. I was walking on air, oblivious to everything but him. She bit her lip, gazed at the ground.

"Speak up! When did the bleeding stop?"

"It's never been regular . . . I've been queasy for about a month . . . While you were away at the island . . ." Mehpare stammered.

"While we were at the summer house. Of course. I should have known. I wish we'd taken you with us. Foolish of me. Are you telling me you're two months pregnant?"

"I suppose so."

"I see. Now get out of my sight."

For a brief moment, Mehpare had to lean on the table for support. Then she returned to the kitchen. She was guilty, and she knew it. But she had no regrets. Once Kemal left the house she'd be left to the mercy of Saraylıhanım, berated daily. When the child was born, anyone who took the time to make a few simple calculations would learn the truth and she could well end up without a friend in the house. She'd be known as the hussy who'd seduced the young master."

Well, wasn't she?

Of course she was. She'd done all she could, first to get Kemal to notice her, then to perpetuate his interest.

No! She wasn't a hussy. She'd hidden her love as she'd tended to her patient, and it was Kemal who'd kissed her. Kemal. It was he who had struck the match. She closed her eyes, remembering.

"Mehpare Abla, are you all right?"

"I'm fine, Zehra. I had a stabbing pain, but it's gone now."

"Where?"

"In my heart."

"There's no fighting that sort of pain at your age," the housekeeper laughed knowingly.

Mehpare placed a pinch of mincemeat on top of a vine leaf and rolled it into a cylinder. Life behind the trenches, with all of those guns, those bullets, would be easier than life in this house. She was sure of that. But she'd endure anything for the sake of the baby. She'd deliver a healthy boy for Kemal. A boy? How did she know? Would it really be a boy? Of course. She would bear her darling a son. She felt it.

– 11 –

October 1920

The wedding was held at home, three days before Kemal's departure. Among the small circle of honored guests was Mehpare's aunt, along with her daughters, Mualla and Meziyet, and her son, Recep, all of them there to spend the night. Around the bride's neck they placed a "five in one," the traditional necklace of five gold coins. Mehpare couldn't help wondering which needy waif had been deprived so that she, the orphaned niece, would be able to receive such a valuable present. Her aunt had often told her how upset they'd been to send her off so young. "It was for your own good, Mehpare, so you wouldn't have to suffer in poverty with the rest of us," she'd always say. But if it was really for her own good, why hadn't they sent one of their own children to Reşat Bey's mansion?"

"Saraylıhanım chose you," her aunt had said. "Out of all the children, it was you she chose."
Had Mehpare been selected because she was prettier than her aunt's girls?
They too were tall, well-formed, comely. Mehpare had wondered long and hard about why she'd been chosen. Finally, she'd

understood: it wasn't because she was prettier, smarter or better behaved; no, it was simply because she was alone in this world. Saraylıhanım had wanted her because she was utterly helpless, completely dependent. Were she to be mistreated, she could complain to no one; were she to run away, there was no home for her to run to, no mother and father to receive her with open arms. Cunning woman. But God works in mysterious ways: she'd been sent to a strange house for her own good, and the wheel of fortune had indeed turned, and something wonderfully good had happened to her: she was now a bride in the same house where she'd arrived as an impoverished stray. Some would say she'd seduced the young master; others would claim that his love for her was that of a kind-hearted man for an orphan. Say what they would, it was a storybook tale, complete with a happy ending. And she was its heroine.

At this very moment, Saraylıhanım was slipping a bracelet of beaten gold onto her wrist, the very bracelet Reşat Bey had brought to his aunt from Damascus many years before. How Mehpare had admired it! She remembered the day she'd stroked it with her fingertips, lingering over the clasp, which was shaped like a pair of serpent's heads with eyes of ruby.

"You're quite partial to that bracelet, aren't you?" Saraylıhanım had said.

"I adore it."

"God willing, one day your husband will provide you with one even finer."

She'd closed her eyes and imagined a faceless husband placing such a bracelet on her wrist. And now, there it was. And as for the husband: for weeks and months she had studied Kemal so intently that even if she weren't to see him for years, she would remember, always, each detail of that beloved face, down to the curve of his lash.

Dilruba Hanım was crying, while out in the hallway Ömer Hodja prayed in a deep bass voice. Kemal was on the other side of the door, with the hodja. When they finished praying, Kemal would respond: "I take Mehpare Hanım at Allah's command, in the name of the Prophet and of my own free will." Words would be spoken, words mysterious and unintelligible to Mehpare, like *mihr-i müeccel* (the part of the wife's dowry paid to her by her husband upon consummation of the marriage) and *mihri-i muaccel* (the part of the dowry agreed to be paid to a wife if divorced or widowed); the papers would be signed and, from that moment onwards, she would be Kemal's wife.

Kemal's lawfully wedded wife! What more could I ask of you, almighty Allah? All I ask is that Kemal return to me, safe, in good health. I don't care if I'm lavished with bracelets, with "five in ones"—I don't care if I'm beaten, degraded. Nothing else matters. Just bring me my husband, God, that's all I'm asking.

Her head bowed, Mehpare glanced out of the corner of her eye at the people sitting in the room. Perhaps she'd been unfair to them? Yes, she'd suffered Saraylıhanım's rebukes, but which of them hadn't had to endure that woman's tongue? Since the day she'd stepped into the house, no one else had treated Mehpare with anything but respect: the children thought of her as an elder sister; Behice Hanım was mild-mannered by nature; Reşat Bey had always been kindly. She'd been scolded on occasion by

Saryalıhanım, that was all. It was she herself who had argued that a stranger would never be able to tend to Kemal's needs, thus preventing the employment of a nurse. No one had expected or even wanted her to shoulder so much work, but she'd voluntarily undertaken every task she could, and, over time, they'd come to take it for granted. If she'd gone from impoverished relative to overworked servant, it was her own doing.

The moment the wedding ceremony was over, all of the women, led by Leman and Suat, rushed over to Mehpare. Lining up to offer their congratulations were her aunt, her aunt's daughters, Behice, housekeeper Gülfidan, Azra Hanım, Zehra and, last of all, Saryalıhanım, who remained seated but reached out her right hand for Mehpare to kiss. Mehpare kissed the hands of all her elders, was practically smothered by the girls and tightly embraced by Azra. Saraylıhanım was even sufficiently moved at last to place a cool kiss in the center of her forehead.

Next, Mehpare received the men. She kissed the hands of Reşat Bey and the hodja, and shook the hand of her aunt's son. The last man to enter the room was Kemal. As he stood facing his bride she made to kiss his hand. But he stopped her, took her hands and gazed into her eyes. Mehpare expected him to say something, but not a word left his lips. He seemed too stunned to speak.

Zehra brought in a tray of mint-scented lemonade. From now on, Zehra would be responsible for running and fetching. Mehpare had risen to the rank of "young bride."

Behice had ensured that the wedding feast was as lavish as the conditions of the day permitted. There was the traditional wedding soup, rice pilaf with chunks of lamb, two cold vegetable dishes drizzled with olive oil, and *hoşaf*, a cold drink made of stewed fruit. No wedding would be complete without the dessert of sweetened, spiced rice—*zerde*—but it had been impossible to find saffron. There hadn't been any sugar for the lemonade and the other desserts either, so they'd been sweetened with the honey sent by İbrahim Bey a week earlier.

After dinner, Leman and Suat played the piano and the violin together and Aunt Dilruba's daughters sang to the accompaniment of the ud. Even so, the gaiety of a wedding party was missing: the atmosphere in the house that day had the solemnity of a funeral. Other than Mehpare's aunt and her daughters, no one seemed to be in high spirits. When the men retired to the selamlık to bubble noisily at their water pipes the women began conversing in the sitting room on the upper floor. Azra sat next to Mehpare on the divan and in a low voice said, "You've changed your mind about going to Anatolia, Mehpare."

"Kemal Bey wouldn't allow it."

"When you said you'd never leave him, I assumed . . ."

"I wanted very much to go, but Kemal Bey thought it would be wrong of me to join him."

"My word! Your Kemal Bey was singing quite a different tune just ten days ago. So, heroism and duty are sacred as long as they're performed by others."

"It's something else, Azra," said Mehpare, "something I can't explain right now. I'll tell you later."

"What is it?"

"A personal matter. Concerning me."

Without another word, Azra carefully studied Mehpare out of the corner of her eye. "When's Kemal leaving?" she finally asked.

"Friday."

"Does Reşat Bey know?"

"He's known for some time. Saraylıhanım has been told as well, but she didn't expect him to be leaving quite so soon. She wept for hours and wouldn't be comforted."

"So there's a reason for her swollen eyes. Well in that case, I'll say farewell to Kemal tonight. I'll be leaving the house first thing tomorrow morning. I suppose you newlyweds will be asleep at that hour."

"You might have the opportunity to see Kemal again at the farm or somewhere in Anatolia. I'm the one you should be making your farewells to." Tears sprang into Mehpare's eyes.

"Don't cry, Mehpare. Keep your composure. Who cries on their wedding day?"

Mehpare wiped at her face. "You're right, Azra. And when are you off to Anatolia?"

"Next week, I hope."

"May God watch over you."

When the men finished chatting over their water pipes they trooped up to the sitting room—at which point Zehra and the housekeeper went downstairs to air out the selamlık and prepare a bed for Aunt Dilruba's son. Dilruba Hanım and her daughters were to spend the night in Mehpare's room, while Azra would be staying in Kemal's room. A double mattress was placed in the large room where Azra had stayed previously, now the nuptial chamber. The newlyweds would have only a few days together, but those few days were among the happiest of Mehpare's life, and would sustain her later, during the hard times. After about half an hour of conversation among the assembled guests, Reşat Bey announced, "All right everyone, the time has come to send the newlyweds to their chamber."

"I'm rather tired myself," Behice said to the guests. "May I request your kind permission to retire to my room as well?"

When Reşat Bey and Behice Hanım had gone to their room, Azra came up to Kemal. "I'll be staying in your bed tonight. Aren't you afraid I'll rummage through your things?" she laughed. "I remember how worried my big brother was that I'd go through his books and papers, or find his love letters."

"Azra, if you knew how much I missed those days, growing up together. The most carefree time of my life . . . but it's only much later that you realize how precious they are."

"Well then, here's a word of advice from me: make sure you appreciate how precious your wife is. Don't leave it till later. She's devoted to you," Azra said.

"I know."

"Is that why you've prevented her from going to Anatolia?"

"It's important she stay at home . . . for health reasons."

Azra gave Kemal a knowing smile, but contented herself with the words, "You're quite the rake, my dear." Then she extended her hand. "I'm leaving early tomorrow. We might not see each other for a long time. Goodbye, Kemal."

"I'll see you to your room," Kemal said. "We'll say goodbye upstairs."

Mehpare's dejected demeanor at the sight of Azra and Kemal whispering and laughing as they left the room together wasn't lost on Saraylıhanım, who, with a slight lift of her chin and arched eyebrows, indicated that Mehpare was to follow them. "Mehpare, why are you just standing there, why don't you take your aunt's girls up to their room? And don't forget to take a candle with you."

Mehpare shot a look of gratitude at Saraylıhanım and turned to her aunt.

"Please follow me, Aunt."

"Follow your husband, Mehpare. We'll find our room on our own," said Dilruba Hanım.

"Mehpare Abla, I'm going down to the kitchen for a glass of water. Will you show me where it is?" asked one of Dilruba's daughters. Mehpare had no choice but to lead the girl downstairs, but before doing so she kissed Saraylıhanım's hand, pressed it to her forehead and bid goodnight to the others.

"Mehpare Abla, he's so handsome! However did you manage to steal his heart? Well done!" enthused Meziyet the moment they were in the kitchen and the door tightly shut. "Saraylıhanım's stewing, but you just ignore her!"

Mehpare's face went bright red. "Come on, get your water and go to your room, Meziyet," she said as she pulled the muslin cloth off the mouth of the earthenware jug.

"Why are you mad at me? I'm only telling the truth. And mother says she'll make me a better match than ever, now you're the daughter-in-law of a minister."

"It's late, Meziyet. I'm tired. We'll talk about all that tomorrow."

"But we're going home tomorrow morning."

Exactly, Mehpare thought to herself.

"Oh, I get it," Meziyet gushed. "The groom's expecting you. I'm so thick sometimes. Quick, run to your room, Mehpare. Better not keep your husband waiting."

Before Meziyet could say another word, Mehpare hastily re-covered the mouth of the jug, left the kitchen and raced up the stairs.

Kemal had already arrived in their room and was performing his nuptial prayers. Mehpare sat on the edge of the bed and waited. When he was done she sprang to her feet to roll up his prayer rug. "Wait," he said, "that can wait till later." He pulled a diamond ring out of his pocket.

"This was my mother's, Mehpare. I never knew her. My father put it on her finger when they were married. It didn't bring her good luck. But—God willing—it will to you."

Mehpare took the ring, kissed it and slid it onto her finger.

"There's something I want to tell you," Kemal said. "I'm leaving on Friday."

"I know."

"If I can't be with you for the birth of our child . . ."

"You'll be there, I'm sure of it . . ."

"We're only human, Mehpare. We don't know what the future will bring. I may be on the road, or far away . . . Anyway, if I'm not with you, I'd like the baby to be named after my mother if it's a girl, after my father if it's a boy."

"We're having a son."

"Then call him Halim."

"You'll be the one whispering his name into his ear, God willing," Mehpare said. But she turned her head so her husband wouldn't see her tears. "Could you undo my buttons?" she asked. "I can't reach them."

For some reason, Mehpare the legally wedded wife seemed much more timid than the bold, uninhibited servant girl she had once been. She didn't even turn to look at Kemal's face as he undid her buttons, gathered her long hair in his hands and kissed the back of her neck. Mehpare shuddered slightly, hastily slipped out her clothing, dashed to the bed so she wouldn't be seen naked, threw on the nightgown beneath her pillow, and pulled the blanket up to her chin.

"So, you're my reluctant bride now, are you?" Kemal laughed. "Carry on then, it's your due." Lifting the corner of the blanket, he slid in next to Mehpare, pulled her close and moved in for a kiss.

Mehpare gently stopped him.

"Can't we lie like this for awhile—can't we just sleep in each other's arms?" she asked. "Please, just like this. Perfectly still and peaceful. Holding each other. Sleeping."

Ahmet Reşat was up early that Friday morning, preparing for a long day that included his participation in the Friday Prayers Procession and a meeting with a few fellow Cabinet members to discuss the most recent news from Anatolia. When he came down to the tiled entry hall he was saddened by the sight of a suitcase resting next to the front door.

"Aren't they up yet?" he asked.

"I heard Mehpare making her way to the toilet. They're awake," Saraylıhanım informed him.

"Shall we send Zehra to tap on their door?"

"Reşat Bey, you and Kemal spoke well into the night. Aren't you tired of conversation yet?"

"I wanted to bid him farewell. He might be gone before I return. Do you know what time the carriage is supposed to come?"

"Barely married and off he goes! To save the country! Well it looks to me like the country isn't going anywhere, Kemal or no Kemal. And even if it does require saving, they can certainly do without him. It defies reason; but then, the boy's always been unhinged. Off he goes again, and back home he'll come, wretched and . . ."

"Grandmother, I can hear every word," Kemal called out, leaning out over the railing on the floor above. "Uncle, wait, I'll be right down." He skipped down the stairs two at a time. "We were up late, and I overslept."

Furious at having been interrupted, Saraylıhanım continued her muttering: "I don't care who hears me. I'll tell you again, to your face. There's no telling what you've been getting up to lately. If I had the strength, I'd give you a good thrashing. It's your uncle who should be giving you a hiding, but he's far too good-natured. Abandoning a bride of three days: I've never heard of such a thing. It isn't as though you're being called up by the army. If you were going away to serve the Sultan I wouldn't care. But you're asking for trouble, the two of you, husband and wife. Listen to me— there'll be no getting wounded and coming back home. We've endured quite enough at your hands."

"Quiet, grandmother. Take a deep breath," Kemal said. "You're liable to burst a vein."

"I most certainly am. And you'll be the cause of it. Your nonsense will be the death of me."

"Why don't you go upstairs and let me and my nephew make our farewells," said Reşat Bey.

"There's no reason you can't do it while I'm here."

"Saraylıhanım, please!"

The force of Reşat Bey's tone had the elderly lady gathering up her skirts and scurrying off toward the stairs. As soon as they were alone, Kemal took his uncle's hands in his own. "I'm indebted to you, Uncle, and I know I can never repay your kindness. Everything good that's happened to me has happened because of you. And now, in order for me to leave with a clear conscience and a light heart, I must ask you to look after Mehpare."

"Mehpare will always be a daughter to me, Kemal."

"I know that. But I wish I'd never upset you . . . I wish everything had been different . . ."

"Kemal, even misfortunes harbor blessings. Go with a clear conscience and a light heart; take care of yourself and come back to us safe and well. And remember, you now have a wife in this house, awaiting your return. Don't court danger. Look after yourself, my son."

Ahmet Reşat embraced his nephew. The two men stood there for a moment and when they stepped apart their eyes were glistening.

"I'll send word, uncle, just as we agreed."

"Don't worry. Things will get better. You'll come back. This land will be ours again. You and I will see brighter days together."

Ahmet Reşat dashed through the door so Kemal wouldn't see the tears streaming down his cheeks. As he strode through the garden he searched his pockets for his handkerchief. He dabbed at his eyes and wiped his nose as he thought about how difficult it would be live in a household of women without Kemal. Who would he confide in, who would he discuss politics with?

He quickly walked to the gate through the cool morning air. A few law enforcement officers, Armenians and Greeks in English uniform, were patrolling the street. He silently cursed as he proceeded towards Sirkeci. A little farther ahead, a gendarmerie battalion composed of men of various nationalities marched in single file. Along with the volunteer members of the modestly-dressed Turkish police force strutted a tall Englishman, stiffly wielding a baton; a Frenchman with a shiny black moustache and a wide black belt cinching his midsection; and an Italian who, in plumed cap and shiny red coattails, resembled an outlandish bird. He also saw homeless Russians huddled under the eaves of the buildings he passed. The prison, barracks, and factories were full to overflowing; there was nowhere to house this many migrants and refugees. Corpses had even begun to appear on the streets.

As he reached Sirkeci he could see the armor-plated warships anchored in the distance. In order to prevent the smuggling of arms and volunteers to Anatolia, the English had begun raiding police stations, and had now reduced Istanbul to the status of captive city. But, as he'd told his nephew, Ahmet Reşat was one of those men who truly believed that every misfortune harbors a blessing. If he hadn't personally witnessed the massacre at Şehzedebaşı Police Station, hadn't learned of the letter written by Fehime Sultan, he would still be firmly on the side of the Sultan. But recent events had shifted his point of view; he now found himself hoping for help from the liberation movement in Anatolia. There was hope, however faint. He wouldn't be able to fight in Anatolia, but, in Istanbul, in his position as Finance Minister, he would do everything in his power to aid the cause.

Turning his head to avoid the sight of the anchored warships, he walked briskly and prayed: "Allah, swiftly deliver us from this degradation. Watch over Kemal. Spare his life and bring him home to his bride."

Prayer had always comforted Ahmet Reşat, but, this time, his heart remained as heavy as before. He wondered if his entreaties had reached God. Very well then, he would go the mosque at noon and repeat his prayers there. And later that day, at afternoon prayers, he would try again. And at last, Allah would hear him, would hear him and would save his city. And his nephew.

By the time the carriage arranged by the organization arrived to take Kemal away, the evening call to prayer was resonating across the city. The first person to spot the phaeton waiting in front of the garden gate was Mehpare, who had been scanning the street from the window for much of the day. She screamed.

"What is it, what's going on?" Saraylıhanım asked.

"There's a carriage at the door," Mehpare moaned. Her face was chalk-white.

"Time to go then," Kemal said.

Behice and Saraylıhanım rushed over to the window; Kemal went to his room on the same floor and shrugged into the maşlah readied for him the night before. Mehpare had restitched the hem so that it would be long enough to cover his feet. As she had busied herself with needle and thread, Kemal had reread the hand-delivered letter directing him to dress in women's garments. Under the worried gaze of Mehpare, he tore the letter into tiny pieces and tossed them into the brazier.

The women and children of the house followed Kemal into the large anteroom. Everyone spoke at once; everyone had something important to say. When Kemal began descending the stairs to the tiled entry hall, there was much pushing and shoving on the staircase. Zehra and Housekeeper Gülfidan had been given the day off; the only servant was Hüsnü Efendi. He stood by the door, frowning deeply, muttering prayers.

First, Kemal kissed the hand of his weeping grandmother, who was too distraught to scold him, too spent even to speak. After they'd exchanged kisses, she stood across from him and muttered a long prayer, which she then ritualistically breathed onto his face. After Saraylıhanım, it was Behice's turn. Now that the nephew she had been so eager to remove from the house was actually leaving, she felt vaguely guilt-stricken. She held Kemal tight and began sobbing loudly. "If I've been at fault . . ." But that was as far as she got.

"Aunt! How can you say that! I'm the one who's been at fault, time and again. I brought trouble into your house, disease . . ."

"All I've done for you, I've done freely, and before Allah, I now release you from any claims I might have on you," Behice said, echoing the leave-taking of her husband.

Leman and Suat were crying, tugging at Kemal's shirt-sleeves. Suat tried to climb up into his arms.

"You're a lot heavier than the last time I picked you up, you little rabbit; I don't think I can manage it now," Kemal said. "When did you get so big?"

Behice pulled her daughters off Kemal. If Mehpare was the only dry-eyed person there, it was because she'd shed her tears in secret over the past few days. She stood in the corner and watched Kemal take leave of his family. Kemal covered his head with the hood of the cloak and squeezed his hands into a pair of women's gloves; before he lowered his veil over his face, he took Mehpare by the arms, pulled her a bit closer, and kissed her neck, cheeks and eyes.

"I'll be back, Mehpare. Don't be upset. Take care of our son," he whispered.

The last person Kemal embraced was Hüsnü Efendi, who opened the door for him. He pretended not to notice the tears in the servant's eyes as he lowered his veil, pulled his cloak close, picked up his small valise, and walked toward the waiting carriage.

Sitting next to the driver was a man with a handlebar moustache of the sort affected by the *kabadayı* of Istanbul—the rough and ready neighborhood toughs led by Cambaz Mehmet of Topkapı. When he saw Kemal coming through the gate, he leapt out of the carriage, took his valise, helped him in, and sat across from him.

Mehpare raced into the garden with a bucket filled by Hüsnü Efendi. Together, they poured out the contents of the bucket as the carriage began driving off.

As the pool of water grew into a dark stain on the street, Mehpare caught a glimpse of Kemal's face and the gloved hand he was waving through the tiny carriage window.

"I entrust you to Allah, my darling," she said. She had never used such a term of endearment in Kemal's presence. She repeated it to herself, again and again: "My darling, my darling, my darling . . ."

The carriage turned left at the bottom of the street, and slid from view.

– 12 –

On the Farm

Arriving at the farm after a grueling journey, Kemal slid his valise under the bunk bed that had been allocated to him, and, as he stacked his books in a neat pile beside it, immediately began looking forward to the day he'd be able to leave this place. The dormitory stank. Though the windows were open, a layer of grey tobacco smoke hovered just below the ceiling and, mingled with the stench of dirty socks pulled on after hasty ritual ablutions, was the overpowering odor of sweat and of breath permeated with garlic. He knew what it was to share a crowded dormitory with other men, but he'd been accustomed to sharing them with the sons of bureaucrats and wealthy tradesmen, men who, like himself, had grown up in stately homes, in mansions. Men who smoked, but whose breath and feet never stank. Men with clean underclothes. Not for the first time, Kemal cursed the years he'd spent shut up in the refined atmosphere of an Istanbul mansion. He thought back to his army days. At the beginning, he'd been struck with a strange sense of regret, as he was now. But when they'd been shipped to the East it was as though a silken cape, white and icy, had obliterated all lesser discomforts. The only thing he remembered from that war was the cold. Endure the cold, overcome the cold, don't succumb to the cold, don't fall captive to the cold! Was it possible that this long and narrow room, this unbearably smoky, packed and airless room, would make nostalgic even for that misery? An hour later, Kemal was astonished to find that he no longer even noticed the reeking, stuffy dormitory. What a remarkable creature, man, he thought. How quickly he adapts to any terrain, no matter how inhospitable, the moment he senses there are no avenues of escape.

And yet he was astonished at how quickly he found himself missing his home. If he had the chance, he'd run back to the house where, despite the presence of Mehpare, he'd been counting the days like a prisoner pining for release. He yearned for the well-aired, well-scrubbed, well-dusted little room in the attic. He felt drained and his head ached here, among these coarse and vulgar men, his bunk-mates. And think how eager he'd been to come!

The journey had gone reasonably well.

The carriage had been stopped a few times by the municipal police, at which the mustachioed fellow sitting across from him and the driver had leapt down to answer some questions before the carriage was allowed to drive on. He'd resented having to sit there in a woman's cloak, absolutely helpless and of no use to anyone, and couldn't help asking his escort why he'd been instructed to do so. Couldn't he have dressed as an ecclesiastic, for example? He hadn't minded putting on a çarşaf the day they'd hidden at Azra's house, but he'd been mortified at being introduced to the men at the farm dressed head to toe in women's clothing.

"Heard about how they've taken to bothering our women, and the big brawl over it?" his companion in the carriage had asked.

"No, I haven't."

"Well, how would you, with the papers censored and all. It's not like the heathens are going to write up their own devilry, is it? Anyway, last week three French officers had a few drinks too many and began hassling some women in Gülhane Park."

"And?"

"And all three of them got knifed. One was hurt pretty bad. I don't know if he croaked or not."

"Their soldiers are out of control, that's what you're telling me."

"That they are. Their commanders don't want any trouble and have warned their men not to do it again. That's why we wanted you to dress as a woman. The stabbings were just last week, and with the memory still fresh in their minds we figured they wouldn't dare touch you."

Satisfied with the explanation, Kemal had kept his coat closed until they reached the inner courtyard of the farm, but he did take off his maşlah before getting down from the carriage. He'd walked through a garden shaded by towering trees, and through the front door of a large house built of yellow stone, out the back door of the same house into a second courtyard, through another garden and, finally, arrived at the building where he'd be staying.

The dormitory housed seventeen men. These fellows in breeches, with bushy moustaches and rough stubble beards, bore no resemblance to any of Kemal's friends from the resistance. They were the sort of men Saraylıhanım would have dismissed as "rabble rousers." As Kemal began lining up the bottles of pills he'd removed from his valise he became aware of scornful sneers from his roommates.

"Got them monthly pains then, do you, brother," one of them grinned.

"My kidneys were damaged and my lungs caught a chill at Sarıkamış. I'm required to take daily medication. If I didn't keep myself healthy, I wouldn't be of any use to you," Kemal explained.

"You fought in Sarıkamış?" asked Dramalı.

"Unfortunately, most of us froze to death before we had the chance."

"Well how did you manage to get home all healthy then?"

"Apparently, Allah wasn't ready to settle accounts with me. I fell captive; then I was sent home."

"You look pretty young, is all."

"Appearances can deceive," said Kemal. And how true that was: these roughnecks and ruffians were already becoming the stuff of legend—weren't at all what they seemed. Most of them were stevedores and coachmen; all of them were prepared to risk their lives to smuggle arms out of warehouses, to give a good dressing down to any of the minority members of the municipal police force who got out of line, to badger and bedevil the occupiers at any time and in any way they could. Black Sea fishermen in single-mast boats had boldly gathered mines laid at the start of the war in the waters of the Bosphorus, turning them over one by one to the War Ministry. Now, in Galata, stevedores and coal porters employed their strong backs for the clandestine shipment of weapons and arms to the resistance forces in Anatolia. If the invasion of Istanbul isn't going smoothly for the invaders, Kemal thought to himself, it's because of these men. He found himself warming to his rough companions. And hadn't Mahir told him that the underground relied not only on porters and carriage drivers, but on pickpockets and crooks as well? These were the common criminals whose light fingers served a noble cause by plundering armories, helping to send the stolen munitions to the Nationalists. How could he possibly look down his nose at them? Still, he couldn't help shuddering as he hoped to himself that there were no thieves among his roommates and decided, on the spot, that he wouldn't ask about their occupations.

And although Kemal did indeed refrain from any pointed questions of a personal nature, his companions had no such scruples, and he was able to learn a great deal about their colorful lives and shady backgrounds, as well as the organization itself, during his stay at the farm. He'd been enlisted into the resistance, which operated on a secretive cell system, by Mahir. All he knew was that an underground shipping line had been established for the sending of people, arms and supplies to Anatolia. The person responsible for running this line so vital to the cause was a footman. Here, the sterling education Kemal had always prided himself on, his courtly manners, which had always been such a source of pride and joy to his grandmother, meant nothing. The tales repeatedly told by the men in his unit were a constant source of amazement and new information.

It was at the farm that Kemal learned that life is neither unfailingly good and true nor unfailingly brutish and misguided. If he was, here and now, working to serve his country in its hour of greatest need, he owed a debt of gratitude to the Committee of Union and Progress, the very party for whom his initial wild enthusiasm had later turned to disenchanted disgust. It was CUP who, by setting up the Special Forces, had trained a generation of secret agents. After entangling the Ottoman Empire in the Great

War, CUP had fallen from power; its leaders had been forced to flee the empire, its members either arrested or exiled, its Special Forces disbanded. But the few party members who had managed to return in secret had also ensured that intelligence-gathering activities continued and a new organization was formed. Kemal was now a member of that restructured organization, which was drawing on its experience to aid the National Independence Army. All across the districts and quarters of Istanbul, men of every description were enlisted in the cause, with each neighborhood attempting to outdo the others in acts of heroism. Local roughs with nicknames like "Rapscallion," "Uncle," "Big Brother," and "Bully," were more than ready to demonstrate their patriotism. Underground cells had filled with oarsmen, fishermen, stevedores, bakers, drivers, craftsmen, laborers, shopkeepers, civil servants, and intellectuals—the unnamed heroes of the resistance who, through their untiring efforts, blazed a path to victory, cobblestone by cobblestone. Kemal knew that without these men, who were smuggling soldiers in civilian clothes and arms stolen from Istanbul depots to the farthest reaches of Anatolia, the war of independence would have remained no more than a dream.

Many was the night an exhausted Kemal climbed into his bunk and said a prayer of gratitude for the CUP, the force behind the new organization known as Karakol and—ultimately—by a multitude of other names.

Kemal wasn't a participant in the street-level actions and activities that were plaguing the occupation forces. He spent his days forging identity cards and decommission papers for the volunteers bound for Anatolia: it was only with the express permission of the Allied Passport Bureau that the citizens of Istanbul were able to travel even within the city limits—say, from Anadolu Feneri, at one extreme, to Pendik, at the other. Kemal was among those busily drawing up papers and stamping them, until his hands were cramped and his fingers numb. And as he prepared counterfeit certificates, records and papers for non-existent merchants, tradesmen, doctors and lawyers, he was counting the days until he would be assigned more dangerous duties.

One evening, as he chatted with his fellows in the dormitory, grumbling about his desk-work, he received an earful from Dramalı.

"Look at him, whining away," Dramalı had said, "you'd think we could do what he does. There's something for everyone. Do all five fingers look alike? No—but they work together, and each does its own thing. Which of us can write all fine and dainty? You! And who can forge those papers? You again! If they tell me to do it, can I? Forget it! The only thing my hand is good for is its trigger finger. So stop complaining and keep at it!"

Without a word, Kemal went over to his bunk and stretched out. A moment later, Dramalı was standing there in front of him. "Have I gone and upset you?" he asked.

"No, I'm not upset. You were right, Dramalı."

"Well, you're right too, Kemal Bey. You've been cooped up here and you're sick of it. I'll tell you what—we're planning to take out this Binit fellow pretty soon. You can join us if you want."

"You mean Bennett? The Chief of Intelligence?"

"The Brit. That's him."

"Dramalı, you'd only be asking for trouble. They'd string you up if you got caught."

"We won't get caught."

"If you kill him they'll simply appoint someone else. But if something were to happen to you, who would raid the arms depots? Don't do it. It's not worth the risk."

"Scared, are you?"

"Not at all. I think it's unnecessary. Is there any need to slog through a cesspool?

"We think there is."

"Does Pehlivan know about this?"

"I suppose you were too busy living it up in some mansion to hear about the torture this Binit character dished out to our Nationalists."

"What's all this about living it up in a mansion, Dramalı? The shortages hit every house in Istanbul. We suffered along with everyone else."

"Never mind all that, what I'm asking is this: do you want to be with us when we take this guy out, or not?"

Kemal was sorry he'd ever opened his mouth. If he refused, his reputation would be in tatters.

"Of course I'll go with you."

"Do you know this guy's language?"

"I speak some English, yes."

"Good, you can tell him why we're rubbing him out," chimed in Börek Vendor Hasan, who occupied the upper bunk, and whose upside-down face swung crazily at Kemal's ear. "We're killing Binit 'cause of what he done to our friends."

"Bennett."

"Sorry about that, it's just that every time I hear his name I picture a pack of dogs. Mind you, he's lower than the claw of the mangiest cur in all Tophane. Tell him what I just said. Do you think you can translate it?"

"I'll do my best," Kemal said, somewhat doubtfully. The thought of committing murder made him nauseous. He reached under his pillow for the lavender-scented handkerchief Mehpare had given him, and inhaled deeply. That same handkerchief had been damp with Mehpare's tears on their last night together. He gently tucked it back under his pillow.

What was his darling doing right now? Was she brushing her long hair or was she sleeping peacefully? Dreaming about him? Did she miss him? How was she coping with Saraylıhanım? Had she told the others member of the household that she was pregnant with his child?

Before Kemal was given the opportunity to help teach Bennett a lesson, he was summoned to his first mission away from the farm. The cauldron of stewed dried beans had just been scraped clean and the dishes were being cleared away when the news arrived that Kemal was to be taken immediately to Eyüp Sultan Mosque. "Can they wait a minute while I perform my ablutions?" Kemal asked.

"You can do them when you get there. Hurry up."

Kemal folded the towel he'd been holding, put it on the bed, rolled down his shirtsleeves, took his jacket and fez, and followed Faik Molla out of the dormitory.

The Algerian soldiers attached to the French army were being housed at the Rami Barracks in the vicinity of Eyüp and would be taken to the mosque that day to attend afternoon prayers. It had become customary for an officer to be on hand to translate the sermon delivered by the cleric into French, for the benefit of the Algerians. The usual translator had suddenly fallen ill and Kemal—who had known for some time that he might be called on to perform the task—would be taking his place.

After prayers had been performed, Kemal knelt next to the cleric and looked at the congregation of dark young men. In their black eyes, he read fear and helplessness. Soldiers of a people who were wealthier, more educated and more knowledgeable than these poor men had come to seize their land, to hold them captive, to lay claim to their very souls. Kemal had no doubt that these young Algerian men kneeling across from him on the carpet of a mosque in Istanbul in ill-fitting French uniforms were wondering why they had been sent to a Muslim country on another continent, and were cursing their fate.

He began by faithfully translating the words of the cleric, who was directing his congregation not to fire upon their Muslim brothers. But then his emotions and thoughts overflowed; he continued speaking long after he'd interpreted the cleric's final words.

His Algerian co-religionists harbored no antagonism towards the Ottomans; they had been sent to a far-away land to fight for French interests in a battle that would leave them maimed and scarred and dead. And to what end? So that the French would get richer. And what about them, the youth of Algeria? What about their families? Would their participation in the invasion of this city, of this land, improve the lives of their mothers and fathers, their siblings back in Algeria? No! Muslim Algerians would continue living under the heel of Christian Frenchmen. And for how long? Until they'd forgotten their own identity, their own language, their own religion. Their French masters might help them fill their bellies but the darkness of their skins and the faith they held dear would condemn them forever to second class status, even in their own country.

At first, the cleric waited for Kemal to finish; then, when Kemal's speech dragged on, the cleric grabbed him by the arm and motioned for him to be quiet. Kemal ignored him and was admonished with the words: "What are you telling them? Be quiet. You'll get me into trouble."

At that, Kemal had no choice but to conclude his impromptu sermon. His Algerian congregation burst into applause.

"What did you say to them?" asked the cleric.

"I told them the truth," replied Kemal. "Their truth."

When Kemal returned to the dormitory that evening, he was astonished to find that the news of his speech at Eyüp Sultan Mosque had preceded him. His roommates surrounded him, eager for more details. He had just sat down on his bunk to begin an impassioned recapitulation when Pehlivan burst into the room.

"Hey, Kemal Bey! Know-it-all! Did we send you there to sermonize, or to translate?"

"I was translating but then I . . ."

"Quiet! Don't talk back to me! From now on, you'll do what you're told and nothing more, understand? Pehlivan planted an enormous finger in the center of Kemal's forehead, and shoved him. Kemal sprang up from his bed, white-faced.

"Hold on, Pehlivan; you've gone too far."

"No—you've gone too far. I call the tune around here. This unit is under my command."

"This isn't the army."

"It's a civilian army. If you don't like it, go back to your mansion. We'll have no trouble replacing you."

"I go where I want, if and when I want. Why am I being subjected to this sort of treatment?"

"I suppose you think you were being clever, right? Well, you weren't. All you did was grab attention. You stood out. Everyone who was attending that mosque is now at the coffee house talking about your nonsense. You'd better pray the invaders don't overhear them. If it meant trouble only for you, I wouldn't care. But you could take us down with you. We're not here to show off. We're not here to fish for cheers. You've got to keep your head down; you should be invisible. This business is nothing like wrestling out on the field. Do you understand?"

"I'm sorry." Kemal said, abashed. "I was wrong; I didn't realize."

"Then stop strutting around and get to bed."

Kemal stretched out on his bunk bed, head resting on his hands, and reflected bitterly on the utter mess he'd made of his first assignment outside the farm. They'd probably never give him another; he'd spend the rest of his life forging papers.

The next day, Kemal realized how wrong he'd been. He was getting dressed in the morning when Pehlivan came into the dormitory and said, "Finish up your deskwork by noon. You've got some work to do in the coffeehouses later in the day."

"In coffeehouses?"

"You won't be going to the mosque all the time. This time, you're being sent to some coffeehouses. We've identified a few places that are frequented by soldiers from the Caliphate Army. You'll go with a couple of friends and ask for a water pipe. You'll start chatting, especially with any soldiers you might see. You'll play a game of cards or some backgammon. As you get chummier, you'll happen to mention that your new soldier friends are bearing arms not on behalf of the Sultan, but because of pressure from the English. You'll bring it up with your friends, real natural, like you're having a heart-to-heart. I don't want you twisting any arms or starting any arguments . . . You're just a couple of guys chewing over politics at the coffeehouse."

"Do you think they'll take our word for it?"

"That's your job, to make them believe you. That's why we chose an upper-class guy like you, someone who has a way with words. Your uncle's the finance minister, isn't he?"

"My maternal uncle, yes."

"Great. You'll repeat what your uncle's told you. One of your companions will be from the State Office; the other one's close to the Palace. If the three of you don't know what you're talking about, who does? Just sit and talk. Grumble about things, how upset you are at the invasion but how there's nothing you can do about it. How you wish your fellow Muslims would stop working for English interests, change sides and go to Anatolia to fight against the Greeks. You won't be telling any lies. Balıkesir, Bursa and İzmit have already fallen, and now the Greeks are invading Tekirdağ. It's God's truth, isn't it? And everyone knows it. And when they've taken İzmir, they're bound to move on to Istanbul, aren't they? Everyone knows how badly the Greeks want Istanbul. And at this rate, it'll be theirs. Are we going to stand for it? Or are we going to do something before it's too late? Wouldn't it be great if these Ottoman soldiers stopped working under the orders of the English, if they went to Anatolia, taking their weapons with them, to help their Muslim brothers? That's what you've got to get across, Kemal Bey! Just talk amongst yourselves so you get the others thinking, open their eyes a little. But not like what you did yesterday: you've got to be cool and calm. That's what I expect of you."

"And then?"

"And then *what*?"

"Fine, I'll do exactly what you told me. But then what should we do? What if we fail to dupe them?"

"You're not duping anyone. You're planting the seeds of doubt. When you finish your chat and your coffee, you'll be going to other coffeehouses to do the same thing. When you leave, others of us will arrive and repeat what you said. We'll keep it up until we've won the soldiers over to our side."

"But what if we fail?"

"Always look on the bright side, Kemal. What if we succeed?"

And at that, Kemal could only nod in agreement.

"You'll need to be dressed as a gentleman when you go out this afternoon. I've had the suit of clothes you wore under your cloak ironed, and your fez is ready," Pehlivan said. "You talked up a storm last night. Let's see how you do today, Kemal Bey."

Late that night, Kemal, a bit dizzy from smoking water pipes at four different coffeehouses, found his companions were still awake. Some were performing their prayers on their rugs, others stood in prayer in a corner. At first he assumed they had waited up for him and launched into an account of his adventures. Kandıralı signaled for him to be silent.

"We'll listen to all that later, bey. For now, join us in prayer."

"What's going on?" Kemal asked. "Has something happened?"

"Has it ever!" Kandıralı confirmed. "Dramalı went off with Cambaz and some of the others to teach that dog Binit a lesson. They still haven't come back. We're praying for their safe return."

"But weren't they going to take me along?"

"How could they! Binit doesn't hang out in coffeehouses. He goes to fancy places and rubs shoulders with dandies like you. They'd know you in a minute."

"Kandıralı, how do you know where I go or who I know?"

"Your mug gives you away. You look like the kind of guy who makes merry up in Pera."

Kemal didn't bother to inform Kandıralı that he hadn't so much as poked his nose out of doors for a very long time indeed. He was tired. He got undressed and climbed into bed. He'd expected to drift off into a deep sleep the moment his head hit the pillow, but he was now too worried to do so. He joined the others as they held vigil for Dramalı and his men.

It was morning before they returned. In order to shake their pursuers, they'd had to run off in the opposite direction, through Kağıthane and over the hills of Istanbul, before daring to return to headquarters. They were deeply disappointed: Binit had been wounded, not killed. Well, by hurting him, they'd avenged their Nationalist friends, at least somewhat, they consoled themselves.

"You promised I could join you. Tell us everything that happened, at least," Kemal said.

"We've had our guys tailing this Binit character for close to two months now," Dramalı began. "He knows how to have a good time and he's got a thing for the ladies. He goes out every night. Whenever he stepped into a music hall, we'd make sure one of our men was sitting at the next table, watching his every move and listening to everything he said. He usually hangs out at a tavern in Büyükdere. Binit's crazy about rakı. He always has a bottle brought over, nice and cold, plates of snacks laid out on the table in front of him, a Greek beauty perched on each knee, and there he sits, drinking the night away. After he's had his fun with the ladies, he gets into his automobile and they drive him off to the Kroker Hotel. But does he go up to his room and conk out? No! If a few Turks have been rounded up he heads down to the hotel cellar, roughs 'em up real good with a horsewhip and then, and only then, has a good night's sleep. If the dungeon of Kroker could only speak, the things it would tell us. What they've done to our men."

"Enough of that. Tell me what happened."

"The leaders of our organization put their heads together and passed a death sentence on Binit. And Pehlivan approved it."

Glancing over at Pehlivan, who was sitting cross-legged on one of the bunks, Kemal seized the opportunity to get even for the previous night. "So you decided it's not always best to remain invisible, did you?"

"My men are patriots, and I can't always control them, Kemal Efendi," said Pehlivan. "Sometimes they've got to do what they've got to do."

Everyone was eager to hear the rest of the story, and Kemal held his tongue.

Dramlı picked up where he'd left off.

"So after his night out on the Bosphorus, he gets into his automobile and the headlights are switched on, like always. That's how we knew he was coming up the hill. There's never anyone else driving around over there at that hour. We'd stationed fifteen of our men there, behind trees and bushes, to keep a look out. We had a few look-outs on top of the hill, too. We planned to stop his automobile; then Mad Hamza was going to start shooting it up. He took up position behind a tree on the side of the road. We were all lying in the field, face down. There wasn't a peep. It was completely dark, there was no moon out last night. The only light was the stars, like diamonds, big as your fist, shining away in the black sky. We were all holding our breath. Then, way in the distance, we saw the lights of his car, coming toward us. He came speeding round the bend. We'd sawed through a huge tree right there on the side of the road. We were holding it up with rope, but it was all we could do to keep it standing. We were going to let it crash down right when the car passed. We only had a split-second to get it right. A split-second! If we were late, his armed guards would mow us down. As the automobile got closer, one of our guys lets out a whistle. Down goes the tree, with a terrible creaking noise . . . I can still hear it. But the tree lands right in front of the automobile, not on top of it. We all start shooting. His guards are shooting back. Sergeant Husam was standing right next to me; with all his might, he lobs a bomb. I heard one of the heathens scream; another one was crying and carrying on something awful. Mad Hamza swore he saw Binit over to one side, lying in a puddle of blood. But it beats me how he managed to see anything on a night that black! And then all hell broke loose. Dogs barking, the watchman blowing his whistle, all kinds of shouting and yelling and cursing . . . We ran down the hill as fast as we could, not looking back once."

"If Bennett's dead we'll read about it in the papers," Kemal said.

"If they don't censor it."

"Even if it's censored, we'll get wind of it, don't worry."

"I hope he's alive," Pehlivan said.

"What? Why? You mean we went through all that for nothing?"

"I hope he's alive, and I hope he knows he was punished for all the torture he dished out. That's worse than death."

"You're right. If he did survive, he'll be looking over his shoulder for the rest of his life. "

No one fell asleep that day until well after morning prayers. They all slept until evening.

– 13 –

At Home

Ahmet Reşat had begun returning home directly from the Ministry when his day's work was done. He wasn't particularly close to most of his fellow Cabinet ministers and had grown weary of the interminable, inconclusive bickering. He kept the fact that his feelings for His Majesty had cooled considerably to himself. In any case, the best way for Ahmet Reşat to gain information of possible use to the resistance was to remain silent, alert. He was pained and somewhat ashamed at the situation in which he found himself, and sometimes felt that his activities were those of a hypocritical traitor. Yet all he asked for was an independent country, at peace. His street encounters with the forces of the occupation were becoming increasingly unbearable and as he set about the government business that frequently brought him face to face with foreigners he struggled to contain his contempt and resentment.

Life at the ministry was tedious at best, and life at home wasn't much better: he felt like a rooster shut up in an overcrowded henhouse. None of his intimate friends or confidants lived nearby, and the conditions of the day prevented visits to far-flung districts of

Istanbul. Talk at home centered exclusively on babies—whenever, on his days off, he ventured into the sitting room on the middle floor, he invariably found Saraylıhanım and Behice seated on the divans discussing names.

"Reşat Bey, naturally we'll be naming him Raif, after your father, but we'll need a second name as well; it won't do to be known simply as "Raif." These days, more contemporary names have become fashionable. Firuzan would do nicely. Or perhaps Kenan, or Bülent."

"You do your own father a grave injustice, my girl," Saraylıhanım would interject. "I think the boy should be called İbrahim Raif. That way, we'll have considered the feelings of both sides of the family." Behice would then begin voicing her objections, and on it went.

Reşat Bey couldn't resist a parting shot as he fled the room that day: "You're measuring nappies for a baby that's not even born yet. Why, we might have another girl."

"No, this time it'll be a boy. I saw it in a dream!"

"May it all work out for the best," he said, as down he went to the shadowy stillness of the selamlık, where he'd busy himself at his writing desk, penning detailed accounts of the most recent state of affairs to his friend, Interior Minister Ahmet Reşit, who was still in France, or by reading books and awaiting news of Kemal.

It had been a long time since anyone had brought news from the farm. If anything bad has happened to Kemal, surely we'd be the first to know, he'd tell himself. Three days after his nephew had left home, someone had arrived at the door to tell them that he'd arrived safely and that they shouldn't be alarmed if there was no more news for a time. Simply traveling to and fro was hazardous, and try as he would to remain calm Ahmet Reşat couldn't help worrying. It was on one of those trying days, as he sat yet again at his desk wrestling with figures and ledgers, that Hüsnü Efendi entered the room carrying an envelope.

"From the postman?" Ahmet Reşat asked as he reached out his hand and took it.

"A lady brought it, sir."

"Who?"

"I couldn't tell. She was wearing a çarşaf."

"Didn't you ask who'd sent it?"

"The bell at the garden gate rang. I went and opened it and a woman handed me an envelope. When I asked who had sent it, she pointed to the envelope and I assumed that it was for you."

"All right Hüsnü Efendi," said Ahmet Reşat, "you can go."

"Efendim, she's still here. That woman is waiting at the gate."

"Waiting for what?"

"For a response, I assume."

When Ahmet Reşat saw that it was Kemal's handwriting on the envelope he deduced that the woman at the gate was in fact a man. Try as he might, there were some things he would be unable to conceal from Hüsnü Efendi. "Show her into the garden," he said resignedly, "and have her sit under the arbor. Offer her refreshments of some kind. I'll read the letter and write a response. It should only take a few moments."

"And if Saraylıhanım or Behice Hanım were to ask . . ."

"Don't get the ladies involved in this! If anyone asks, tell them a relative has come to visit you."

When Hüsnü Efendi had left the room, Ahmet Reşat opened the envelope, held it under the desk light and began reading. Kemal informed his uncle in covert terms that he was in good health, and enquired as to the welfare of the family, to whom he sent his greetings. Then he got to the point: The Nationalists had managed to locate munitions, but were short of funds for them. Kemal indicated the quantities of 'sugar' that were needed and employed similar code words to signal where payment should be made. The next paragraph was sufficient to cause Ahmet Reşat to break out into a cold sweat: they wanted to have the munitions shipped to Anatolia on an Italian vessel. To facilitate the loading of the clandestine cargo in Istanbul it would be necessary to make contact with Harbormaster, Pandikyan Efendi, who was known to be trustworthy and a friend of the Turks. Ahmet Reşat could apply to him without hesitation.

Ahmet Reşat carefully reread the cryptic letter three more times to ensure that he'd understood it correctly. After he'd taken notes, he folded the sheet of paper, thrust it into his pocket and walked over to the outdoor kitchen on the other side of the garden. Simply tearing the letter to tiny shreds would be inadequate with the likes of Saraylıhanım in the house. Hüsnü Efendi was mopping the tiles of the outdoor kitchen. When he saw Reşat Bey, he came straight up to him.

"Is she gone?" asked Ahmet Reşat.

"I invited her into my room so no one else would see her. She's waiting there."

"You've done well," said Ahmet Reşat as he entered the kitchen.

"Is there anything else, efendim?"

"Is the stove burning?"

"I lit it a moment ago for lunch. It's not blazing yet. Did you want a cup of coffee? We've got some of that chickpea coffee left. I'll have them make some inside."

"I don't want any coffee, Hüsnü Efendi. Slide open the stove, would you?"

The servant rushed over and opened the lid of the cooking stove. The heat struck Ahmet Reşat in the face as he bent over it. He removed the letter from his pocket and shredded it; then he threw the pieces into the stove and closed the lid. When he stood up, he saw Saraylıhanım Hanım staring at him from the doorway.

"What are you doing here, my dear?"

"I had a sudden desire for coffee."

"Reşat Bey, my boy, why do you suppose there's a kitchen inside the house? You won't find so much as a coffee pot out here. You do realize that this stove is used only for grills and strong-smelling foods, don't you? You haven't been yourself since Kemal went away."

"You're right, Aunt," Ahmet Reşat agreed, "I've been terribly absent-minded of late." Avoiding Hüsnü Efendi's eyes, he went straight to the selamlık.

He could understand why Kemal needed money for arms. Only a week earlier the British, having found themselves powerless to prevent frequent raids on the arsenals of Istanbul, had dumped any remaining munitions into the waters of the Sea of Marmara, near the Prince's Islands. With the clandestine supply of weapons from Istanbul thus eliminated, the resistance movement would be forced to explore other avenues. Which meant purchasing arms from the French or the Italians.

Establishing contact with Pandikyan Efendi would be far more difficult than simply raising funds. The Finance Minister himself couldn't simply stroll into the office of a harbormaster. Nor could Pandikyan Efendi be summoned to his own office. It would attract undue attention. And inviting him to the house was unthinkable! He would have to find a way to send word to Pandikyan, but how? First, he would respond to the letter and dismiss the veiled courier waiting even now in Hüsnü Efendi's room. He pulled a sheet of paper out of the desk drawer, opened the lid of the inkstand, dipped his pen into the well, and composed his thoughts. Kemal had not referred to him as "uncle." The letter had begun with "My esteemed efendim," and he would respond as though he were replying to an old friend. He indicated that everyone at home was well and forwarded in clandestine terms the latest developments. The government had received news that Kâzım Karabekir Pasha was poised to reclaim Sarıkamış and Kars from the Armenians. That was the good news. But there was some bad news as well: The Greek occupation had encroached as far as Bursa. Ahmet Reşat concluded his letter, signed it, and gave it to Hüsnü Efendi to pass along to the courier. Then he went up to his room to change his clothes. He should get in touch immediately with the Minister of Marine, who had never concealed his sympathy for the Nationalists. He should also sound out any other ministers who shared their sentiments. They would have to find a way to finance the flow of arms into Anatolia.

Most of the funds allocated to the Red Crescent found their way onto the battlefields of Anatolia. The association had even gone so far as to sell some of its own holdings, with the proceeds going to the National Army. Perhaps he could channel funds to Anatolia by making it appear that they had been earmarked for the Red Crescent? Damat Ferit was still in France, and he would have considerably more room for fiscal maneuvers while the Grand Vizier remained at a safe distance.

Finally, he would have to find a way to meet with Pandikyan. Ahmet Reşit Bey sighed deeply as he wished more fervently than ever that his closest colleagues and confidants hadn't all been abroad at a time of such need.

As he got dressed, he contemplated the various ways he could reach Pandikyan without attracting unwanted attention. He suddenly remembered that Pandikyan had been among those in attendance at the games of cards and chess he'd played with the French officers. That was it: he'd send Hüsnü Efendi with a note inviting the harbormaster to join a bridge party. But where was the card game to take place? He contemplated the home of his old friend Caprini Efendi. No, that wouldn't do at all. Friendship or not, they were on opposing sides. Could he fully trust an Italian? Finally, he hit upon a place: they could meet in a room at the Şahin Pasha Hotel, in Sirkeci. It was a hotel popular with wealthy landowners, and they should go largely unnoticed among the bustling crowd.

Just after late afternoon prayers, Ahmet Reşat and Pandikyan Efendi met in a room on the first floor of the Şahin Pasha Hotel. Reşat Bey had reserved the room in advance and sent the number to Pandikyan. He'd had a samovar of tea and two tulip-shaped glasses brought up to the room.

The harbormaster was quite nonplussed when he arrived at the room all prepared for bridge and saw only one person awaiting him.

"I beg your pardon, Pandikyan Efendi," Ahmet Reşat said, "but I was forced to take precautions. I've invited you not for cards, but because there's a matter I wish to discuss."

"I should have guessed as much, efendim," said Pandikyan, "but as we had played bridge previously, well, I thought it possible that . . ."

The two men studied each other for a moment. "I need your help," said the host, wasting no time.

"I would be honored to be of any small service, Reşat Beyefendi."

Ahmet Reşat poured them both tea from the samovar, indicated that Pandikyan Efendi was to sit in the chair and himself perched on the edge of the bed.

"Pandikyan Efendi, it hasn't escaped my notice that you're a cooperative and loyal citizen of the Ottoman Empire. Your contribution to the war of independence in Anatolia has been great. It was you who notified the relevant authorities of the secret storehouses under British control, the amount of munitions they contained, and even the destination of the ferryboats used to transport arms."

"God forbid, efendim. God forbid. I have always remained outside politics. I am a mere civil servant. All I'm able to do is ease formalities."

Ahmet Reşat understood how badly he had alarmed his guest. He would have to act quickly to gain his confidence.

"Certain close acquaintances of mine have dedicated themselves to the resistance. It was they who furnished your name. We had already formed an acquaintance, as you know . . . We've played bridge at the same table." Ahmet Reşat lowered his voice to a whisper and mentioned a few people from Karakol.

Pandikyan Efendi was sufficiently reassured to ask, "What would you like me to do?"

"We'll be boarding a few passengers on the next Italian ship to sail from this harbor. Their freight is rather heavy. We'll require your assistance to load it."

"No ships flying the Italian colors are scheduled to set sail over the next week."

"Time is of the essence. If we were to increase the boarding fee, perhaps?"

"It's not a question of money. I would advise you not to rely on Italian ships at this time. The English raided one of them and the Italians found themselves in quite a difficult position. Their ships are now being closely monitored."

"But this is an urgent shipment. As you know, the Greeks are advancing . . ."

"I can recommend another ship. I know the captain."

"Which ship? Do you foresee any difficulties?"

"The *Ararat*."

"Are they deserving of trust?"

"I wouldn't recommend them otherwise. But you'll have to agree on fees."

"When can you provide me with more information?"

"Within the week . . ."

"There's no time. Would tomorrow be out of the question?"

"Would you be able to find out the amount and weight of the freight by tomorrow?"

We're in trouble now, Ahmet Reşat sighed to himself.

Thanks to Kemal, he was getting more and more involved in this business. With each step, he sank a little deeper. Even worse, he was endangering others. He'd begun using Hüsnü Efendi as a courier, and the poor man would now have to be sent to the farm, both to receive the information required by Pandikyan and to get approval for the loading of the arms onto a different ship. Fortunately, vegetables and chickens were being raised at the farm. In the event of any unpleasantness, Hüsnü Efendi would be able to claim that he had gone there to buy seedlings or poultry.

"I'll find out immediately,Ē Reşat said, "and have the information delivered by the same person who brought you the bridge invitation. And as far as the matter of payment, you can have full confidence in me."

"If I can't place my in trust you, who can I trust, efendim?" Pandikyan said. "And I'm honored that you've placed your trust in me as well."

"Thank you, my friend."

"Beyefendi, we're all on the same ship. If it goes down, we're done for, all of us. I'm doing everything in my power to help keep it afloat. I see that you're doing the same."

"Let me say, once again, thank you and God bless you," said Ahmet Reşat. He was overcome with emotion as he offered his hand to Pandikyan. So, there were men like this: while some Armenians may have donned a French uniform and turned on their neighbors of centuries, others were prepared to put the Muslims to shame by risking all they had to help liberate the country they shared.

– 14 –

Call of Duty

Early one morning, before he'd even breakfasted, Kemal was somewhat taken aback to learn that he'd been summoned to the main building. He washed his hands and face without delay and slipped into a fresh, collarless shirt. Wetting his hair, he attempted to plaster it to the sides of his head. He was escorted to the main building by the same man who'd brought word that his presence was requested. Assuming that he'd be going to the room on the second floor where he'd been taken on his first day at the farm, Kemal headed for the stairs and had already climbed two of them when his companion said, "We're not going upstairs, bey. Please follow me." Kemal came back down the stairs and the two men quickly walked to the end of the corridor. A tap on the large wooden door elicited instructions to enter and the man stepped aside to allow Kemal to go in alone.

Kemal found himself in a spacious room organized into a makeshift military headquarters. There was a writing desk to one side and a large table in the middle of the room, covered with maps. A few men were leaning over the maps deep in conversation. Kemal snapped his heels together and nodded in response to the salute of a young man in civilian clothes.

"I'm Captain Seyfi of the General Staff, here from Ankara for the night. After a few appointments I'll be returning immediately."

"And I am Kemal Halim."

"Please sit down," the man said, gesturing to a chair opposite the writing desk as he sat himself down behind it. "I have learned a great deal about you," he said, "from extremely trustworthy sources. I'll get straight to the point. You're a veteran of Sarıkamış."

"Yes, if you can call me that. As you know, most of us froze to death without firing a shot."

"The fact that you volunteered for battle indicates a certain fearlessness. We need people like you. The Greeks are advancing through Thrace . . ."

"Am I to take up arms?"

"If necessary, yes. But the gathering of intelligence is of far more importance to us at the moment. It's vital that we establish lines of communication between the battlefield and Ankara."

"Then how unfortunate that the postal system is under the control of the Allies," Kemal said.

"Not entirely under their control," interjected the man in the kalpak on the other side of the desk. "We do have access to a few secret telegraph lines. When the British requested detailed sketches of all our telegraph networks we told them we had none. We explained that a few clerks had simply memorized all the networks, and that we managed as best we could. They believed us—such is their contempt. They had our telegraph employees reserve a few lines for Allied use and cut all the other lines to Anatolia. That is, they imagine all the lines have been cut. In fact, we have a few secret lines in operation. But they're inadequate. We also need couriers."

Kemal listened attentively.

"Kemal Halim Bey, we'd like to use you immediately, for both our telegraph and our courier networks. Highly confidential reports and battle plans can't be sent by telegraph. I'm aware that you're working at the documents department here and wonder if you would agree to . . ."

"I agree," Kemal blurted out. "I agree to undertake anything you ask. I'm also prepared to go to the front."

"Your health won't allow that. I also ask you to bear in mind that if you are captured while performing your new duties you could well face torture, even death. Think carefully. If you do agree to become a courier, we'll have the necessary documentation prepared for your journey to Anatolia."

"I'm ready. When do I go?" Kemal asked. "You'll set out at the beginning of the week."

"Sir, would it be possible to send word home? They don't need to know where I'm going, but they should know that I'm leaving Istanbul."

"As you wish. I'm afraid there's no time to make your farewells in person. These are difficult days. We have to do whatever we can to prevent the Greeks from advancing any further, and we have to do it at once."

"Right. I'll be ready the moment you want me."

There was nothing left to say. Kemal nodded a salute to the assembled men and left the room. This was the moment he'd so eagerly awaited. As if all those months in confinement, listening to the idle chatter of women, hadn't been bad enough, his evenings now consisted of listening to the exploits of a dormitory full of men who conducted daring raids he was unable to join. Soon, he wouldn't have to content himself with the stories of others. He would have his own tales to tell. Tales he would pass on to his children and grandchildren: daring feats, acts of heroism, perilous adventures . . ."

But he was still troubled. He'd be leaving without having made his farewells to his uncle, his grandmother, the girls . . . And then there was Mehpare . . . Never mind, when he did get back he'd most certainly enjoy her every chance he got. Kemal headed to the dormitory to write a letter of farewell to his family.

— 15 —

Reunion

As Hüsnü Efendi ventured out of the house and into the early morning darkness, where a carriage and neighing horses were waiting for him at the garden gate, a shadow leapt straight at him from behind the apple tree near the front door. "Hey! Who's that?" he shouted, brandishing his cane.

"Wait, Hüsnü Efendi . . . Don't hit me . . . It's me."

"Oh, Mehpare Hanım! What are you doing out here at this hour?"

"I'd like to ask you the same question."

"I have some business to attend to."

"But Hüsnü Efendi, the sun's not even up yet. What kind of business?"

"I'd suggest you return to the house immediately, Mehpare Hanım. Were Saraylıhanım to see you out here with me I don't want to think what she'd do!"

"You're off to visit Kemal Bey, aren't you?"

"Go back inside, Mehpare Hanım. It's none of your business!"

"Hüsnü Efendi, it's my husband you're going to visit."

"Who told you that?"

"Well, where are you going then?"

"I can't say. It's top secret. I'm simply following the Master's instructions."

Mehpare extended the Koran she was holding in her hand and said, "Well then, swear on the Koran that you're not going to Kemal Bey."

"What do you want from me, Mehpare Hanım? Why are you doing this?"

"Take me with you."

"That's out of the question!"

"Aren't I entitled to see my husband?"

"Get permission from the Master first."

Absolutely certain now of the servant's plans, Mehpare became even more insistent. "If you had any human kindness at all you'd take me with you."

"I can't take you, Mehpare Hanım," Hüsnü doggedly insisted as he worked to release his arm from Mehpare's grip.

"Hüsnü Efendi, my husband left the house just three days after we were married. I may never see him again. He may be martyred. I'm begging you."

"I couldn't possibly!"

"I have something very important to tell him."

"I'll tell him for you."

"It's very personal."

"Quick then, write a letter. I'll wait till you're done."

"I want to tell him in person."

Hüsnü Efendi freed his arm and began striding towards the carriage. Mehpare ran after him. "Hüsnü Efendi, for the love of

God . . . I'll kiss the soles of your feet . . ." Tears began sliding down her cheeks. "I think I may be going to faint . . ."

Hüsnü Efendi turned round just in time to clasp Mehpare round the waist. The Koran had slipped from her fingers. Muttering a quick prayer, he picked it up, kissed it, pressed it to his forehead, and handed it back. "Take your Koran and go back into the house, Mehpare Hanım. You've gone all pale and you look ill. You'll catch a chill and make it worse. Go on."

"I'm not ill. Look, I'm going to share a secret with you. I'm pregnant. That's the news I want to tell my husband. He'll be going to Anatolia soon. He may or may not be coming back. Please, I'm begging you. Have you no heart, Hüsnü Efendi?"

The servant squirmed helplessly.

"Then go and ask Reşat Beyefendi for permission. I can't take you without his knowledge."

"He mustn't know. Let me go with you. On the way back, you can drop me off at the corner. We'll return to the house separately. I'll tell them I visited my aunt," Mehpare said, as she once again seized him by the arm. "Hüsnü Efendi, this may be the only opportunity Kemal will ever have to caress his child, even if is only through my belly. If something were to happen to him before I delivered the good news, it would weigh on your conscience forever."

A short time later, as Mehpare took a seat next to Hüsnü Efendi and the carriage rattled off, the poor man couldn't help asking her how she had known he was about to leave for the farm.

"Every day, from the moment I wake up until I go to bed at night, I wait for news from my husband. This morning, too, I got up early and was sitting in the chair in front of the window, reading the Koran. At the sound of horses neighing, I looked out of the window and saw a carriage had arrived. Clearly, something odd was going on. When I saw you in the garden I grabbed my çarşaf and ran straight out of the front door. In my haste, I was still carrying the Koran."

"I'm going to get into trouble because of you," Hüsnü Efendi grumbled.

"No you won't. My lips are sealed. The arrival of that woman the other morning did not escape my notice either. But did I mention it to anyone?"

"You mean you saw her!"

"I did. And later, when Reşat Bey told us that Kemal was in good health, I was convinced that she'd come with a message from my husband. God will bless you, Hüsnü Efendi, for reuniting man and wife."

Hüsnü Efendi said nothing in response, nor did he speak for the rest of the drive: he was too preoccupied with wondering what Reşat Bey would do when he found out that Mehpare had accompanied him to the farm.

Kemal was seated at his desk early that morning preparing documents. They'd had another exciting night and no one had been able to sleep until dawn. This time, a twelve-man team led by Pehlivan had pilfered a naval factory and hauled all the gunpowder they could carry to the Aynalıkavak Shipyard on the Golden Horn. The English had recently begun locking up and sealing armament plants to prevent further thefts, but Pehlivan's men had succeeded in entering through the roof, leaving the sealed door fully intact and unlikely to arouse suspicions later. The acrobats and rope-walkers on the team had utilized their skills to stealthily remove the clay roofing tiles, allowing everyone to slip inside unnoticed. Five of the men in Kemal's dormitory had joined the operation and those left behind had spent the night with rapidly beating hearts, praying for their success. They were still listening to accounts of the daring raid from their newly returned roommates when the morning call to prayer started. Eyes bloodshot but spirits high, Kemal was busy at work on a consignment document when the dormitory cleaner walked into the room and announced, with a barely suppressed smile: "Sir, you have a visitor."

Kemal ignored him.

"Sir, it's a shame to keep your visitor waiting . . ."

"Were you talking to me, Sülo?"

"You mean you weren't expecting a visitor?"

"No, I wasn't."

"There's a woman here for you. She's waiting in the side garden." Assuming the woman in question was yet another male courier, Kemal walked straight to the end of the long corridor and out into the side garden. He could barely make out Hüsnü Efendi standing some distance away under a plane tree. There was someone next to him, someone quite tall and dressed in a çarşaf. He wondered if it was Azra. He knew she was about to be sent to Antep and decided she must have come to say good- bye. As he walked closer he began to get butterflies in his stomach. It wasn't Azra. He started walking faster. When the woman pulled open her *ferace* Kemal thought his heart would stop beating. He broke into a run. Mehpare raced towards Kemal and threw her arms around his neck.

"Don't Mehpare . . . They'll see us . . . Stop it," Kemal said as he unclasped Mehpare's arms and took her hands in his. Yes, it was his wife, trembling and in tears.

"So what if they see us? Aren't I your wife? How wonderful it is to see you again! The nightmares I've had. But you're well, praise God."

"I'm fine. Why have you come here? Does my uncle know?" Kemal asked.

"I followed Hüsnü Efendi." She took Kemal's hand and placed it on her belly. "We've missed you terribly. When we guessed that Hüsnü Efendi was likely to come here, the two of us, mother and son, began tracking his every move. And now here we are, both of us."

"Mehpare, your powers of intuition are incredible; you never cease to amaze me—you can't imagine how anxious I was to see you last night."

"Are you saying I've appeared in your dreams as well?" asked Mehpare, whose moment of intimacy with her husband was brought to an abrupt end by Hüsnü Efendi:

"Beyefendi has sent you a letter. Please read it and write back quickly. We don't have much time." Pulling the letter out of his sash, he handed it to Kemal.

Kemal squatted at the base of the plane tree and read the letter. "I'm going inside to write my reply," he said. "Please wait for me here."

Mehpare made to follow him as he strode off.

"You can't come inside, dear. Strangers aren't welcome here, let alone women. As a matter of fact, I still can't fathom how you dared to come. What if you'd been followed? What if something had happened to you?"

"We weren't followed. And anyway, I'd risk anything to see you."

"You're carrying a child in your womb; you're responsible for two lives now. Hüsnü Efendi was mad to bring you here."

"Please don't be angry with him. I insisted. Tell him that if he's asked to bring you another letter he should take me along. If I'm informed in advance I can bring food and clean clothes."

"It won't happen again, Mehpare. I'm leaving within a week."

"No!"

"Tell my uncle. I'm being sent to the Western front, as a courier."

"So I was right! I should have gone with you. I should be at your side."

"What are you talking about! I'm worried enough as it is at your having come here." Kemal was silent for a moment; then, taking his wife's hands in his, "Mehpare, don't mind what I just said, I'm glad you've come," he said. "I didn't want to leave without making my farewells. Tell my grandmother, my uncle, my aunt and the girls . . . Tell everyone in the house to send me off with their prayers and blessings. I won't be on the front lines, but I will be in some danger. If anything were to happen to me, I entrust you to my uncle. I'm going to write a letter to him now and send it with you."

"Don't entrust me to anyone. Come back to me, safe and sound. I'll be waiting for you. So will your son."

"God willing!"

Kemal released Mehpare's hands and began walking towards the inner courtyard. Mehpare stumbled back to Hüsnü Efendi's side and leaned against the plane tree. "I'll never forget this kindness," she said. "Thanks to you, I've been able to see my husband one more time."

"Did you give him the good news?" Mehpare nearly asked him what he meant, but caught herself. "God bless you," she said. They awaited Kemal in silence. A short time later he returned with a few envelopes. Two of them were addressed separately to his grandmother and uncle, the other bore an unfamiliar name. Mehpare placed all three of them in her bosom.

"Come on, efendim, let's get back," Said Hüsnü Efendi, "we've got a long way to go."

"Just a little while longer. Please." Mehpare slipped her arm through Kemal's and led him a short distance away. At first, Hüsnü Efendi was touched at the sight of the whispering couple, but he began fidgeting as the minutes passed. Mehpare had placed Kemal's hands on both sides of her belly. The servant didn't wish to disturb them, but there were burly men wandering about with guns stuck in their sashes; a little further ahead, through the oak apples, he could see a regiment of men going through drills; behind him, an injured man doubled up in pain was being carried into a large yellow building. Wherever he directed his gaze he saw things he felt he wasn't meant to see. Finally, he could bear it no longer. "Come on, Kemal Bey, we've got a long trip back," he called out.

Mehpare and Kemal came up hand in hand and the three of them walked together as far as the inner courtyard. After embracing his wife and placing a kiss on her forehead, he bade farewell to Hüsnü Efendi. "Take care of Mehpare Hanım. Make sure she doesn't get bounced about too much in the carriage, won't you?"

he said with a look of gratitude. For the first time that day, Hüsnü Efendi was glad he'd brought her.

Mehpare reluctantly released Kemal's arm. "Leave me an address. I'll send word of our son's birth."

"I'll write as soon I know."

"Until we meet again, darling . . . Godspeed."

As though anticipating that Mehpare would cry all the way home, Hüsnü Efendi took a seat next to the driver for the ride back. When, many hours later, they had arrived in their neighborhood, Hüsnü Efendi ordered the carriage to stop at the top of the street and suggested Mehpare walk the rest of the way home.

"I've decided to tell them the truth," Mehpare said.

"Beyefendi will be extremely angry."

"I'll tell him you had no idea, that I secretly climbed into the back of the carriage. I'll take the blame."

"There's no stopping you," sighed Hüsnü Efendi. "Well, you can get out here. Give the letters to me and I'll take them to beyefendi at the Ministry."

"I'm coming with you. There's something I have to tell Kemal Bey's uncle."

"I'm dropping off the carriage over by the bridge, that was the agreement. But you can't walk all that way."

"Yes, I can."

"Do what you have to!" Hüsnü Efendi muttered to himself resignedly as he returned to the driver's side to pay the fare.

By the time Mehpare and Hüsnü Efendi arrived at the Finance Ministry, many of the civil servants were already departing for the day. Hüsnü Efendi went up to Reşat Bey's personal secretary and informed him that the finance minister had a visitor. Then he entered the building with Mehpare, who marveled at the grand marble staircase as she ascended to the floor above, where Reşat Bey had his office. When the clerk asked who she was, she replied: "His daughter-in-law. I've brought some urgent news from home." The clerk ushered her into an adjoining room and a moment later she was standing in front of the minister himself.

Ahmet Reşat started at the sight of Mehpare in his office. "Has something happened to Behice? Or my aunt?"

"Everyone's fine. Forgive me, efendim," Mehpare said, "but I'm afraid I've done something I shouldn't, yet again. As Hüsnü Efendi was leaving today to visit Kemal Bey, I climbed into the carriage without his knowledge or consent; I went to the farm and saw my husband."

"How dare you presume to do such a thing? Are you mad?"

"I had some important news for him, efendim. And I was determined to tell him myself. Please forgive me."

"And what news is that? Or is it that you're intending to go off to Anatolia? You knew I wouldn't allow it so you went to Kemal instead, is that it?" Ahmet Reşat had risen from his desk, and was standing in front of Mehpare, looking directly into her eyes.

"No, efendim. I . . . I'm pregnant, efendim. I wanted to be the one to tell Kemal, efendim."

Ahmet Reşat softened. He returned to his desk. "Are you certain, my girl?"

"Yes I am."

"May Allah bring the infant to term. My congratulations. Presumably you managed to see Kemal?"

"I did. He sent you three letters." She pulled them from her bosom and placed them on the desk. Ahmet Reşat couldn't help reproving Mehpare one last time before he read the letter addressed to him.

"Mehpare, you should have informed me that you wished to go to the farm."

"You wouldn't have allowed it, efendim. And I wouldn't have wanted to disobey you."

"And so, even in your condition, you didn't hesitate to place yourself in possible danger. You're no different from your husband! Small wonder that he married you. A perfect match."

"With your permission, I'd like to go home now; I don't wish to detain you any further."

"You've been traveling the better part of the day. You must be exhausted. I'll arrange a carriage and we'll go home together. I've finished here in any case."

Ahmet Reşat scanned the letter and summoned Hüsnü Efendi, but not before arranging for Mehpare to wait outside in the clerk's office. After about ten minutes Hüsnü Efendi rushed out to get a carriage. After a considerable wait, Ahmet Reşat and Mehpare set off for home. Meanwhile, Hüsnü Efendi stuck one of the letters into his sash and walked off in the opposite direction.

As they drove along in the carriage Reşat Bey asked, "How did you find Kemal? Has he grown thin?"

"No, he looked well," said Mehpare, "the color has come back to his cheeks. He wrote to tell you that he was going to the front, efendim."

"Indeed he did. May God watch over him."

Both of them sat in thoughtful silence the rest of the way home. When the women of the house saw the missing Mehpare getting out of the carriage with Reşat Bey, they flocked round, peppering her with questions. "Leave her in peace," said Ahmet Reşat. "Mehpare left with me this morning; she's been to see Kemal. She had some news for him."

"What news?" demanded Saraylıhanım, infuriated that something had happened in the household without her knowledge.

"I'm going up to my room. Mehpare will tell you herself."

Mehpare walked into the sitting room on the second floor, the other women and girls hard on her heels, and sat down on the divan in front of the bow window. Looking directly at Behice she murmured, "I too am expecting a child, Behice Abla."

"All this fuss about that?" Saraylıhanım snorted.

"Saraylıhanım!" Behice exclaimed as she rushed over to kiss Mehpare. The girls were delighted that the house was to be enlivened by the addition of two babies, and everyone began talking at once. This time, Behice would be having a boy, so how wonderful it would be for Mehpare to have a girl. And if it was a girl, she should be named "Leman". The elder Leman would immediately begin knitting a set of pink baby clothes for her namesake, which was just as well because, to tell the truth, she was tired of knitting blue rompers for her younger brother . . .

"When are you due?" Behice asked.

"Simply calculate the number of days they've been married," Saraylıhanım volunteered. "Unless of course, the baby were to arrive early . . ."

"Why ever would it?" said Behice. "She's a healthy young woman."

"My dear, one can never be sure in these matters. Weren't you a healthy young woman yourself, once? And yet you miscarried. Or had you forgotten?"

Biting her tongue, Behice thought to herself: *You'll never let me forget, you old sow. Given any opportunity you fling it in my face: the loss of a male heir.* She turned to Mehpare, who was looking pleased and proud, and said, "In any case, there'll be something of an age difference between the babies; mine will be a protective older brother to your little girl."

"Why did you visit Kemal?" Saraylıhanım whispered into Mehpare's ear, the moment she spotted an opening.

Mehpare blushed as she replied, "I missed him, efendim."

"Tell me the truth! He's not ill is he?"

"No, I swear he's not. I kept dreaming about him. I had to see him, and I'm glad I did. I found him well."

This time, Saraylıhanım's whisper was conspiratorial: "Tell me the next time you go. I'll come with you."

Not wishing to distress Saraylıhanım with the news of her grandson's imminent departure, Mehpare turned her attention back to the lively babble of female voices. Those were the days when the women of Reşat Bey's mansion were still able to enjoy pleasant conversation.

– 16 –

Birth

Behice's contractions began in the first week of October, the same week Ahmet Reşat was coping with Wrangel's army. The abdication of Nicholas II and the subsequent rise to power of the Bolshevik-dominated Soviets had plunged Russia into civil war. Among the generals leading the anti-Bolshevik White Army was Pyotr Nikolayevich Wrangel. Facing the prospect of massive defeat in the Crimea and the decimation of his troops by an unusually early and bitter winter, Wrangel had begun organizing a mass evacuation to the lands of the Ottoman Empire. Soldiers of the White Army joined the waves of White émigrés fleeing for their lives to the opposite shore of the Black Sea. And so they came, by the tens of thousands, huddled in their black coats, packed onto the decks of ships bearing pestilence and vermin, until the barracks and the hospitals, the camps and the churches of Istanbul were overflowing with refugees. An exhausted city still straining to accommodate the previous waves of immigrants from the Balkans and the Caucasus now had to contend with Wrangel's wandering bands of soldiers as well.

Two Russian warships were in dry dock at the Haliç Shipyard on the Golden Horn. Ahmet Reşat had received information that the Russian soldiers under Wrangel's command were to embark on them, along with a number of Greek soldiers, for Ottoman ports on the Black Sea. Their objective was twofold: to prevent small sailing vessels from smuggling arms and volunteers to the Nationalist Army in Anatolia, and to occupy the Black Sea coast.

After this intelligence was passed along to Ahmet Reşat, he found himself sitting in the offices of the Minister of Marine. Ahmet Reşat had hoped his colleague would share his sympathies for the movement in Anatolia, and he was not disappointed. And thus it came to pass that two Ottoman ministers put their heads together to figure out a way to help the resistance forces.

The Nationalist movement was besieged on all sides. Not only were they threatened by the army of the Istanbul Government, great swathes of Anatolia were occupied by Allied forces, and, to complicate matters further, the Armenian, Kurdish, Circassian and Greek peoples of the Ottoman Empire were each bent on establishing their own states. The Nationalists would be unable to withstand a flanking movement by Wrangel; they'd have to be informed immediately. And it wasn't only Mustafa Kemal and the leadership of the national resistance movement who had to be notified: the people of Anatolia needed to know too. The traditionally hospitable and generous Turks living along the Black Sea needed to be informed of the danger posed by the ships bearing Greek and Russian sol- diers. Were they to be caught unawares, their lands would be seized.

But how were the Ottoman ministers to convey this news to the Black Sea Turks? The Minister of Marine proposed that it be announced in the newspapers. It was a good idea. That way, the information would be conveyed directly to the people. Without delay, the announcement was written up and sent to all the newspapers. What they had failed to take into account, however, was that the Allies would simply censor any reference to Wrangel.

Ahmet Reşat had arrived at his office early and was scanning the newspapers in vain for the report he himself had helped to write when his office boy conveyed news of a far more personal nature: His Excellency would please be informed that his manservant was downstairs and requested an audience. Ahmet Reşat was astounded. Hüsnü Efendi had opened the garden gate for him that very same morning. Why had he said nothing then? Behice wasn't due for another month. Something must have happened to Kemal. Had he been caught and arrested? He had Hüsnü Efendi showed into his room at once. The troubled face of his servant immediately told him something was wrong.

"Anything wrong? Has something happened?" he asked with a tightening in the chest.

"Hanımefendi has gone into labor," Hüsnü Efendi said. "I raced over to the midwife and sent her to the house, then I came straight here to tell you."

Ahmet Reşat blanched. "But there's still time . . ." he managed to say.

"Saraylıhanım says it's begun."

"Go home directly, Hüsnü Efendi. Stay with them, they may need you. I'm attending to some urgent business at the moment and I have a meeting scheduled shortly. I'll come the moment I'm free," he said. "And be sure to let me know if there's anything I can do."

"I won't disturb you unless it's absolutely necessary, efendim," said Hüsnü Efendi, as he took the roll of bank notes handed to him by his master in case of emergency and left the room. Ahmet Reşat was distraught at not being able to be at his wife's bedside, but in a few moments he would be attending a meeting of the Ottoman Public Debt Administration, after which he was scheduled to meet with the manager of the Imperial Ottoman Bank in order to apply, yet again, for a moratorium on Ottoman arrears of debt . . .

Women tend to give birth in the early hours of the morning, he muttered to himself. Why on earth has Behice chosen business hours? Was it to make his life more difficult?

As he opened the door of his office to go to his meeting, he nearly bumped into Doctor Mahir.

"Mahir Bey? Can it be? You're back in Istanbul!"

"Yes I am, efendim. For a short time. The typhus and cholera cases . . ."

Ahmet Reşat interrupted: "My friend, God must have sent you in my hour of need. There's no other explanation. You can tell me about typhus and cholera later. You've arrived in the nick of time, Mahir Bey: Behice is in labor even as we speak. I can't go to her; I'll be attending some critical meetings until this evening. But my thoughts are back at home. Unless you have urgent business, I wonder if I could possibly ask you to attend my wife. It would put my mind at ease."

"I'll go immediately," Mahir said. "And don't worry about a thing. I won't leave your house until you arrive."

The two men hurried down the stairs and raced off in opposite directions.

It was an exhausted and guilt-ridden Ahmet Reşat who finally arrived home that evening, although his sense of remorse was somewhat alleviated by the presence of Doctor Mahir. The only birth Ahmet Reşat had been able to attend was that of Leman. He had bitterly regretted not being by his wife's side when Suat was born and it had been even worse when their third child had been stillborn: but what could he do! They hadn't even been in the same city. And now, today, he had been so close to home, yet equally unable provide comfort or assistance. He prayed that there was still time; Behice might still be in labor. If the baby had been born, surely Hüsnü Efendi would have sent someone with the good news?

He'd been unable to locate a carriage when he left the ministry and had fought his way onto a teaming platform and into an overflowing tram. Then he'd run all the way from the stop on Divanyolu to the top of his street, where he'd paused for breath as he rounded the corner before breaking into a trot the rest of the way. He slid open the gate's latch and stepped into the garden. The house was strangely silent. He couldn't hear the cry of a newborn baby. He looked up at the second floor. The sitting room was dark. The bedroom curtains were drawn but there was a light in the selamlık. Mahir must be waiting for him.

As he strode through the front garden Hüsnü Efendi opened the door and waited for him to enter. No one was in the tiled entry hall. Houses with newborn babies were usually scenes of celebration. He was filled with a sense of foreboding.

"Has the baby been born yet?" he asked, dreading the answer.

"Yes, this afternoon," said Hüsnü Efendi.

"But why didn't anyone tell me?"

"Hanımefendi didn't wish it." Ahmet Reşat went from merely alarmed to devastated. He flung open the door of the selamlık, only to find Mahir sound asleep, an open book resting on his knees.

"Mahir Bey!"

As Mahir leapt to his feet the book fell to the floor with a thud.

"Has something happened? Something terrible has happened, hasn't it? Tell me, is Behice alright? Is the baby alive?"

"Everyone's fine. Behice and the baby are both in good health."

"Then why is the house so quiet? Why didn't anyone send me word? Where's my aunt? Where are the girls?"

"Behice Hanım is recovering. I gave her a sedative; she's asleep."

"What about the others?"

"They've gone to their rooms."

"Mahir, what's the meaning of all this? Was it a difficult birth? Is something wrong with the baby, a defect of some kind? For God's sake, tell me."

"Reşat Bey, please sit down. Nothing terrible has happened . . . It's just . . ."

"Just what?"

"Well, everyone's a bit disappointed. Saraylıhanım and Behice Hanım are most upset because . . ."

"Because what?"

"Because it's a girl. You have another daughter."

"Is she healthy?"

"Yes. And she's beautiful."

"Ah, thank God," cried Ahmet Reşat. "I was terrified. I thought something had gone wrong. Where's the baby?"

"Saraylıhanım placed the baby's cradle in Mehpare's room so she wouldn't disturb her mother. Behice Hanım was inconsolable. We did all we could to comfort her, but forgive her if she's still a bit cantankerous. New mothers tend to suffer severe mood swings. Be gentle with her, Reşat Bey."

"You can't be imagining I'll be cross with her simply because she gave birth to a girl. Don't you know me at all, Mahir Bey?"

"That's not what I meant, efendim. It's just that the women were all so upset; I assumed you'd had your heart set on a boy. Even Leman Hanım seems quite miserable. Apparently, the baby things are all blue."

"Has everyone in this house lost their senses?"

Ahmet Reşat opened the door and called for the housekeeper, who came running up to kiss his hand in congratulations.

"Tell Saraylıhanım, Mehpare Hanım and the girls that I'm expecting them all in the sitting room," said Reşat. "Housekeeper Gülfidan, what is the meaning of this? Is this any way to welcome the latest addition to our family? Have you prepared the sherbet?"

"Of course I have, sir."

Hand it round in the upstairs sitting room. Tell Zehra to help you make the necessary preparations. What ingratitude! It would try the patience of the Lord himself," said Ahmet Reşat. "You'd think we were holding a funeral in this house."

A short time later, Mehpare arrived on the middle floor with a swaddled baby in her arms. The proud father pulled back the blanket and peered at her face.

"My God, just look at her!" said Ahmet Reşat. "She's so tiny!"

"She's slightly premature," Mahir told him. Then, at the worried frown on Reşat Bey's face, he added, "There's absolutely no cause for concern. She'll be just fine before you know it."

Smiling broadly and—for reasons of her own—not at all displeased that the birth had been premature, Mehpare said, "Just look at all that golden hair and that milky white skin; her button nose and rosebud mouth look like the work of an artist. She's a real beauty, praise God!"

"Then it's done, we'll name her Sabahat—beauty," Ahmet Reşat said.

"God willing, her fortune will be as fair as her face," said Saraylıhanım as she entered the room.   Reşat Bey kissed his aunt's hand and asked, "You're not upset that it's not a boy, are you, dear aunt?"

"It is you who should be upset, not me; it's you who has his bloodline to consider," she replied in a voice that was positively waspish. "Behice is awake. She's been asking for you." Ahmet Reşat took the baby from Mehpare's arms, held her close to his chest and started carefully climbing the stairs as Leman and Suat were clattering down.

"Careful ladies, you'll wake your sister," he whispered.

"Oh, father! It's another girl, you know that don't you?" asked Leman.

"I'm extremely pleased with my daughters. It's wonderful."

"What are we going to name her?"

"Unless your mother has any objections, Sabahat."

"Doesn't that mean 'morning breeze'?"

"No, it refers to beauty, to the fine features of the face. Your sister will grow up as beautiful as you. That much is obvious even now."

"What, are we beautiful?" giggled Suat.

"Indeed you are, although I also expect you to be clever, learned and well-mannered," said Ahmet Reşat.

Behice's head rested on her embroidered pillow like a faded magnolia. Her eyes were swollen and bloodshot. When she saw Ahmet Reşat she weakly said, "I've failed you again. I've disappointed you."

"What kind of talk is that, Behice! You given me a little girl more beautiful than I could have imagined. I'm happy, so happy: just look at the delicacy of her face! And she's already got golden curls, just like you. I've named her Sabahat, in honor of her fine features – that is, unless you have any objections."

"I was expecting to name him Raif İbrahim, I hadn't thought of any girl's names."

"We'll name the next one Raif İbrahim."

"God won't grant me a son."

"It's best not to meddle in the Lord's work, Hanım. For now, we ask only that Allah grants us an auspicious son-in-law when the time comes. And may this lovely little girl bring fortune to our family and to our country," Ahmet Reşat said as he placed Sabahat in his wife's arms.

"I'm exhausted. If I nod off, she'll slip out of my arms. Give Sabahat to Mehpare, would you? Keep her contented until it's time to nurse."

Ahmet Reşat kissed his wife on the forehead and took the baby back into his arms. "Get some rest, my dear," he said. "Tomorrow we'll summon the hodja to come and bless our little girl."

He left the room, and as he went downstairs he pressed his nose against his newborn daughter's neck. "Tiny Sabahat Hanım," he said, "you've already gone and upset your mother for not being a boy, but I'm going to ensure you're educated as though you were one. And God willing, when you're all grown up, you'll be a dynamo." Then he sat down on the stairs, whispered the name Sabahat and a brief prayer into his daughter's ear, and ritually breathed on her.

In the anteroom on the second floor, Leman was seated at the piano playing a love song she'd recently memorized for Mahir.

"Play something proper, my girl," Saraylıhanım called out as she passed by. "Enough of that jingle-jangle. Play something that sounds like music."

"It's a *chanson*, nana."

"Shamson! Play something with a decent melody. Something Mahir Bey will enjoy."

"Don't mind nana, efendim. She objects to everything," said Leman, slightly embarrassed that her grandmother was ignorant of the latest French songs.

"Ah, the children these days," groused Saraylıhanım, "so disrespectful to their elders. God save us, and it's all Reşat Bey's doing, he does spoil them so. May he not come to regret it one day!"

In order to avoid the squabbling of Saraylıhanım and the girls, Ahmet Reşat had descended to the selamlık. When he found himself alone there with Mahir Bey he said, "Saraylıhanım is having difficulty adapting to the changing times, bless her, and she insists on taking it out on the girls. If only we'd all managed to adapt and modernize none of this would have happened. But we resisted change of any kind and we failed to adapt to the new age. And because we've failed to develop on our own, we've been forced to develop by those same countries we're forced to borrow money from. But coercion only achieves so much . . . It can't do any more."

"Neither the public nor the Sultan look favorably upon the idea of freedom and independence. I can understand the Sultan's objections. Who would possibly curb his own power?"

"The Europeans have, efendim! Their kings all have parliaments and legislative assemblies. They share their power with parliament. We're the only ones who have failed at that."

The two men spoke at some length on state affairs. Both were deeply saddened by the humiliation of their empire and sat for a time with heads hung, in silence. "You know," Ahmet Reşat finally said, "the best piece of luck we have is that neverending enmity between the French and the British. Their rivalry is our opportunity. Had they unfailingly agreed with each other, we'd have been finished long ago."

"We've also benefited enormously from the rivalry between Greece and Italy. Otherwise, the Italians would never have helped us smuggle weapons into Anatolia."

"I've always been rather fond of the Italians," said Ahmet Reşat," and count some of them among my closest friends. Look, why don't you spend the night here. I'll have a bed made up for you here in the selamlık."

"Your household is busy as it is. I wouldn't want to inconvenience you any further," Mahir protested.

"Neither the tramway nor the ferryboats are running at this hour. You've got no choice."

"That's what happens when you get engrossed in conversation," Mahir said. "Well, we did have a lot of catching up to do."

"I'll have Gülfidan make up your bed straight away."

When Ahmet Reşat had left the room Mahir reflected on their conversation. As far as he understood, the recent matter of Wrangel was deeply troubling to Ahmet Reşat, who was already contending with a thousand and one other problems. Even as the movement in Anatolia desperately battled the enemy, new troubles seemed to be emerging from every quarter. Everyone with a secret agenda seemed to be swarming into what remained of the empire. Naturally! Wolves stalk when the air is hazy. And at that moment in history, a dusty miasma lay over the land of the Ottomans.

Ahmet Reşat returned with the housekeeper.

"Let's go upstairs for a moment," he said, "while they prepare your bed."

"You're tired too, efendim. Aren't you ready for bed yet?"

"Not yet. We've talked over so much but I still have no idea why you've returned to Istanbul. Surely you didn't come all this way to deliver Behice's baby!"

Mahir laughed. "Actually, no. Cholera may well spread to the barracks, so I've come to take precautions."

"Has there been an outbreak of cholera?"

"It'll start any day now."

"Surely you can't simply order the outbreak of cholera?"

"That's precisely what I'll do. It'll be ordered to start and then it'll spread to all the barracks."

"Well I'll be damned!"

"That way, all of the barracks will be evacuated. The officers will have to get out of the way for me to apply disinfectants. I'll have to disinfect the warehouses as well, of course. The reason I'm here is to confirm the presence of cholera. I'll identify a serious case, write it up and recommend that measures be taken. Have I been able to make myself clear, efendim?"

"I understand exactly what you mean, Mahir Bey," said Ahmet Reşat. "Might I suggest we celebrate Sabahat's birth and the successful prevention of a cholera epidemic by each drinking a cup of linden tea? Then it's off to our beds and a restful night's sleep."

"That sounds perfect."

"Housekeeper Gülfidan, could you brew us up some linden tea? You can make up the bed later," said Ahmet Reşat. As they walked to the sitting room upstairs Mahir peeped over at the piano. The lilac shawl wrapped around Leman's shoulders as she'd played was now draped over the piano stool and in danger of touching the floor. Mahir picked it up and placed it on top of the piano. Then he brought his hand to his nose and discreetly breathed in the scent of lemon cologne.

– 17 –

The Raid

Sick of his paperwork and eager for deployment to the front, Kemal was ecstatic to be summoned one day as he was napping in his bunk just before mid-afternoon prayers. He hurriedly threw on his clothes and it was with a quick step and a light heart that he followed the now familiar path to the main building. Was he going to Anatolia at last? Awaiting him were the architects of a night-time raid. One of them, a man everyone addressed as Major, was known to Kemal as the commander of the farm; but the two men sitting on either side of his desk were strangers. Major pointed to a chair. Kemal sat down.

"Kemal Bey," Major began, "Two motorboats are leaving for Karamürsel tonight. You'll be on one of them. You'll then travel overland to Ankara for a few days of training on how to set up telegraph lines, after which you'll immediately be sent to the Aegean front."

"Right, efendim."

"We have an additional request to make of you."

"I'm at your service."

"Since you'll already be in one of the motorboats, you could be of great use to us."

"How?"

"Let me introduce you to captains Mustafa and Ahmet, in whose boats tonight we will be getting guns and ammunition from the Karaağaç depot for transport to our friends on the front in Anatolia."

Kemal nodded at the two captains, whose rough and ready looks marked them out as men from the Black Sea region.

"When we were deciding who to choose for this assignment, we realized we needed men who were patriotic, capable and—most important—able to keep a secret. You met all of our requirements. We don't expect you to help carry the munitions, but undertakings of this nature require meticulous records. The men carrying the weapons will be too busy for that. That's only one of the reasons we would like you to be aboard one of the boats tonight. If, God forbid, anything were to go wrong, we want you to talk to the occupation police in their own language and stall them with a cover story we will provide."

"Yes sir."

"This raid is a dangerous business. It could end in death."

"I understand."

"Do you accept?"

"Yes."

"That's precisely the answer I would have expected from a veteran of the Battle of Sarıkamış," Major said. "Your name is Gaffur Abdullah and you're a merchant in the cloth and underclothing trade. You're shipping some goods to the Asian Shore and returning to Istanbul with vegetables and grain. You own a trading firm.

All your documents are ready; you'll have them tonight. Now go to the dormitory and pack. Then come back here and get dressed in the clothes we've chosen for you. The captains will brief you once you're on your way."

Kemal ran all the way back to the dormitory, where, from among his possessions, he took only his medicine and the hand-kerchief embroidered for him by Mehpare. He entrusted his books to Hemşinli Osman, from the next bunk over, and made his fare-wells to his roommates. Once he'd returned to the main building and dressed in his costume, as instructed, he reentered the room and saluted Major and the others.

Kemal and the two captains traveled by carriage to a jetty on the Sea of Marmara, from where they set sail for Ahırkapı, just below the palace at Saray Point.

There was a strong wind, and as the small sailboat bobbed and dipped Kemal became increasingly seasick. He fought back the urge to vomit and silently gave thanks that the deepening dusk concealed what must have been his decidedly greenish color. Terrified of disgracing himself, he fixed his gaze on a point in the distance and tried to remain as motionless as possible—he re-membered having read somewhere that that might help.

As the sky darkened the sea grew calmer, and Kemal began to feel better. The captains took turns describing in more detail the raid that was to take place later that night. Kemal listened with the rapt attentiveness of a pupil.

When it had became obvious that the Ottomans were on the losing side in the Great War and the probability of foreign inva-sion strengthened, CUP partisans had begun stockpiling weapons across the city. The 500 crates of ammunition known to be at the Karaağaç depot on the Golden Horn were now needed to counter the Greek invasion. With God's help, all 500 crates would shortly be on their way to Anatolia. The risk involved was believed to be minimal, since the Karaağaç storekeeper, one Nazmi Bey, was himself involved in the underground and had prior knowledge of that night's raid.

Once they reached Ahırkapı, they would be driven by horse and cart to a pier on the Golden Horn, where two motorboats would be waiting. Captain Ahmet's boat would lead the way with the raiders; Captain Mustafa's would follow with Kemal.

In celebration of his newly settled stomach, Kemal took a drag on the cigarette offered him. Damn, it was foul! Captain Ahmet took over the briefing from Captain Mustafa. Once again, Kemal hung on every word. They'd had difficulty finding forty men to cart off the heavy guns. Not just anyone would do. No, they needed men who were brave, strong, quick and tight-lipped. And you couldn't find one of them on every corner, could you? So they'd told five of their captain friends to be on the lookout for men who fit the bill. With God's help they'd been rounded up in no time and would be joining the raid. Both captains were as calm and confident, as though they were discussing a regularly scheduled ferryboat service from the European shore to the Asian. Their self-assurance was contagious, and Kemal, who was anxious not to offend, took a final drag on the nauseating cigarette and tossed it into the sea.

"We'll be handing out pistols and daggers to all the men, just in case something goes wrong. Kemal Bey, I'm giving you a pistol too. I hope you won't need it, but it's best to have one, just in case," said Captain Mustafa. "Here you go—you know how to use it, don't you?"

"Yes," said Kemal as he silently prayed he wouldn't disgrace himself that night and considered, with a sinking heart and a churning stomach, how much younger and stronger he had been just five years earlier, marching off to Sarıkamış. So much had happened since then: he was no longer healthy, nor was he in his twenties. Seasickness was a horrible thing! He decided right then and there he'd never again take on more than he knew he could handle. Having honorably discharged the duties he'd accepted that night, he would go straight home, where he'd find refuge in Mehpare's arms and spend the rest of his life studiously penning articles and shunning adventure of any kind, devoting himself instead to being a wise husband and a loving father, just like his uncle.

As planned, they disembarked at Ahırkapı and traveled to a pier on the Golden Horn. Both motorboats were ready. Small bands of men, their faces swathed in cloth, came stealing out of the surrounding buildings, and materialized from behind bushes and trees. Everyone seemed to know exactly what was expected of them. They must have been old hands at this sort of thing. Most of the men crept into the first boat; a few boarded the second with Kemal, disappearing into the hatches and holds, where they crouched without a whisper, a sneeze, a cough. The engines had been muffled by towels, the exhaust pipes lowered into the sea. Kemal had forgotten all about seasickness. He nervously scanned the area, the only sound the beating of his own heart. The boat sliced through the dark waters, past Karaağaç, and drew up to a landing in front of the depot. "Gangway! Don't come near the landing!" the watchman shouted.

"Friend, we're not strangers . . . Didn't they tell you we were coming?" asked Captain Mustafa.

"No. Don't come any closer!"

"Tell Nazmi Bey we're here. He's expecting us."

"I told you not to come any closer." The watchman pointed his gun at the captain.

"What the hell! What are we, enemies? Don't go pointing that gun at me; save it for the real enemy. Shame on you."

As Captain Ahmet kept his boat well back, Captain Mustafa drew up to the landing. "What's your name, matey? Come aboard. Everything's shipshape. The English gave us a permit to clean out the depot. You know what it's like, they can't keep the thieving under control . . . So they decided to dump everything into the sea, to keep it from the Ottomans. That's why we're here. To load it up and dump it a bit further along. Straight into the sea with the whole lot, I say, no use to them and no use to us. I hate to do it, but we're just following orders." As the captain was speaking he steered closer to the landing until he was able to grab it with his hand.

Kemal could barely make out the stock-still shadows that had appeared some distance behind the watchman, facing the sea. Who were they?

"Captain Mustafa, look over there . . ." Kemal was about to blurt out when the captain gripped his arm as he continued talking:

"Kemal Bey, give me a hand, would you? Keep the motorboat still," Captain Mustafa said as he leapt up onto the landing to continue his chat with the watchman on dry land. The shadowy figures had crept even closer. Kemal leaned out and clutched the metal rail of the landing with both hands. As he held on for dear life, the boat started drifting away from shore and he found himself being transformed into a sort of human gangplank, with his feet precariously planted on the boat and his overextended arms stretched to breaking point. He was just about to fall into the water when a sailor jumped onto the prow, gripped the wooden landing with powerful fingers and managed to draw the boat closer.

"I thought my arms would be ripped off," Kemal said.

"They're fine, they're just a bit longer now, brother, is all. New to this kind of thing, are you?"

"I'm not a sailor . . . Hey, what's going on?" As Kemal had struggled to keep the boat close to the landing, men from the other boat had silently jumped ashore and, smooth as clockwork, immobilized the watchman, tying his arms behind his back and wadding a handkerchief in his mouth. Men began leaping out of Captain Mustafa's boat as well, and to Kemal's right and left shadows streamed ashore and towards the depot. In the darkness, Kemal could make out English watchmen tumbling off the wall, their feet pulled out from under them.

Four men were approaching Kemal's boat. "Grab my hand and come ashore," one of them said.

"Who are you?" Kemal asked.

"We organized the raid. We were expecting you. Come on." As Kemal took the extended hand and jumped ashore he felt deeply grateful to have left the sea behind. "Nazmi Bey opened the doors. Our men are inside right now. You were told to take delivery of the crates and count them, weren't you? Hurry up and get to it."

Two of the men waited in the boat while Kemal followed the other two a short distance back. Crates were being swiftly and soundlessly passed from hand to hand toward the boat. As Kemal furiously scribbled in a notebook, unable to see what he was writing, a large youth he'd met on the boat ride, who went by the name of Gendarme, kept his gun trained on a few gagged and bound soldiers, his eyes alert to the tiniest movement. Lookouts kept the raiders posted on any vessels that passed close to shore, at which time they'd stop their work, only to resume it with intensified speed once the coast was clear.

Kemal had some burlap sacks opened and, with the help of Nazmi Bey, sorted munitions in order of importance, with cartridges going into one bag, bullets and ammunition into other bags and crates. Once filled, everything was immediately loaded onto the two motorboats.

Once the depot had been emptied of munitions, the captains ordered their men and their prisoners onto the boats, which began cruising toward the bridge, heavily laden with the small arsenal, as well as the raiders and their captives.

The bound and gagged prisoners had all been marched at gunpoint into the bows of Captain Ahmet's boat, under the watchful eye of their guards, talkative now that the raid was done. The captains had been undecided on what to do with them.

Captain Mustafa had suggested that they be dropped off on a secluded stretch of rocky coast a safe distance away.

"I think you should take them all the way to Karamürsel and surrender them to the Nationalist Forces. On the way, we'll impress upon them that they're the native sons of these lands, not of England," Kemal weighed in.

"But are they likely be swayed?" Captain Ahmet asked doubtfully.

"Yes, very likely. I've been preaching a similar message to everyone from the Senegalese and the Algerians to the Muslim Indians.

That was one of my duties, and I've been fairly successful. And these boys are Turks, after all," Kemal said.

"A few of them are English."

"Good God! Why'd we bring them along?"

"What were we supposed to do? Let them go, so they could report the raid and identify our boats? That would have been asking for disaster."

"You're right, but now we'll have to feed them. These foreigners aren't like us; they're not used to going hungry."

"Well, even in the worst weather it shouldn't take more than two nights to get there. Don't worry, whether we give them food or not, they're not going to starve," said Captain Ahmet.

After a long debate, a decision was reached: the prisoners would be taken to Karamürsel and surrendered to the National Forces. And the English hostages might well prove useful as bargaining chips.

They made a short stop on the banks of the Golden Horn to load boxes of canvas, curtain fabric, and underwear onto one of the boats, sacks of grain onto the other. Most of the raiding party disembarked and slipped off home. When they resumed sailing, the remaining men carefully stacked merchant Gaffur Abdullah's goods on top of the munitions.

The second part of the adventure was about to begin.

The surface of the sea was smooth and inky, and it was no coincidence that no moon shone that night.

Kemal decided he was getting his sea legs, and that he might even be enjoying the bobbing of the boat and the murmuring of the waves as they gently lapped and plashed . . . His thoughts drifted back to the rowboat excursion he'd taken with his uncle on the Sea of Marmara.

He'd leaned over the side and trailed his hand in the water, keeping it there until it was creased and puckered. Then he'd gleefully shouted: "Look Uncle, I've got old man hands, just like you!"

His uncle had laughed and stroked his hair with the words, "Here's hoping you live to a ripe old age, and acquire a pair of them in earnest." As he remembered, Kemal couldn't help laughing aloud at the realization that his uncle had only been in his twenties at the time.

"You seem to be feeling better now, Kemal Bey, but the real danger's just about to begin," the captain told him. "We're approaching Unkapanı Bridge."

Kemal's smile died on his lips. There were no impediments at that bridge and they continued cruising unhindered towards Karaköy Bridge—the checkpoint controlling all maritime traffic into and out of the Golden Horn. Even in the darkness Kemal could see the anxiety on the captain's face.

"Will they search the boat?" he asked.

"If one of our men is on duty, no."

"And if he's not?"

"Then we might be in for a little trouble."

They'd reached the bridge. A man signaled the boat with a lamp. Captain Mustafa let out a shrill whistle. The shadow up on the bridge responded in kind. The boat slowed and the captain steered it toward the checkpoint. Kemal felt his heart pounding. Cruising across the water may not have been as excruciating as trudging across the ice in Sarıkamış, but he sensed that he was as close to death as he had ever been in his life. The slightest false move would be met with a hail of bullets. And what a tragedy that would be. Not because they would die—no, they were all prepared for that: but because they'd die before surrendering the munitions, and all their work would have been in vain. Kemal silently prayed for success. If he were to die, he asked that it be for a purpose. Unlike the lives squandered in Sarıkamış, with not a single shot fired. As he prayed, a deep voice reached his ears.

"Password?"

"Crescent."

"Signal?"

"Destination."

"Move along. Safe journey to you."

"Thanks."

Moments later, they were past the bridge and chugging toward the Sea of Marmara. Drained from all the excitement, Kemal sat in the stern of the boat, his back propped against a pile of nets, looking out over the murky water. Captain Mustafa came up to Kemal and rested his hand on his shoulder, "Shouldn't be any trouble now! Why don't you go below deck and have a nap," he suggested.

"I'm fine here."

"My nose is telling me we could have some stormy weather. If we do, you'll get awfully sick below. You'd better get some sleep now, while it's dead calm."

Kemal glanced over to his right, at a coastline etched in indigo, dark but for one or two lights straining weakly somewhere in the distance. There was nothing to look at; he got up to do as the captain had advised. And as the first welcoming corner presented itself, Kemal curled up and fell fast asleep.

Frantic cries and shouts, someone yelling, "Light a bonfire," comings and goings, hurried footsteps overhead . . . half-real, half-dreamed as Kemal lay sleeping. A heavy crate dropped with a thud and he opened his eyes. At first, he had no idea where he was. Was he in the dormitory, in his bunk? Instinctively ducking his head, he sat up. It was stuffy. Getting to his feet, he walked, clutching anything he could for support. The strange noises in his dream continued, even though his eyes were open. He climbed the three rungs of the ladder, stepped on deck and looked up at a starless sky leached by the milky light of early dawn.

"And a good morning to you, sir," Captain Mustafa greeted him. "They dropped a crate of rifles and woke you up." The pieces of information in his confused mind came together and Kemal knew where he was.

"Have we reached our destination?"

"We have, thank God. That was quite some snooze, Kemal Pasha."

"You mean I was promoted to pasha while I slept?" Kemal laughed.

"Pasha of the whole navy."

The band of men still on the boat had busied themselves all night long lugging sacks and crates to shore. There were also some new men, who had come aboard to help.

"Where's the other boat?" Kemal asked.

"It hasn't arrived yet. We're still waiting."

"How long have we been here?"

"Almost an hour."

"I was out like a light, Captain Mustafa. I wish you'd woken me up. Why are the others so late? You don't think there's been any trouble, do you?"

"They were right behind us. Then we lost them over by Darıca . . . They might have had engine trouble."

"God help them."

"Maybe they overshot the dock," said one of the men carrying off a crate of munitions.

"That's what the district governor thinks, which is why he suggested lighting a bonfire on the shore. Of course, now that it's getting light outside a fire won't do any good."

Kemal shivered slightly as he stepped off the boat. There was a fresh breeze. A mountain of crates and sacks rested on the dock. He pulled his notebook out of his pocket and leaned against a post trying to read it. Still too dark. He gave up. A huge fire blazed on the shoreline, the bonfire the governor had ordered. Kemal walked back and forth on the dock. The sky was growing brighter by the second. He pulled out his notebook again and started cross-checking the list of items from the depot.

As the hours passed everyone grew increasingly nervous about the missing second boat. The entire consignment had been loaded onto carts waiting on the dock and the cargo hold had been refilled with sacks of grain. Also stacked on the dock were Kemal's boxes of cloth and underclothes.

Captain Mustafa came up to Kemal and said, "It's time the traveler was on his way. You'll have to be leaving us now."

"And you should go immediately and help the others if their boat's broken down," Kemal said.

"Aye aye, Navy Pasha," chuckled Captain Mustafa. "But the sea's too deep for them to drop anchor if they've had engine trouble, Kemal Bey. They'll have drifted off to God knows where."

Not for the first time, Kemal felt rather sheepish at his ignorance. The captain thrust out his hand and said good-bye. The mooring lines were untied and Captain Mustafa's motorboat chugged off into an open sea glazed here and there with shimmering shades of red and yellow, until he and his boat were no more than a pinpoint on the distant horizon. Kemal felt as though his last link to the city had been severed. As the boat bound for Istanbul disappeared, he was keenly aware how far he was from home. He felt oddly empty but curiously elated as he sat on a box of underclothes and began to stocktake in his notebook as he patiently waited for the second boat.

As noon approached, those around him began to lose hope. The sun was now high above the horizon. The district governor of Karamürsel and his men were openly speculating that the boat had been stopped by an English assault vessel out on the open sea. Everyone was grim-faced.

"At any sign danger, they would have dumped all the weapons into the sea," Kemal said, still holding out hope. Then he remembered the prisoners that had all been loaded onto the second boat. They could hardly throw all of them overboard!

"There's no sense waiting out here in the open," the governor said. "Let's go back to town. There may be word from Istanbul."

As they trooped dejectedly off of the dock someone noticed a tiny speck on the horizon. Their hearts in their mouths, they waited. Yes, it was them.

The boat was welcomed with whoops and cheers. Their engine had broken down near Darıca and they'd spent all these hours trying to repair it. The freight was unloaded and the prisoners turned over to the commander of the National Forces when he arrived to pick up the weapons.

Another raid successfully concluded.

The British response was harsh. Many of the men rounded up by the occupation authorities were tortured to extract confessions. The Istanbul Government was threatened with reprisals and, from that day onwards, all vessels of all sizes and descriptions were categorically forbidden to pass under any bridges after nightfall.

– 18 –

December 31, 1920

Dilruba Hanım didn't join her chattering daughters in the sitting room after dinner. She performed her ablutions and her prayers, got into bed and read the Koran well into the night. Then she placed it on her nightstand, said a final prayer, and lay down to sleep in the hope that, in her dreams that night, God would show her the best path. Two weeks earlier, a family living on the street behind hers had asked for Mualla's hand in marriage. They were good people, honest and simple. She'd first met the mother of the family some years earlier at the corner grocery; they'd since visited each other for morning coffee and to exchange holiday greetings, shared recipes for jam and börek, and generally got along well. While she couldn't easily refuse such a family, Dilruba was a mother first and foremost, and neither was it easy for her to forget that she had a relative, however distant, who served in the cabinet and lived in a mansion in Beyazit. If Reşat Beyefendi were to confide to one his clerks that he had relatives of a marriageable age, any of them would doubtless be eager to take as his wife a girl as virtuous and well-connected as her daughters. And if Mehpare had successfully beguiled the young master of the house under whose patronage she had been sent to live, surely her own girls could turn the head of one Kemal Bey's distinguished friends. Mualla and Meziyet would then be sent from the peeling house on a humble street in Beşiktaş to become the mistresses of grand mansions all their own.

Their home hadn't always been in such a state of disrepair, of course. When her father had bought it some forty years earlier, it had been a typical Istanbul house, a three-storey wooden structure, painted white, with a red-tiled roof and charming bow windows. Dilruba Hanım had been a child at the time. Like so many Circassians, her family had fled to Istanbul to escape the bloody massacres in the Caucasus after the '93 War. The house had been bought with the gold pieces they'd sewn into the hems of their skirts and the linings of their cloaks and even hidden in their hair. They'd hoped to build a peaceful new life in their new homeland, but they'd arrived just as the Ottoman Empire was entering a period of decline and disintegration. And so they lost their men to war, their women to childbirth, and their children to epidemics. They may have become poorer, sadder, but they were still grateful not to have to face slaughter and rape, and grateful for their prosperous relatives here, always prepared to lend a helping hand. If one of the girls were to make a favorable match, employment might even be arranged at a government office for her son Recep.

When, gift in hand, daughters in tow, Dilruba Hanım had made her way to the mansion to present her congratulations on the occasion of the birth of Behice's third daughter, and dutifully stayed on for a few days to help with the flood of well-wishers, she'd casually dropped a hint to Saraylıhanım.

"Reşat Bey is in such a temper these days that I fear he's in no condition to act as matchmaker," Saraylıhanım had said, adding, "But when the time comes for Mehpare to give birth I do hope you'll come again for a night or two, at which point I'll be certain to broach the subject with him."

Saraylıhanım relished the role of marriage broker.

Dilruba Hanım found herself on the horns of a dilemma: should she wait until the birth of Mehpare's baby and the prospect of a distinguished and possibly wealthy suitor for her daughter, or should she settle for the neighbor's son? Life had repeatedly taught her that when in the presence of running water, one should wash one's hands. Furthermore, she was worried that Mualla would gain a neighborhood reputation as a fussy, stuck-up girl. Kismet may come to your feet; but, once turned away, might never return. As Dilruba Hanım pondered long and hard, it never occurred to her to ask her daughter for guidance. No one had asked her when her own husband had been arranged. The task of choosing a spouse fell to elders, relatives, and even neighbors. And as she wrestled with her weighty responsibility, deeply conflicted and unable to reach a decision, she hoped her dreams would show her the way.

Dilruba Hanım was awakened from a deep sleep by a series of explosions. She'd been dreaming about a double wedding and was smiling contentedly at a low rumbling which she'd taken to be the pounding of the ceremonial drums. That smile was still on her face as she sat up in bed. Those were no drums—no, it was a bomb . . . and another. She leapt out of bed so abruptly that her head spun and she nearly toppled over. Lurching to the window she pulled back the curtains. The sky above the two- and three-storey houses was illuminated with an unearthly red light. There must be a fire nearby! The streets had filled with frantic people running to and fro. Bombs continued to explode, one after another. Were they being shelled? Had the enemy invaded their street? Would they burst into the house? Would they loot and pillage? Would they kill everyone? She ran out of her room and bumped straight into her daughters, both of them quaking with fear.

"What's going on, mother? Are they dropping bombs on us? What's that racket?"

"Where's your brother? Where's Recep?"

"He hasn't come back yet."

"He hasn't returned? At this hour? My God, what if something's happened to him? He may have been shot, or arrested!"

"Don't even say such a thing!"

"Quick, get dressed girls, into your çarşafs. Everyone's running for their lives. Let's go."

"But where can we go at this hour, mother?"

"We'll go to Reşat Bey's house. We can shelter there. It's the home of a minister; we should be safe."

"But how will we get there?"

"We'll find a rowboat to take us as far as Sirkeci. Or we'll walk. Hurry up and get dressed. Write a note to Recep saying where we've gone. Leave it on the console in the hall. Got that, Meziyet? Quickly now!"

The blasts were deafening and unremitting. Dilruba went to her room, rummaged through a wooden trunk and pulled out a tin box containing her valuables and the deed to the house. Groping through the contents of a dresser drawer, she located a key, opened the box and began rummaging around for something. She hastily stripped the pillow of its case, tossed in the few jewels and gold pieces from the box, tightly knotted it and secured it to her waist with a long sash, and slipped into her cloak and çarşaf. "Are you ready, girls?" she called.

Dilruba Hanım and her daughters raced down the stairs to the street door and outside. The street was heaving with panicked neighbors, screaming women, wailing children, howling dogs, watchmen blowing whistles. People were hanging out of their windows. Everyone was shouting at once and it was impossible to tell what anyone was saying.

"Take hold of my hands, hold tight," Dilruba Hanım shouted to her daughters, "and if anyone gets lost in the crowd we'll meet at the Beşiktaş Ferry Station, all right?"

The crowds were surging towards the main street, pushing and shoving, trampling each other, stepping over and onto the fallen. Dilruba Hanım realized she'd forgotten to put on her shoes. Not only was it difficult to walk in backless slippers, her feet were cold. Trying as best she could to keep hold of her daughters' hands, she checked to make certain the bundle strapped around her waist was still there. It was—she relaxed slightly. The bombs were still going off in rapid succession, and each explosion painted the sky a garish red, then other colors, one after the other. Flashes of blue and yellow, orange and purple.

"It's Doomsday," cried a man with a grey beard. "It's not bombs, it's the end of the world!"

The panicked crowd surged forward. Dilruba stumbled and nearly fell when someone stepped on the hem of her çarşaf; her headscarf slid to the ground. It would be impossible to bend over and pick it up. Well, they were all going to die, she no longer cared what the neighbors said, she thought as she tugged at her daughters and was swept along by the hordes of people. There was someone just ahead, going against the crowd, arms outstretched as he fought his way through. He was nearly upon Dilruba Hanım before she cried, "My God, it's you!"

"Mother! What are you doing—your hair's uncovered! Where on earth are you going?"

"Oh, Recep! My boy! All hell's broken loose. Look at the sky! All those colors! We're running for our lives."

Halted as they were in the middle of the street, Dilruba Hanım and her family were shoved and elbowed from behind. Recep managed to pull his mother and sisters out of the crush and into the safety of a doorway.

"Mother, have you lost your mind? Get back to the house at once!"

"But son, what about the bombs? Don't your hear them? We'll be safe at Reşat Bey's."

"What bombs?"

"Look! Everyone's running away!"

"We're going home," Recep said. "I hope you haven't forgotten to close the door. Otherwise, thieves will have long since cleaned us out."

There was a long explosion. "See? They're dropping bombs!" Meziyet said.

"That wasn't a bomb. They're fireworks. If you'd made it as far as the coast you'd have seen for yourselves," said Recep with an odd look on his face, as though he didn't know whether to laugh or to cry. "The heathens are celebrating their new year. There's a cruiser anchored off Beşiktaş. They've been setting off fireworks for an hour. Now go on, get home!"

"Whatever do you mean?" stammered Dilruba Hanım. "No one sets off fireworks in the winter!"

As Dilruba Hanım limped back to her house, shivering in a single slipper, her head bare, her hair disheveled, her bundle of valuables threatening to slip to her knees, she decided that her dream that night had shown her the correct path. Allah had given her a glimpse of Armageddon; she'd been forced to confront death; then, he'd restored her to normal life. If she really had remembered to shut the door tightly against thieves, she would immediately inform her neighbors, first thing tomorrow, that she would indeed agree to give her daughter Mualla's hand in marriage to their son. And may it all work out for the best.

Spectacles perched on his nose, Ahmet Reşat sat in his room reading a letter in the daylight coming in from the window. When he'd finished, he folded it, placed it in his pocket and went downstairs to join the women in the sitting room.

"Mehpare, tell Gülfidan to make us each a nice cup of coffee, would you?" he said.

"Her hands smell of onion at the moment, I'll go make some and bring it up to you, efendim," Mehpare said. "And you'll have to excuse me, please. I find I'm unable to enjoy the aroma of coffee these days."

"Make some for Saraylıhanım and Behice then. They'll have some."

"Don't make any for me, Mehpare, too much coffee is bad for my milk," Behice said. In actual fact, the women were economizing so that their guests and Reşat Bey could drink coffee. And that wasn't the only way they scrimped: Behice would pretend not to want meat on those days meat dishes were prepared, ensuring that her share then went to her daughters, who were growing, and Mehpare, who was pregnant. At first Saraylıhanım had been quite prickly with her fussy daughter-in-law; but when she came to understand Behice's true motives she began treating her more kindly.

Mehpare left the room to prepare coffee for Reşat Bey and Saraylıhanım.

"What's going on my boy? Why the sudden desire for coffee service?"

"It's conversation I want; the coffee was a pretext," Ahmet Reşat explained.

"Reşat Bey, since when have you been interested in sitting down to conversation with us?" Behice asked.

"Why wouldn't I sit down with you when there's something to discuss?"

"Is there something to discuss?"

"There certainly is."

"I'm dying to know what it is, tell us for God's sake."

"Wait for Mehpare to come back," said Reşat Bey.

"Reşat, my boy! Is it really necessary that Mehpare be here?"

"It is," Ahmet Reşat said, "considering that it concerns her husband."

"Oh, is there news of my lion? Tell us this minute. I'm bursting with curiosity. Is he in good spirits? Is he in good health? Has he reached the front?"

"I'll answer all your questions . . . when Mehpare's here."

A short time later, Mehpare walked into the room with a mother-of-pearl tray containing a coffee cup and a tea glass. She handed the coffee cup to Reşat Bey and walked over to Saraylıhanım. "I know how you like your coffee sweet; but we're out of sugar, so I've brought you tea, efendim," she said. "I added a spoonful of honey."

"The abundance of İbrahim Bey's honey is remarkable," Saraylıhanım said, "are you saying we haven't finished it yet?"

"We've used it sparingly. There's still a bit left."

"Wonderful. Now sit down and listen, my girl, there's some news from Kemal."

Mehpare's knees shook. She sat down on the divan next to Behice, who had placed her baby on her outstretched legs and was lightly rocking her.

"This letter was written while Kemal was in Ankara." Ahmet Reşat said, "He was able to get there only after two days, traveling by horse and cart and posing as a cloth merchant. They'd prepared all the necessary papers for him and there were no obstructions or difficulties of any kind. He says he's willing to put up with rain and hail—even snow—as long he's allowed to keep his feet on dry land. I think we can assume he didn't think of much of traveling by sea."

"Oh, my poor boy," Saraylıhanım said, "he's never been one for the water, ever since he was little. Do you remember, Reşat Bey, when he was three and there was that terrible storm as we were coming back from the island? He had nightmares for months."

Mehpare wished that the elderly woman would keep quiet and not speak again until all the news of Kemal was finished. Reşat Bey resumed his reading.

"There's a school building of some kind in Ankara. They stayed there for a time. Kemal was taught how to read and write telegraphs, as well as how to set up telegraph stations. Then they sent him off to the Aegean region with coils of wire and some insulators."

"And?"

"From what I understand, they plan to set up telegraph stations in areas invaded by the Greeks, so they can communicate with Ankara."

"Good lord, what on earth does that boy know about telegraphy?" cried Saraylıhanım. "They'll get him into trouble, I just know it. What if he gets dizzy stringing up all those wires and falls . . ."

"Bless you, Mother," Behice said, "Kemal won't be stringing up the wires himself, someone else will be doing it."

"Ladies," said Ahmet Reşat, "I'd greatly appreciate it if you'd kindly stop conversing among yourselves and pay attention. There's some news you'll all welcome."

"What news?"

"Guess who Kemal met in Ankara?"

"Who, who?"

"Gazi Pasha?" Mehpare asked.

"Wrong."

"Come on, tell us son."

"Azra Hanım."

Mehpare was unable to restrain a cry.

"What's Azra doing in Ankara?" Saraylıhanım asked. Then she stood up and walked directly over to Reşat Bey. "What's Azra doing in Ankara?" she repeated.

"She's learning telegraphy as well."

"Is she going to the Western Front?" asked Mehpare, who despite her affection for Azra couldn't help but speak in slightly brittle tones.

"No. She's working in Maraş. She's learned all she needs to learn and is returning to Maraş."

As Mehpare fought to conceal her relief, Behice muttered, "Is Azra mad?"

"She's not a woman she's a tomboy. God protect our girls," Saraylıhanım said.

"Is there any other news of my husband?" asked Mehpare.

"I'll give you the letter and you can read it yourself. But he's used a lot of code words, so there's a lot you won't understand."

Mehare found herself at Ahmet Reşat's side. She very nearly snatched the letter from his hand.

"There are two letters addressed to you, Mehpare," said Ahmet Reşat.

All three women looked up, wide-eyed.

"One of them is from Kemal. What's the second one?" Saraylıhanım asked.

Reşat Bey pulled two envelopes out of his pocket and handed them to Mehpare. At the sight of Kemal's handwriting, she tore one of them open.

"Who's the other letter from? Tell me at once!"

Eager to mollify Saraylıhanım, Mehpare opened the second envelope and checked the signature. "Azra has written to me as well," she said, "and if you'll excuse me I'd like to read both letters in my room."

"No good has ever come of careless correspondence, mark my words," said Saraylıhanım.

Mehpare ignored the elderly woman's insinuations, as well as the transparent look of envious hurt on Behice's face, and ran off to her room. With the tips of her fingers, she caressed Kemal's words. Then she kissed the sheet of paper and began reading.

The letter opened with Kemal's greetings to everyone in the household. Mehpare skimmed through the questions about everyone from Saraylıhanım to Sabahat and reread, several times, the bit about the chance meeting with Azra in Ankara. No, there wasn't the slightest indication of anything untoward. Kemal had sincerely enjoyed running into an old friend and wished to share his happiness with his wife. That was all. In any case, Azra had returned to Maraş after two days and Kemal was just about to be posted to the Aegean, to a town whose name he didn't reveal in the letter. Her beloved husband wrote that there had been signs in his dreams that pointed to happier times ahead and that he was convinced fate would unite them within the year. He called on Mehpare to remain light of heart and to be extremely careful with their baby. When Mehpare finished the letter she wiped her eyes and moved on to the one addressed to Reşat Bey. The letter to Kemal's uncle was much more specific concerning Kemal's duties, but, as she'd been warned, was full of code words that made it difficult for her to decipher. Once she'd reread Kemal's letter several more times, she felt ready for the one from Azra.

"To Mehpare Hanım, my long-suffering and self-sacrificing Sister," the letter began. Next, Azra described her coincidental encounter with Kemal in Ankara. She had found him healthy and well. There was no cause for Mehpare to be concerned about her husband's health. He was proud of and pleased with his duties and even blamed his extended illness in Istanbul upon his having been confined to the house, where he was of no use to anyone.

Next came the most important section for Mehpare. A very important piece of news.

Last autumn, as the two of them were walking home together from Şayeste Hanım's lecture, Azra had confessed that her heart had been empty for a very long time and that she wished she were able to love a man with all the passion and longing Mehpare felt for Kemal. Mehpare had said that she felt certain Azra would soon meet such a man. Mehpare had been right. Azra was in love with a major she'd met in Maraş. When she'd seen Kemal in Ankara she had spoken of this man and was now sharing her secret with Mehpare as well. While a part of her wanted to trumpet her love to the whole world, she preferred for the moment that no one knew about it and asked that Mehpare promise to keep it a secret. One day, God willing, they would meet in Istanbul and she would reveal his identity, if he survived.

If he survived! Mehpare sat on the edge of the bed, held up her cupped hands and prayed, "Please, may all of you survive."

Mehpare was getting ready to reread all three letters, again and again, when the bell to the garden gate rang. She walked over to the window and was surprised to see her aunt and her aunt's daughters, followed by Recep, whose arms were full of parcels, traipsing through the garden, all smiles. No one had told her Aunt Dilruba would be visiting. She slipped the letters under her pillow and ran downstairs.

Dilruba Hanım had arrived both to give the news of Mualla's engagement and to share with her beloved relatives, while it was still fresh in her mind, the distress and sufferings of an event that had happened some ten days earlier. With frequent interruptions from her daughters and her son, accompa- nied by impromptu reenactments, she related how, very late one night, the infidels had begun celebrating one of their new years, the terrific explosions, how everyone had taken to the streets, fearing for their lives, and how she'd lost a slipper and headscarf in the panic and mayhem. Leman, Suat and Behice were in stitches over the whole affair, but Saraylıhanım more or less successfully banished the traces of a smile that had crept into the corners of her lips. Her mind still on the letters she'd put under her pillow, Mehpare was unable to con- centrate. She wanted nothing more than to return at once to her room and to the world of her letters, but was incapable of commit- ting such a blatant discourtesy while there were guests.

After repeating her tale several times to the general mirth of her hostesses, Dilruba turned to Mehpare and remarked, "Are you sure you aren't expecting twins, my girl? Your belly is absolutely enormous."

Mehpare, who had grown accustomed to that question, merely answered with an enigmatic smile.

"We don't have any twins in my family but Mehpare might on her mother's side. Do you know anything about that, efendim?" Dilruba Hanım asked.

Saraylıhanım was preparing an appropriate response when they were interrupted by the entrance of the housekeeper.

"There's someone downstairs. He's brought the master a mes- sage," she said.

Reşat Bey raced for the door; Mehpare went pale; Saraylıhanım clutched her breast. The women anxiously awaited Reşat Bey's return. For so many years, all news had been bad news: they expected nothing else. A few moments later they heard Reşat Bey's step on the stairs. "He's walking up the stairs quickly, so it can't be bad news," Mehpare said to herself. She was proven right when Reşat Bey appeared in the doorway with a broad smile waving a telegraph.

"Dilruba Hanım, you've brought good fortune with you. Kemal sends us fresh news. The National Army has succeeded at last in holding the line against the Greeks. And this despite the Greeks' twenty thousand rifles to our six thousand. It happened at a place on the Western Front called İnönü."

"In on who?" asked Saraylıhanım, who was hard of hearing.

"I don't know who's on what; all I know is that Reşat Bey is smiling for the first time in months, so it must be good news," Behice said.

- 19 -

February 1921

It was evening. The women and children had just finished dinner. Mehpare was in the kitchen preparing a tray for Reşat Bey, who was late, as usual. Typically, Saraylıhanım couldn't resist meddling, calling down the stairs to Mehpare, who was arranging slices of börek on a plate: "Mehpare, Reşat Bey doesn't care for potato börek; be sure and give him the one with parsley, won't you."

"That's just what I'm doing, efendim," Mehpare replied.

Mehpare had grown heavy-limbed and her ankles were swollen; even so, she'd been doing her best to assist the housekeeper ever since the irregularly paid salary of the master of the house had left them no choice but to dismiss Zehra. Poor Housekeeper Gülfidan was getting too old and fat to manage the stairs. Not that the heavily pregnant Mehpare could take them two at a time herself, any longer. Her belly was so big that Suat and Leman were convinced she was carrying twins. If they were boys, their names were ready: in her capacity as honorary elder sister, Leman had decided on Selim for the younger boy: it would go well with Halim, the name reserved for the elder.

As the girls chattered on, Mehpare would tilt her head slightly to one side and listen in resigned silence. She could easily foresee the girls' disappointment when she didn't bear twins; what she couldn't predict was how Reşat Bey and Behice Hanım would react to the early arrival of the baby. Would there be much scratching of heads and counting of fingers? Would they reproach her; fling it in her face, even? Or had the ever crafty Saraylıhanım long since hatched an explanation of some kind?

Having placed a dish of stewed prunes and a mug of ayran on the tray with the börek, Mehpare set it on the marbletopped table in the entry hall. When Reşat Bey arrived he could take the tray either to the selamlık or to the upstairs sitting room, whichever he preferred.

No one had done the shopping that day, so there weren't any newspapers in the house. Hüsnü Efendi had lost a relative and would be away for several days attending the village funeral. As Reşat Bey had left that morning, Mehpare had asked him to bring home a newspaper from the ministry. She had begun studying the newspaper every day to see if there was anything that might involve Kemal.

At Saraylıhanım's insistence, Behice had descended to the pantry so the two women could take inventory. The sugar was long gone. There was very little cooking oil. It was only through much sifting of the remains of a sack of flour that they had been able to bake börek that day. Behice would write to Beypazarı that night and request that her father send some grain, oil and cottage cheese.

Clutching the banister, Mehpare began climbing the stairs. The girls were in the anteroom singing to the accompaniment of the piano and violin.

"Come and join us, Mehpare Abla," Leman called out, "bring your ud and we'll switch to something *à la Turca*."

Mehpare declined. She had a twinge in her lower back and wanted to lie down in her room. She'd just reached the second floor landing when she heard the bell to the garden gate. It would be far too much trouble to go back down two flights of stairs, she decided. Let Gülfidan open the gate for a change.

Mehpare got to her room and walked over to the window. The housekeeper was waddling through the garden. So, she'd heard the bell. The women of the house had been led to believe that Gülfidan was quite deaf and certainly unable to hear bells and knocks, but they'd all chosen to turn a blind eye to the servant's little ploy. The housekeeper opened the gate and began talking to two unfamiliar men. Even from her vantage point at the window, Mehpare could tell from the men's stiff movements and stern demeanor that whatever had brought them to the house was of a serious nature. Mehpare left the window and sat down on the edge of the bed, her hand pressed to her chest. Her heart felt heavy and troubled. And it wasn't just her heart. Even though she'd eaten nothing but a bowl of rice, she'd been burping all day. She felt listless; nothing appealed. She uncovered her head, unbuttoned her blouse, to relieve herself of the weight pressing onto her chest, reached out her hand to get the bottle resting on the nightstand, splashed cologne on her temples and breasts, kicked off her slippers and was just stretching out in bed when something told her to get up and walk back over to the window.

The housekeeper was gone. Standing at the garden gate with the strange men were Saraylıhanım and Behice. One of the men pointed into the distance as he explained something. Mehpare watched as Behice began beating her knees; Saraylıhanım swayed for a moment, tilted forward and fell to her knees on the grass. The men took her arms and tried to pull her to her feet.

Hair uncovered, blouse unbuttoned, feet bare, Mehpare bolted down the stairs and toward the two men propping up Saraylıhanım, one on each side, as they half carried, half dragged her to the house, Behice immediately behind them, talking continuously:

"Mother, please mother, I'm begging you, try to remain calm. Mehpare mustn't hear of this or, God forbid, something could happen to the baby, I implore you, mother, please . . ."

Mehpare darted out of the front door and straight up to the men. "What happened to Kemal?" she screamed. No one spoke. No one moved. The four people standing across from her were frozen in place, like a photograph, staring at Mehpare as she stared back at them. Mehpare stretched out her arms and with a fluttering motion gently fell forward and down, collapsed on the marble slab in front of the door.

"My God, I hope she hasn't bumped her belly," Behice shouted as she knelt and put her ear to Mehpare's breast to listen to her heartbeat.

A growing pool of pinkish fluid was staining the white marble by Mehpare's legs.

"She's losing the baby!" Behice shrieked.

"It's not a miscarriage; she's giving birth," Saraylıhanım managed to say.

"Help!" Behice shouted at the men propping up Saraylıhanım. "Help us! For God's sake, go tell the housekeeper, tell the girls. Call the midwife. Get a doctor, quick! Don't just stand there, run! Run!"

The men dashed into the house, leaving Saraylıhanım on the ground. Unable to stand up unassisted, she crawled on all fours across the lawn to Behice and Mehpare. Pulling off her headscarf she folded it, handed it to Behice and said, "Put it under Mehpare's back, my girl. Bend her knees and pull her legs a little apart."

Mechanically, Behice did as she was told. Saraylıhanım crawled closer to Mehpare, leaned over and, with the back of her hand, slapped hard on each cheek. Mehpare opened her eyes and stared blankly.

"Mehpare, you're giving birth. Think of nothing but the baby. Only the baby. You expected a boy, didn't you? Think about your son. Take a deep breath. Now breathe in and out. In and out. That's it, dear. And another. And another."

The two men and the other women of the household came rushing out and gathered around Mehpare, everyone talking at once. The housekeeper fluttered about, wringing her hands; both girls were crying.

The men leaned over, hoisted Mehpare and began hauling her towards the house. Now fully conscious, she started screaming and shouting. Helped to her feet by her grandchildren, Saraylıhanım followed the men inside, barking instructions all the way, trailed by the others. "As soon as you get her inside, lie her down in the selamlık, the first room on the right."

Behice turned her attention to Leman, who was confusedly running circles around her. "First, run to the midwife's, then go to Belkıs Hanım's house, the next house down. Tell her what's happened. Get them to send a servant to your father. Perhaps they can take the coupe and go all the way to the ministry. But whatever they do, someone has to get word to your father. We need him here immediately and he's got to inform Mahir Bey as well," she said.

"I'll just get my çarşaf . . ."

"Don't make me repeat myself, Leman! Get going this minute. It's an emergency. I don't give a toss about your çarşaf. Run!" Leman stared at her mother, normally so courteous and such a stickler for propriety. Smoothing back her hair, she headed for the garden gate, thanking God that the midwife was a next door neighbor.

With Leman gone, Behice turned on Suat, who was still sobbing. "What are you crying about?" she said.

"Mehpare Abla's dying."

"She's not dying. She's having a baby."

"But what if she dies?"

"Stop being ridiculous and make yourself useful. I left poor Sabahat in my room. Go wait with your little sister."

"I want to wait with Mehpare Abla. The housekeeper can look after the baby."

"She's helping deliver the baby, boiling water and preparing strips of cloth. She's got work to do."

"But mother, I . . ."

For the first time ever, Behice lifted a hand against one of her children. "Suat, I told you to go and look after your sister. I left the balcony door open. A cat might come in. Look, if anything were to happen to her, as God is my witness I swear I'll tear you to pieces with my own two hands!"

Suat darted off to the house, so eager to avoid the first smack of her life that, for the first time, she was willing to do exactly what she was told. Mehpare's screams echoed beyond the garden and into the street.

Ahmet Reşat and Mahir didn't arrive home until several hours later. He had been at a privy council meeting and they'd waited until it was over to give him the news. All he knew was that Mehpare had gone into labor, meaning the baby, which by his calculations was only five months old, was certain to be stillborn. Why, he wondered, did the children of this family seem fated to arrive in the world before their time. Perhaps there was truth in the saying "an overprotected eye is certain to be pricked." That is, perhaps the premature births could be blamed on the over-coddling of the women during their pregnancies.

As Ahmet Reşat considered how he would break the news of the stillborn baby to Kemal, his ears started to burn and his head began throbbing. Pulling himself together, he sent one of his clerks to Mahir's house, the other to the hospital where the doctor was working. Fortunately, Mahir was working on the European shore at that time and Ahmet Reşat prayed he would be found quickly. He himself dashed down to the street and began looking for a coupe. When none appeared, he jumped onto a passing tram, one hand clutching the metal door handle, his foot on the running board, looking for all the world like a student. He silently prayed no one would see him. When the tram reached Divanyolu he leapt off and began running home. When he arrived at the top of the street, he found Mahir paying a driver.

His first words were, "The baby's unlikely to have survived. It's stillborn, isn't it?"

"Just let me get my foot in the door and we'll see," said Mahir.

"Even at seven months, premature babies can be kept alive these days."

Ahmet Reşat didn't have the heart to tell him that the baby wasn't even six months yet.

They quickly walked to the house without speaking. Behice opened the door. Her eyes were red, her face chalk white. As Ahmet Reşat removed his fez he asked:

"Is the baby alive, Behice?"

"Yes, yes," she said, sobbing as she threw herself into his arms.

"And Mehpare? Is she well?"

Still sobbing, Behice responded, "Yes . . . as well as can be expected."

"I'll go upstairs and see how they are," Mahir offered. Doctor's bag in hand, he was heading for the stairs when Behice said through her tears, "Mahir Bey, Mehpare is in the selamlık."

Mahir opened the door to the selamlık. A sheet had been spread over one of the divans and Mehpare lay there, arms at her sides in the narrow space, still as a corpse. In a cradle next to the divan lay a tiny infant, obviously premature, swathed in cotton. Its cries were so weak they were barely audible. The midwife sat on a cushion at Mehpare's feet, reading the Koran. When she saw the doctor she collected herself. "It was premature," she whispered. "She's going through a bad time. She doesn't want to see her son."

Mahir went over to Mehpare and asked, "Are you all right, Mehpare Hanım?" She didn't open her eyes.

"Mehpare Hanım . . . Mehpare . . . It's me, Doctor Mahir. Are you all right?"

When there was still no response he assumed Mehpare was sleeping and went over to the cradle. He leaned over, took the baby in his arms, set it on the divan and began examining it. To the midwife, who was standing over him, he said, "The chances of survival are good."

He went upstairs to say he thought it would be a good idea to keep the baby under observation at the hospital for up to ten days and that, if they permitted him, he would take both mother and baby to the Italian Hospital in Beyoğlu, where some of his close friends were working. He opened the door to the sitting room and poked his head inside. Ahmet Reşat was sprawled in his chair and when the doctor saw the expression on his face he forgot all about Mehpare and the baby. "Reşat Bey!" he whispered.

Saraylıhanım was sitting cross-legged on the divan in front of the window, hands folded in her lap, rocking back and forth and repeatedly muttering something unintelligible to Mahir. He listened carefully for a moment, but when he still couldn't make out what she was saying he set his bag on the floor and carefully looked around the room. Behice and Suat weren't there. It was Leman who stood at her father's side, massaging cologne into his temples and his arms; it was Leman whose face was as pallid and drawn as her father's. Leman came up to Mahir, leaned forward as though she was about to tell him a secret, and said, in a near whisper, "We received some painful news today . . ."

Mahir stared at Leman's face. She'd aged at least ten years that day and it was only now that he could make sense of Saraylıhanım's repeated lament: "There's not even a grave for me to visit!"

– 20 –

Broken Wings

Azra had put down her pen and leaned back in her chair when, in the weak, flickering light, she saw that her tears were smudging the ink. She closed her eyes and waited for a time. Then she allowed herself to sob long and loud.

She was living in a primitive dwelling—impossible to heat in the winter and maddeningly short of water in the summer—located on one of the narrow lanes in the impoverished outskirts of the city of Maraş. Sitting there at her desk, the shutters still closed against the morning sun, wearing her nightgown, her shawl slipping off her left shoulder, her hair uncombed, the dark circles under her eyes mute testimony to yet another sleepless night, she was the very picture of misery and dejection—she suspected she looked like an actress ineptly performing some melodrama in a provincial theater. And yet, she still seemed completely out of place in the utter wretchedness of that room.

She'd believed that it was love of country that had brought her to this distant city. That is, she'd believed it until months of hardship had given her the courage to examine her true motives, forcing her to conclude that she had come not for country but to inject excitement into her empty life.

How envious she had been of Mehpare! And it was only now, as she composed a letter of condolence, that she acknowledged an envy that astonished her. Feeling genuine affection for that uninformed young woman living in the house of Reşat Beyefendi in the role of poor relation, a status so much lower than her own, Azra's friendship had nonetheless been tinged with envy for Mehpare's intense love for Kemal, and later, with envy for the fertility God had granted so generously to Mehpare while denying it so completely to herself.

Kemal, however, had always implied that it was Mehpare who might be envious of Azra. Which was only natural. After all, Azra was well-educated, wealthy, esteemed and independent: everything Mehpare aspired to, but would never attain. Kemal had cited Azra's many fine qualities as precisely the reason she should be tolerant of any discourtesy evinced by Mehpare.

But Mehpare had never been discourteous, had always shown Azra the greatest respect—except for that one day when they'd all gathered at the mansion. And now it was Azra who would give anything to change places with Mehpare—anything. But God disposes.

Fate had sent Mehpare into Reşat Bey's house and into Kemal's arms; it was fated that they would marry, and it was also fated that she would be left a widow before she'd fully learned what it was to be a wife.

Had Azra's envy, then, been misplaced?

No, Mehpare had a child in her arms. And she would always have her great love, even if she yearned for him till the day she died.

She, Azra, had nothing.

She and Necdet had married because their families had deemed it suitable. It was a sensible marriage with benefits on both sides. When she looked back and tried to remember their happiest moments together, she'd see the docile, hazel eyes of her husband looking at her with great tenderness, if not great love. There had been moments of deep contentment: sitting side by side listening to music or reclining on lawn chairs under the chestnut tree in the garden discussing books they were reading.

But passion?

If there were moments of erotic desire, they belonged to Necdet alone. Lying under her husband's strong, youthful body, her legs parted, her silk nightgown hitched to her waist to spare the lace, she'd surreptitiously wipe away the drops of sweat falling from her husband's forehead onto her face and, if there was enough light, study Necdet's face with disgust. When his eyes began rolling behind half-closed lids she'd know the end of her torment was near. And that's when she'd begin the work of murmuring *ah's* and *oh's* to hasten his climax. She sometimes wondered if her failure to conceive had been due to her inability to give love to her husband, to take pleasure from him. On that day when Kemal and Mehpare had hidden at the mansion, Azra had been staggered at the raw desire she noticed in the girl's eyes every time she looked at him. The act of sitting in the same room as Kemal was enough to produce an intensity of feeling in Mehpare that far surpassed anything Azra had ever felt for her husband, even in their most intimate moments. Azra had observed their every move; she'd taken their measure. She'd seen how Kemal would "inadvertently" brush against Mehpare's hand, her arm, her hair, even her breasts and her thighs. And as for Mehpare, she was forever gazing at him, lingering over his eyes and his lips, and Azra had recognized the look of a woman recalling private moments. And when Mehpare wasn't actually looking at Kemal, she would still drift off to thoughts that were, no doubt, of Kemal, always of Kemal.

She'd been envious. But it wasn't them she'd envied—it was that heightened emotional and physical state, one that she recognized while realizing it was something she herself had never experienced.

Now, as she dipped her fountain pen into the inkwell and struggled to compose a letter of condolence, she had no idea what to say.

I am greatly saddened, dearest sister. May God grant you the patience to endure. Your husband was martyred for the motherland. Be proud of him. Try to find solace in your son.

Azra crumpled up the sheet of paper and started again.

Dearest Mehpare, my beloved and most unfortunate sister,

Would you take consolation in an account of the last two days I spent with Kemal? We were both excited by having arrived in Ankara to learn a new skill, one that would be helpful in driving the enemy from our lands. Kemal was elated. He had married the woman he loved, he was awaiting the birth of his child, he had been given an important duty he was thrilled to discharge, and he was, in his own words, "of use at last." Once the Greek advance was repulsed, he planned to return home with his head held high. Neither of us had any idea how the Greeks would be driven off, but we'd both dedicated ourselves to just that end, and we believed, with every fiber of our being, that a miracle would happen . . .

Mehpare, on that night in Ankara, Kemal and I talked until dawn. We returned to our childhood. We were both moved to tears. By what we've lost, by what we've lived, by our mistakes...

No, she could never send that to Mehpare. Another crumpled ball of paper tossed into the waste bin . . .

She began again.

You're absolutely determined to learn more of that horrific event. I don't know of what use such knowledge will be to you, but I'll do as you ask nevertheless: Kemal was traveling with a bag of telegraph conductors when he was detained by the military police near Eskişehir. He refused to open the bag. He tried to send them on their way, saying he was a traveling salesman, and producing the relevant papers. They insisted he open the bag. Left with no choice, he agreed. But instead of opening the bag he flung it into a nearby ravine. The Greek police looked down at the bag at the bottom of the ravine. Then they pulled out their guns and emptied their bullets into his slender, defenseless body . . .

Why am I writing this, Mehpare? Am I out of my mind? Another sheet of paper was crumpled and tossed. No, this would be more than a letter of condolence. Azra wanted to confess her love. She needed to unburden herself. Perhaps by confiding her love to someone else she would free herself from this nightmare. That was her real and fervent desire.

. . . and so, as I wrote to you earlier, I've at last found a love like the one you shared with Kemal, the love I so envied and admired. But Mehpare, I'm afraid I've bungled things badly, yet again. There was a desperate hopelessness to your early love for Kemal and I, too, am now hopelessly and passionately in love with this man . . . This man . . . This man . . .

In the letter you wrote to me, you said how pleased you were that I had found love at last. Don't be pleased for me, sister. There is nothing pleasing about this love of mine . . .

As Azra stood up the chair tipped over. She began a frenzied circling of the room. What to do with this man and this love? Could she accept the offer he'd been making day after day? Could she run away with him? Obliterate her past, dismay and disgrace her mother, her relatives and her friends . . . Could she abandon her homeland?

The night before, she'd come to Jean Daniel's house dressed like a local villager, thrown herself into his arms, too enraptured to make sure the curtains were drawn, felt his weight pressing down on her, been maddened by his exploring lips and later, lying in his arms, released and fulfilled, had promised to leave with him. And then came morning and a cool head and now, as she sat writing to Mehpare, she realized how agonizing it would be to tear up roots... She couldn't decide if the tears streaking the page in front of her had been shed for Kemal or for herself.

Perhaps the only solution was for Jean Daniel to die fighting for his cause, just as Kemal had. That way, she would be free. But what was she doing? Was she really hoping for her lover's death? For the sake of her own peace of mind? She would never amount to so much as the nail on Mehpare's little finger, Mehpare who was ready at any moment to give up her life for Kemal! Azra paced back and forth, the whole length of the room, wide-eyed and waving her arms as though deep in argument.

Mehpare, if you only knew what a fortunate woman you are! You'll be loving the ghost of Kemal for the rest of your life. Which means that he'll always be yours. He won't be there to see you age and fade and grow old. But if I abandon my country and my family to pursue this love for a French officer, and if he betrays me ... If he leaves me one day ... How could I return across a bridge of ashes? And to whom would I return?

Azra poured water into her cupped hand from the pitcher on the desk and splashed her face. She pushed up the guillotine window and opened the wooden shutters. She drew aside the calico curtain, blinking in the morning light and attempting to draw fresh air into her lungs. But her chest was tight and soon enough she'd have to get dressed and leave. She was to report to the provincial governorship and edit the Turkish commanders' correspondence with the French. When the Greeks had defied the Allies by continuing their advance into Anatolia, there had been a subtle but perceptible change in the attitude of the French and the Italians towards the Turks, a shift that accelerated after the Ankara Government had signed a friendship treaty with Soviet Russia in March

If only Kemal were alive to see these developments for himself. If only. But just as Azra knew that a life full of "if only's" wasn't really a life worth living, she also knew that the rest of her days would be spent in regret. If she left, one day she'd wish she'd stayed; and if she stayed, one day she'd wish she'd gone.

She rolled a cigarette and lit it. When she'd smoked it she felt marginally better, well enough to sit down, place a clean sheet of paper on the desk in front of her, and write a letter of condolence to Mehpare.

– 21 –

September 1922

My Dearest Sister, Mehpare,

I'm writing this letter to you from İzmir. Please send all future letters to the new address that I'll forward to you. I read your most recent letter with close attention. Believe me when I say that I know as well as you that grief and longing will be with you forever. Try to accept the painful truth. It's true that death didn't take my lover from me, but the pain of separation is as acute as the pain of losing a loved one. And furthermore, I don't have a baby binding me to life.

Dearest Sister, life goes on. And while you rear Halim and Sabahat in Istanbul, I'll be occupying a position at a school in İzmir, where I plan to settle. We have no other choice. This is our lot in life, the way the women of our land have always lived. Let's pray that our children have happier lives than ours.

Believe me, sister, your letters are a source of great comfort to me here in the uproar and upheaval. They bring me the colors and smells of my city. But I'm afraid the letters I send to you are always accounts of fighting, of the war.

As you know, hostilities with France ended last October. The French troops stationed in and around Adana have all been demobilized and Jean Daniel has returned to France at the head of his regiment. I refused his offer of marriage—refused to accompany him. He left these lands disappointed and angry. He desires no further correspondence with me and says he wishes only to forget me and to get on with his life. He'd hoped for us to return to France together, to marry and start a family. If it weren't for this war, that might have been possible. He'll never understand why I couldn't bring myself to marry an officer from an army that was occupying my country. So be it, I have no regrets. And, like you, I now have a great love I will never forget. I will love Jean Daniel for as long as I draw breath.

While he was still in Maraş I requested transfer to a place other than Ankara. My transfer to the Western Front coincided with King Constantine ordering his Greek troops to march on Ankara. Vehicles and wagons loaded with soldiers, the wounded and the fleeing filled the roads. It was a grinding journey but it was worth the hardship. I was there to share with others our great victory in Sakarya.

I stayed in Eskişehir for a while. As our National Army launched a major offensive I was given a position as a nurse at a field hospital behind the lines.

It was smart of us to attend those classes at the Red Crescent in Istanbul, Mehpare. If I hadn't learned how to dress wounds, how to change bandages and give injections, what would I have done? There were other women here from Istanbul, seven of us in all, nursing amid the shelling and gunfire, sometimes for days on end, with virtually no sleep. During twenty days of continuous counter-attacks, we did everything we could to help, from working in the field hospitals and kitchens to gathering fruit from the trees and vegetables from the fields, from rolling bandages to assisting at surgeries. With God's help, every single counter-offensive ended in victory.

Undoubtedly, Reşat Beyefendi has long since been informed of the most recent development, but I'll share it with you nonetheless: Greek Commander in Chief General Nikolaos Trikoupis and his retinue were captured last week. We wept in the streets, embracing one another and singing together. Then we all followed the army corps as it advanced towards İzmir, which is how I eventually came to be in this beautiful place. As we neared İzmir, the entire city was in flames. They wouldn't allow any women to go to the port, where there were reports of utter chaos. We waited at a village not far from Manisa and were able to enter İzmir only two days later. I don't know if you'll believe this, but as I looked out over İzmir for the first time, from a hilltop, I felt as though Ali Riza and Kemal were there with me, shedding tears of joy. They have not died in vain. Every life we lost brought us a step closer to liberation.

Mehpare, this might not be of much comfort to you, but the telegraph lines Kemal successfully put in place are now proclaiming victory to the four corners of our land.

By the end of this month, Western Anatolia is expected to be purged of the Greek army. I'm preparing to rent a small house in the district of Karantina, not far from the school where I will become an English teacher. I'm arranging for my mother to come and live with me. The summers here are said to be sweltering, but for the rest of the year the climate is mild. When school is re-cessed for the summer, we'll be coming to Istanbul in any case. We'll probably rent out part of our enormous house. And we'll have the opportunity to see you all.

There is much talk of eventually expelling the enemy forces from Istanbul as well. I would like to be there with you when it happens.

Please reply soon. Send me news of Halim and Sabahat, of Behice Hanımefendi, Reşat Beyefendi and the girls. Has Leman improved on the piano? Has Suat grown taller and more beauti-ful? I wonder about all of them. I learned from my mother that Saraylıhanım has not been herself since the news of Kemal's death. I'm terribly sorry. May Allah heal her.

May God bless us all; I kiss the hands of all my elders and the eyes of all the children.

Thinking of you always, your devoted friend,

Azra

When Mehpare had finished reading the letter she folded it and put it in the pocket of her apron. Saraylıhanım's voice was rever-berating down the stairs.

"Mehpare, have you brewed Kemal some linden tea?" she cried.

Walking over to the foot of the stairs, Mehpare replied, "I have. I'll bring it in a moment."

There were days when Saraylıhanım's faculties were clouded, when she thought Kemal was still alive. The rest of the household would placate her by acting as though Kemal was still with them.

Mehpare had even begun to enjoy this little charade: it pleased her to imagine that her husband was still among them.

When Behice had noticed that Mehpare was behaving like Saraylıhanım, she'd alerted her husband and Reşat Bey had spoken to Mahir.

Mahir had been deeply concerned by Mehpare's behavior. Saryalıhanım's delusions could be put down to her advanced years, but he strongly advised that Mehpare be put under immediate psychiatric observation. A nerve specialist had been contacted and a thousand and one pretexts found to send Mehpare for a consultation with the renowned doctor.

It's difficult for any woman to cope simultaneously with the loss of a husband and the birth of a child. Would it be possible to arrange a change of scene for Mehpare, some place far away, unconnected with her memories?

The household discussed various alternatives. But Mehpare was nursing two babies. Where could she go and who could take her? Behice thought of sending Mehpare and the babies to Beypazarı. She'd go with them, see her father and return to Istanbul. Mehpare could stay on at the farm for a couple of months, benefiting from the clean air and the fresh food.

But when they brought up the subject with Mehpare she was vehemently opposed. She was not going anywhere, she told them. No one could tear her away from the lingering scent of her husband and the memories kept alive in the rooms he'd once inhabited.

"Mehpare dear, we only want what's best for you," Reşat Bey had pleaded. "It's not right to shut you up here with my old aunt, whose mind isn't what it used to be. The dead are gone, my dear, and the living must go on with life. Think of your son if not your-self. You need to be healthy for his sake."

"I am healthy, efendim."

"Spiritually healthy then."

"I'm spiritually healthy as well. If I act as though Kemal is alive, it's only to make Saraylıhanım happy. It does me good as well."

"And that is precisely the danger. He's dead. You mustn't pre-tend he's still alive."

"Fine then! I won't do it again!"

Mahir advised them not to push her, and they didn't insist she go to the farm. And for her part, Mehpare stopped acting as though Kemal was alive and never again played along with Saraylıhanım. And now, as Mehpare poured out a glass of brewed linden from a long-handled copper pot, she smiled to herself. They all thought she was crazy. Well let them. She heard Saraylıhanım's tread on the stairs.

"Why are you coming down here, dear? I'm bringing up the tea."

"You've remembered to add some honey, to soften up his chest?"

"I have," Mehpare assured her in a low voice. "Now go back upstairs, don't let them see you down here."

She watched as the elderly woman dragged her feet back up the stairs. It was as though the authoritative woman who had taken over the birth of Halim until the midwife arrived and who had single-handedly managed the administration of the household over the following weeks had decided her duties were done, and become a *deli saraylı*, a former palace woman gone typically mad.

As Behice and her daughters become increasingly exasperated with Saraylıhanım, Mehpare's love and tenderness grew by the day. She knew that Kemal's death had scorched the elderly woman's heart just as intensely as it had her. They understood each other. Mehpare would not leave this house until Saryalıhanım—may Allah grant her a long life—had been recalled by her maker. And when she did leave, she wouldn't go to Beypazarı, but to İzmir, to live with Azra.

And they would take to the air together, on broken wings.

– 22 –

Flight

It had been seventeen days since Sultan Vahdettin had lost his title as the thirty-sixth *padişah*, or "Master Shah" of the House of Osman. Ever since he'd received notice of the abolition of the sultanate on the night of November 1, 1922, he had remained in the palace in his remaining capacity as Caliph. And as the Caliph sat in one of the pavillions in the royal park of Yıldız, his eyes traveling across the hundreds of domes under which his illustrious ancestors had gone to their eternal rest on the seven hills of Istanbul, it was impossible to know if he was lamenting the treachery of the Arab leaders he'd always believed would eventually come to the aid of the "Commander of the Faith," or if he was bitterly regretting the missteps and miscalculations of the past years. It was impossible to know because the normally taciturn Vahdettin was no longer speaking at all. His despondency spoke for itself: in the deep lines etched on his face, in his sagging shoulders.

He hadn't been particularly surprised when he'd been notified of the decision to abolish the Ottoman Dynasty.

The Sultan's first aide-de-camp had greeted National Government representative Refat Pasha in Kabataş with the words, "Welcome, efendim. I convey to you—and to the National Government which you represent—the royal salutations of His Majesty."

Refat Pasha had responded with the words: "Please convey my respects and gratitude to His Exalted Shelter of the Caliphate."

Sultan Vahdettin was astute enough to infer from the wording of that greeting that the sultanate had come to an end. And as he considered his future, he would have found it impossible not to ponder the violent end suffered by other European rulers.

The French monarch Louis XVI had been guillotined; King Charles I beheaded with an axe; the Russian Tsar Nicholas II shot, along with his entire family. Those would have been the first murders that came to the former Sultan's mind. The sovereigns sitting on the thrones of overturned empires had all shared a common fate: execution. And, closer to home, hadn't many of Vahdettin's own ancestors and relatives also been murdered?

Most had been killed on the orders of their brothers—but some had been dispatched at the request of sons and mothers, and one had even been put to death by his own father. If that was to be his fate, he should accept it with dignity and grace.

In this modern age, surely more humane methods would be visited upon him than those reserved for his ancestor Genç Osman, in 1622. Surely, Sultan Vahdettin would either be shot or hanged.

But then again, there were no signs of preparation for his execution. There was nothing to do but wait patiently. And so he waited. He hadn't yet considered either suicide or flight.

Then he was informed of a deplorable incident and changed his mind.

Ali Kemal Bey, a leading journalist at *Peyam-ı Sabah*, a pro-sultanate gazette that had consistently opposed the Ankara Government throughout the occupation and the war of liberation, had been having a shave at a barber's shop in Beyoğlu when agents from the Special Force had abducted him, taking him first to Kumkapı, then by motorboat to İzmit.

There, this burly and defiant columnist had been attacked by an angry mob armed with sticks and stones, and finally—when Nurettin Pasha, the commander of the unit assigned to protect him, had failed to issue orders to keep him safe from the crowd—he had been lynched.

The day of the Friday Prayer Procession was fast approaching. Vahdettin was terrified at the thought that he too would be thrown to the crowd: was his execution to take the form of a public lynching? Under no circumstances should he mix with his subjects. After all, the people had been slowly crushed under the boot of the foreign enemy for four long years and had every right to demand a reckoning from their sovereign. If only Sultan Vahdettin could tell the people of his own sufferings, could explain that he had taken the only possible course of action, could describe the torments he had endured as he resigned himself to his fate.

If only he could tell them that he regarded the victory of the National Army as a miracle wrought by Allah and that he was at least as grateful for this triumphant army as they themselves were. But Vahdettin knew he would never have the opportunity for any of this. Some lunatic would leap out of the crowd, others would follow, and God forbid . . . He couldn't bear to think about it. He couldn't allow his royal station to be degraded by a repeat of that mob scene in İzmit.

So he decided to flee before Friday Prayers.

From what he'd been able to ascertain, the National Government would not object to abdication and self-exile. No one wanted any bloodshed, unrest or harm to the Caliphate. Ankara had deeply regretted the lynching of the journalist. The best solution was to flee the country with the security afforded by the title of Caliph.

On November 17th, dressed in ceremonial costume, and prepared, along with his fellow dignitaries, to join the procession, Ahmet Reşat took his place in front of Yıldız Mosque in the area reserved for Ottoman ministers. Standing at attention as they awaited the arrival of the Sultan's carriage were the Royal Guard, in colorful uniforms and white gloves, and the officers, with their gilded decorations, kalpaks and shiny boots. The carriage was behind schedule. The call to prayer echoed from the minarets. Minute followed minute, one after another. An impatient gelding began kicking and stamping under a mounted guard. Others joined in.

Ahmet Reşat and his fellow ministers continued to wait respectfully for the imminent arrival of their sultan, even though they knew he would never again be coming to the Friday Procession. And as he waited, Ahmet Reşat studied the faces of the crowd: the enduring, the long-suffering, the deceived people of Istanbul.

He felt like embracing each and every one of them, these people filling the courtyard of the mosque; he wanted to tell them to stop waiting in the rain and to go home.

Because Ahmet Reşat knew that even as the people of Istanbul were standing in the rain at the Friday Prayers Procession, Sultan Vahdettin VI Mehmet Han was abandoning his country as part of an escape plan devised by General Harrington.

Early that morning five former government ministers and three former Grand Viziers had gone to Yıldız Palace. The Sultan had first bid farewell to his family and relatives in the harem; he had then gone to the selamlık to make his farewells to the personages gathered there to see him off. Wearing an official uniform bedecked with Ottoman and foreign decorations, and dark glasses that might have been meant to conceal his tears, he gravely shook the hands of those assembled and spoke in a qua- vering voice.

Five minutes after the Grand Viziers and ministers had proceeded to the courtyard of the mosque in their personal carriages, he and his retinue would board two automobiles with drawn curtains, exit the Beşiktaş gate of Malta Pavilion, and drive down an avenue lined with British soldiers to Dolmabahçe Palace.

After resting briefly in the harem of Dolmabahçe Palace, he would proceed to the royal pier, board a motorboat flying English colors, and, in a last cruel twist of fate, be conveyed to the waiting British battleship, *Malaya*.

With him were his two wives, his favorite concubine, his son, Ertuğrul, his private physician, Reşat Pasha, and a few trusted men who handled his personal affairs, chief among them first aide-de-camp Çerkez Pasha. Twelve people in all. And most probably, at that very moment, a military band was striking up *The Sultan's March* as a double row of British sailors lined up on the deck of the battleship Malaya and took aboard the last Ottoman Sultan.

Ahmet Reşat hastily pulled his watch out of his breast pocket and checked the time. Yes, the ship bearing the Sultan was probably weighing anchor just about now. He put his watch back in his pocket. Bowing his head slightly, arms folded over his chest, he discreetly paid his respects to all of the illustrious sovereigns, and, in particular, to the last sovereign, of an empire whose glories and dignity had once been legend. When he lifted his chin there were tears in his eyes. He hadn't felt this wounded, hadn't felt a stab of pain quite this acute, since Kemal's death.

Ahmet Reşat joined the grumbling throngs shuffling towards the outer gate of the courtyard. The rain was falling more heavily than before. Which was good, because the tears were rolling down his cheeks, tears he was helpless to contain, tears that seemed such a natural part of him at that moment that he was barely aware that they were there at all. He felt like Emir Abdullah of Granada, who'd wept from the safety of the mountainside as he'd watched Spanish soldiers swarming the streets of a city going up in flames. Abdullah's mother had turned to him and spoken those words that would go down in history: "That's it, cry—crying suits you. Snivel like a harlot for the city you failed to defend like a man!"

Ahmet Reşat's tears had come too late. Unlike Kemal and his friends, he'd failed to put his heart and soul into defending his city. But, thanks to those brave young men, Istanbul was on the verge of becoming, once again, his city. Insolent foreign troops would no longer be wandering the streets in colorful braided uniforms, and Ottoman officers . . . how foolish . . . which Ottomans? Were there any Ottomans left? In the handful of land remaining from a mighty empire that had once spanned three continents, Turkish officers would no longer be forced to salute those strutting invaders.

"And thank God for that," he said to himself.

Ahmet Reşat walked all the way to Beyazit. By the time he reached the garden gate he was exhausted, physically and spiritually. Too tired to bother with a key, he rang the bell. He nodded a silent greeting to Hüsnü Efendi and they walked to the house together without a word. The front door swung open. It was Behice, looking utterly drained as she helped him out of his coat, took his fez and flashed a meaningful glance in the direction of the selamlık. "Caprini Efendi has been waiting for you for over an hour," she said. "Count Caprini Efendi."

"Good heavens! I wonder what he wants?"

"I can't say I understand exactly. There's a list of some kind . . . He insisted on seeing you himself. My word, Reşat Bey, today, of all days, why on earth did you have to come home so late?" asked Behice.

− 23 −

Farewell

Ahmet Reşat studied the early morning, mist-shrouded vision of Istanbul rising from the waters of the Bosphorus, minarets reaching for the skies. He stood tall and unblinking on the shore, imprinting upon his mind a spectacle he'd probably never see again. Drawing the cool sea air deep into his lungs, he closed his eyes and listened to the city. He would impress Istanbul upon all five of his senses. Later, much later, in his mind's eye, he would behold the minarets and domes, the Bosphorus shading blue to green; his nose would fill with the richness of kelp, the tang of salt, of coal smoke; his ears would ring with the metallic rattling of a tram, the deep moan of a passing ferryboat, the raucous cry of street vendor and gull. He would remember.

He would never forget.

Mahir was standing a little way off, and when Ahmet Reşat sensed the doctor approach, he lightly coughed to clear the disquieting lump from his throat, turned to his friend, and said, "Mahir Bey, I can't expect you to watch over my family while I'm gone, but it would greatly ease my mind if you'd concern yourself with the health of the two newborns."

"Rest assured, efendim. I will be caring not only for the babies but for your entire family. If my work in the city is done before you return, I'll request appointment to a hospital in Istanbul. And if they still insist on posting me to the countryside I'll resign immediately."

"I have no right to burden you with such a responsibility. I only ask that you look in on them from time to time. Behice Hanım doesn't have a head for figures. If you could help her, perhaps. Ah, if only Kemal were alive . . ."

The lump was back; Ahmet Reşat went quiet.

"Reşat Beyefendi . . . I'm having some difficulty putting this into words . . . I'm rather discomfited, but I really feel I must speak to you about a certain matter, and there's so little time . . ."

"Yes, do go on, Mahir Bey."

"I'm well aware of the difference in our ages, but I do feel that, in your absence, in order to still the wagging tongues of the ladies and to preclude any unsavory speculation, that... were I to request Leman Hanım's hand in marriage . . . were we to become formally engaged and marry only upon your return . . ."

"Mahir, asking you to take care of my family is one thing, but this is something entirely different. How could you assume such extravagant generosity? And furthermore, Leman is but a girl."

"Leman Hanım is sixteen years old. She'll be seventeen by the time you return. We can wait."

"You mustn't sacrifice yourself like that on our behalf."

"Reşat Beyefendi, it would be no act of self-sacrifice. You see, I greatly admire Leman Hanım."

"Oh!"

"Please don't misunderstand. She's a young woman now, and I'm very fond of her. If events hadn't unfolded in the way that they have, I would never have been bold enough to admit you into my confidence. My admiration would have remained a secret. But circumstances have changed. You shouldn't leave your house without the protection of a man."

"I never noticed that my girl was grown up. Between work and state affairs, it seems like I've never even had time to look at my children. I've missed out on life, Mahir. And now, life is sending me to a strange land . . ." Ahmet Reşat stared into the distance through tears.

"Is your response in the affirmative, efendim? Do you consent to take me as your son-in-law?"

"Could there be a more agreeable groom, Mahir? You're my dearest friend. Our families have been intimate for generations. Still, I have to consult my wife and daughter first. After all, it's Leman who's getting married."

"If they consent too, we can be betrothed this evening, before you leave."

"I'll go home and discuss it with my family. If there are any objections, our friendship won't suffer, surely?

"Never. I would still look after your family and remain in Istanbul until you returned."

"I can't ask that of you. Let me speak to my daughter . . . then we'll talk again."

"Reşat Beyefendi, you will let me know, won't you? Even if . . ."

"Of course I will. I'll have Hüsnü Efendi deliver a letter to the hospital."

"I'll be waiting at home," Mahir said. "It's closer."

"Very well. I'd like to walk along the shore for a bit. The letter will be in your hand right after noon prayers, Mahir Bey."

Mahir said good-bye to Ahmet Reşat and strode off towards Sirkeci, his cape fluttering behind him; but whether he was walking or flying, he himself couldn't have said.

When Mahir was out of sight Ahmet Reşat sank onto a boulder and gazed into the distance. The sun had not yet risen; the sea stretching out before him had not yet been irradiated a brilliant blue: it was opalescent and shot with rays of red piercing through the low bank of clouds on the opposite shore. The ancient peninsula behind him seemed to enfold Ahmet Reşat, blanketing him in its glories, its transgressions and its virtues. He had been born and grown to manhood here in this city of narrow lanes flowing down to the water's edge, of crimson vines and dark-green cypresses, of simple wooden houses garlanded with the magenta blossoms of the judas tree, of great lonely squares and a bustling bridge linking the Muslim and Christian quarters: this was a city old, proud and unrivalled.

Tomorrow, at about this time, the strip of coast now under his feet would slowly pass before his eyes, above it the domes of the old palace and minarets like pens pointing to the sky, as he stood on the deck of an Italian ship, bound for exile, leaving behind his home, his family, his relatives and his friends. He wouldn't be there to admire Leman in her bridal veil or to dandle his grandchildren on his knee. He wouldn't be there to see Suat blossoming into young womanhood, the crinkles forming in the corners of

Behice's beautiful eyes and lips, Sabahat and Halim taking their first steps, his aunt's last years on this earth: in short, he wouldn't be there to witness any of the ordinary things that give life meaning and consequence.

His rigorous education, his years of hard work and duty on three continents on behalf of the empire, the orders of merit he'd always made light of, his devoted and dedicated service . . . to a Sultan he had blamed just days ago for having fled on an English destroyer, like a traitor.

No, he couldn't blame His Majesty any more than he could blame himself. The poor Sultan had been forced to shoulder problems that had been accumulating for centuries. Finally, the volatile accumulation of lies, the tricks, the plundering, the ignorance, the greed, the cronyism, the bigotry, the thousands of missteps committed in the name of religion, the corruption, the profiteering, in combination with the insatiable appetite of the European states, had exploded in his hand, burning one and all.

The Sultan was gone. And he too would be going. He repeated the same question to himself: Where was he going, and why?

Was he running off just to live among strangers, his identity and character in tatters as he struggled to survive . . . To breath in and breath out . . . To eat, drink, and sleep?

To eat and drink?

With what money and for how long? Trying to survive on the bit of money he hoped to obtain from the family income . . . What if he lived for a long time? And if the properties he'd pinned all his hopes on were seized—something that could happen at any moment—how would he and his family scrape by? There were six females to consider, two of them babies, one of whom was still in swaddling clothes, an elderly woman, a child, and, perhaps, only Mahir to look after them! Mahir! Had Allah sent Mahir to protect and look after his family? Actually, he could surrender his family to the care of his father-in-law, but İbrahim Bey was now too old to leave his small town and settle in the big city. And he couldn't even imagine Behice and his daughters at the farm.

He gazed at the red ripples on the surface of the water, now becoming marbled with yellow, as though an invisible hand was doing *ebru*, drawing sharp lines that suddenly softened and merged. If he were to walk out into the sea . . . lift the boulder he was sitting on and walk out… if he were to let himself be slowly swallowed up, sink into the shimmering, marbled water, just off shore. To sink, like the empire he was preparing to abandon. Was his soul so very precious? Wasn't God going to claim it one day, anyway?

Ahmet Reşat stood up. Stumbling slightly, he walked the length of the shore, gazing out over a sea now, finally, turning a deep blue. His shoulders sagged and his neck was lost inside his coat. He'd lost his hope, his expectations and his future. The only thing he would be able to give his family from now on was sorrow. And sadness, worry, and maybe even—God forbid—shame. Some would brand his daughters the children of a traitor. That's what they'd call his loved ones: the wife of a traitor, the aunt of a traitor, the relatives of a traitor. He thought back to the terrible scene with Kemal. "You'll have me known as the uncle of a traitor! Get out of my sight!" he'd said to his helpless nephew.

"Allah," he prayed to himself, "Allah, what have I done that I'm destined for such a life?"

As he considered once again the safety of his family, he hoped with all his heart that his daughter would accept Mahir's marriage proposal.

Tearing open the envelope the moment Hüsnü Efendi handed it to him, Mahir skipped straight to the last lines.

"Hüsnü Efendi," he shouted to the servant, who had begun to descend the steps but now stopped, turned round and asked, "What is it sir?"

"Come here." Fishing through his pockets Mahir extracted every coin he could find and dumped them into the palm of the servant, who was standing at the front door again. Hüsnü Efendi's bewildered eyes traveled from his cupped hand to Mahir's face.

"Is there something you'd like me to purchase for you, sir?"

"No. That's a tip."

"Sir, that's rather a lot of money."

"You've brought me wonderful news, efendi. Tell everyone I'll be around the moment afternoon prayers are read." When Hüsnü Efendi had dutifully trotted off the doctor raced inside, sat on the first chair that presented itself and began savoring each word of the letter. Leman had accepted his proposal. Behice Hanım and Saraylıhanım had voiced no objections; on the contrary, they were most pleased. He was expected for dinner.

When Mahir arrived at the house, he was ushered by the housekeeper not into the selamlık but directly upstairs to the sitting room. A dinner *à la française* had been laid on the table in the anteroom. No one was there yet. Mahir set an enormous box of *lokum* on the console, took a seat on the divan in front of the window and looked outside. The street was in darkness, the lone streetlight at the top of the hill wasn't burning. Dark streets for dark times. But Mahir was inwardly radiant, if slightly ashamed to be so amid the gloom of everyday life.

When Ahmet Reşat entered the room he sprang to his feet.

"My dear man, I'm quite relieved to inform you that my daughter apparently returns your feelings. So, my Leman has reached an age where she's able to have feelings for men, it's all quite astonishing for me," he said.

Mahir flushed. Reşat Bey was saying that Leman had feelings for him. He was saying other things, too, but, for a moment, Mahir didn't hear a word above the pounding of his heart.

" . . . So, what do you think of my idea, Mahir Bey? Since there are no longer any men at home, there's no need for a selamlık. As I was saying, if you'd like to remain in Istanbul after the nuptials and open your own clinic, you can use the selamlık."

"We'll hold the wedding only after your return, efendim."

"I might never return. Our families will hold the engagement ceremony, then you can wait a bit for the wedding, until Leman is at least seventeen."

"We'll all be there at the wedding."

Ahmet Reşat sighed, but didn't give voice to his doubts. A few moments later, Saraylıhanım, Behice and Suat came into the room. Disappointed to see that Leman had not yet made an appearance, Mahir rose to his feet and greeted the ladies, kissing Suat on both cheeks.

"Oh, you needn't have bothered, Mahir Bey," said Behice as she accepted the box of lokum and handed it to the house- keeper with instructions to arrange its contents in the silver bowl reserved for sweets. "Mehpare's taken a curling iron to Leman's hair. They'll be down shortly," she reassured Mahir as she sat down.

"Mahir Bey," she continued, "Saraylıhanım had noted your interest in Leman but I, for the life of me, wouldn't have thought such a thing possible. Well, may it all be for the best. Now we'll have a man at the head of the household and we women won't go unprotected until my husband returns."

"I remain forever at your disposal, efendim," Mahir said.

"You're too kind, Mahir Bey."

"With your permission, I'd like to become engaged tonight, while Reşat Bey is still here."

"Aren't we rushing things a little?" Saraylıhanım protested. "Shouldn't we wait for my Kemal?"

"If we act in haste, it is only because Reşat Bey is leaving," Mahir said.

"It might be the last such occasion on which I'm able to share my daughter's joy," said Ahmet Reşat.

"How can you say such things, Reşat Bey," Behice cried. "Please don't wear yourself down with such unhappy thoughts. You'll be back in a few months. You'll prove your innocence . . ." Her eyes filled with tears.

"Have I committed a crime that I'm now forced to prove my innocence?" asked Ahmet Reşat. "Is it a crime not to betray an institution of which you yourself are a part?"

"Reşat Bey, you were on the losing side. That's your crime. It's as simple as that. And if Kemal were alive, he'd be on the winning side," Behice said.

"Kemal's alive. You'll see, he'll be here soon, within a few weeks."

No one took any notice of Saraylıhanım.

"It's not as simple as that, efendim," Mahir explained to Behice. "Reşat Beyefendi may not have actively opposed the Sultan but he was of great service to the winning side and to the liberation of our country . . . Behind the scenes, of course. And none of us expected the Sultan to flee."

"It was suggested that he might," said Ahmet Reşat. "That may well be. But he didn't have to flee."

"Anyone in his position would have done the same. Am I not fleeing myself?"

"You're not the sultan."

Behice tactfully changed the subject. "Mahir Bey, the army barracks have always harbored resentment for the Sultan. Why is that?"

"That hasn't always been true, efendim. Only since the reign of Abdülhamit. And, really, can you blame them?"

Ahmet Reşat was preparing to weigh in when Leman and Mehpare arrived. Leman's long hair curled down past her shoulders; a hint of kohl had brought out her eyes; she wore a pale lilac dress with a lace collar. All else forgotten, Mahir stared at the girl framed in the doorway, smiling at him.

Ahmet Reşat was as impressed by his daughter's beauty as Mahir—and considerably more surprised. He thought back to the swaddled baby in his arms. He'd missed so much of his eldest daughter's life and now he might not be there to see his younger girls grow up.

"Welcome, efendim."

Both men snapped out of their reveries at the sound of Leman's voice. Mahir drew her extended hand to his lips. Leman seemed equally taken aback and pleased to have received her first kiss. Pleased to be the center of attention and perfectly aware that her beauty had enchanted Mahir, she realized that everyone in the room had now accepted her as an adult.

"Now that everyone's here, we can go in to dinner," Behice said.

Mahir stood up. "This morning, I received your permission to propose to Leman Hanım," he said. "And so, here and now, in your presence, I would like to formally request the hand of Leman Hanım in marriage." He turned, looked into Leman's eyes and asked, "Would you accept me as your husband?"

Saraylıhanım stirred furiously on the divan, outraged that a marriage proposal would be made directly to a girl, even as her elders were present and available to give their consent. So, the family would have yet another member recklessly enraptured with all things modern! Everyone was silent for a moment. Leman kept her eyes bashfully lowered. Mahir's heart leapt to his throat.

Finally, in a low voice: "If my father deems it suitable . . ."

"But what about you, Leman Hanım?" After a momentary show of reluctance, prettily feigned, "Yes, efendim," she said.

Turning to Reşat Bey, Mahir asked, "In that case, would you now permit us to be become engaged?"

"They already have," said Saraylıhanım. "But anyway, Kemal was always so fond of you."

Mahir smiled and pulled a diamond ring out of his pocket. "Then may this engagement bring blessings upon us all." Mahir slid the ring onto Leman's finger. He pulled a second ring out of his pocket and handed it to her. With shaking hands she slid the silver ring onto Mahir's finger. It was the first time Saraylıhanım had seen a girl place a ring onto the finger of her betrothed. The family elders were supposed to do it! Was the man mad!

"Leman Hanım, in two days I will be coming to visit you again, accompanied by my elder sister, Şahber Hanım, to bring our family jewels and our engagement gifts. Forgive me for not having been able to complete all the preparations today," Mahir said.

"You've prepared everything wonderfully, efendim. All right everyone, please go in to dinner," Behice said, leading the way.

They were all just about to sit down at the table when they heard a baby crying overhead.

Mehpare rushed off.

"Is that Halim crying?" asked Mahir.

"No, that would be Sabahat. It's feeding time, you see," Leman said.

When Behice remained seated Mahir murmured, "Behice Hanımefendi, we'll wait for you to come back . . . I trust I'm now considered a member of the family . . ."

"You've always been like a member of the family, Mahir Bey," Behice said. "There's no need for me to go upstairs. Mehpare's nursing Sabahat, bless her. My milk has been in short supply."

"Poor Mehpare has a baby at her breast all day long," Leman said. "And they're both so chubby."

"Mehpare Abla's turned into a cow," Suat giggled.

"Suat! If your father wasn't leaving tomorrow I'd send you straight up to your room! Not another word out of you, do you hear!" scolded Behice, who had gone red with embarrassment.

"Mahir Bey, you've been deceived by the outer appearance of my daughters into thinking they've grown up; they're still children, I fear," Ahmet Reşat said.

"Impertinent children," Saryalıhanım added for good measure. Leman's eyes filled with tears.

"Then I'm a lucky man indeed to have a fiancée with the guilelessness of a child," Mahir said.

"Come on," Ahmet Reşat said, "Let's speak of pleasant things at dinner this evening. I want to smile when I look back at this, my last meal with my entire family."

"What do you mean 'last meal'? We'll have many more meals together," Behice said. Her husband's decision to flee abroad had already begun the transformation of a coddled, delicate creature into an iron-willed woman prepared for adversity of any kind. Ahmet Reşat flashed his wife a look of gratitude.

Despite their best efforts, the dinner that evening was shrouded in sadness. They all knew it could well be their last meal together. Mehpare didn't speak at all. Ever since Kemal's death, she'd taken to speaking only when necessary. Try as she might to maintain a veneer of gaiety, Behice's spirits were clearly sagging. Conversation at the somber engagement dinner was mostly between Reşat and Mahir, and focused almost exclusively on the state of the nation and the future of an empire without a sovereign. An empire?

"We should stop referring to the Ottomans as though they still had an empire," Ahmet Reşat said at one point. "We've lost our empire; a handful of land is all that remains to us. God willing, Mustafa Kemal Pasha will be better at defending it from the rapacity of foreign states than we were."

Immediately after dinner, Mahir made his excuses and asked permission to go home. He would, of course, be getting up early the following morning.

"Mahir Bey, please don't trouble yourself tomorrow. I'll slip out of the house first thing in the morning. I'm joining some colleagues at the quay," Ahmet Reşat said.

"I will most certainly be standing on the quay to wave you off, efendim."

Ahmet Reşat accompanied his future son-in-law as far as the garden gate. Leman waited in vain for him to turn round and wave. But as he strode off into the darkness that night, Mahir's thoughts were solely of Ahmet Reşat's dawn journey into what could be permanent exile.

When Ahmet Reşat returned to the sitting room he found Leman in front of the window.

"Why haven't you gone to your room yet, my dear?" he said, stroking his daughter's hair.

"Father, why do you have to go? No one's given me a proper explanation. I'm an engaged woman now, not a child. Can't you tell me?"

"Sit down, Leman" Ahmet Reşat said wearily. Father and daughter sat across from each other on the divan.

"There's a list, Leman. The men on the list are considered traitors to their country. I haven't seen the list myself, but I'm absolutely certain that all of the members of the last cabinet and all of the signatories to the Treaty of Sevres are on it. The Ankara Government has issued a death warrant for everyone on the list."

"Father!" Leman stifled a scream with her hand.

"You must never lose your fortitude, my girl. You've got to look after your mother, your grandmother and your sisters. Keep your composure at all costs. Having entrusted the entire family to you and Mahir Bey, I'm able to leave with a heart less troubled. One day, they'll understand that we're not traitors and we'll be able to return. You're the daughter of an honorable man who has given his life to the service of his country. Never forget that."

Leman leaned her head on her father's chest, her body wracked with sobs. Ahmet Reşat allowed her to cry for a moment, then, in a soft voice, he said, "Come on, let's go to our rooms. Don't let your mother see you crying like that."

Leman composed herself, wiping away her tears and the first kohl she had ever worn with the back of her hand. With her streaked face and elaborately curled hair, she resembled neither a child nor a woman. Still in mourning for her beloved uncle, she'd suddenly become engaged and learned of the death warrant against her father. Her large eyes looked perplexed, as though she had not yet puzzled out how she was meant to endure all that had come her way. It was with both sorrow and love that Ahmet Reşat gazed at the sixteen-year-old girl whose shoulders, at the fall of a single sentence, had been burdened with the responsibilities of a lifetime.

Once Mehpare had finished nursing Halim, changed his diapers and put him in the cradle at the foot of her bed, she leaned over the decorative cradle to her right. Eyes tightly shut, Sabahat appeared at first glance to be sound asleep, but her tiny lips puckered and worked, a sure sign that she would soon wake up and cry. Mehpare wiped her nipple with some moist cotton, bent over the cradle and picked up the tiny girl. Eyes closed, the baby snuffled hungrily, nuzzling and craning its neck until she soon found her wet-nurse's nipple and began sucking noisily. Mehpare ran her fingertips over the downy hair. She'd loved the other girls, especially naughty, talkative Suat. But there was a special place in Mehpare's heart for the baby now in her arms—this little girl, who, like her own Halim, would grow up without knowing the love, the tenderness, the well-meaning gruffness of a father. Mehpare herself knew only too well what it was like to be viewed by others with that subtle mix of pity, scorn, and disdain reserved for fatherless girls.

In her first years in this house she'd been so envious of the way the girls were spoiled and petted by Reşat Bey. While everyone else would rush about making themselves and the house presentable if they knew the master of the house had turned into the street on his way home, the girls had never been the least bit scared of him. They'd come tumbling down the stairs and leap straight into his open arms.

"*Où est mon petit cadeau?*" Suat would ask, and each time she'd be praised for having added a few more words of French to her vocabulary. Saraylıhanım had always objected, warning, "You're spoiling the girls, Reşat Bey, my boy. They'll never be able to adapt when they go off to live with their husbands."

"I'm not sending my girls away," Reşat Bey would say. "When they get married, their husbands can come here and live with us." He'd finally notice the pair of eyes peering through the crack of a door or down from the landing, and turn his attention to the dejected little girl who wasn't his daughter. "I'd even have second thoughts about giving Mehpare away to just any suitor." Mehpare's nose would tickle and her eyes sting. She'd wanted so much to be Reşat Bey's real daughter. That had been impossible, of course; but now here she was, not only his daughter-in-law but his daughter's wet nurse. And if God had taken Kemal away from her, he'd also given her two babies to hold close to her heart. It was early still, the sun hadn't yet risen above the horizon; a time said to be the most auspicious for prayer. If she vowed to God never to suckle Sabahat again, never to hold her or so much as caress her silken skin, would He allow Reşat Bey, the man she now regarded as her father, to stay here in this house?

After twenty minutes of nursing, she sat Sabahat on her lap and burped her. Then she gently put her down in the cradle, nappies unchanged so that she wouldn't wake up, and drew aside the curtain. A coupe was waiting in front of the garden gate. Soon, Ahmet Reşat would walk through the front door, small valise in hand, board the coupe and disappear into the morning gloom. And, just like Kemal, those who remained behind would never know where he'd gone, what he'd endured, where he was buried. As Mehpare fought back her tears she heard a creak on the stairs. Someone was tiptoeing down those stairs, careful not to wake anyone. It could only be Reşat Bey.

He'd wanted to leave without any fuss, leave the house as everyone slept. Later, they would all wake up at the usual hour as though nothing had happened and go on with their daily lives. That's what he'd wanted . . . what he'd requested of each of them . . . asking that his last wish in this house—until he returned, of course—be honored.

When Mehpare was certain he had descended as far as the ground floor, she threw on her dressing gown and rushed down the stairs to the kitchen. She paused at the door. In the dimness she could make out a ghostly apparition in a white nightgown: it was Behice, doing exactly what Mehpare had come down to do. Mehpare crept inside and fumbled for a basin; finding one, she filled it at the faucet. As she left the kitchen with Behice, they came across Saraylıhanım. A moment later, the three women, none of them speaking, all of them bearing a basin of water, stepped through the front door and silently followed in the tracks of Ahmet Reşat. He didn't look back, either because he actually didn't hear them or because he simply chose not to. Nodding to the driver holding open the door, he stepped into the coupe. The previous night, his wife had wept in his arms. He didn't have the strength to look upon that face drawn with pain and into those eyes shot with blood, to bid her farewell yet again. The driver climbed up onto his seat and flicked his whip at the horse's bony hindquarters. As soon as the coupe began rolling away, the lips of the three women formed soundless prayers as they splashed their basins onto the street.

"Go like water and return like water, my husband." Behice's anguished cry mingled with the receding clicks of hooves on cobblestones, and was gone.

The minute the coupe turned the corner onto the main street, Behice, who had been able to remain on her feet only with the support of Mehpare and SaryalıHanım, sank to the ground and burst into tears.

Mahir was agitatedly pacing back and forth in front of the port authority when he saw a coupe drawing up to the curb on the opposite side of the street. He hurried over and took the small valise from the driver.

"Mahir . . . What have you done! You shouldn't have come," said Ahmet Reşat.

"How could I not come, Reşat Bey! How could I let you go without saying goodbye?"

"Have any of my colleagues come?"

"I see a few of them. Look, just over there on the corner; it's Cemal Beyefendi and Hazım Beyefendi."

"Let me go and say hello to them; I'll be right back." Ahmet Reşat had only walked a few paces when he suddenly spun on his heel and returned to Mahir's side. "Come with me, Mahir. I'd like to introduce my new son-in-law to my friends," he said. A smile spread across Mahir's troubled face. The two men walked side-by-side towards the gathering crowd.

An official from the Lloyd Triestino shipping company came up to a small group of passengers chatting on the quay as they waited to board an Italian ship bound for Brindisi; he informed them that he'd brought their travel documents. With long faces, the last Ottomans followed the official into the customs house. The disgraced ministers of a defunct empire were to travel with papers arranged by Count Caprini, who had enjoyed close ties to the palace and was a personal friend of many of the men he was now helping to flee.

When Count Caprini had heard that the Ankara Government had drawn up a list of men condemned to death, and that it contained the names of every minister in the last cabinet, he'd called on his old friend Ahmet Reşat, personally traveling all the way to the mansion in Beyazit.

Most of the cabinet members and members of parliament had already left on the British steamer, Egypt, bound for the country of that name. Among those still remaining were several of the Count's friends. A steamer would be leaving for Brindisi in two days. If Ahmet Reşat and his friends missed that boat they would have to flee by train, meaning identity checks at every border they crossed. That could be dangerous.

A decision was hastily made. Those unable to obtain passports in the brief time allotted would have to get them on the quay, just before the ship sailed.

As Ahmet Reşat and his friends followed the Italian official into the customs house, Mahir began walking towards the stern of the anchored steamer. The ship stretched on and on, like a vast floating apartment block. It was only when he reached the end of the ship that he was able to see the opposite shore. A few lights were still burning over by Yenicami; in the twilight of early dawn, the city was slowly shaking itself awake with mutters and murmurs and groans. Welling up into the morning sky, drowning out the clacking of the first tram, the *putt-putting* of motorboats heading for harbor, the weary cries of fishermen unloading their catch, was the call to prayer. Eyes closed as he listened reverently to the melodious chanting of the muezzin, Mahir entreated Allah to help Ahmet Reşat.

At the touch of a hand on his shoulder, he jumped.

It was Reşat Bey, now standing next to him, saying, "It's time to say good-bye."

Mahir looked at his friend's face, that kind, handsome face, now worn and sallow in the pearly first glow of dawn. But when Ahmet Reşat spoke, his voice was as strong and firm as ever.

"Mahir, I'm entrusting my family to you. I'm certain you'll cherish Leman. Don't delay the wedding on my account. And my offer remains. You'll be discharged from the military for being my son-in-law. I urge you to set up a clinic in the selamlık."

"Thank you. Don't allow your heart to grow heavy, efendim. Know that all will be well here. Your family is now my family."

"I may be overstepping here, but Mehpare and Halim are also members of this family, Mahir, and I must ask you, please, not to view them any differently than you would Behice Hanım, Sabahat or Suat."

"Of course not, efendim."

"Now make your farewells."

Ahmet Reşat placed one hand on his future son-in-law's shoulder, gripped his arm with the other and looked for a time into his face, as though to draw strength from those honest, brown eyes. Then, without a word, he turned and swiftly climbed the gangplank to the ship.

Mahir was suddenly very much alone at the base of the enormous steamer, the welfare and security of an entire family resting on his shoulders. He didn't even notice the other passengers ascending the gangplank. He gazed up, seeking a last glimpse of Ahmet Reşat, but there was no sign of him.

Reşat was at the back of the ship, both hands resting on the rail as he looked out over the sea, the domes and the minarets. Seagulls dipped their white wings into the water as they scavenged for food. Soon, the rising sun would paint the domes gold. The city would awaken, coming to life with its stevedores, its vendors, its civil servants, its students, its fishermen. After the steamer had slowly moved away from the quay, turned toward the open sea and bid its farewell to Istanbul with a strange animal cry, the city would soon be left behind.

He'd blamed the Sultan for having fled aboard a British warship; it was wrenching to think about that now. Ever since his twenties,

Ahmet Reşat had been serving the state as an honorable, judicious, industrious subject of the empire and now, like a traitor, like a criminal, he was forced to abandon his country, holding a foreign passport. It was a dagger in the heart, twisting. He couldn't still the pain, the shame, the outrage. The previous morning he'd imagined walking into the sea with a boulder. Now he imagined jumping off the ship. If he didn't strike his head on the way down, would he reflexively start swimming the moment he hit the water? He could imagine the screaming headlines the following day: *Disgraced Finance Minister Botches Suicide!* What would Behice do when she heard about that? Or his aunt?

He reached into his pocket for his cigarette case and was startled when his fingers came into contact with something. Strange, he only carried his tobacco in that particular pocket! He pulled out a hard object wrapped in a handkerchief. Fingers trembling with excitement he unraveled the silken knotted corners, upon one of which "BR," his wife's initials, were embroidered in silver thread. Gleaming in his hand was the family heirloom Behice had worn on their wedding night, a diamond-studded brooch shaped like a bird. A tiny slip of paper had been carefully folded and placed in the bird's beak.

"I realize your funds are limited and if you ever find yourself in need please don't hesitate to sell this bird. My heart is with you, always."

He was moved to tears. Banished were the dark thoughts that had been swirling in his head just a moment earlier. He didn't have the courage to kill himself while there were people he loved, and he was too pious to betray the soul Allah had entrusted to him for safekeeping. So, until the time came to surrender that soul, he would endeavor to survive in a foreign land. He might obtain a position somewhere, perhaps as a translator. His French and Persian were good, and he spoke some Italian. Or he might become an accountant. Surely a man who had once managed the finances of a vast empire would be sufficiently versed in figures to attract the attention of a merchant. He'd work and meet his needs, exchange letters with his family, follow his children's lives from afar, miss them and Istanbul terribly, be filled with longing but go on living. And maybe one day he would pin the brooch back onto his wife's breast with his own hands.

Suddenly, there was a deep-chested, full-throated, drawn-out hoot: the ship was leaving port. Ahmet Reşat tightened his grip on the wooden rail and, confident that he would be drowned out by the ship whistle and oblivious in any case to possible onlookers, he roared with all his might:

"Farewell Istanbul! Farewell my city!"

– 24 –

The Letter

June 1924, Bucharest

To my beloved wife, Behice,
I wept with joy as I read your most recent letter about of the birth of Sitare; how sorry I am that I couldn't have been with you. May her name, the Persian for 'star', herald a life and destiny forever bright. I ask God that the child be healthy, dutiful, long-lived.

As I near the second year of my exile my heart is filled with sorrow and anguish. So this is my compensation for thirty-five years of service to my country. It is only as joyful news in a letter that I learn of the birth of my only grandchild. I was not at all upset to learn of Mahir's resignation. If it is agreed that he is to be pensioned off, his return to Istanbul will be favorable, God willing. Official duties and matters of state are no longer the source of any pleasure.

It is the necessities of life that are important and may God provide for him and my family in Istanbul. Behice, I too would very much like to see you, but you wouldn't be comfortable here, and in view of the severe winters I couldn't agree to your coming. I won't let you suffer for my sake. Perhaps in November we could go to Rome and winter there together. Or I could go to Pest and wait for you. If I can find suitable housing there, and we decide we'd be able to live cheaply enough, we could consider moving. I beg you again not to let anything trouble you. Some good comes out of everything—even in all of this misery there is good, have no doubt. It is enough that God grants our family health, wellbeing. Up to now, we've enjoyed a comfortable life. I have faith that God will not deprive us in the future, either. Let us stay alive. We have so much left. If my return to Istanbul proves possible, we'll figure things out by letter—and then, by ship or by train, I shall return.

At present, all we can do is continue to be patient.

To my venerable aunt, to Mehpare and to you, my dear, I wish God's blessings and patience. Convey my affectionate greetings to my dear lamb, Suat, and especially to that great source of pride, my daughter Leman, and to my son-in-law, Mahir Bey. I kiss the eyes of Sabahat and Halim. May God grant my tiny granddaughter Sitare a long and auspicious life.

Your affectionate husband,
Reşat

Notes

p. 6   *handed his coat to Hüsnü, and entered the* selamlık: The part of a large Muslim house reserved for the men.

p. 9   *The disastrous misadventure of Sarıkamış*: Located near Kars, Sarıkamış was the scene of a battle between Russia and the Ottoman Empire, in which İsmail Enver's army (90,000 men) was defeated by the Russian force (100,000 men; the engagement lasted from December through January, 1914–1915. In the subsequent retreat, tens of thousands of Turkish soldiers died. This was the single worst defeat of an Ottoman army during World War I. On January 1, 1919, the new Ottoman government expelled Enver Pasha from the army after he led the Army of Islam in an ill-fated campaign in the Caucasus region. He was tried *in absentia* in the Turkish Courts-Martial of 1919-20 for the crimes of "plunging the country into war without a legitimate reason, forced deportation of Armenians, and leaving the country without permission," and condemned to death.

p. 9   *the partisans of the Committee of Union and Progress:* (Turkish: *İttihat ve Terakki Cemiyeti*) A political party in power from after the revolution of 1908 until 1918, when many of its members were court-martialed and imprisoned.

p. 14   *she was poked in the shoulder by a* madam: a title generally reserved for non-Muslim women.

p. 20   *secretly reached an agreement to give the Twelve Islands to Italy:* After several centuries of special semi-autonomous status within the Ottoman Empire, the Dodecanese archipelago—which includes Rhodes, Kos and Patmos—declared independence in 1912, only to be occupied almost immediately by Italy.

p. 23   *In moments of tenderness, she occasionally managed* valide: A formal term for "mother," in the sense of "Queen Mother."

p. 37   *in Crete during the massacre of the Muslims there:* Ottoman forces were expelled in 1898 and an independent Cretan state founded only after several years during which Cretan Muslims faced massacres, particularly in the four coastal cities.

p. 39   *When the cabinet of Ali Rıza Pasha ratified the National Pact:* Misak-ı Millî (English: National Oath or National Pact) was the set of six important decisions made by the last term of the Ottoman Parliament. The Parliament met on 28 January 1920, and published their decisions on 12 February 1920. These decisions resulted in the occupation of Istanbul by the British on 16

February 1920 and the establishment of a new parliament, the Grand National Assembly, in Ankara.

p. 44   *positions of responsibility at Karakol*: Karakol (police station): code word used for the underground resistance.

p. 52   *Get into your* çarşaf: An outer garment covering a woman from head to foot.

p. 57   *I miss your* gözleme *terribly*: a flat savory cake cooked on a griddle, typically with a cheese, spinach or potato filling.

p. 86   *Ziya Pasha's harem*: Here, harem simply refers to a man's wife or wives, and female relatives.

p. 102   *The name Suat had been chosen when Behice thought she was expecting a boy*: Suat, derived from the Arabic for happiness, Sa'd, is normally a boy's name.

p. 137   *The Minister arrived in the Sublime Porte*: Known in Turkish as *Babıâli*, Sublime Porte referred to the Central Office of the Imperial Goverment of the Ottoman empire in Istanbul, comprising of the offices of the Grand Vizier, the Minister of Foreign Affairs, and the Council of State.

p. 153   *Naime Sultan, the daughter of Sultan Abdülhamit*: The wives, daughters, sisters and mothers of the Sultan also hold the title of "sultan"; used after their names rather than before.

p. 155   *In fact, girls were now able to receive university degrees even from Dar'ül-Fünûnu*: The Women's University was founded in 1914, but when female students boycotted classes in 1920 the school was merged with Darülfünun and co-education introduced. When, in 1922, the Medical School began accepting women, all of its schools, with the exception of Theology, adopted mixed male and female classes.

p. 158   *most of the women had removed their* maşlah: An open-fronted cloak.

p. 172   *posted to Thessalonica during the Balkan War*: Thessalonica and the surrounding area were part of the Ottoman Empire until 26 October 1912, when the Ottoman garrison surrendered to the Greek Army during the First Balkan War, which pitted the combined forces of Serbia, Montenegro, Greece, and Bulgaria against the Ottoman Empire.

p. 185   *when we formed the Kuva-I İnzibatiye*: Literally "Forces of Order"; also known as the Hilafet Ordusu, or "Caliphate Army"; an army established on April 18th, 1920, by the imperial government of the Ottoman Empire in order to fight against the Turkish National Movement in the aftermath of World War I.

p. 187   *the final death blow to the Ottoman Empire*: Grand Vizier Damat Ferit was one of the signatories to the Treaty of Sèvres (August 10th, 1920): a peace treaty prepared by the Allies following WWI that imposed disastrous conditions upon the Ottoman Empire, it included partition and capitulations. The

Treaty of Sèvres was annulled in the course of the Turkish War of Independence and the parties signed and ratified the superseding Treaty of Lausanne in 1923.

p. 192 *She's making* ayran: a cool drink made of yogurt and water.

p. 192 *The Freedom and Unity Party*: The Freedom and Unity Party (Turkish: *Hürriyet ve İtilaf Partisi*) re-emerged in 1919 after being banned in 1912. The party embraced close ties with England , expressing its preference with the maxim: "If you fall into the sea, embrace a serpent and you'll survive; but if you embrace Germany, you'll drown."

p. 213 *the Association of Anglophiles*: (Turkish: *İngiliz Muhipleri Cemiyeti*; literally, "Society of the Affectionate Friends of the English") As the name implies, an organization whose members, many of them from prominent Istanbul families, supported an English mandate. The association was accused of having a hidden agenda aimed at denigrating Islam, spreading Christianity, belittling Turkishness and attempting to turn public opinion against the rebellion building in Anatolia. Atatürk himelf referred to the society as "nefarious" and "treacherous."

p. 243 *a* tekke *on the Asian Shore*: A dervish lodge.

p. 273 *let me and my nephew make our farewells*: To make one's farewells in this sense is much more than simply saying good-bye.

It's a ritualistic leave-taking (usually performed on death beds, before battles, or before long separations) in which both parties mutually forgive all that has been unjustly taken or done.

p. 278 *they poured out the contents of the bucket*: Water and fire both figure prominently in Turkish folklore and custom. Water is poured onto the road as a guest departs, both to make the journey "as smooth and fluid as water" and to ensure their safe return.

p. 287 *every time I hear his name I picture a pack of dogs*: Here, Börek Vendor Hasan is indulging in a bit of onomatopoeic word-play: the Turkish pronunciation of Bennett is similar to Bin-İt (Bin: 1000; İt: dog); hence, "A Thousand Dogs" Bennett.

p. 353 *after the '93 war*: The Ottoman-Russian War was fought in 1877-1878, but is known as the '93 War because it took place in 1293, according to the Rumî Calendar.

p. 361 *Gazi Pasha*: Before Mustafa Kemal took the surname Atatürk, he was often referred to as Gazi Pasha (Gazi means war veteran).

p. 382 *a friendship treaty with Soviet Russia*: The Moscow Treaty established the eastern borders north of Iran. It was also concrete evidence of continued Bolshevik support for the anti-imperialist movement in Anatolia and the rival government established in Ankara.

p. 391   *those reserved for his ancestor Genç Osman*: Osman II, or "Young Osman," so called because he ascended the throne at age fourteen, was reportedly either strangled with a bowstring or killed by "compression of the testicles."

p. 402   *as though an invisible hand was doing* ebru: *Ebru*, or water marbling, is formed by drawing designs with dye on the surface of water and then transferring the whirled image onto paper placed on the water.

p. 403   *an enormous box of* lokum: A soft, bite-sized, flavored sweet: so-called "Turkish delight."

p. 406   *since the reign of Abdülhamit*: Sultan Abdülhamit II was deposed on April 27, 1909, two weeks after the conservative-backed military overthrew the cabinet.

AYŞE KULIN was born in Istanbul in 1941. A fiction writer and essayist, Kulin has been awarded the Haldun Taner Short Story Award, the Sait Faik Story Prize, and has twice been named writer of the year by the University of Istanbul Communication Faculty. In 2011, *Farewell: A Mansion in Occupied Istanbul* was longlisted for the International IMPAC Dublin Literary Award.

KENNETH J. DAKAN has translated work by Buket Uzuner.

TURKISH LITERATURE SERIES

Turkish literature, from the time of independence to the present, has characterized itself by focusing on the struggles of everyday Turks and also by integrating modernist styles from the West, a trait most notable in translation in the work of Nobel prizewinner Orhan Pamuk.

This volume is the first in Dalkey Archive Press's Turkish Literature Series, established in cooperation with Barbaros Altug and Everest Yayinlari, which will make available Turkish writers and their works who have previously had little exposure in the Anglophone world.

Acknowledgement is also due to the Ministry of Culture and Tourism of Turkey, for its support through the TEDA subvention project.

Forthcoming in the Turkish Literature Series:

Music by My Bedside by Kürşat Başar

PETROS ABATZOGLOU, *What Does Mrs. Freeman Want?*
MICHAL AJVAZ, *The Golden Age.*
The Other City.
PIERRE ALBERT-BIROT, *Grabinoulor.*
YUZ ALESHKOVSKY, *Kangaroo.*
FELIPE ALFAU, *Chromos.*
Locos.
JOÃO ALMINO, *The Book of Emotions.*
IVAN ÂNGELO, *The Celebration.*
The Tower of Glass.
DAVID ANTIN, *Talking.*
ANTÓNIO LOBO ANTUNES, *Knowledge of Hell.*
The Splendor of Portugal.
ALAIN ARIAS-MISSON, *Theatre of Incest.*
IFTIKHAR ARIF AND WAQAS KHWAJA, EDS., *Modern Poetry of Pakistan.*
JOHN ASHBERY AND JAMES SCHUYLER, *A Nest of Ninnies.*
ROBERT ASHLEY, *Perfect Lives.*
GABRIELA AVIGUR-ROTEM, *Heatwave and Crazy Birds.*
HEIMRAD BÄCKER, *transcript.*
DJUNA BARNES, *Ladies Almanack.*
Ryder.
JOHN BARTH, *LETTERS.*
Sabbatical.
DONALD BARTHELME, *The King.*
Paradise.
SVETISLAV BASARA, *Chinese Letter.*
MIQUEL BAUÇÀ, *The Siege in the Room.*
RENÉ BELLETTO, *Dying.*
MAREK BIEŃCZYK, *Transparency.*
MARK BINELLI, *Sacco and Vanzetti Must Die!*
ANDREI BITOV, *Pushkin House.*
ANDREJ BLATNIK, *You Do Understand.*
LOUIS PAUL BOON, *Chapel Road.*
My Little War.
Summer in Termuren.
ROGER BOYLAN, *Killoyle.*
IGNÁCIO DE LOYOLA BRANDÃO, *Anonymous Celebrity.*
The Good-Bye Angel.
Teeth under the Sun.
Zero.
BONNIE BREMSER, *Troia: Mexican Memoirs.*
CHRISTINE BROOKE-ROSE, *Amalgamemnon.*
BRIGID BROPHY, *In Transit*
MEREDITH BROSNAN, *Mr. Dynamite.*
GERALD L. BRUNS, *Modern Poetry and the Idea of Language.*
EVGENY BUNIMOVICH AND J. KATES, EDS., *Contemporary Russian Poetry: An Anthology.*
GABRIELLE BURTON, *Heartbreak Hotel.*
MICHEL BUTOR, *Degrees.*
Mobile.
Portrait of the Artist as a Young Ape.
G. CABRERA INFANTE, *Infante's Inferno.*
Three Trapped Tigers.
JULIETA CAMPOS, *The Fear of Losing Eurydice.*
ANNE CARSON, *Eros the Bittersweet.*
ORLY CASTEL-BLOOM, *Dolly City.*
CAMILO JOSÉ CELA, *Christ versus Arizona.*
The Family of Pascual Duarte.
The Hive.
LOUIS-FERDINAND CÉLINE, *Castle to Castle.*
Conversations with Professor Y.
London Bridge.

Normance.
North.
Rigadoon.
MARIE CHAIX, *The Laurels of Lake Constance.*
HUGO CHARTERIS, *The Tide Is Right.*
JEROME CHARYN, *The Tar Baby.*
ERIC CHEVILLARD, *Demolishing Nisard.*
LUIS CHITARRONI, *The No Variations.*
MARC CHOLODENKO, *Mordechai Schamz.*
JOSHUA COHEN, *Witz.*
EMILY HOLMES COLEMAN, *The Shutter of Snow.*
ROBERT COOVER, *A Night at the Movies.*
STANLEY CRAWFORD, *Log of the S.S. The Mrs Unguentine.*
Some Instructions to My Wife.
ROBERT CREELEY, *Collected Prose.*
RENÉ CREVEL, *Putting My Foot in It.*
RALPH CUSACK, *Cadenza.*
SUSAN DAITCH, *L.C.*
Storytown.
NICHOLAS DELBANCO, *The Count of Concord.*
Sherbrookes.
NIGEL DENNIS, *Cards of Identity.*
PETER DIMOCK, *A Short Rhetoric for Leaving the Family.*
ARIEL DORFMAN, *Konfidenz.*
COLEMAN DOWELL, *The Houses of Children.*
Island People.
Too Much Flesh and Jabez.
ARKADII DRAGOMOSHCHENKO, *Dust.*
RIKKI DUCORNET, *The Complete Butcher's Tales.*
The Fountains of Neptune.
The Jade Cabinet.
The One Marvelous Thing.
Phosphor in Dreamland.
The Stain.
The Word "Desire."
WILLIAM EASTLAKE, *The Bamboo Bed.*
Castle Keep.
Lyric of the Circle Heart.
JEAN ECHENOZ, *Chopin's Move.*
STANLEY ELKIN, *A Bad Man.*
Boswell: A Modern Comedy.
Criers and Kibitzers, Kibitzers and Criers.
The Dick Gibson Show.
The Franchiser.
George Mills.
The Living End.
The MacGuffin.
The Magic Kingdom.
Mrs. Ted Bliss.
The Rabbi of Lud.
Van Gogh's Room at Arles.
FRANÇOIS EMMANUEL, *Invitation to a Voyage.*
ANNIE ERNAUX, *Cleaned Out.*
SALVADOR ESPRIU, *Ariadne in the Grotesque Labyrinth.*
LAUREN FAIRBANKS, *Muzzle Thyself.*
Sister Carrie.
LESLIE A. FIEDLER, *Love and Death in the American Novel.*
JUAN FILLOY, *Faction.*
Op Oloop.
ANDY FITCH, *Pop Poetics.*
GUSTAVE FLAUBERT, *Bouvard and Pécuchet.*
KASS FLEISHER, *Talking out of School.*

FORD MADOX FORD,
The March of Literature.
JON FOSSE, *Aliss at the Fire.*
Melancholy.
MAX FRISCH, *I'm Not Stiller.*
Man in the Holocene.
CARLOS FUENTES, *Christopher Unborn.*
Distant Relations.
Terra Nostra.
Vlad.
Where the Air Is Clear.
TAKEHIKO FUKUNAGA, *Flowers of Grass.*
WILLIAM GADDIS, *J R.*
The Recognitions.
JANICE GALLOWAY, *Foreign Parts.*
The Trick Is to Keep Breathing.
WILLIAM H. GASS, *Cartesian Sonata
and Other Novellas.*
Finding a Form.
A Temple of Texts.
The Tunnel.
Willie Masters' Lonesome Wife.
GÉRARD GAVARRY, *Hoppla! 1 2 3.*
Making a Novel.
ETIENNE GILSON,
The Arts of the Beautiful.
Forms and Substances in the Arts.
C. S. GISCOMBE, *Giscome Road.*
Here.
Prairie Style.
DOUGLAS GLOVER, *Bad News of the Heart.*
The Enamoured Knight.
WITOLD GOMBROWICZ,
A Kind of Testament.
PAULO EMÍLIO SALES GOMES, *P's Three
Women.*
KAREN ELIZABETH GORDON, *The Red Shoes.*
GEORGI GOSPODINOV, *Natural Novel.*
JUAN GOYTISOLO, *Count Julian.*
Exiled from Almost Everywhere.
Juan the Landless.
Makbara.
Marks of Identity.
PATRICK GRAINVILLE, *The Cave of Heaven.*
HENRY GREEN, *Back.*
Blindness.
Concluding.
Doting.
Nothing.
JACK GREEN, *Fire the Bastards!*
JIŘÍ GRUŠA, *The Questionnaire.*
GABRIEL GUDDING,
Rhode Island Notebook.
MELA HARTWIG, *Am I a Redundant
Human Being?*
JOHN HAWKES, *The Passion Artist.*
Whistlejacket.
ELIZABETH HEIGHWAY, ED., *Contemporary
Georgian Fiction.*
ALEKSANDAR HEMON, ED.,
Best European Fiction.
AIDAN HIGGINS, *Balcony of Europe.*
A Bestiary.
Blind Man's Bluff
Bornholm Night-Ferry.
Darkling Plain: Texts for the Air.
Flotsam and Jetsam.
Langrishe, Go Down.
Scenes from a Receding Past.
Windy Arbours.
KEIZO HINO, *Isle of Dreams.*
KAZUSHI HOSAKA, *Plainsong.*

ALDOUS HUXLEY, *Antic Hay.*
Crome Yellow.
Point Counter Point.
Those Barren Leaves.
Time Must Have a Stop.
NAOYUKI II, *The Shadow of a Blue Cat.*
MIKHAIL IOSSEL AND JEFF PARKER, EDS.,
*Amerika: Russian Writers View the
United States.*
DRAGO JANČAR, *The Galley Slave.*
GERT JONKE, *The Distant Sound.*
Geometric Regional Novel.
Homage to Czerny.
The System of Vienna.
JACQUES JOUET, *Mountain R.*
Savage.
Upstaged.
CHARLES JULIET, *Conversations with
Samuel Beckett and Bram van
Velde.*
MIEKO KANAI, *The Word Book.*
YORAM KANIUK, *Life on Sandpaper.*
HUGH KENNER, *The Counterfeiters.*
*Flaubert, Joyce and Beckett:
The Stoic Comedians.*
Joyce's Voices.
DANILO KIŠ, *The Attic.*
Garden, Ashes.
The Lute and the Scars
Psalm 44.
A Tomb for Boris Davidovich.
ANITA KONKKA, *A Fool's Paradise.*
GEORGE KONRÁD, *The City Builder.*
TADEUSZ KONWICKI, *A Minor Apocalypse.*
The Polish Complex.
MENIS KOUMANDAREAS, *Koula.*
ELAINE KRAF, *The Princess of 72nd Street.*
JIM KRUSOE, *Iceland.*
AYŞE KULIN, *Farewell: A Mansion in
Occupied Istanbul.*
EWA KURYLUK, *Century 21.*
EMILIO LASCANO TEGUI, *On Elegance
While Sleeping.*
ERIC LAURRENT, *Do Not Touch.*
HERVÉ LE TELLIER, *The Sextine Chapel.*
*A Thousand Pearls (for a Thousand
Pennies)*
VIOLETTE LEDUC, *La Bâtarde.*
EDOUARD LEVÉ, *Autoportrait.*
Suicide.
MARIO LEVI, *Istanbul Was a Fairy Tale.*
SUZANNE JILL LEVINE, *The Subversive
Scribe: Translating Latin
American Fiction.*
DEBORAH LEVY, *Billy and Girl.*
*Pillow Talk in Europe and Other
Places.*
JOSÉ LEZAMA LIMA, *Paradiso.*
ROSA LIKSOM, *Dark Paradise.*
OSMAN LINS, *Avalovara.*
The Queen of the Prisons of Greece.
ALF MAC LOCHLAINN,
The Corpus in the Library.
Out of Focus.
RON LOEWINSOHN, *Magnetic Field(s).*
MINA LOY, *Stories and Essays of Mina Loy.*
BRIAN LYNCH, *The Winner of Sorrow.*
D. KEITH MANO, *Take Five.*
MICHELINE AHARONIAN MARCOM,
The Mirror in the Well.
BEN MARCUS,
The Age of Wire and String.

SELECTED DALKEY ARCHIVE TITLES

WALLACE MARKFIELD,
Teitlebaum's Window.
To an Early Grave.
DAVID MARKSON, Reader's Block.
Springer's Progress.
Wittgenstein's Mistress.
CAROLE MASO, AVA.
LADISLAV MATEJKA AND KRYSTYNA
POMORSKA, EDS.,
Readings in Russian Poetics:
Formalist and Structuralist Views.
HARRY MATHEWS,
The Case of the Persevering Maltese:
Collected Essays.
Cigarettes.
The Conversions.
The Human Country: New and
Collected Stories.
The Journalist.
My Life in CIA.
Singular Pleasures.
The Sinking of the Odradek
Stadium.
Tlooth.
20 Lines a Day.
JOSEPH MCELROY,
Night Soul and Other Stories.
THOMAS MCGONIGLE,
Going to Patchogue.
ROBERT L. MCLAUGHLIN, ED., Innovations:
An Anthology of Modern &
Contemporary Fiction.
ABDELWAHAB MEDDEB, Talismano.
GERHARD MEIER, Isle of the Dead.
HERMAN MELVILLE, The Confidence-Man.
AMANDA MICHALOPOULOU, I'd Like.
STEVEN MILLHAUSER, The Barnum Museum.
In the Penny Arcade.
RALPH J. MILLS, JR., Essays on Poetry.
MOMUS, The Book of Jokes.
CHRISTINE MONTALBETTI, The Origin of Man.
Western.
OLIVE MOORE, Spleen.
NICHOLAS MOSLEY, Accident.
Assassins.
Catastrophe Practice.
Children of Darkness and Light.
Experience and Religion.
A Garden of Trees.
God's Hazard.
The Hesperides Tree.
Hopeful Monsters.
Imago Bird.
Impossible Object.
Inventing God.
Judith.
Look at the Dark.
Natalie Natalia.
Paradoxes of Peace.
Serpent.
Time at War.
The Uses of Slime Mould:
Essays of Four Decades.
WARREN MOTTE,
Fables of the Novel: French Fiction
since 1990.
Fiction Now: The French Novel in
the 21st Century.
Oulipo: A Primer of Potential
Literature.
GERALD MURNANE, Barley Patch.
Inland.

YVES NAVARRE, Our Share of Time.
Sweet Tooth.
DOROTHY NELSON, In Night's City.
Tar and Feathers.
ESHKOL NEVO, Homesick.
WILFRIDO D. NOLLEDO, But for the Lovers.
FLANN O'BRIEN, At Swim-Two-Birds.
At War.
The Best of Myles.
The Dalkey Archive.
Further Cuttings.
The Hard Life.
The Poor Mouth.
The Third Policeman.
CLAUDE OLLIER, The Mise-en-Scène.
Wert and the Life Without End.
GIOVANNI ORELLI, Walaschek's Dream.
PATRIK OUŘEDNÍK, Europeana.
The Opportune Moment, 1855.
BORIS PAHOR, Necropolis.
FERNANDO DEL PASO, News from the Empire.
Palinuro of Mexico.
ROBERT PINGET, The Inquisitory.
Mahu or The Material.
Trio.
A. G. PORTA, The No World Concerto.
MANUEL PUIG, Betrayed by Rita Hayworth.
The Buenos Aires Affair.
Heartbreak Tango.
RAYMOND QUENEAU, The Last Days.
Odile.
Pierrot Mon Ami.
Saint Glinglin.
ANN QUIN, Berg.
Passages.
Three.
Tripticks.
ISHMAEL REED, The Free-Lance Pallbearers.
The Last Days of Louisiana Red.
Ishmael Reed: The Plays.
Juice!
Reckless Eyeballing.
The Terrible Threes.
The Terrible Twos.
Yellow Back Radio Broke-Down.
JASIA REICHARDT, 15 Journeys Warsaw
to London.
NOËLLE REVAZ, With the Animals.
JOÃO UBALDO RIBEIRO, House of the
Fortunate Buddhas.
JEAN RICARDOU, Place Names.
RAINER MARIA RILKE, The Notebooks of
Malte Laurids Brigge.
JULIÁN RÍOS, The House of Ulysses.
Larva: A Midsummer Night's Babel.
Poundemonium.
Procession of Shadows.
AUGUSTO ROA BASTOS, I the Supreme.
DANIËL ROBBERECHTS, Arriving in Avignon.
JEAN ROLIN, The Explosion of the
Radiator Hose.
OLIVIER ROLIN, Hotel Crystal.
ALIX CLEO ROUBAUD, Alix's Journal.
JACQUES ROUBAUD, The Form of a
City Changes Faster, Alas, Than
the Human Heart.
The Great Fire of London.
Hortense in Exile.
Hortense Is Abducted.
The Loop.
Mathematics:
The Plurality of Worlds of Lewis.

FOR A FULL LIST OF PUBLICATIONS, VISIT:
www.dalkeyarchive.com

SELECTED DALKEY ARCHIVE TITLES

The Princess Hoppy.
Some Thing Black.
LEON S. ROUDIEZ, *French Fiction Revisited.*
RAYMOND ROUSSEL, *Impressions of Africa.*
VEDRANA RUDAN, *Night.*
STIG SÆTERBAKKEN, *Siamese.*
LYDIE SALVAYRE, *The Company of Ghosts.*
Everyday Life.
The Lecture.
*Portrait of the Writer as a
Domesticated Animal.*
The Power of Flies.
LUIS RAFAEL SÁNCHEZ,
Macho Camacho's Beat.
SEVERO SARDUY, *Cobra & Maitreya.*
NATHALIE SARRAUTE,
Do You Hear Them?
Martereau.
The Planetarium.
ARNO SCHMIDT, *Collected Novellas.*
Collected Stories.
Nobodaddy's Children.
Two Novels.
ASAF SCHURR, *Motti.*
CHRISTINE SCHUTT, *Nightwork.*
GAIL SCOTT, *My Paris.*
DAMION SEARLS, *What We Were Doing
and Where We Were Going.*
JUNE AKERS SEESE,
Is This What Other Women Feel Too?
What Waiting Really Means.
BERNARD SHARE, *Inish.*
Transit.
AURELIE SHEEHAN, *Jack Kerouac Is Pregnant.*
VIKTOR SHKLOVSKY, *Bowstring.*
Knight's Move.
*A Sentimental Journey:
Memoirs 1917–1922.*
Energy of Delusion: A Book on Plot.
Literature and Cinematography.
Theory of Prose.
Third Factory.
Zoo, or Letters Not about Love.
CLAUDE SIMON, *The Invitation.*
PIERRE SINIAC, *The Collaborators.*
KJERSTI A. SKOMSVOLD, *The Faster I Walk,
the Smaller I Am.*
JOSEF ŠKVORECKÝ, *The Engineer of
Human Souls.*
GILBERT SORRENTINO,
Aberration of Starlight.
Blue Pastoral.
Crystal Vision.
*Imaginative Qualities of Actual
Things.*
Mulligan Stew.
Pack of Lies.
Red the Fiend.
The Sky Changes.
Something Said.
Splendide-Hôtel.
Steelwork.
Under the Shadow.
W. M. SPACKMAN, *The Complete Fiction.*
ANDRZEJ STASIUK, *Dukla.*
Fado.
GERTRUDE STEIN, *Lucy Church Amiably.*
The Making of Americans.
A Novel of Thank You.
LARS SVENDSEN, *A Philosophy of Evil.*
PIOTR SZEWC, *Annihilation.*
GONÇALO M. TAVARES, *Jerusalem.*

Joseph Walser's Machine.
*Learning to Pray in the Age of
Technique.*
LUCIAN DAN TEODOROVICI,
Our Circus Presents . . .
NIKANOR TERATOLOGEN, *Assisted Living.*
STEFAN THEMERSON, *Hobson's Island.*
The Mystery of the Sardine.
Tom Harris.
TAEKO TOMIOKA, *Building Waves.*
JOHN TOOMEY, *Sleepwalker.*
JEAN-PHILIPPE TOUSSAINT, *The Bathroom.*
Camera.
Monsieur.
Reticence.
Running Away.
Self-Portrait Abroad.
Television.
The Truth about Marie.
DUMITRU TSEPENEAG, *Hotel Europa.*
The Necessary Marriage.
Pigeon Post.
Vain Art of the Fugue.
ESTHER TUSQUETS, *Stranded.*
DUBRAVKA UGRESIC, *Lend Me Your Character.*
Thank You for Not Reading.
TOR ULVEN, *Replacement.*
MATI UNT, *Brecht at Night.*
Diary of a Blood Donor.
Things in the Night.
ÁLVARO URIBE AND OLIVIA SEARS, EDS.,
Best of Contemporary Mexican Fiction.
ELOY URROZ, *Friction.*
The Obstacles.
LUISA VALENZUELA, *Dark Desires and
the Others.*
He Who Searches.
MARJA-LIISA VARTIO, *The Parson's Widow.*
PAUL VERHAEGHEN, *Omega Minor.*
AGLAJA VETERANYI, *Why the Child Is
Cooking in the Polenta.*
BORIS VIAN, *Heartsnatcher.*
LLORENÇ VILLALONGA, *The Dolls' Room.*
TOOMAS VINT, *An Unending Landscape.*
ORNELA VORPSI, *The Country Where No
One Ever Dies.*
AUSTRYN WAINHOUSE, *Hedyphagetica.*
PAUL WEST, *Words for a Deaf Daughter
& Gala.*
CURTIS WHITE, *America's Magic Mountain.*
The Idea of Home.
Memories of My Father Watching TV.
*Monstrous Possibility: An Invitation
to Literary Politics.*
Requiem.
DIANE WILLIAMS, *Excitability:
Selected Stories.*
Romancer Erector.
DOUGLAS WOOLF, *Wall to Wall.*
Ya! & John-Juan.
JAY WRIGHT, *Polynomials and Pollen.*
*The Presentable Art of Reading
Absence.*
PHILIP WYLIE, *Generation of Vipers.*
MARGUERITE YOUNG, *Angel in the Forest.*
Miss MacIntosh, My Darling.
REYOUNG, *Unbabbling.*
VLADO ŽABOT, *The Succubus.*
ZORAN ŽIVKOVIĆ, *Hidden Camera.*
LOUIS ZUKOFSKY, *Collected Fiction.*
VITOMIL ZUPAN, *Minuet for Guitar.*
SCOTT ZWIREN, *God Head.*

FOR A FULL LIST OF PUBLICATIONS, VISIT:
www.dalkeyarchive.com